Lost Creek Books presents
Wesley Murphey's books (as of 2015)—

Fiction

Trouble at Puma Creek: A Vietnam vet, a deadly hunt

While hunting deer in Oregon's Fall Creek Forest in 1980, Vietnam veteran Roger Bruington is murdered by an Oregon State Police officer after discovering a suspicious shack. Did finding the shack get him killed? Or was this a government hit because Bruington was finally going to reveal the U.S. Government's cover up of the evidence he turned over in 1974 proving American POWs were still being held captive in southeast Asia a year after all POWs were supposedly released? (338 pages)

A Homeless Man's Burden

Based on the actual still-unsolved 1960 bean-field murder of little *Alice Lee* near Pleasant Hill and Dexter, Oregon. Wesley Murphey picked in that very field for many years and, as a teen, worked for Alice's father. Murphey's father was Alice's school bus driver and the mail carrier in the area for 25 years. This somewhat autobiographical story begins on the McKenzie River in 2010 with a dying homeless man's confession. (302 pages)

Girl Too Popular

Being the most popular girl in town is not all it's cracked up to be—Carly Cantwell finds out why when she is kidnapped to a remote location in the forest. Is her abductor connected to her ex-stepfather who she rejected? Or is someone or something greater at work here? (178 pages)

To Kill a Mother in Law

When Dan Thurmond married Brenda, he got Maureen Muldano, the mother in law from hell. Now, with his marriage on the rocks, and shut out by his wife's restraining order, Dan's hypocritical, pseudo-spiritual, controlling mother-in-law and other wolves in her family are going to reap what they sowed. (302 pages)

Nonfiction:

Blacktail Deer Hunting Adventures (Revised/Expanded Edition 2014))

A classic. The only true adventure account ever written on hunting the Pacific Coast's blacktail deer. Well Illustrated. "Anyone who has ever hunted blacktail deer can relate to this book and can gain some good hunting lore from reading it." -- Boyd Iverson author of Blacktail Trophy Tactics (184 pages, 60 illustrations)

Conibear Beaver Trapping in Open Water (Revised 2014)

Master Beaver Trapping Techniques. Recognized as one of the top beaver trapping books in America. 115 illustrations. (110 pages)

Fish, Hunt & Trap a Little

Volumes **One** and **Two** (180 pages, and over 60 illustrations in each)

True Tales and Tactics by Wesley Murphey and his deceased father, Don Murphey. These volumes include many articles previously published in national and regional publications—and many great never-before-published articles that will charm you, teach you, entertain you, make you laugh and remember when, and inspire you to get out into the great outdoors to fish, hunt and maybe even trap a little.

See and order all Wesley Murphey books at **lostcreekbooks.com**

Disclaimer:

The photo on this fictional book's front and back covers depicting an Oregon State Police trooper is an approximation to the actual uniform and is deliberately not an exact representation. The character in this book's story who is depicted by this person wearing this uniform represents a fictional rogue Oregon State trooper and is not a reflection on any actual OSP troopers. Oregon State Police troopers are among the finest in America.

TROUBLE AT
PUMA CREEK

A Vietnam Vet - A Deadly Hunt

Wesley Murphey

Lost Creek Books

La Pine, Oregon

TROUBLE at PUMA CREEK: A Vietnam Vet-A Deadly Hunt

By Wesley Murphey

Published by Lost Creek Books, La Pine, Oregon

Website: http: lostcreekbooks.com

Trouble at Puma Creek is a work of fiction, though the idea for the book came from an actual double homicide that occurred at Puma Creek. Names, characters, businesses, organizations, places, events, and incidents either are the product of the author's imagination or are used fictitiously. The OSP uniform as used on the book's cover is deliberately not an exact representation of an actual OSP trooper.

Cover Design- Howard Rooks Graphic Design, Pleasant Hill, Oregon
Cover photo subjects: Dale Tweedy and Cody Murphey, all 2010.

ISBN 978-0-9641320-5-4
Library of Congress   LCCN 2011900092

Printed in the United States of America by Sheridan Books

Fiction: Vietnam Fiction
        Historical Suspense, Thriller, Murder- Mystery

1

The Buck

The big blacktail buck moved cautiously down the draw, unaware of the hunter eighty yards uphill to its right.

Last night the hunter had camped at Puma Creek Campground. Before daylight he hiked the two miles back into the old-growth forest, hoping to get a crack at the trophy buck before it bedded down for the day. Things hadn't gone according to plan. In the five hours since dawn, he hadn't seen the buck or any other deer in his mile-long swing up the mountain and across several springs on the Bedrock and Slick Creek drainages.

Now, as he worked side-hill amongst the sword-fern and sparse Oregon grape bushes beneath the canopy of the giant firs overhead, suddenly, he spotted movement downhill to his right. Instinctively, he froze, silently released his safety, and slowly turned his head toward the motion, hoping not to spook whatever it was.

It was the buck. *His dream buck.*

He couldn't believe it. He had the elevation advantage, and the wind was in his favor—late-morning thermals carried his scent uphill away from the buck. But the buck's body was mostly obscured by vine maple bushes. He was a good shot, but he was trembling now and wanted to get a rest for his rifle if possible.

Ten feet to his right was a huge fir, six feet in diameter at the butt. In the giant tree's shade, he inched his way forward, careful not to step on any of the dry branches lying near the tree's base. He moved up to the tree and located the deer below him. He slowly raised the gun up, and braced his left wrist against the tree's bark. But he didn't have a clear shot. He prayed the deer would continue its present course which would take it into an opening in the brush twenty feet ahead.

Seconds crept by as the deer gradually moved toward the opening, then suddenly stopped. It raised its head and looked up the hill in his direction. It couldn't possibly know he was there, could it, he thought. The deer funneled its ears around in various directions, listening for any sound that would betray a predator. It licked its muzzle and sniffed the air. The hunter wondered if it had heard him. That was the only possibility. The deer seemed to take forever to satisfy itself that there was no danger. Then, as suddenly as it had stopped, the deer once again began moving forward, toward the precious opening.

The hunter had bragged to his hunting buddies that he was coming back up here to get this buck. They all laughed and said, "That old boy will never give you another chance. You were lucky to see him the first time."

They were wrong, and he couldn't wait to show them the monster in the back of his truck that evening.

As the buck approached the opening, the hunter took long deep breaths to calm himself. The buck's head and majestic antlers came clearly into view, then the neck. Only two more steps to go. He could take a neck shot now, but opted to wait for the sure-thing lung shot.

One more step.

Patience. Breathe. Hold.

Finally, the buck's chest was clear. With his cross hairs centered behind the buck's right shoulder, half-way down its body, he took up the slack in the trigger. A loud blast echoed up and down the canyon and in the trees above.

The buck ran off, like mortally-wounded deer often do.

The hunter crumpled to the ground among the twigs, needles and cones at the base of the huge tree. Blood soaked the forest floor around his head and began oozing down the hill through the needles and moss. His rifle lay eerily silent three feet to his right. His buddies weren't going to see his big buck tonight, *or any other night*. Nor would they ever laugh at him again, or get to hear his hunting stories. Neither would his wife and two young daughters.

The buck was gone. The hunter was dead.

A branch snapped seventy yards uphill above the dead hunter. Two men made their way down the steep incline toward the victim. The man in front carried a .243 Remington, while the second man had a 270 Winchester rifle. The lead man—wearing an old, green, camouflaged army jacket, slick-brown leather-pants, and a green army ball cap—was a wiry-built, straggly-looking, full-bearded, long-haired hippie, about five-foot eight, in his mid-thirties. The second man, wearing a blue Oregon State Police uniform and a blue wide-brimmed, OSP hat, was a clean-cut young trooper, in his mid-twenties, about six foot and stockily built. They were an unlikely pair, yet they were obviously a team. Neither had spoken since the gun blast had shattered the peaceful quiet of the woods.

As they approached the still body, the hippie said, "You could have been a sniper in 'Nam with a shot like that."

The trooper didn't answer. It was his first kill.

Both men stared at the bloody mess at the base of the giant tree for several seconds, then suddenly the trooper wretched and gave up his breakfast. He wiped his mouth and nose off, then said, "I actually killed a human. I didn't consider how hard it would be afterwards."

"You don't know the half of it yet," said the hippie. "But we had no choice. You could sweat over when you were found out, or do away with the witness, and remain a free man, free to uphold the law and keep the poachers from raping our forests of wildlife."

"But what about the man's family?"

"What about them? Sometimes innocent people get hurt in the crossfire. Your dad understood that, just like I did and still do. In 'Nam there were a couple times when we had to kill a civilian or two to get them to expose the gooks. There was no way to justify that fully, but sometimes you just had to do what was necessary to protect your own ass. And half the time, we never knew whether the civilians were Viet Cong (VC) or not; *they all looked alike*. For our own safety, the motto was, "When in doubt, waste the mothers.""

"I should have let you do it."

"That wasn't the plan. You needed to get your feet wet some time. Get a taste of what your dad went through."

"But he was a soldier in a war."

"This is war too. Just a different kind of war."

Wearing a pair of blue-green rubber gloves, the kind used for cleaning toilets, the hippie took out a plastic pint bottle from his pack. He removed the lid, then stuck the bottle, containing a couple ounces of water, where it could catch the blood that continued to slowly drain from what was left of the man's face.

"Boy, your hollow point sure did the job," said the hippie, talking like they did in the Nam, which only deepened the trooper's remorse.

The trooper didn't answer him, as the trooper searched the area downhill from the corpse for some bone and skin fragments. He thought, I bet you guys never had to try to find enemy body parts after the fact, or try to disguise the evidence.

On a patch of green moss, fifteen feet away, the trooper found a piece of cheek bone with the bloody skin still attached. Wearing rubber gloves, he picked it up and carefully placed it in a zip-lock sandwich bag and put it in his pack.

"We've got what we need," he said, without letting the hippie see it. He had no desire to show off the bone as if it was a trophy.

Next, using moss, the hippie wiped his gloves off thoroughly, then unzipped the hunter's green canvas backpack, to pull everything out.

"Look here. He's got several things from the shack, including notebook pages with formula's written on them in mine and your hand writing. No doubt there's fingerprints too."

After retrieving what came from the shack, the hippie replaced the hunter's stuff inside the pack and zipped it closed.

"Come on, let's get this body packed up to your truck and moved down near Fall Creek. We don't want anyone poking around up this drainage at all."

The trooper removed a military-type tarp from his backpack. It was the same style the soldiers used on the battle field to remove wounded or dead men. They stretched it out on the ground next to the dead hunter, then picked him up by his arms and legs and laid him on it. They then pulled out a turkey-sized clear bag, put it over the man's head, and secured it around his shirt collar with a piece of torn white sheet. They took out another bag and scooped up the blood soaked moss and needles from the ground and bagged them so they could place them next to the body where they intended to leave it lay.

Next they moved the tarp and body ten feet away from the tree, and scattered moss, needles, and branches around to cover up the sign that there had been a bloody accident there. Finally, they slung their rifles over their shoulders. Each grabbed an end of the tarp and—after the trooper grabbed the sling of the hunter's 30.06 with his gloved, free hand—began the laborious pack up hill with it. The state trooper's white Dodge Ram was parked nearly a mile away. It was a rough pack; they had to stop to rest numerous times.

It was nearly three by the time they reached the trooper's pickup. They wasted no time in getting the dead hunter loaded and covered in the back. The trooper knew that no other troopers were scheduled to be in the area today, so there shouldn't be any trouble getting to the drop-off point three miles away as the crow flies, though much farther by the winding logging roads.

They jumped in the truck and took the Clark Butte Road to the east-northeast around to the Alder Creek logging road, which took them south toward Fall Creek Road. A half mile above Fall Creek Road, they passed a blue, late-model Ford pickup headed up the road they had just come down. Two rifle barrels pointed toward the truck's ceiling between the two hunters in the pickup.

After they reached Fall Creek Road they headed west until reaching the winding Jones Creek Road and took it northwest for two miles. They pulled down a grown-over skid road and stopped three-quarters of a mile north of Puma Creek Campground. From there the two men carried the corpse downhill to the south for almost a quarter mile.

"Let's put it at the edge of that creek there," said the hippie, pointing to his right, twenty feet away. "The water will help confuse things when they find him. Let's set him down for a second and you get that bag off his head. Save the blood, we can shake it around here."

The trooper unwrapped the sheet from around the hunter's neck and swallowed hard as he carefully removed the bloody bag.

"Don't you dare puke here," said the hippie. "Now, let's lift the sides of the tarp and lay him so his head and shoulders are in the water." They moved the man over to the creek. "That's it. Now let's just slide the tarp out from under him."

"How do you do all this so easy, as if the guy is just a dead animal?" asked the trooper, as they pulled the tarp away.

"Believe me, when you've seen as much death as I did in the Nam, you have to disassociate yourself from it or you go crazy."

"It seems to me you're crazy either way then."

"You weren't there. You can't possibly know what it was like."

"The way this whole thing is bothering me right now, I don't know how you guys could stand it."

"They were the enemy," said the hippie, not considering that would only lay more guilt on the young trooper. "The U.S. Army paid your dad and me, and all the other grunts, to kill gooks. Not to ask questions. It'll help us both right now, if you would stop asking questions too. I'm sorry for what you're going through. But we had no choice. Get that through your head. Your dad told me if anything ever happened to him in the Nam to take care of you, your mom and your sister. I've done that the best I can. But we are in this situation now, like it or not. There's no turning back, so you've got to accept that and deal with it. Alright?"

"OK. I just wish my dad was here right now."

"I'm the only dad you have left, Butch," he said, using the nickname that he only used when they were alone, and then rarely. It was the closest the hippie ever came to an expression of intimacy with his surrogate son, at least it was since he left for Vietnam in December 1965, a few months ahead of Butch's dad. Butch was only nine then. "I know I'm not much, but it's the way it is."

After the tarp was out from under the body, the hippie handed his two corners to the trooper and said, "Now dunk it in the creek below the body. Get that blood washed out."

The hippie then grabbed the turkey bag and dumped the blood around by the dead hunter's torso. Next, he grabbed the zip-loc bag from the trooper's pack and removed the skull fragment, crossed the creek by way of a three foot boulder in the water halfway across and placed the fragment on the green, moss-covered ground several feet up the other side of the stream. He then took out the quart bottle filled with the slightly-diluted blood and what little brain matter he had recovered earlier, shook it up, removed the cap and replaced it with a spray nozzle. He then walked about ten feet up the other side of the creek and began spraying the mixture all over the ferns, moss, needles and grass, while walking backwards toward the corpse.

"Get that bag washed out now," he said to the trooper. "Then we'll fold that tarp and get out of here." He looked up at the sky and noticed some large cumulous clouds forming in the distance. "Let's hope it doesn't rain before they find the body."

For the final touch, the hippie laid the hunter's rifle beside the body, with only the wooden stock out of the water. He had seen that same picture plenty of times in the rice paddies and swamps when he was in the Nam.

2

No Show

On the telephone the next night, **Sunday, October 26th, 1980**—

"Dick, Roger hasn't gotten home from hunting. I'm very worried that something has happened to him? He went hunting up Fall Creek Friday afternoon."

"Jan, it's only 9:30. If he got a big buck down in some canyon just before dark this evening, it could take him until midnight or even tomorrow to get the buck out and get home."

"But he said—"

"I know. But trust me, from my own experience I know what I'm talking about. I know it's easy to think the worst, but things happen sometimes when you're hunting that you don't anticipate."

"Alright, but if I don't hear from him by mid-morning tomorrow, I'm going to call you again."

"I'll call to check with you by ten," said Dick. "If he isn't back, I'll round up Dave and Aaron and go see if we can figure things out. Where'd he go hunting up there anyway? He told us he was going back after a big buck. But you know him, he keeps his honey holes

9

to himself. All we knew was that it was some place up Big Fall Creek."

"He told me he would be camping at Puma Creek Campground."

"Okay, we'll be in touch. Call me as soon as he comes in."

"Alright. Thanks."

After Jan hung up the phone, she walked down the hall to her daughters' bedroom, went in, and knelt down on the carpet in the narrow space between the beds. She gazed into the face of sleeping eight-year-old Mandy, on her right, for a minute and thought back to the day she went to her gynecologist to have a pregnancy test.

When Roger arrived home from his sawmill shift, she ran out and—just as he got out of his truck—jumped up on him, wrapped her legs around the back of his waist, hugged his neck, and kissed him. Then, with a huge grin on her face, she looked into his beautiful blue eyes, and said, "We're going to have a baby!"

"We're going to have a baby?"

She nodded her head, "Yes."

"We're going to have a baby!" he said again, bursting into tears of joy as he hugged her tight. "We're going to have a baby! I love you so much, Jan. I love you so much."

She wiped a tear from her cheek and then looked into six-year-old Emily's still baby-like face as she snored softly. She remembered when Emily was a year old. Jan was sitting on the love seat next to Roger who had Emily on one knee and Mandy on the other. He bounced them up and down and said, "Humpty Dumpty sat on the wall. Humpty Dumpty had a great fall." On the word fall, he bounced both girls extra high, and they giggled with joy. "All the kings horses, and all the kings men," and then speeding up the bouncing, said quickly, "couldn't put Humpty together again." The girls laughed their heads off, and so did she and Roger, as they all hugged in one of their famous family hugs.

"Roger loves them so much, God," Jan cried. "And I love him so much. Please don't let anything be wrong."

1:15 the next afternoon, Monday—

"Jan, I'm calling from the Unity Market. We found Roger's pickup at Puma Creek Campground, like you said. But there was no sign of him. And judging by his stuff in the campsite, it doesn't look to me like he's been there for quite a while."

"Oh no, Dick," she said, breaking into sobs. "We've got to call the police."

"I was going to do that as soon as I got off the phone with you."

"I'm coming right up, Dick. Will you wait for me there at the market?"

"I think you better call some family members and stay by your phone. There isn't much you could do up here right now anyway. I'm sure the police will get a search and rescue operation going right away."

"Oh, Dick, what am I going to do?"

"Just get on the phone to your sister or brother and have them come over to your place. Call Wanda (Dick's wife) too. I'm sure she'll be glad to come over. We'll get back to you as soon as we know anything. Oh, you better dig out some more photos to give the police. I'm sure they'll send an officer over to talk to you right away. I forgot to ask you earlier, what was Dick wearing?"

"You know what he hunts in, his red and black plaid shirts, black jeans and an orange ball cap. You know how he is about not wanting someone to accidentally shoot him. You can't miss seeing that cap."

"Well that's right. So we know he couldn't have been accidentally shot. Chances are good that he's probably twisted an ankle real bad or something. Try not to worry. It's been warm enough at night, and dry, so if he is laid up somewhere in a canyon, he'll be fine, other than maybe being real thirsty and hungry. I'll call you when we know something."

"Okay. Good luck," she said, still sobbing.

Dick immediately called the Oregon State Police and reported

Roger missing. They said they would send a couple troopers up to meet him at Puma Creek Campground, and they would also contact the Lane County Sheriff's Department to see what kind of help they could send.

The Lane County Sheriff sent a deputy to Roger's house in Springfield to talk to his wife and to get some photos of him. They also sent a deputy up Fall Creek to Puma Creek Campground, 18 miles northeast of Lowell and about 30 miles southeast of Springfield.

As Dick drove along Fall Creek Reservoir on his way back up to Puma Creek Campground, he thought back to a baseball game in seventh grade.

His and Roger's team was down by one run with two out in the bottom of the seventh and last inning. Dick was up to bat, with Roger on second base, taunting the pitcher by stretching his lead out farther with each pitch. The count was full after Dick had fouled two straight pitches back. The pitcher came out of his stretch and delivered to the plate. Roger broke hard for third base as the fast ball headed toward the catcher. Dick swung with everything he had and crushed the ball over the left field fence.

When Dick crossed home plate with the game-winning run, Roger slapped his hand with a high-five and said, "You did it, Babe!"

"Yes I did," answered Dick.

At Puma Creek Campground half an hour later—

Two state troopers pulled their pickups next to the three men standing near two pickups parked next to the campsite where Roger's green 1976 GMC pickup sat forebodingly.

"Are you guys Roger Bruington's friends?" asked Trooper Bryan Wilson in the first rig.

"Yes we are," answered Dick Eastbrook, Roger's best friend.

Both troopers then parked their rigs behind the second of the two parked trucks on the paved campground drive-through, got out and walked to the three men.

Oregon State Troopers Wilson and Martin were handsome young men in their mid-twenties, with similar stocky builds, both between five feet eleven inches and six feet tall. They knew each other only through their contact on the force, where they both worked general law enforcement, along with game enforcement in separate areas within Lane County. Their jurisdictions overlapped only in the Fall Creek drainage. Trooper Wilson had all of Lane County from Fall Creek north and then west to Interstate 5, whereas Trooper Martin had all of Lane County from Fall Creek south and also west to Interstate 5. Several other Oregon State Police officers also shared these same jurisdictions, though only a few were also game wardens.

All five of the men—Bruington's friends and the troopers— walked to the picnic table in Bruington's campsite to discuss things. Majestic Douglas firs provided the bulk of the overhead canopy in the campground, with some alder, a few large maples, and some cascara mixed in. Sword fern, salal, rhododendron and salmon berry bushes made up the majority of the ground cover.

Puma Creek Campground, a Willamette National Forest campground, the last campground in the upper end of the Fall Creek drainage, had eleven campsites. But Bruington, who was camped in site 6, was the only camper there now. It was unclear whether any other people had camped in the grounds over the weekend. No one besides Bruington had signed the camp register.

A Lane County Sheriff's deputy pulled up in his four-wheel drive a few minutes after the state troopers. He got out and walked up to the five men gathered around the picnic table. Already they had a topographical map spread out and were looking at it.

As the deputy approached, Trooper Martin glanced up, and said, "Afternoon, deputy." He reached out his hand, and said, "I'm Trooper Martin, this is Trooper Wilson, and these are Roger

Bruington's buddies."

"Nice to meet you guys. I'm Lieutenant Dowdy. Two teams of volunteer search and rescue crews should be arriving from Springfield shortly, as should the deputy that was sent to Bruington's home to talk to his wife."

Addressing the civilians, Lieutenant Dowdy asked, "Do any of you guys have a photo of Bruington or know what he was wearing?"

"I'm Dick Eastbrook, I dropped by his house on my way up here and picked up a few photos from his wife. Roger and I go way back to our grade-school days."

Dowdy could see immediately that Eastbrook, at six-foot two-inches and 210 pounds, was a strikingly handsome, self-confident man, and guessed he was probably a leader in everything he did.

Aaron Howe, another friend, folded back the geological survey map, revealing a five by seven photo and a pair of three by fives of Bruington that were lying on the table. The larger photo showed Bruington with a huge grin as he was positioned behind the body of a nice three-point blacktail buck he had killed a couple years earlier. He was wearing a red and black plaid long-sleeve shirt and an orange ball cap that was tilted back slightly for the photo. His Savage .06 rested across the deer's belly, with the butt in the foreground. A typical proud-hunter photo.

"I understand Bruington was deer hunting on this trip," said Dowdy. "Was he wearing the same colored clothing and hat he had on for this photo?"

"According to his wife, he was," answered Eastbrook. "We looked through his tent and found three long-sleeved, plaid shirts identical to the one in the photo, so I think we can safely assume that he was wearing the same thing. He's definitely a man of habit."

"Had any of them been worn?" asked Trooper Wilson.

"Yeah, one had. Roger is a stickler for changing his hunting clothes every day. He didn't want any more odor on his clothes than necessary. The other two shirts were neatly folded, along with three colored tee-shirts, some underwear, and a couple pairs of black jeans."

"Have any of you guys hunted with Bruington?" asked Dowdy.

"Sure we have," answered Aaron Howe. "The four of us hunt elk together on the coast every year."

"So you've hunted deer in this area with him?"

"No, actually we haven't. You'd have to know Roger to understand that one. When it came to deer hunting, he actually did most of his hunting alone. The rest of us often hunted deer together, though."

"So why would he hunt elk in a party with you guys, but not deer?" asked Dowdy.

"I know it always seemed odd to us too. Roger is a bit superstitious. Nothing particularly out of the ordinary or anything, really. Kind of like the way baseball players who are on a hitting streak will often follow the exact routine the day of the game."

"From the time Roger was twelve," Eastbrook broke in, "he hunted deer with his father every year, that is, until he turned seventeen. He had only taken one shot at a deer up until that time." Knowing what the law officers were thinking, he said, "Don't worry, I'll get right to the point." The troopers looked at each other with a look that said, *good*. "Opening day, when Roger was seventeen, he went out hunting alone in the woods up hill from his house and within an hour of daylight spotted and killed a beautiful fourpoint buck. He's been hunting deer mostly alone since then.

"I should probably tell you guys," said Eastbrook, "that Roger once told me another reason he preferred hunting deer alone was that he always had a twinge of fear that if he hunted with a partner he might get shot by them. I had asked him, 'Then why don't you insist on hunting elk alone?' He said, 'It's the size of the animal. No one's going to mistake a man for an elk.'"

"I guess he never read the annual hunting-accident summary," said Wilson. "There have actually been a few hunters shot and wounded, or killed, by hunters who said later they mistook the hunter for an elk. But there's no doubt about it, it is much rarer that hunters are mistaken for elk than for deer."

"Were any of you guys hunting up here in this area this weekend?" asked Lieutenant Dowdy, barely beating Trooper Wilson to the punch with that question.

Instantly, the air around the camp table got thick. There was an awkward silence, then careful not to seem the least bit defensive, Eastbrook spoke up. "No sir. Stevens and I went hunting out the other side of Creswell, and Howe didn't hunt. He got his deer two weeks ago in the same area we hunted this weekend."

Lieutenant Dowdy had a reputation for not mincing words, but he somehow blended that with the ability to easily establish rapport with people in his investigations.

"That's just a routine question, so you guys need not take any offense to it. If I didn't ask it, someone else would." said the salt and pepper haired, forty-four year-old, seventeen-year-veteran of the Lane County Sheriff's Department.

Lieutenant Jim Dowdy—a sturdy built, five-foot ten-inch, handsome, rugged-looking man with a heavy black and gray mustache that covered his upper lip—grew up locally and was a three-sport star throughout his high-school career at Lowell, where he graduated with sixteen classmates in June 1953. Wanting to be one of "the few and the proud," and to get some combat experience, he joined the marines two weeks later but wasn't shipped to South Korea until the end of the year, just in time to do some cleanup duty. Not quite what he had in mind. He completed his three year hitch in 1956, and would have gladly shipped over for another tour if there had been a war to fight. Vietnam was still years away.

Of course, he didn't know there would even be a Vietnam—nor did any other Americans. In fact, very few Americans had even heard of Vietnam in 1957, let alone had any clue that they or someone from their family, or someone they knew, would fight there and be one of the 58,000 plus who would die in a rice paddy or jungle, so far from home. Or be one of hundreds of thousands of other soldiers and medical personnel that would be forever scarred by the physical or psychological wounds they suffered there. Nor did any Americans know that war would prove to be a lost cause before it ever began because of the complicated political factors involved in fighting it.

By the time things heated up in Vietnam, Dowdy was already on the streets and highways of Lane County as a rookie sheriff's deputy, after having spent the years since his discharge from the marines working in a couple different saw mills in Lane County. He hadn't looked back, and had no regrets. In his seventeen years on the force, Dowdy had completed ten years on patrol, two years as an undercover agent, and several years as detective. He was happily married to his rally-queen, high-school sweet-heart, still a beautiful, shapely, five-foot seven-inch blonde. The two of them had three teenagers, two boys and a girl. The kids attended Thurston High School, and followed in their parents' footsteps as good athletes. The daughter was also a cheerleader.

"Do any of you guys know where he hunts up here?" asked Dowdy.

"We know he has camped here at Puma Creek before, and at other times just camps somewhere comfortable off the beaten path. But we don't know specifically where he hunts. He's more than happy to tell us his hunting stories, but he never tells us the locations. And he seems to enjoy holding that over our heads."

"I take it he is a pretty successful hunter?" said Wilson.

"You got that straight," said Eastbrook. "He gets a branch-antlered buck every year, and they are usually three or four points."

"And you guys have never been curious enough to follow him up to his hunting spots?" said Dowdy.

"Don't think we haven't thought long and hard about that. But if you can't trust your friends, what do you have?" said Stevens.

"You have a point there. Do you guys get your deer each year?" He was just making small talk, but the three buddies weren't sure if they were being interrogated or not.

"Generally we average two deer between the three of us," said Eastbrook. "We do pretty well elk hunting, too. We get at least one nice bull each year, and two years we filled three of our tags."

"That's a good record," said Wilson.

Just then two green vans, bearing the yellow words, "Lane County Search and Rescue," on their sides, pulled up to the camp-site and parked behind Lieutenant Dowdy's rig. Fourteen people, including two women, poured out of the vans and walked over to the campsite where the others were gathered. Pulling in right behind them was Lane County Sheriff Deputy Mike Bradshaw, who also parked his rig and proceeded immediately to the campsite.

Lieutenant Dowdy, the senior lawman, took command, filling the SAR crew in with the information he had gleaned from Bruing-ton's friends.

Then he said, "Since we have no way of knowing which direct-ion Bruington went hunting from this camp, I'm going to go with my gut based on my own hunting experience. Looking at these topo maps, we can see that all the area to the south of this campground is way too steep and is mostly on north facing slopes, which are far-less attractive to deer because of poorer quality foliage for them to feed on. As a general rule, deer prefer the browse that gets a lot of sunlight on southeast, south and southwest facing slopes. Plus at this time of year, when the weather has begun dipping below the freez-ing mark some nights, deer like to be where they can catch the morning sunrays. With all that in mind, I want us to focus our entire search in this area to the north of Fall Creek." He used the end of a small branch to trace the perimeter of a six square mile area to the north and northwest of Puma Creek Campground.

One of the OSP troopers felt ill-at-ease upon seeing Lieutenant Dowdy point out the extent of the area of interest. Both troopers, and Bruington's three hunting partners, knew Dowdy's instincts were right-on for knowing where a good hunter would likely hunt for deer in the area surrounding the campground. They also knew that much of the area of interest was made up of old-growth Douglas fir which, though preferable to the sterile, dark-timbered north slopes south of the campground, was definitely not an area that would hold a lot of deer. But sometimes the oldest bucks could be found in just such an area, away from the succulent foliage that attracted large numbers of deer, and more hunters. Perhaps that was what lured Bruington to the area in the first place.

"We only have a little over two and a half hours until sunset," said Dowdy. "We'll lose a lot of light in the big timber before that, so we need to get started. We all know the odds of a positive outcome drop off on a steeper slope with the passage of every hour. Some points that could mean a better outcome, or, unfortunately, may indicate a poorer one, are that Bruington is thirty-three, in good physical condition, and is an experienced outdoorsman with excellent survival skills. He did a couple of tours in Vietnam with the Army."

Those last words pierced like a bayonet through one OSP trooper's heart, adding to the deep remorse he already felt.

Dowdy held up the photo of Bruington with the deer, then passed it around. "From what Bruington's wife and friends have said, and from the evidence in his tent, we can assume he was wearing red and black plaid upper clothes, black jeans and an orange ball cap."

The OSP trooper suddenly thought, *I don't remember the ball cap,* at least not after the shot.

"Because of the limited daylight, I want us to begin our search in the timber just north of the Jones Creek-Fall Creek confluence." He pointed to the area on the map lying on the table. "We'll spread out to the north, spacing ourselves at twenty-yard-intervals. The sword fern patches are dense and tall in this timber. We don't want to take a chance of walking by him." Tracing across the map with the stick, he said, "We'll move east to west, then west to east, back and forth between Jones Creek and Slick Creek. That's a distance of nearly two miles in each direction. I figure we can make one pass down and back before dark. After dark, we'll have to tighten our intervals by half. If you find anything that looks like human sign, blow four times on your whistle then communicate your findings to me by radio. Is that understood?"

"Yes, sir!" they said collectively.

"I will be on the outside farthest to the north, Trooper Martin will be the middle man, and Trooper Wilson will bring up the bottom. Bruington's friends will be mixed in among you. Deputy Bradshaw, you'll be our base man monitoring the radio here at the campsite."

"Yes sir, Lieutenant."

"Let's go." Lieutenant Dowdy led the way down the gravel footpath to the beat down trail that followed Fall Creek to the west and then crossed over the creek on the wooden footbridge joining the trail along the north side of Fall Creek. He took it east two hundred yards to Jones Creek, all the while keeping an eye out for any signs of someone having hiked up the bank.

"Okay, let's spread out. Follow me." He headed up the creek's west bank while scanning the east bank.

The search and rescue operation proceeded according to plan, with the team making a full sweep down and back with no one blowing four times on his whistle. Lieutenant Dowdy, however, blew twice on his at regular intervals, and was answered by Troopers Martin and Wilson each time. Not only did that help keep the search party oriented to one another, if Bruington was within ear shot and conscious, it would alert him that help was in the area. If he was able to respond, he could shoot his gun three times or blow on the whistle that his wife and hunting buddies said he always kept in his fanny pack when hunting.

3

The Body

After one complete sweep, the search team had covered one square mile of timber. It was 6:45 and almost dark when they moved up the hill, positioned for the final sweep of the evening.

Then one of the SAR team members shouted, "I see a body in Jones Creek!" He was shining his bright flashlight off to his right where it reflected off the flowing brook.

"Where?" shouted Dowdy.

"Right there, lying partly in the water by those ferns." He moved his beam around in a circle bringing it back to the body each time.

"I can't see it from here," said Dowdy.

He blew his whistle four times, then got on his field radio, which was being monitored by everyone on the hillside, as well as the deputy at Puma Creek Campground.

"Everyone stay put where you are. One of the SAR members has spotted a body in Jones Creek. I can't see it from my position, but will move in carefully so I don't disturb any potential evidence." Then, speaking by radio to the member who spotted the body, he asked, "What is your name team member who has a visual on the body?"

"I'm Dave Wells, team member four," answered the twenty-seven year-old, ex-Oregon State track star. The team members had each been numbered and positioned for the search accordingly, with number one being the member next to Lieutenant Dowdy, number two just downhill from him, and so on.

"Stay where you are Wells, and keep your light on the body. Are you certain it's a human?"

"There's no doubt about it, sir."

"Okay, Troopers Martin and Wilson carefully proceed up the hill along a direct path until you reach Wells. Keep your eyes open for potential evidence. Especially, keep your eyes open for any disturbed soil between you and the creek that would indicate a human walked there."

"Yes, sir," they both responded.

"Deputy Bradshaw?"

"Yes sir, Deputy Bradshaw here."

"Report to dispatch, that one of the SAR members has located a body, and that I am approaching it now. We'll keep them posted on the status of our search. You better tell them to inform the coroner. Tell them we'll let them know if we find any evidence indicating it wasn't a death by natural causes."

"Aye, sir."

Lieutenant Dowdy, sweeping his flashlight beam back and forth across in front of him, slowly made his way past bunches of fern as he moved toward the light beam at the creek. In two minutes he spotted the body. "I see it now, Wells. You're right, it's definitely a human. It looks like a male. He's laying belly down. Good eyes."

As Dowdy got to within twenty feet of the body, approaching from the west bank, he began seeing blood drops smattered on fern leaves. "Troopers Martin and Wilson?"

"Yes, sir," they both answered on their radios.

"I'm about twenty feet from the body now, and I'm finding blood splattered on fern leaves. It definitely looks like a gunshot incident to me. After you reach Wells, I want you both to break off to your right toward the creek. One of you approach my position on the west bank. The other one cross over and come up the east bank. Keep a close eye out for any blood or signs of human footprints. Let me know the second you find something." They both acknowledged.

"Deputy Bradshaw, are you staying on top of this?"

"Yes, sir, I am. Do you want me to radio in your latest findings?"

"Yes, we need to get the coroner team out here ASAP. It looks like it's going to be a long evening."

"Get the coroner out here, yes sir. I'm on it."

Deputy Bradshaw immediately used the CB in his patrol car to call dispatch and request the coroner team to come to Puma Creek Campground.

Two minutes later, over his radio, "Lieutenant Dowdy?"

"Dowdy here."

"The coroner team will be here in about forty minutes. Will you have someone come down here to escort them into the woods to your location?"

"If this proves to be Bruington, I'm going to release most of the SAR team. I'll get a couple of them to bring the coroner up here. We're on the bank of Jones Creek about six hundred yards north of the Fall Creek confluence.

I've got my camera with me, so I'm going to take a bunch of photos. Hopefully the body will have some ID on it, or I will be able to confirm by visual whether it is Bruington or not."

"Yes sir. Keep me posted."

"I will."

"SAR team, for now, I want you all to get comfortable where you're at. We're dealing with a dead body here involving a gunshot incident. At this point, I don't know whether it was a self-inflicted accident or if the guy was shot by someone else. And I don't know for certain that it's Bruington. From here out, we'll treat the whole area as a crime scene, which means you need to take a seat and hang tight for a bit. As soon as we figure a few things out, we'll decide when you can return to base. I appreciate your help tonight. I know this isn't the outcome any of us was hoping for."

Bruington's friends were deeply saddened, anticipating the confirmation from Dowdy that the body was Bruington's.

When Dowdy had the body in clear view, he removed his camera from his backpack and began taking photos from different angles. A rifle was laying a foot away on the right side of the body, with only the wooden stock visible above water. Troopers Wilson and Martin arrived fives minutes later. Martin had observed nothing he would consider evidence of human activity, though he reported by radio that he could see where a herd of elk had followed down the east bank of the seven-foot-wide Jones Creek for a short distance, then turned back to the east. He figured they came through last night some time. Wilson had seen nothing until he got to the same bloody ferns that Dowdy had noted.

Martin asked, "Can we approach the body now, sir?"

"Yes, come on in. I've got over two dozen photos. There's plenty of blood splattered over there," he pointed to the west side of the creek below the body, "but I haven't been able to find a gunshot wound on him. That moss washed onto the back of his head and neck may be covering it up."

After reaching Dowdy and the body, Wilson said, "He's wearing the same clothes Bruington was supposed to be wearing. That's really eerie, the way that rifle is laying mostly in the water there. It looks like a scene out of a war movie." The red and black plaid, long-sleeved shirt was partly covered by a green, canvass backpack, still strapped over the dead man's shoulders.

"It's definitely unsettling, isn't it. I'm going to see if I can find some ID," said Dowdy, as he reached for the right back pocket of the man's black jeans.

Dowdy dug the wallet out and unfolded it. The driver's license was right there with his picture on it. "It's Roger Bruington. I guess we already knew that though, didn't we?"

While Dowdy was bent down looking at the wallet, he took a closer look at the back of Bruington's head, which was barely out of water, mostly covered by stringy moss, with a couple brown maple leaves washed up against the right ear which was facing upstream. He noticed a bit of blood.

"There's a hole in the back of his head. It's a gunshot. And it's no exit wound. He's been shot in the head from behind."

Both Staters squatted down close to see what Dowdy was pointing at.

"You're right, sir," said Martin. "I hate to think what his face looks like."

They all stood up, Dowdy pulled his radio from his belt and, keying the mike, said, "Deputy Bradshaw?"

"Bradshaw here, sir."

"You can report to dispatch that we have a positive ID on the victim. It's definitely Roger Bruington. He's been shot in the back of the head with a high-powered weapon. It's a homicide."

"Yes sir."

Bruington's friends—Eastbrook, Howe and Stevens—heard Dowdy's report over the SAR team-members' radios on either side of them, and felt a wave of grief come over them. Eastbrook wept; it was like losing a brother. He and Bruington had been best friends since third grade.

Over the radio, Lieutenant Dowdy said, "SAR members— including you Wells, and Bruington's buddies, gather together at SAR 16's position and return to base. I'll need a couple of you to bring the coroner team up here when they arrive at Puma Creek. Those same two can also help carry the body down after the coroner has completed his examination at the scene. They should be here in about half an hour. You can decide among yourselves who's going to help. Thank you all for your help this evening. Hopefully the next time we meet it will be under more favorable circumstances."

"Lieutenant Dowdy, this is SAR eight. Dick Eastbrook wants to know if he and his buddies can come up there to your position to see their friend."

"I understand what he's asking, but there's no point in that. They don't need to see the way we found Bruington. Besides, I need to keep traffic here to a minimum. If they want to wait together at SAR 16's position for now, and accompany the body down the hill later, that would be fine."

"Yes sir. I'll let them know."

The SAR team and Bruington's buddies gathered together. Just before heading downhill, SAR eight said over the radio, "Lieutenant Dowdy, SAR eight here. We'll leave a radio with Bruington's friends, and stay in contact with you. Wells and I are going to bring the coroner team back up."

"Alright, let me know when you're back at base. I imagine it'll take the coroner close to an hour on the scene to get his photos and whatever other evidence he can find. The state troopers and I will hang here."

4

Coroner Arrives

An hour later, the Lane County Coroner and his assistant, who had both hiked up through the timber along the west edge of Jones Creek following SAR members Wells and number eight, Langly, pushed their way through the final ten feet of sword fern thirty yards below the waiting lawmen, and then crossed the creek to the east bank by way of a natural log dam.

"You can approach through that area there," said Lieutenant Dowdy, tracing a path with his flashlight in ferns below him. We've already looked that area over thoroughly and found no sign of evidence."

As the coroner stepped into view of the body lying partially in the creek, Dowdy said, "Heck of a way to spend a Monday evening, huh, Doug, hiking a steep hill through the brush in the dark?"

"This is nothing compared to some places I've been," answered LC Coroner Doug Villard. "What do you know so far, Lieutenant?"

"We didn't want to do anymore in the dark than necessary to get access to the body, but I can tell you that it appears to me Bruington was standing right here facing the creek to his southwest and was shot from somewhere up there to the northeast behind him. There's a lot of blood splattered on the ferns just across the creek in a direct line with how the body is lying. I got down close enough to see the bullet hole in the back of his head, which is mostly covered in that moss there. You'll have to get close to see it yourself. I took about two dozen photos of the body and the area within ten feet of it."

"Alright, hang tight for a few minutes. I've got to get my own photos and take some measurements."

The two troopers and the SAR members stepped back away from the little flat where the coroner and his assistant started taking photos and measurements. The assistant, Mike Baird, held a medium-bright light on the body as Villard directed, while Villard obtained various measurements and photographs from numerous angles. The two of them had worked together in the Lane County Coroner's Office for the past four years and barely had to say a word while going about their tasks. Villard spoke periodically into a miniature cassette tape-recorder, giving various descriptions of his findings.

"Okay, Mike; that should do it. Now paint around the body and around the rifle stock."

When Baird finished painting, he stepped away.

"You can get him out of the water now, Lieutenant," said Villard. "Keep him face down and place him a few feet away from the water."

"I'll get the rifle first," Dowdy answered, as he reached out with his gloved hands and carefully lifted the rifle from the water. Its barrel had stringy moss dangling from it. He expected to see blood all over the scope and front portion of the rifle, but found none. "I guess the water dissolved any blood that would have been on it, because I don't see any." Looking the gun over, he said, "It's a Savage 30.06. That's funny, the safety's not engaged."

The coroner took two pictures of that before Dowdy opened the bolt, and drew the round out of the chamber. Surprised, he said, "This gun was fired. The chambered shell is empty."

One of the troopers was shocked at that revelation.

The other one said, "That's very odd, don't you think, Lieutenant."

Dowdy immediately unloaded the rifle's magazine. "There are four loaded shells here. He only fired the chambered round. That raises some interesting questions, doesn't it?"

"It sure does," said the coroner. "Like was this empty round fired at the man who killed him?"

"Or, did he shoot at a deer that the other hunter was also hunting, and then got shot because of it?" said Trooper Martin.

"Or is it possible that he had fired his weapon at an animal earlier, missed and simply forgot to extract the spent casing and inject another one?" said Trooper Wilson. "I've done that before, myself."

"I can tell you this," said Martin. "The year I switched from using a semi-automatic deer rifle to a bolt action, I made the same mistake. I had gotten so used to the follow-up rounds being loaded in automatically, that I forgot to work the bolt after missing with my first shot. Cost me a nice deer, too."

"What you troopers are saying makes a lot of sense. But does a very experienced, successful hunter, and Vietnam veteran, like Bruington make that kind of mistake?"

"I doubt it," said the coroner.

"Anyone could make that kind of mistake," countered Wilson.

"Well, let's get him out of the water," said Dowdy, as he handed Bruington's rifle to the coroner's assistant.

Wilson grabbed Bruington by his ankles, while Trooper Martin and Lieutenant Dowdy each grabbed an arm pit and elbow. "Lift," said Dowdy. They lifted the rigid body and moved it several feet away from the creek, then set it down on the mossy ground so the top of the head was three feet away from the water.

Villard snapped several photos of the body in that position. Then he gently pulled all the moss and crud away from the head and shoulders, and took more photos. Both troopers, Dowdy, and the two SAR members all watched with curiosity while remaining silent. They were all nervous about what they were about to see.

"Alright, you can turn him now, Lieutenant," said Villard.

Martin and Wilson stepped forward. One grabbed a leg, the other an arm, and pulled him over onto his back. Immediately, Martin turned away and vomited.

"Oh my Gosh," said Wilson. "There's nothing left from his nose up."

Dowdy and Wilson just stared at what was once a human face. Dowdy had seen plenty of gore in his life, but this was the first time he had seen a dead body with a crawdad and periwinkles attached to bone-white flesh inside a man's skull. The crawdad quickly climbed out of the brain cavity, made a hasty move toward the water, and disappeared into the dark shadows of the creek. At that, Wilson turned away and puked.

"That's not quite like seeing dissected frogs in your biology course is it, you guys?" said Dowdy.

Villard stared at the mangled face for half a minute, then remembered he needed to take some photos.

As the three lawmen continued to look at the body, trooper Martin said, "Wasn't Bruington reportedly wearing an orange ball cap?"

"Yes, he was," said Dowdy. "It's got to be around here somewhere, but since we haven't run across it already, we better wait until daylight to look for it. We don't want to take a chance of skewing the evidence. With his head laying in the creek the way it was, the best bet is that the cap is somewhere in the creek. It might have washed off his head and ended up downstream under some sticks or something."

"Yeah, that sounds logical," said Wilson. "I'm just curious, Lieutenant, do you think there is any chance this was an accidental shooting by another hunter mistaking Bruington for a deer?"

"That's definitely a possibility. Judging by the blood splattered on the ferns across the creek, and from all indicators here at the scene, I believe Bruington was standing at the edge of the creek, facing the southwest, and was shot from somewhere up there to the northeast." He pointed in that direction. "He may have bent down to get a drink, then stood back up. If a hunter from somewhere up there saw that movement, especially with all these high ferns behind Bruington, he may have thought he was seeing a deer, and shot before positively identifying his target."

"What about the hat?" Martin asked. "How could another hunter not see the hat? And that red and black plaid shirt should have been fairly easy to see also. Of course he may have taken the hat off to get a drink."

"What do you think, Doug?" Dowdy said."

"Here's what we know for certain," said the coroner. "The bullet entered the back of Bruington's head, four inches below the crown, and took off all of his face from just above his mouth to mid-forehead. That suggests a slight upward trajectory from the back of his head to the front, where the bullet exited the skull. Of course, until we get him back to the lab and insert a rod with the bullet's diameter through the skull hole, we won't know for sure what the angle of entry was. And even then, if the bone around the inside of the hole is fractured, we'll never know for sure what the exact angle was."

"Now assuming that I'm correct about the bullet-trajectory, and because all of the terrain behind where Bruington was standing is slightly uphill, he would have been looking down at a slight angle when he was shot. Do you guys follow me so far?"

"That sounds good to me," said Dowdy.

"Me too, sir," said Martin. "But what does that have to do with whether Bruington had an orange hat on or not, or whether another hunter would have seen the hat if Bruington was wearing it?"

"Consider this," said Villard. "Trooper Wilson, go stand right over there, face your body toward the creek and look down toward the water, tilting your head slightly; not just your eyes."

Trooper Wilson, wearing a blue OSP ball cap, walked to the water's edge ten feet below Bruington's body and did what the coroner requested.

"How much of Wilson's hat do you see from that angle, Trooper Martin?" asked Villard.

"I see what you're getting at, sir. I can see very little of the hat."

"And you're standing only fifteen feet away," interjected Dowdy. "Of course, if the shooter had a scope, then his being farther away may not have been much of a factor. But even with a scope, very little orange would have been visible. Then consider that if the hunter happened to be startled by Bruington's movement as he raised up from getting a drink, got a sudden case of buck fever, quickly swung his rifle toward the target and fired.... Well, I think you get the picture."

"Aren't you assuming an awful lot?" asked Martin.

"I'm only speculating. But that's part of investigating these things. You look at the available evidence and come up with some theories. When all the evidence is in, sometimes your theories prove to be right on, and other times they stink. The important thing is to never let your theory prevent you from objectively considering all the evidence in the case. As soon as you get locked in on one theory, you end up trying to prove it to yourself and others."

"I didn't know we were going to get an investigative lesson when we hit the brush today, Lieutenant," said Martin.

"Well, you wouldn't have if things had turned out the way we all hoped they would, with Bruington stranded up in a ravine with a broken ankle or some other non-life-threatening injury."

"That would have been a great thing to be able to report to his wife," said Wilson. "I sure don't envy the person who has to give her this news. It's probably going to be his friend, Eastbrook."

"I'm dreading the first time I have to do it," said Martin.

"Whether it's the first or fifth time, troopers, it doesn't get any easier. Trust me."

As the coroner and his assistant continued getting photos, the three lawmen continued their discussion.

Then finally, "Lieutenant Dowdy," said the coroner, "we're all through here. Let's get the victim's body out to our van now."

Dowdy hung several strands of orange surveyor ribbon from some nearby branches to make it easier to relocate the site in the morning.

Assistant Baird positioned the field stretcher beside the body, and then laid the open transport bag on top of it. He, Troopers Martin and Wilson, and Lieutenant Dowdy, each grabbed an extremity, while the coroner lifted the head. They then hoisted the body onto the bag and stretcher. After zipping the bag closed up the middle from the feet to the head, the coroner's assistant strapped three belts tightly around the bag, through the handle loops, securing it to the stretcher.

Dowdy radioed Bruington's buddies informing them that the investigative team was on the way out. Then said to those with Bruington's corpse, "It's crucial that none of what any of you saw or heard here at the scene be repeated to anyone. I mean that— especially the part about Bruington's rifle having been fired and not reloaded. If anyone finds out about that it will only complicate our investigation. Do you all understand?"

"Yes, sir," they each acknowledged.

"Good. I *am* going to tell the buddies and family that we haven't found his hat yet, but that we fully expect to find it tomorrow," said Dowdy. "Alright, let's get him out of here."

The state troopers then each grabbed a front handle, and the SAR members each took hold of one at the back, lifted the body, and followed Lieutenant Dowdy and Coroner Villard. Assistant Baird followed behind shining his light to assist the men with the stretcher. They made their way to the log dam just downstream and crossed carefully on the parallel twin three-foot-diameter logs that seemed to be spaced perfectly for just such a venture.

Bruington's friends joined them a minute later—heavy with grief that became heavier when they saw the bagged form—and followed along behind. The extraction party reached Puma Creek Campground at 10:50 PM. Each of the SAR members felt grief come over them upon seeing the bagged body, which was immediately loaded into the coroner's van and taken to the county morgue.

Lieutenant Dowdy arranged for the investigative team to meet back at Puma Creek at eight in the morning. Deputy Bradshaw would remain at the base camp until then. Dowdy would follow Bruington's three friends to Bruington's house and be there when Dick Eastbrook broke the news to his wife.

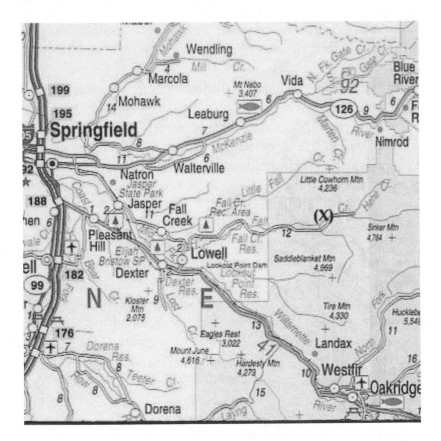

The (X) marks the map area on page 35

Map showing Puma Creek Campground, Roger
Bruington's hunt path, the shack, location where Bruington
was killed, the area searched, and spot where Bruington's body
was discovered.

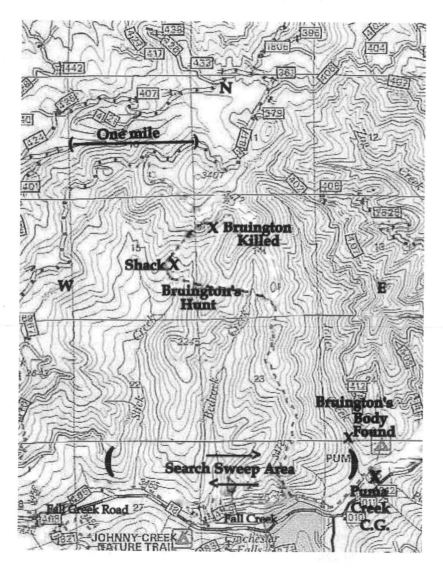

5

A Quandary

The Oregon State troopers headed home for the night knowing they had to return to Puma Creek the next morning. One of them would barely sleep. As soon as he got home to Springfield, he got on the telephone and rousted the hippie from his restless sleep.

The hippie had rarely gotten a good night's sleep in over fourteen years, and when he did it was under the influence of marijuana, beer or wine. Every night he faced the demons of his memory. He'd spent too many nights alone in the jungle after making a kill. Many nights then, and since returning to the states, he'd held a loaded pistol to his head longing to put "him" out of his misery. But each time he couldn't complete the squeeze. Even that taunted him, mocked him, that he could only kill someone at a safe distance where he couldn't hear the victim's gurgling gasps for his last breaths.

"What are you calling me at this hour for?"

"We found the body tonight."

"What do you mean you found the body?" asked the hippie, in a fog.

"That hunter!"

"What hunter?"

"Don't make this any harder for me than it already is. You know what hunter. The one we wasted."

"Oh, now I'm following you. My mind takes a little to get hitting on all cylinders."

Does it ever hit on all cylinders, the trooper wondered.

"The hunter was wearing an orange hat. Do you remember picking that up and moving it with the body?"

"Hold on there a minute. You're coming at me with too much information. Let me get a cup of coffee and wake up a minute," said the hippie.

"I'm not going to wait until you brew a pot of coffee to talk about this."

"Hold the fort, big boy; I'm not going to heat it up. I just need to get the caffeine in my system." The hippie rolled out of his filthy, worn-out sleeping bag that lay on the cot a foot above the wooden floor of the old run-down house.

The trooper often wondered why the hippie even had a phone in the house when he didn't have much else. Tonight he was glad he did have the phone.

In a minute the hippie came back on the line. "Now what's this about you found the body and an orange hat?"

"We found the dead hunter, you know, from Saturday." He was doing his best to disassociate himself from the hunter, from the fact that he had killed the hunter. He was already learning, or trying to learn, how the killing game was played. How the killer lived with killing, with taking the life from another human being. How it had been for the hippie, and for his own dad, so many years ago. But *they were in a war.* He wasn't. He couldn't escape that fact no matter how many different ways the hippie had tried to convince him otherwise.

"Ok. That's good. We wanted them to find him, right."

"It's good that they found him, but his hat is missing."

"What do you mean his hat is missing?"

"He was wearing an orange ball cap. He was hunting with an orange ball cap on, to keep anyone from accidentally shooting him."

"Well he got shot anyway, didn't he?"

"Quit messing with me. Do you remember him wearing an orange ball cap?"

"Yeah, now that you mention it. He was definitely wearing an orange hat."

"So where is the hat?" asked the trooper. "Did you see the hat after the hunter was dead?"

"No, it didn't even cross my mind. I never had to keep track of hats before."

"Well this hat may prove to be a big problem for us."

"I'm not following you."

"Before me and the other law officers, the man's buddies, and the search and rescue people began our search for the hunter above Puma Creek Campground, it was established that he was wearing everything he had on when we moved him, and he was also wearing an orange ball cap. And I'll tell you something else I found out about him. He did two tours in Vietnam in the Army."

"He did?" the hippie answered, with that "oh no," quality in his voice. If that was true, thought the hippie, they had killed a fellow Namvet. They had added to that long list of vets that had survived the war, only to die "back in the world." And he had been involved. Not just involved, he made the decision that it had to be done.

"Are you okay?" asked the trooper, after too much silence. He knew the Vietnam connection wouldn't set well with the hippie, just as it hadn't set well with him. But he couldn't imagine how deeply wounded the hippie would be at the knowledge they had killed a Namvet. Even at that, he knew the hippie would deal with it like he seemed to deal with everything, by telling himself, "It don't mean nothin'."

"I'm fine," the hippie finally answered. "So how is the hat going to be a problem?" The hippie's normally paranoid mind still hadn't put the pieces together.

"Tomorrow, they're going to be looking all around the area where the body was found to try to come up with that hat. And when they don't find it, something isn't going to add up for them. They're going to get hung up on what happened to his hat, don't you think?"

"People lose hats all the time." The hippie just couldn't get his mind up to speed.

"Yeah, but they don't get shot in the head when they're wearing a hat that is supposed to prevent that. Are you getting it yet?" said the trooper, physically and mentally tired after a very long day, but growing more tired by the second with the hippie's inability to think clearly tonight. Of course, he had never tried to hold a rational conversation with the hippie this late at night before, at least not since the trooper grew up and moved away from home.

"Yeah, I think I'm finally getting the picture. That is a problem, isn't it? We need it to look like a hunting accident. But if the hunter who was shot was supposed to be wearing the hat to prevent getting shot by accident isn't wearing the hat and then gets shot... This is complicating my mind," said the hippie, as he gulped down some more cold, black coffee, drug the base of the phone with his left foot to the limit of its twenty-foot long cord, and poured another cup. "So what's the worse thing that will come of not finding the hat?"

"You really don't think well at this time of night, do you? The worst thing that can come of it is that someone decides to do a relentless search to turn up the hat and stumbles on to the same thing we had to kill the hunter for."

"Uh. I'm suddenly feeling sober. We do have a big problem, don't we?"

"Now you're getting the picture. But our situation is even worse than that?"

"What do you mean?"

"When the sheriff's deputy checked the hunter's rifle at the scene, its safety was off, and it had a spent shell casing in the chamber, and four loaded rounds still in the magazine."

"That is a problem! How could that have happened?" asked the hippie.

"Maybe if you weren't drunk or high so much of the time, it wouldn't have happened."

"What's that supposed to mean? I sense a great lack of respect in that comment, and I don't like it one bit."

"I'm sorry about that. I didn't mean to be disrespectful. But how is it that we didn't think to check the man's weapon when we moved it?" said the trooper.

"I guess we were pre-occupied with everything else."

"Well, that oversight may come back to bite us in the butt. What are we going to do about it?"

"Damn it. Give me a minute. That's a little heavy for me yet."

"While you're trying to sort things out, I'll tell you that the coroner and the deputy came up with a good scenario for how a hunter wearing a blaze-orange hat could still get shot in the head, accidentally."

"Yeah, and what's that?"

"If the shooter was directly behind the hunter and the hunter had his head bent down slightly, the orange on the hat would have been barely visible to the shooter. And then they speculated that the hunter could have been crouched down getting a drink and suddenly stood up, startling another hunter into mistaking the movement for a deer. He got buck fever and made a quick off-hand shot."

"That sounds plausible to me," said the hippie, who was thinking much better now. "So is that what they think happened?"

"That was just a good hypothetical explanation for how someone could accidentally shoot another hunter who was wearing an orange hat. There was also some discussion on the possibility that the hunter wasn't wearing his hat. But the hat aside, the bigger problem is why a hunter who is shot in the back of the head has a rifle loaded with an empty shell casing."

"What did the sheriff say about that?"

"We had a little brainstorming session and the ideas that were thrown out there were that, one way or another, the hunter could have taken a shot at something earlier and simply forgot to re-chamber a live round, or that it's possible he actually took a shot at his killer prior to being shot."

"And then he gets shot in the back of the head by the guy he first took the shot at?" said the hippie. "I doubt that one."

"So did we, so there's a better chance that the dead hunter just forgot to reload after shooting his gun earlier," said the trooper.

"I don't remember hearing any shots before the hunter went where he shouldn't be, do you?"

"No. But you know how it is up in the heavy timber with canyons and such. Sometimes you can't hear a shot from just around the ridge."

"You've got a point there," said the hippie. "Do you think the sheriff is leaning one way or the other?"

"I'm not sure, but he seemed to favor the accidental shooting theory. He said they'd know more after tomorrow's investigation. One problem I see for us is if they get stuck on the hat missing. From what I could discern, the hunter's friends are convinced the guy would never have hunted without his hat on, and so until they find that hat to prove it, we have a big problem."

"You mean the hunter's friends are going to look for the hat?"

"They didn't say anything about doing that yet. Right now everyone is assuming that in daylight the hat will be found some-where nearby. There's a bunch of brush and logs laying all over in the water downstream from where the body was. They're almost certain the hat will be in there somewhere."

"So if we could get back up there tonight and get that hat into the creek below the body's position," said the hippie, half-excited, "that problem would be solved."

"If I didn't run across the hat during broad daylight when I was looking for bone fragments below the body before we moved it, how do you think we could possibly go up there tonight—check that, there's no way I could go back into that area tonight. But how do you think you could go up there tonight and find a hat we didn't even see during daylight hours?"

"I guess you don't have much experience in the dark, do you?"

"Why do you say that?"

"In the Nam I did a lot of stuff in the dark. And believe me, in the thick jungle, dark is really dark. But when you shine a flashlight around, it's surprising the things you can see that you would never see by daylight. And over there some of the things you see by flashlight scare the hell out of you."

"I can imagine."

"Shining a flashlight beam around in the dark causes certain things to light up like a Neon light. Things like metal, glass, and orange ball caps."

"You're right. So can you get up there tonight and find that hat and get it into the creek below where the body was discovered?"

"I haven't had much sleep, but I'll get up there and give it my best shot." said the hippie.   Throughout his entire childhood, the hippie had a "can do" attitude about anything he did. In high school, he starred in cross country in the fall, and played shortstop on a good baseball team in the spring. He was also very bright, graduating as the valedictorian of his senior class at Cottage Grove High School in 1964.

His time in Nam had broken his go-getter spirit, and he had never recovered it since returning home to the states. The cold reception he received from the flower children in the airports and people in general, had only caused him to sink deeper in his defeatist attitude of: "What is the point to any of it? I spent over four years of my life doing what my country called me to do, and I come home and nobody even wants to know I was over there. In fact, they all want to pretend that 'over there' doesn't exist, that it is a figment of some people's imaginations."

"When you go up there," said the trooper, "you need to come in over the top from the Little Fall Creek side so no one sees your vehicle in the area. There's no telling exactly what kind of coverage the Sheriff's department might have up there tonight."

"Roger that. What are you going to do?" asked the hippie.

"I'm going to try to get some sleep. Tomorrow isn't going to be any fun."

"We'll connect tomorrow night then, to see what the score is. Hopefully, by then, I will have retrieved the hat and gotten it down into the creek at the crime scene. If I have, I'm sure you're little investigative party will have found it, and our worries on that front will be over."

"I sure hope so. We can't take a chance of them traipsing around up in the hills above there," said the trooper. "Let's just hope they become convinced the shooting was accidental by another hunter."

"Yeah, that's the way it has to turn out. Any chance you can steer them to that conclusion?"

"I'm afraid I can't do much without someone wondering why. When we were close to the body in the dark this evening, I wanted to suggest they look the creek over behind the search party's perimeter, but I didn't dare. And I couldn't be the one to find the body. Then, fortunately one of the SAR members had the smarts to shine his beam around down in the creek and spotted the corpse. If he hadn't done that, we would have a lot more to sweat right now than we do."

"Well, just do what you can. I better get going if I'm going to have any chance of finding that hat and getting it into the creek before morning. Call me tomorrow night."

"Okay," said the trooper. "Good luck."

"I'll see you later."

6

Daylight Search

At fifteen minutes before eight the next morning, Tuesday, October 28th, Sheriff's Investigator Lieutenant Dowdy and Deputy Lohner, drove into Puma Creek Campground. Deputy Bradshaw had a pot of coffee heating over the fire at Bruington's campsite. OSP troopers Wilson and Martin arrived in their rigs a few minutes later, followed immediately by Deputy Cardwell, Bradshaw's relief.

At Bruington's picnic table, coffee was served, and Dowdy opened up a couple Winchell's donut containers exposing two dozen donuts of different makes and models. He also set out a half-gallon container of orange juice. The setting couldn't be better, with huge firs overhead and a smattering of alder and maple trees nearby. The air was crisp and fresh, typical of late October in the foothills on the western slope of Oregon's Cascade Mountains.

The lawmen shot the bull for ten minutes, while sipping coffee, orange juice and wolfing down donuts. Then Trooper Wilson said, "Did you go to Bruington's house last night, Lieutenant Dowdy?"

"Yes, I accompanied his three hunting buddies. It was a very sad thing to watch. The only thing harder was when I've had to tell a

44

parent their child was killed, either in an accident or otherwise. Mrs. Bruington bawled her eyes out and so did her young daughters who are six and eight. All the relatives there were torn up over it. It really hit me hard thinking how my wife and family would respond the same way if something happened to me.

"She kept asking how anyone could have shot him accidentally while he was wearing that bright ball cap. 'How could they not see that?' I assured her we would be up here today trying to get some answers. Then she suddenly stopped crying, looked me right in the eyes, and asked, 'Are you sure it was an accident?'"

"So how did you answer that, Lieutenant?" Martin asked.

"By then the kids had been taken into another room by a relative. I told her we always consider all the possibilities. Then I said, 'Since you opened that door, Ma'am. Can you think of any reason why your husband would have been the target for murder?'"

"'Of course not,' she said. 'Roger was a friendly guy who had lots of friends.' Then it was like she forgot for a few seconds that he was dead, and said, 'He works in the shipping department at Weyerhauser. He's just your average Joe.' Then she burst into tears again, back to reality, and cried out, 'He wasn't just the average Joe to me and my girls, he was our everything! What are we going to do without him?'"

"'That had to be rough, Lieutenant," said Deputy Lohner.

"I was dying inside."

At 8:20, the four men of the investigative team left Puma Creek for the 600 yard hike back up hill along Jones Creek to return to the scene of the crime. At 8:30, Dowdy radioed Cardwell that the team was on site and beginning the investigation.

"You weren't kidding about all the blood splattered on the ferns over here, were you, Lieutenant Dowdy," said Trooper Martin. "It's not just on the ferns, it's on the moss and grass here too." Each team member took plenty of photographs.

After several more minutes, Martin said, "Lieutenant, I've found some bone fragment over here with skin still attached."

"Hold it up directly above where you found it so I can get the angle in relation to where the body was laying."

"Yes, that lines up perfectly. Our shooter had to be directly back up in there somewhere," said Dowdy, pointing to an area in the shade, seventy-five yards to the northeast behind the body's fallen position. "Lohner, make your way up there to look for footprints or other disturbance that would be human-caused. Be careful not to walk on any sign in getting there."

"Yes sir, Lieutenant."

Trooper Wilson put on his neoprene waders and began searching the creek for the ball cap. The water in the deepest portion of the pool was nearly two feet deep. He used a four-foot-long, half-inch bar with a hook on the end to probe underneath brush, sticks and logs.

Ten minutes later, over the radio, "Lieutenant Dowdy?"

"Yes, Deputy Lohner, what is it?"

"Much of the ground up here has been chewed up by elk hooves. I'm afraid we aren't going to do much good trying to find human prints in this mess."

"Well, do the best you can, look for anything. Look for a spent shell casing. That would be the best evidence we could find. Of course if the hunter was using anything other than an auto-loader, he would have had to eject the shell manually after the shot. And then, after he found that his target was a human and not a deer, he most likely would have gone back up there to recover the spent shell. I'm not holding my breath on finding a shell, but if it is there, we sure as heck don't want to miss it."

"Trooper Martin, I'm going to stand right where Bruington would have been standing when he was shot. You stand where you found the bone fragment. Lohner, line yourself up in a straight line with Trooper Martin and myself. There. Now move back another twenty yards.

"Trooper Martin, keep yourself in a direct line with me and

Deputy Lohner and walk away from me to the southwest. I want you to see if there is anything out there that could hold a bullet or a bullet fragment, any trees, downed logs, or stumps. If we can find the bullet, we'll have a huge piece of evidence."

"Yes sir." Trooper Martin walked slowly away.

Five minutes later, "I'm sorry, sir, there's nothing out here that would have stopped a bullet."

"I was afraid of that," answered Dowdy. "Trooper Wilson, are you finding anything in the water?"

"No, sir," he said, continuing to wade around in the twenty-feet-long by seven-feet-wide pool, probing every nook and cranny.

"Don't quit until you find that hat. I'd bet my right arm, it's in that creek."

Half an hour later, nothing more had been found by any of the four.

"How long are we going to keep looking, Lieutenant?" asked Wilson.

"If I have to get a snorkel mask, we're going to find that hat."

"With the logs at the bottom of this pool holding everything back, there's no way I've missed the hat if it's here. You're welcome to try for yourself. Why are you so certain the hat has to be here?"

"If you had watched and listened to Bruington's wife last night, you'd understand."

"I guess you're probably right, Lieutenant. But, suppose he set the hat down somewhere earlier to cool his head off, maybe while he sat on a stump and ate a sandwich or something. Maybe he even dipped the hat in the creek somewhere else, then accidentally walked off and left it. We've all done that. I mean, honestly, it makes a whole lot more sense that he would have been shot accidentally if he wasn't wearing the hat.

On the radio, "Deputy Lohner, come on down here."

"Be right there sir," answered Lohner, who had searched the area to the northeast out to over a hundred yards.

The four lawmen huddled near the spray-painted outline of Bruington's body.

"Did you find anything up there, Deputy Lohner, that can be considered evidence?"

"No, sir, I didn't. If there was any human activity there on Saturday, the elk scuffed it all up."

"Trooper Martin found no sign of a bullet or fragment lodging anywhere on the opposite side of the creek. Nor did he find anymore bone fragments or skin," said Dowdy. "Trooper Wilson did not find the hat or anything else in the creek. Of course if there had been any bone or skin there it would have been all but impossible to find, and besides that some crawdads would have carried it into a dark crevasse to feast on it. So let's sum up what we do have, what we do know, and what we can conclude regarding this shooting.

"Okay, we know Bruington was shot while wearing black jeans, and a red and black plaid shirt. Supposedly he was wearing an orange ball cap, too. But since we can't find that, we have to accept the possibility that he wasn't wearing it and didn't have it with him when he was shot. Or whoever shot him took the hat so it would appear he wasn't wearing it and was, therefore, more likely to be mistaken for a deer when he was shot. What do you guys think of that?"

"I think your idea that the shooter could have taken the hat sounds like a definite option, Lieutenant," said Lohner. "Though I personally have a hard time seeing how anyone wouldn't have seen the red plaid shirt and identified it as human and not a deer."

"With all this high sword fern around here, I have no problem believing the shirt could have been obscured," said Wilson. "And another consideration is that the shot was made from the northeast toward the southwest. If the shot was made anytime during the middle of the day, the shooter would have been contending with the sun, possible glaring or shading issues. It could have been difficult for him to see any colors on the shaded side of Bruington's body."

"That's a great observation, Deputy Wilson," said Dowdy. "Now let's consider this. Accepting that Bruington was shot from probably seventy-five to a hundred yards away and hit dead center in the back of his head, what does that tell us about the shooter?"

"Either he was a skilled marksman hitting exactly what he was aiming at," said Wilson, "a less-skilled shooter getting lucky, or the head shot was made completely by accident by another hunter throwing his rifle up in a hurry and popping off a quick shot at what he believed was a deer."

"I concur with that," said Lohner.

"Here's a consideration, sir," chimed in Martin. "How many hunters pop off shots at deer during a buck-only hunt, without confirming the animal has the necessary fork on one antler? There are no antlerless hunts up here in this area right now, and the Northwest Hunter's Choice Season doesn't begin until this next weekend."

"That's a good point, Trooper," said Dowdy.

"The percentage of accidental, mistaken for game, shootings is always much higher during the seasons that allow for shooting does," Martin added. "You can go into almost any bar in a small-town during the hunter's choice seasons, in plain clothes of course, and listen to hunters loosened up with several beers joke about taking brush shots at anything that moves. It's scary. That's one of the reasons I'm a strong proponent of mandating hunters to wear hunter orange over much of their torsos while hunting big-game."

"What are they going to do, mandate all the hikers and bikers in the woods during any big game hunting season to wear hunter orange, too?" asked Wilson.

"I don't want to talk politics right now," said Dowdy. "Let's get back on point. In order for someone to deliberately shoot Bruington out here in the woods, he would've had to have motive. I'm going to question a number of people, including Bruington's wife, his relatives, buddies, and co-workers to see if any of them know anything that could point a finger toward someone having a motive.

I'll tell you guys right now, I'm leaning toward this being an accidental shooting, just as I described last night. I think Bruington got down to get a drink from the creek, then raised up and startled another hunter, who thought he saw a deer and wheeled around and took a quick shot. Then upon seeing his mistake the hunter left the area immediately, probably taking Bruington's hat with him."

"Before we call it a day, let's do a thorough search of the perimeter of the crime scene out to seventy-five or a hundred yards, just in case an animal carried the hat off. It probably wouldn't have carried it any farther than that. Also keep your eyes open for footprints."

After over an hour of searching the perimeter, Martin said, "Lieutenant, if the hat was here, don't you think we would have found it by now?"

"Yeah, I think you're right. And I think we've found all the evidence we're going to find from this crime scene. With no footprints to go on, no shell casings, no bullets, and nothing else, this could turn out to be the perfect crime. What better time to kill someone—either by accident or on purpose—if you want to get away with it, than during a big-game season? Did either of you troopers have game duty out this way on Saturday?"

"No sir, I was covering the Middle Fork Willamette area above Hills Creek Reservoir," said Martin.

"I wasn't here either, Lieutenant. I covered Walterville north, Camp Creek and the Mohawk River Drainage."

One of them—or both—were lying. But unless Dowdy could get a reliable witness to state that one of the troopers was seen in the area, there was no way to prove it. And since they weren't suspects, Dowdy wouldn't even check their logbooks. Both state troopers had great leeway in how they covered their territories, and they didn't always keep the OSP dispatcher apprised of their location.

"I just thought if either of you had been in the area Saturday, you might have taken down some license numbers of various vehicles here. It was just a stab in the dark. I'm afraid our chances of figuring out who the shooter was are slim, unless we get a break outside the crime scene. We could put out a public appeal for anyone having any knowledge of people out here on Saturday to call the sheriff or state police, but we'd get little or no response." It didn't occur to Dowdy that what he should ask the public is whether anyone saw an Oregon State Police officer in the area on Saturday.

"I think you're right, sir," said Martin.

"Well, let's get back to base and call it good," said Dowdy. "I'll need all your film when we get back. I've got the cheekbone and skin that Martin found, and numerous fern leaves, fir needles and grasses with blood on them, so we can confirm the blood type as matching Bruington's. That's just a formality. We all know it's his."

Upon arriving back at the station, Dowdy spoke with Coroner Villard, "Have you come up with anything good from Bruington's body?"

"Yes, I've completed my examination. The bullet that killed him was from a .270 caliber rifle and, based on the damage it did, it was undoubtedly a hollow point. There was enough damage to the bone on the inside of the entry hole that I was unable to determine the exact angle of entry. But judging by the area missing from the face, I'm sure we had it figured about right in the woods: a slight up angle from back to front of the skull. I didn't find any bullet fragments in the skull or anywhere else on the body. As we already knew, the cause of death was the headshot. There were no other wounds on the body. But as we expected, there was gunshot residue on both of his hands, his lower face and neck, as well as his shirt-sleeves and around the shirt's collar area.

"The time of death, near as I can determine, was between eleven in the morning to one in the afternoon Saturday. Since his stomach only had, what looked like, some cereal, an orange, and maybe half a ham and cheese sandwich, I don't think he had eaten lunch yet. Plus his pack contained two and a half ham, cheese, and lettuce sandwiches, an apple and a Pay Day candy bar."

"Good work Villard."

"Thanks. Did you guys find the hat and other evidence?"

"Nothing."

"Nothing?"

"Yes. Nothing. No hat, no shell casings, no bullets lodged in wood, and no foot prints. The ground around the whole area is covered in heavy moss and fir needles. And to make matters worse, the elk had been all over the perimeter."

"Tough luck, huh? So where does that leave you?"

"Empty handed. A dead body, no hat, nothing to go on except what we already determined last night. He was probably shot from a position seventy yards to the northeast. Whether it was an accident, or murder, is hard to say. Oh we did find part of a cheek bone with the skin attached on the opposite side of the creek where all the blood was splattered. I'll get that over to you right away."

"That's good. If you were a betting man, Lieutenant, where would you place your money?"

"That's the frustrating part. Everything about it screams murder, but I have no evidence to go on other than the bullet hole in the back of his head, and the peculiar circumstance of the rifle being off safe and containing a spent round in the chamber."

"So what are you going to assume, or theorize?"

"The problem is, why would anyone murder him? And in the woods while he is hunting? From the little bit I've learned about him, he was just your average Joe. I'm going to dig into his background to see if there is anything that would indicate where someone would have motive. I think it's going to be a difficult case to solve, unless we get some unexpected break?"

"I tend to agree with you on that."

"Well, thanks for the information. I better do some digging. If you come up with any new ideas or theories, let me know," said Dowdy.

"I will. Good luck."

"I'll definitely need it."

7

The Buddies

At 4 o'clock, Tuesday afternoon, Dick Eastbrook called the Lane County Sheriff's Office from work and requested to speak with Lieutenant Dowdy regarding the Roger Bruington death.

"This is Dowdy."

"Yes, Lieutenant Dowdy. This is Dick Eastbrook. Have you guys learned anymore about Bruington's death?"

"Mr. Eastbrook, we're doing everything we can. Of course, I can't give you specifics regarding our findings."

"Come on, Lieutenant. I was Bruington's best friend. You don't have to give me the same line of bull you have to give everyone else. I was on that hill when you found him, for crying out loud."

"I'm sorry if you think I'm giving you a line of bull, Mr. East-brook. I'm not trying to put you off. I know how difficult losing your best friend must be. But there are procedures that must be adhered to in an investigation like this in order to not compromise any potential evidence or witnesses."

"You've got your lines down well, don't you, Lieutenant. You

53

and I know damn well something is fishy about this whole situation. At least answer me this one, did you find his orange ball cap?"

"Why is that hat so important to you anyway?"

"I've hunted elk with Roger Bruington for eight years and hunted deer with him some too. He's always worn that hat. If you didn't find the hat, that raises some serious questions in my mind. Now did you find the damn hat or didn't you?"

"I understand that your emotions are on edge right now, Eastbrook. But getting mad at me isn't going to help the situation. I will answer any questions that I feel I can answer and not compromise the integrity of our investigation. So, about the hat: *No, we did not find the hat.*"

"You looked the whole creek over and the banks around the area completely?"

"Yes we did. One of the state troopers waded in the water and probed under everything, and still found nothing. You're not the only one that is stuck on why that hat wasn't with Bruington's body. But the truth is, whether the hat is ever found may not have any bearing on this case. I mean, he could have taken the hat off to sit on a stump and eat a sandwich hours before he was shot. The hat could be anywhere in those woods."

Dowdy didn't tell him the hat was actually a small piece of the puzzle compared to Bruington's rifle being chambered with a spent round.

"Are you guys going to search some more for the hat?" asked Eastbrook.

"I don't expect so."

"What else did you guys learn or find up there today?"

"I really can't tell you anymore, Mr. Eastbrook."

"Did you find any shell casings, or bullets lodged in logs, trees, or stumps?"

"It sounds like you should be a homicide investigator, Mr. Eastbrook. I can't tell you what else we found, but I will tell you we looked for all those things as well as footprints and any other clues that could lead us to the killer."

"So you didn't find any shell casings?"

"That's not what I said, is it?" said Dowdy, running out of patience. "Look, Eastbrook, we're doing, and will do, the best we can to figure out what happened and to find the shooter. You have to trust me on that. I'm on you're team, and I need you on mine. I'll tell you this. We have completed our investigation of the crime scene and the surrounding area. A herd of elk trampled through the area where the shot came from. You being an elk hunter, I don't think I have to say anymore. You've seen how they tear things up."

"So are you done at Bruington's campsite also?"

"Yes, though I still have a deputy there. As a matter of fact, just as you called, I was getting ready to call Jan Bruington to see if someone could get up there and get the truck and other stuff."

"I'll call her myself and tell her Dave Stephens and I will get it as soon as I get off work."

"Thanks," said Dowdy. Before you go, Mr. Eastbrook, you need to realize that this is going to be a difficult case to solve unless we catch an unexpected break. A man was killed in the forest during deer season while he was hunting. Chances are no one witnessed it, and probably no one paid attention to who was in the area at the time of the shooting. The fact that we found Bruington two days after he was killed makes it even less likely we'll ever get the answer to who did it."

"You mean to tell me someone is going to get away with killing my best friend, and there's nothing you, I or anyone can do about it. That's bull!"

"No, I'm not saying that at all. I'm just being realistic about that possibility."

"So why don't you go over to Bruington's house and tell his wife that 'he shouldn't have been walking through that area there' when some trigger-happy hunter got a bad case of buck fever and blew her husband's brains all over the forest with a sniper-quality shot to the back of his head."

"I can feel your pain, Mr. Eastbrook. I really can. And I wish I could do something about it, something to ease it. Believe me when I say I am a long ways from being done on Bruington's case. I will be questioning his family members, friends and co-workers to try to get some answers. I'm going to do my darnedest to figure out who did it and why. But it may take some time."

"Well I'm glad to hear you at least say that," said Eastbrook, who was cooling down a little. "My hunting buddies that you met yesterday and I will go up in that area and do a thorough search for his hat in a day or two. We believe that hat holds some answers."

"I know the hat is a puzzle," admitted Dowdy. "It's even possible a wild animal carried it away. If that was the case, it could be in some badger or coyote hole seven feet under ground."

"Well, we have to give it a shot anyway. Not finding the hat may not prove anything, but if we can find it, we will at least know it wasn't taken away by the shooter."

"You do have a good point there," conceded Dowdy. "Now I need to get back to work. If you learn anything that might help the case, Mr. Eastbrook, will you call me immediately?"

"You can count on it."

Dick Eastbrook on the phone with Dave Stevens half an hour later—

"Dave, I talked to Lieutenant Dowdy and learned that they did not find Roger's hat. And from what I could determine, they didn't find any other solid evidence in the area either."

"They didn't? So what's that mean?"

"To be honest, I think they're already leaning hard toward this shooting being little more than another hunter mistaking Roger for a deer and killing him accidentally."

"Are you serious? They're going to let it ride like that?"

"I didn't say that, Dave. What I mean is that's their best guess right now. But Dowdy told me they're treating it as a possible murder and have every intention of questioning Roger's friends, family and co-workers."

"What kind of questions did he ask you, Dick?"

"He didn't. I kind of kept him on the defensive."

"Not you, Dick?"

"Is that supposed to be funny?"

"Not at all. Just if the shoe fits most the time, you wear it very well."

"Funny. I am very curious what happened to Roger's hat. We all assumed it would turn up in the creek. That really only leaves three other possibilities. One, whoever shot him took it, possibly to make it look more likely that he could have been mistakenly shot. Two, a wild animal carried it away. And three, Roger took it off and accidentally walked away from it some time before he was shot. What do you think, Dave?"

"When did Roger ever lose a hat when he was hunting or fishing with us?"

"Never."

"Right. And now the day there is a trigger-happy hunter in the woods with the fever, he leaves it lay somewhere? I don't think so."

"Me either."

"A wild animal carrying it away is a possibility. But chances are if an animal took the hat, it only would have carried it a short distance and then lost interest. I think the first possibility is the most likely. If you accidentally shot and killed someone when you were hunting alone, Dick, and no one else was around, would you turn yourself in?"

"That's a real tough one. And I darn sure never plan to pull a trigger fast enough to find out. You don't really believe Roger being shot in the head could be an accident anyway, do you?"

"I can't imagine anyone having a reason to murder Roger."

"Either way, Dave—you, me and Aaron need to search those woods for that hat. At least we'll feel like we're doing something positive."

"Have you talked to Jan?"

"Yes. I talked to her this morning. She said the memorial service is scheduled for Saturday at one."

"How's she doing, anyway?"

"She's doing as well as can be expected. She has lots of family around, but she's worn out and very emotional."

"I can't imagine my wife having to deal with something like this."

"Me neither. Well, I'll talk to you between now and Saturday."

"Okay. Hang in there."

"I'll try."

Roger Bruington, Dick Eastbrook, Dave Stevens and Aaron Howe had hunted elk together in the Southern Oregon Coastal Mountain Range for the last eight years. Roger and Dick, friends since grade school, met Dave and Aaron while attending Lane Community College in Eugene, Oregon in the winter of 1971-72. At the time, Roger was fresh out of the Army, and had only returned to the States weeks earlier from his two consecutive tours in Vietnam totaling twenty-four months. Aaron was the only other military veteran, though he never served in Vietnam.

Roger and Dick were laughing and cutting up in the college cafeteria one day at lunch when Dave and Aaron were drawn to their table. Dick was sharing his latest deer hunting tales and Roger was swearing he was fabricating the whole thing, calling him a BSer, who was full of it and full of himself. When Dave and Aaron walked up to the table, Aaron thought things were about to get out of hand. Roger, sporting his military-cut, short, black hair, was obviously no match verbally for the larger, long-haired, handsome Dick Eastbrook; and Aaron wasn't about to stand by and see a fellow ex-grunt get the short end of the stick with any long-hair.

But he and Dave quickly discovered they were witnessing two best friends enjoying their time together like they hadn't been able to do in a long time. Dick invited the two to have a seat, then continued to let his hunting tales flow freely. In no time, Dave and Aaron knew they had met their matches. Dick soon invited them to join him and Roger that evening at one of the local pubs near the University of Oregon for some brews. They never looked back.

The four of them fished and camped together several times the following summer, hunted deer together in October, then hooked up for the seven-day second-season Roosevelt Elk hunt in the Sixes Unit inland from Bandon on the southern Oregon coast in late November.

At the time the four met in the cafeteria, Roger and Dick were the only ones who were married. Roger had married his beautiful, dark-haired, petite wife, Jan, on a fourteen day leave home from Vietnam at the end of August 1970. Dick, on the other hand, married his high-school sweetheart, Wanda Rhodes, the summer following their graduation in 1966. Dave got married in 1975, and Aaron was still single the day Roger was killed.

8

The Hat

Late that evening, the state trooper, wearing blue jeans and a brown short-sleeved shirt, pulled his green Ford pickup into the long, gravel driveway of the run-down old house in the woods at the edge of a large field near Wallace Creek outside of Jasper. He wasted no time getting out and knocking on the partly open front door.

"Del, we didn't find the hat this morning. What happened? Weren't you able to find it?"

"I had a flat tire on the way up there, and when I went to put the spare on it was flat, too."

"So you didn't even get to look for the hat?"

"No. I had to wait at my truck for several hours until some logger came by and gave me a lift to the Fall Creek Service Station. The gravel road on Little Fall Creek isn't exactly Interstate 5 during the middle of the night."

"What did you tell the logger about what you were doing there at that hour?"

"I told him the Oregon State trooper that covers Fall Creek murdered a hunter over the weekend and asked me to cover it up for him."

"That's not the least bit funny."

"Sorry. Actually, he wasn't the talkative type. Didn't ask me anything, and I didn't volunteer. I'm sure he figured I was just a dumb-ass hippie out looking for some psychedelic mushrooms or something."

"So now they've completed their investigation in the area and have no hat. That leaves us in a precarious position."

"Why? What are they saying about the hat?"

"The investigating Lieutenant, Jim Dowdy, thinks one of three things happened to the hat. One, the shooter took the hat to make it look like the dead hunter had been hunting without it and was, therefore, more likely to be accidentally shot. Two, the dead hunter left it somewhere earlier in the day and wasn't wearing it when he was shot. Or, a wild animal may have carried it away."

"So, the law is done looking for the hat then?" asked the hippie.

"Well, the law is, but you can be sure the hunter's buddies aren't done looking. They believe the hat missing is a big piece to the puzzle of what actually happened to their friend."

"So we still have a problem, right? If the hunting buddies are going to search those woods for the hat, sooner or later they're going to stumble into the wrong area."

"That's what I'm afraid of."

"I'm curious, has there been any hint that any of the lawmen suspect the shooting didn't actually take place where they found the dead hunter?"

"No. I think we did a nice job of staging the scene. I'm sure they've bought that part of it hook, line and sinker. And we can thank a herd of elk for helping cover our butts by trampling around the area in the time between our plant and when the body was discovered."

"I told you I had a way with wild animals. One time in the Nam, I had a 300 pound tiger prowling around this patch of elephant grass I was sleeping in on one of my sniper runs. The damn thing was sniffing and pawing my whole body. I lay as still as anything living can, breathing super shallow, just knowing at any moment he was going to take a huge chomp out of me. That went on for at least two minutes. Finally, he got right up near my neck, and I couldn't take it anymore. I gave a big spray of bug repellant right in his eyes. He coughed and snarled and ran away."

"You never told me about the tiger before. Geez, I thought the snakes and other poisonous reptiles were bad enough. How did you guys ever get any sleep?"

"I don't know if we ever did. It all seemed like one bad dream, and it still does. Everyone and everything over there conspired to kill American soldiers by any and every means possible. If that didn't make you paranoid, you were already dead. The only way to survive it mentally was to accept that *you were already dead just being there*, even if your body hadn't found that out yet."

"Why are you opening up to me about that stuff now, after all these years?"

"Because you have blood on your hands, you've killed. You're now one of us—*a killer.*"

"Don't say it like that. I hate myself for what I've done, not only for what I did to that hunter, but to his wife, to his girls, to his family, and to his friends. And then knowing he was a soldier over there just like you and my dad, I haven't slept more than a few hours a night since it happened."

"You've got to tell yourself, we had to do it. Tell yourself, it don't mean nothin'. Trust me, it works. When you told me the hunter you shot was a Vietnam vet, this horror tried to take me over. It haunted me. But I told myself, it don't mean nothin'. It always works. That's how you live with it. That's the only way to live with it when you have stopped the heart of another human being. Say it with me now. It don't mean nothin'. Come on say it."

Together they said it. "It don't mean nothin'. It don't mean nothin'. Nothin' means nothin'.'" Then they hugged for the first time in years; they were one now. The trooper cried. The hippie cried. Then the hippie lit up a joint and handed it to the trooper.

The trooper, who hadn't used marijuana in over two years, took two light tokes, and got a slight high. He then handed the joint back to the hippie, who took several long, deep drags and got good and high.

Finally, the trooper said, "Del, we've got to find that hat and get it down near the crime scene before the buddies get back up there."

"No problem. I'm feelin' so good. I'll find that hat for you. I'll go back up in the morning and find it. It's probably in the bottom of a fern patch not far from where you shot the hunter. Since they've already looked all around the area where the body was found, where should I put it?"

"You need to make it look like an animal carried it off. You'll need to get one of those raccoon skulls at the shack and use the skull's teeth to make it look like an animal chewed on the hat a little.

"Then take the hat over the ridge about 150 yards to the north-west and lay it next to a tree or a stump. We didn't search that area at all, and it's very likely the hunter's buddies will give the area closest to the scene the most thorough search and work up hill from there. At least we better hope they do."

When the trooper was done giving instructions, he said, "Do you think you can handle that?"

"Look, kid, I may be high, but you damn well still better treat me with respect. I heard every word you said. It's cool. I have it handled."

9

The Investigation

First thing Wednesday morning, Lieutenant Dowdy began doing his background investigation on Roger Bruington. He knew if the shooting was, in fact, an accident there was little chance he would ever find the hunter who had accidentally shot him. But he felt if it wasn't an accident, his chances of figuring out who the shooter was were better.

Three things bothered him: Bruington's rifle's safety not being engaged; the empty shell in the chamber; and the hat not being found anywhere around the crime scene.

He made up his mind that he had to go back up into those woods himself and look for that hat some more, whether the hunting buddies did or not. In fact, he had to do it before they did. As much as he wanted to give everyone the benefit of the doubt, and wanted to believe Bruington's hunting buddies were on the level with him, as a cop he had learned years ago that people can surprise you.

Dowdy wanted to learn more about Bruington as a person, and part of that included learning about his military record, particularly his two tours in Vietnam. So he got on the phone to military records, explained that Bruington had been killed and that he thought Bruington's military record might help in his investigation. After a little convincing, the woman at the records office agreed to express forward a copy of Bruington's service record to Dowdy.

Dowdy then called the homes of the hunting buddies to arrange individual meetings with them, then called Roger Bruington's widow, Jan, and set up a meeting with her.

At two o clock, Dowdy arrived at the Bruington's place off of South 32nd Street in Springfield. When Jan answered the door, he greeted her, and she invited him into her living room. She asked if he minded if her sister and brother-in-law sat in on the interview. He consented, knowing their presence would be a comfort to her.

He took a seat in a brown rocking chair across from the couch that the sister and brother-in-law were sitting on. Immediately he noticed the two foot by two foot photo of Jan, Roger, and their two young daughters on the wall over the couch, but didn't comment about it. Jan sat down in the blue easy chair near one end of the couch.

"I know this is a very rough time for you, Mrs. Bruington. I am deeply sorry for your loss. But I also want to get whatever information you can give me that might assist in my investigation into your husband's death."

"I appreciate your sympathy, Lieutenant" she said. "And please call me Jan."

"Yes. Jan. So Jan, if I ask any questions today that you don't feel comfortable answering, feel free to decline. Of course anything I ask, I'm asking for a reason. The more you can tell me the better."

"Okay, I'll do the best I can," she said, glancing from the Lieutenant to her sister and brother-in-law and then back to the Lieutenant.

"Do you know if your husband had any enemies, or any relationships that seemed strained?"

"No, he didn't have any enemies. He was an easy-going man. Anyone could get along with him."

"How was your marriage relationship?"

She appeared puzzled at that question and squinted her eyes, while looking at her brother-in-law. He gave her a slight nod.

"Roger and I never had a fight in the ten years of our marriage. A woman couldn't ask for a better husband than he was to me."

"I'm sure that only makes losing him more difficult," said Dowdy. "What kind of father was he?"

"He was an excellent father. What do these questions have to do with his death?"

"I'm just trying to get an overall feel of the kind of person Roger was.

"I understand."

"What do you know about his military service?"

"Not much, really. He didn't talk much about it. He did two tours in Vietnam from 1969 to 1971. We were actually married on his two-week leave home between the two tours."

"Most soldiers had a thirty-day leave between tours in Vietnam, though most soldiers didn't serve two consecutive tours there. Why was Roger's leave so short?"

"That was a huge disappointment to me at the time," she said. "We were engaged for well over a year before that. A few months before leaving for Vietnam in 1969, he asked me to marry him. That was when he was stationed at Fort Lewis, Washington. We saw each other all the time during his six months there. Anyway, originally his leave between tours was scheduled to be thirty days. But three weeks before he came home, he wrote and told me the operation he was involved in wouldn't allow that long a leave. The Army had cut it to two weeks. It was against his wishes. But he still wanted to get married while he was home.

"And so on the fifth day after he got home on leave, we got married in a nice church wedding. Believe me when I say, it killed me to see him fly away back to the war two days after we got back from our honeymoon. I was so afraid I was going to end up one of those broken-hearted war-widows. Over the next year, I wrote him three times a week, but only heard from him half a dozen times. The operations he was involved in kept him away from any place where he could send me any mail.

Thirteen months after Roger left, he arrived at my front door in his dress green uniform, all proud and everything. No phone call, anything. He just showed up one day. I latched on to him and cried tears of joy all over him. He was home for good, though he had to return to Fort Lewis a couple weeks later to get his discharge."

"Well you obviously had a very loving relationship, Jan," said Dowdy. "Did Roger ever say what the special operation was that he was involved in that cut his leave short?"

"Oh no, it was one of those classified things. I guess everything they do in the military is classified to some extent, isn't it?"

"Yes, I suppose that's true. But a lot of things become unclassified years afterward, and even at that, there are plenty of soldiers that do talk about those things with their wives."

"Trust me, Roger wasn't one of them. So there really isn't anything more I can tell you about his service. Maybe you can get some information from his official Army records, or maybe his friend Aaron Howe can tell you more."

As a matter of fact, the Army is sending me copies of his service record. I should receive them in a couple of days. Why would Aaron Howe possibly know something more about Roger's military duty?"

"He was in the Army, too, though I don't think he served any time in Vietnam. I thought he and Roger had sort of a special camaraderie because of them both being Army veterans. I sometimes heard them talk a little about the Army when it was just the two of them."

"Thanks for that piece of information. Did Roger ever say anything about being involved in any private activities, or did you ever hear him talking on the phone about what might have sounded like something private that he wouldn't talk to you about?"

"No."

"Well, I think you've answered all my questions for now, Jan. Oh there is one other thing."

"Yes."

"The rifle that Roger hunted with, that he was using on this trip, was that a new gun to him? I mean, was this the first season he has hunted with it?"

"Why do you ask?"

"I'm just curious, that's all."

"I honestly can't tell you what gun he took with him. I've never paid much attention to his gun collection or which guns he uses for what. But I do know he hasn't bought any new or used guns in several years now. So I guess the answer to your question is, no, it wasn't a new gun to him. Does that matter?"

"No, like I said, I was just curious." Getting up from the rocking chair, he said, "Again, I really am sorry for what you're going through. If there is anything I can do, let me know."

"I appreciate that, Lieutenant Dowdy. Let me walk you to the door."

That evening, seated in the living room of Dave Steven's home in Springfield, after several questions had been asked and answered, and the topic of the missing hat had been discussed, Dowdy said, "Dave, has Roger ever hunted with a semi-automatic rifle when hunting deer or elk with you guys?"

"No. He doesn't have any semi-automatic big game rifles. Well, at least none that he uses. He does own an AR-15. And he has a Ruger semi-auto twenty-two that he hunts varmints and target shoots with. Why do you ask?"

"I was just curious, that's all."

"Seems like an odd question, under the circumstances."

"I know it probably does. But I've learned over the years to go with my instincts in these investigations."

"So what do your instincts have to do with whether Roger ever used a semi-auto big game rifle?"

"Nothing in particular. Just a question," said Dowdy. "Do you know if he did any target shooting with one of his semi-auto's recently?"

"No, I don't. I'll say this, he often shot the Ruger for target practice because the shells are so much cheaper and he just liked that gun a lot. But I can't see how any of this has anything to do with his death."

"It doesn't. It's just something I was curious about."

Neither Dowdy nor Stevens spoke for thirty seconds, as each took another sip of the coffee Dave's wife had brought them earlier. Stevens felt Dowdy searching into his inner being as if trying to find a missing puzzle piece. He felt as if he was part of a Lieutenant Columbo investigation. One in which the Lieutenant plays dumb and asks seemingly stupid questions, but is gleaning special meaning from every word, every nuance in the conversation.

Dowdy took another sip from his coffee cup and then put it down on the stand beside his chair. He looked directly into Stevens eyes, smiled a close-mouthed smile, and then said, "Well, Mr. Stevens, if you think of anything that might help in this investigation, you'll let me know, won't you?"

"You can count on it," Stevens heard himself say.

Dowdy got up from the chair and walked to the front door, with Stevens following a few feet behind him. Dowdy opened the door, then turned part-way around and said, "Have a good evening, and thanks for the good coffee."

10

Aaron Howe Interview

After leaving Steven's place, Lieutenant Dowdy dropped by Aaron Howe's place on the off chance he might catch him at home, since he hadn't connected with him by phone earlier in the day.

When Howe answered the door, obviously surprised, Dowdy said, "Mr. Howe, I tried to contact you by phone earlier today, but I guess you were at work. I have a few questions to ask you regarding Roger Bruington's death. Do you mind if I come in?"

Getting over the initial surprise, Howe said, "Sure, Lieutenant. Come on in. I'd be happy to help you in any way I can."

Howe led Dowdy into the living room, gestured toward a brown chair for him to have a seat, while he settled into his favorite chair, a wine-red, Lazy-Boy easy-chair. Then suddenly remembering his manners, said, "Can I get you a cup of coffee, a soda, or a beer? Well I guess you can't drink beer on duty, can you?"

"I'm fine," answered Dowdy. "I just came from your friend Dave Stevens place and had coffee there."

"You just came from Dave's house? What did he tell you?" he

said, without thinking how that might sound.

"I just asked him some questions, like I'm going to ask you. Just routine stuff. I'm trying to get a good background on Bruington and pick up any information that might be helpful in solving this case."

"I see. Go ahead and ask away," said Howe, doing his best to maintain his composure. "Monday, Dick Eastbrook said that you weren't hunting with him and Stevens because you already got your deer."

"That's right."

"It was a forked horn, wasn't it?"

"Maybe not anything to brag about, but the meat is excellent."

"I can imagine. The does, spikes and forks I've killed have all been more tender than the big bucks. Do you ever smoke any of the meat?"

"You bet. I always smoke up all the meat from the neck, and some of the other scraps. As a matter of fact, I'll get you a couple pieces." Before Dowdy could respond, Howe jumped up from his chair and went to the kitchen and retrieved four good-sized pieces from a quart mayonaise jar and returned to the living room with them.

"Here. This is some excellent stuff," he said, handing a couple pieces to Dowdy and keeping the other two for himself. Both of them began chewing on the end of a piece.

"That is good. What do you use for your brine and wood?"

"I use Soy and Teriyaki sauces, brown sugar and pepper. And of course, salt. And I use some cherry-tree bark for the smoke."

"If I don't leave here with anything else tonight, it was worth the stop for this jerky," said Dowdy.

"Thanks. I'm glad you like it."

"Jan Bruington told me you served in the Army during Vietnam."

"That's right, though I didn't have to go to Vietnam." Immediately he wished he hadn't said it like that, because he didn't know whether Dowdy was for or against the war, and Stevens didn't want to come across in the wrong way.

"I was in the marines myself—just in time for the end of Korea."

"Did you see any combat?"

"Nothing to write home about," he answered, then chewed on the jerky some more.

"How is Jan Bruington doing, anyway? I was going to call her some time this evening. It's not easy, you know. I mean, I care deeply about what she's going through and all. But what do you say?"

"I know what you mean," said Dowdy. "It can be quite awkward. Her sister and brother-in-law were there when I was by early this afternoon. She seems to be holding up okay. But since I don't know her, it's a hard read."

"She's a strong woman. Always has been, no matter how small she is physically. I always envied Roger for what a beautiful, wonderful wife he had." He regretted saying that as soon as it left his mouth, knowing how it might be interpreted. "I mean, not that I envied him, in the sense of wishing she was my wife or anything. Just that he had a woman like her and I didn't. Well, you know what I mean, I'm sure."

"Oh yeah, I know what you mean," answered Dowdy, though he logged Howe's statement in his memory bank as potential motive. Then he felt guilty for doing so, while eating the man's home-made jerky. He reminded himself that he was a cop first and had to pay attention to any possible clues, whether he wanted to or not.

Howe wondered how he could possibly dig himself out of the hole he had just dug, then Dowdy made it a little deeper.

"Where were you last Friday and Saturday, Mr. Howe?"

Howe knew that question was bound to come up, since Dowdy had already been told by Eastbrook at Puma Creek Campground on Monday that he wasn't hunting with Eastbrook and Stevens those days. But the fact that Dowdy was following it up immediately after his blunder regarding Jan Bruington caused his stomach muscles to suddenly grow tight.

He had never been what most people would call a quick thinker, though he was plenty smart. Smart enough to figure out how to stay out of Vietnam while so many of his Army buddies were being sent there. It was just that sometimes he blurted out what was on his mind without weighing the potential consequences

"I stayed home Friday evening after work and watched the Friday Night At the Movies on TV."

"What movie was on? My wife and I like to watch the Friday night movie ourselves, but we missed last Friday because we were over playing cards at my brother's house."

Howe felt like this informal session had turned into an interrogation. And he had been the cause of it with that stupid comment.

"Saturday Night Fever," he managed to say, "starring John Travolta."

"Oh, I guess we didn't miss much."

"You don't like disco, Lieutenant?"

"My wife and I tried it, and honestly tried to like it. But it just doesn't do anything for us. I don't think it will last long. In fact, I think it's on the way out now."

"Well, you're probably one of those 50's rock and roll people aren't you? I don't mean any offense. Believe me, I love that 50's and 60's rock. But I like the disco, too."

"To each his own. I personally think John Travolta is a little full of himself?" said Dowdy.

"You being an ex-marine, aren't you one of *the few and the proud* yourself?" said Howe.

"That's hilarious." Dowdy chuckled. "Yeah. You bet I was one of the few and the proud. But that has a whole different meaning in the marines than when some young guy like Travolta struts around on a dance floor."

Howe laughed. "I'm with you on that, Lieutenant. And I didn't mean any offense."

"Don't worry, I didn't take any. So what'd you do Saturday?" he said, getting things back on track.

"I got up at eight and took the boat out to Dorena Reservoir. Fished for bass all day."

"Can anyone alibi that for you? Trust me, I'm only covering the bases here."

"No one can alibi for me Friday night or Saturday. Wouldn't you know it? I used to always have a babe with me on the weekends if I wasn't doing something with the guys. But I reformed myself in the last year—at least a little. Oh, I did catch several decent bass and one beauty—over five pounds. I have it in the freezer if you want to see it. Would that serve as an adequate alibi?"

"Don't worry about it. I don't consider you a suspect, and I'm sure no one else does either," Dowdy assured him. "Maybe I'll take a look at it before I leave."

"Since I'm sure Dick Eastbrook probably told you of his conversation with me yesterday, I'm sure you already know that we didn't find Bruington's hat."

"Yes, Dick told me that."

"Do you have any thoughts about the hat?" asked Dowdy.

"Pretty much what yours are, that it was either the shooter or an animal that took it." Since he felt like a possible suspect, he wasn't in the mood to talk about the hat or anything else.

"Jan Bruington seemed to think you and her husband talked about the Army days sometimes. Is that right?"

"Oh, yeah. We talked about it from time to time. You know how it is."

"Yes, I do. I have a few buddies that served in the marines that I get together with occasionally for old times' sake. They didn't serve at the same time I did, but we're all 'Semper Fi'.'"

"I hear you," said Howe. "I've never had the same sort of camaraderie with anybody since I got out, except for other Army vets."

"I don't know why that is, but it's true," agreed Dowdy. "Do you know if Bruington was still in communication with anyone in his Army unit?"

"Yes, he was. Why do you ask?"

"I was just curious. I'm just following any thought or question that comes through my mind surrounding his death, possible sour connections or anyone with a possible motive to kill him."

"I see. And what would an Army connection have to do with his death?"

"I haven't thought that far ahead, to be honest. I just want to cover all my bases. Leave no stone uncovered. Can you tell me who in his old unit he was in contact with?"

"Sorry, I can't help you with that one. Roger never told me any of their names, nor did I ever meet them."

"So Roger got together with them?"

"Yes—about once a year."

"And you don't know anything else about it?" asked Dowdy.

"No, I don't."

"And Roger never invited you to his get-togethers with his old Army buddies?"

"No, and I didn't invite myself. I figured if he wanted me to meet them, he would have asked me to. Just like what we told you Monday regarding Roger's peculiar ideas about hunting deer alone, Roger had some funny ways about him. There were just certain things you knew you didn't probe into any deeper."

"I'm beginning to get a better picture of him. So is there anything more you can tell me about his military experience? Did he ever tell you what he did during his two tours in Vietnam?"

"No. When it came down to what his operations were there, he didn't get into that at all. Said it was top secret."

"Weren't you curious?"

"Yeah, in about the same way we were curious about his special deer hunting spots. But we respected him too much as a friend to push him for information. It's not like it affected any of us anyway."

"On Monday one of you mentioned Roger's fear of getting shot by a hunting partner if he had one while deer hunting. Didn't that strike you as odd for a Vietnam combat veteran?"

"I don't know for sure that he was a combat veteran. Like I said, he didn't give up any of that information. I always figured that some time in the future, when Roger was ready to talk about that stuff, he would bring it up."

"That's one thing I've noticed about Vietnam vets more than vets from any other war," said Dowdy.

"What's that?"

"A lot of them simply don't want to talk about their war experience at all. I mean not at all," said Dowdy. "I know it's only been half a dozen years or so since the last Americans left Vietnam, but still there's a silence about the whole war that hasn't been true of any other war in American history. Only Korea has come close."

"It's sad, isn't it." said Howe. "It's almost like America wants to forget it ever fought the Vietnam War."

"It's a terrible travesty," Dowdy agreed. "Some of the bravest men to ever fight a war served proudly over there. Even in the end, the last two years, there were still some tremendously brave actions that were performed by American servicemen."

"Well, let's hope someday, and hopefully not too far in the future, this country can acknowledge that what the American soldiers did in the Vietnam War was every bit as important on an individual basis as what the heroes of World War II and all the other wars did."

"Let's hope so. Well, I better get going," said Dowdy, as he got up from his chair, still holding the piece of jerky he hadn't yet started chewing on. "Thanks for the jerky, and your patriotism."

"You're welcome on the jerky. I don't know about the patriotism."

Howe then reminded Dowdy of his bass. When Dowdy saw it he was impressed, and Howe felt he had at least given some kind of alibi.

Dowdy then left without bringing up the automatic rifle issue, perhaps he learned all he needed to know about it from Stevens. Or maybe it never meant anything to him at all and it was just a ploy—like those used by Lieutenant Columbo.

11

Search for a Deer

Lieutenant Dowdy, in his bed next to his beautiful, sleeping wife Wednesday night, contemplated the facts of the Bruington case, as well as all the unknowns. The hat missing bothered him some. But Bruington's rifle being off-safe and having a spent casing in the chamber, haunted him, mocked him, as if to say, you'll never solve this one. He knew those mocking thoughts had a better than even chance of being true. Knowing there were a lot of unsolved deaths on the books in Oregon, even in Lane County, including a few he had investigated, only served to make him more determined to get to the bottom of the Bruington case.

As he lay there tossing and turning, mulling the possible scenarios over in his mind, he considered what if Bruington actually took a shot at a deer just before he was killed? He had to get back up to the scene of the crime, first thing in the morning.

He would take Deputy Buddy Easton with him. Easton was the best tracker on the force, and an experienced big game hunter. If there was blood to find, they would find it. Dowdy was thankful it hadn't rained since Saturday. From his past experience, he knew dried blood could be found days after an incident if it hadn't been washed away. He jumped out of bed and went to the phone in the living room to call Easton at home to alert him to his plan. Easton, always up for a challenge, was enthusiastic about Dowdy's plan and agreed to meet him at the station at seven sharp.

While Lieutenant Dowdy drove the sheriff's four-wheel drive along the north side of Fall Creek Reservoir, Thursday morning, October 28th, he filled Deputy Easton—a thirty-two-year-old, six-foot one-inch, medium built, red-head—in on the details of the case.

Then Dowdy said, "I already told you we would be looking for blood and possibly a dead deer or a gut pile. But I didn't tell you why."

"And the blood or deer would have something to do with why Bruington's safety was off and his rifle had a spent cartridge in the chamber?" said Easton.

"Yes. Why would Bruington's rifle have a spent round chambered and the safety off and he got shot in the back of the head like he did?"

"That is puzzling. So you're thinking maybe he shot at, and hopefully hit, a deer sometime before he was killed?"

"That's what I'm thinking. If we find blood away from the area where Bruington's blood was splattered, then we'll take samples and have it tested to see if it's from a deer. Of course the best scenario would be for us to find a dead deer with an entry bullet hole and no exit wound. Then we could recover the bullet and see if it matches Bruington's rifle. If we find a dead deer and the bullet wasn't from Bruington's gun, we might have a piece of evidence matching the shooter's gun."

"But wouldn't the guy have taken the deer?"

"That's why I'm thinking possibly a gut pile," said Dowdy. "But he might have panicked after killing Bruington, and decided just to beat foot out of the area. Who knows how a guy that would do something like that would think."

"You've got a point there, Lieutenant. I'm sure you've considered the possibility that Bruington actually took a shot at his killer before he was shot, haven't you?"

"Yes, that's one of the first things we considered. But it doesn't add up that he would take a shot at the killer and then get shot in the back of his head."

"But what if he fired a round at the killer, then turned to try to get away?"

"Bruington is a Vietnam vet. I don't know if he did any combat duty, but you can be sure he knew how to handle a weapon in a hostile environment. So how likely is it he would have taken a shot at someone shooting at him, and not immediately reloaded?"

"How many live rounds were still in his magazine?" asked Easton.

"Four, exactly what it holds. And we found no spent casings anywhere in the area."

"But he could have taken more shots and then reloaded the magazine."

"I thought of that. But he still wouldn't have turned his back to his assailant without ejecting and re-chambering a live round. Especially being a Vietnam veteran. And still you have no casings on the ground in the area."

"Yeah, I see your point. None of that adds up, does it?"

"No," said Dowdy.

"I can't wait to get up on that hill."

"Me either. And I sure hope we find a dead deer."

"With no exit wound," said Easton.

As they reached the upper end of Fall Creek Reservoir, crossed the bridge over the gorge and continued along Fall Creek Road to Puma Creek Campground, the lawmen continued conversing about the case. Dowdy decided to bring Easton in on the entire investigation. He really liked his insight and confidence.

After they had climbed up along the east bank of Jones Creek to within two hundred yards of the crime scene, Dowdy said, "We want to keep our eyes peeled for any sign of blood from here up to the scene. I already know there's no deer carcass, because the troopers, the SAR team and I, were all over this area looking for Bruington. I want to get you oriented to Bruington's position when he was shot."

They found no blood between there and the bloody ferns below the body's position. Upon seeing the extent of the dried blood and brain matter on the vegetation at the scene, Easton said, "This is horrible. I can imagine what it was like the night you found him."

"I don't know if you can. Bruington's face was mostly gone when we pulled him out of the water. The skull cavity even had a crawdad and some periwinkles in it. I've had that face come to my mind more times than I can tell you the last two days, and nights."

"That's the part I hate most about being a law man," said Easton, "whenever we have to deal with a dead body that has a face that's been mangled. But that's almost always been in a car wreck. I think I've only been out on one murder where most of a person's face was gone."

"The suicides are what I hate the most. Of course, the victim's face is never blown away like Bruington's was. Usually it's the side, back or top of the head that is gone."

"I think what I hate most about suicides is that the person chose to take their own life. At least in car wrecks, no one made a conscious decision to kill someone. And the sad thing about most suicides is if the person would've gotten the professional help they needed, many of them wouldn't have killed themselves."

"It's a permanent solution to a temporary problem," said Dowdy.

"It's not much of a solution is it?"

After they got across the creek, Dowdy described the crime-scene scenario. They then began their search across the creek to the west of Bruington's body's position working back and forth, east and west, gradually making their way up the hill among the sparse six-to seven-foot diameter Douglas fir trees, ferns and Oregon

Grape. Most of the forest floor was covered in thick, green moss. Neither spotted any blood or anything that looked human in the first half hour, though Easton commented about the moss and dirt being turned up by the elk.

Then, as Easton turned to his left, ready for the next pass, he saw something that immediately caught his attention about thirty feet to the north, near a stump.

"You're not going to believe this, Lieutenant Dowdy. I think I see the orange hat."

"You're not serious."

"Dead serious."

"Let's mark our positions, then move in on it."

"Done."

"You spotted it. You go ahead and lead the way, Deputy. But keep a look out for any blood between here and the hat."

They moved deliberately up to the stump beside the hat, careful to look for any human sign. There was none, but in the heavy moss bedding, human tracks don't show up even if a human has walked through.

"Let me get my camera out and take some pictures before we move it," said Dowdy. The hat was laying right-side-up a foot to the side of the three-foot-wide, four-foot-high rotting, moss-covered stump, that had some licorice fern about ten inches high growing out of its sides and off its top. There was also a three-foot-high western-hemlock tree, with its drooping leader, growing out of the top of the stump. The fallen and broken, old hemlock tree lay in pieces, spread out down the hill to the east toward Jones Creek. Numerous white mushrooms were growing out of portions of it.

After taking six photos of the hat from various angles, Dowdy said, "Go ahead and pick it up. Let's get a closer look at it."

Easton, wearing the rubber coated gloves he brought with him, picked the hat up by the side of the bill, careful not to squeeze any firmer than necessary.

"Look at all that blood and brain matter," said Easton, as he tipped the hat upside down. "It looks like some teeth marks there on the side of the bill, doesn't it?"

"It sure does. I guess this answers at least two questions, doesn't it? Bruington was obviously wearing the hat when he got shot, and a wild animal picked it up and carried it up here. Is there any blood on the back of the hat?"

"No." Easton handed the hat to Dowdy, who had his rubber gloves on now.

Scanning the hat, Dowdy said, "The only blood is on the underside of the bill, and there's plenty there. Since the hat is dry and the blood and brain matter don't look like they've been diluted by being soaked in the creek, I think it's safe to assume the hat was blown clear across the creek when Bruington was hit."

"I concur, Lieutenant."

"From where he had to have been standing, that's a distance of about ten feet to the other side of the water. We've seen hats blown farther away from a victim than that."

"Well, maybe you have."

"Yeah, I forgot, head shots aren't your cup of tea." They both chuckled. "I guess Bruington's buddies haven't been up here yet. I know they all work during the day, so they probably haven't had a chance. I heard Bruington's funeral is on Saturday. Maybe they were going to try to get up here some time after that. Now the question is, do I tell them I found the hat?"

"Well, consider how things would go if you don't tell them and they come up here, spend hours looking for the hat that we already found, then find out you didn't tell them."

"You're right. I need them as allies, not enemies. Especially since I know I put Howe on the defensive yesterday by questioning him about his alibi situation for Friday and Saturday."

"You did that?"

"Yes, I did that. I had to do it to try to clear him entirely."

"Well, did you clear him?"

"Not exactly, but I got to eat some excellent deer jerky he had made, and to see a five pound bass in his freezer that he caught out of Dorena Reservoir."

"Do you actually consider him a suspect?"

"Not really. Actually not at all. But I got the impression he thinks I do."

"Why would you suspect him at all?"

"You know the old rule: don't overlook the area right under your nose. He made a comment, just out of the blue, that he always envied Roger for having the beautiful, wonderful wife he had."

"He said that?"

"Yes. And it was obvious he regretted it immediately and tried to do some back pedaling."

"Do you think it means anything?"

"No, other than that he's like every other man that can recognize a good woman when he sees one. And maybe that he has a tendency toward foot-in-mouth disease."

They both burst out laughing, partly responding to the humor and partly out of satisfaction at finding the hat. Both were sitting on the old hemlock log now, Dowdy still holding the hat and looking it over, but not focused on it.

"It must be tough to be a non-cop and be put on the spot by a lawman? In fact, I know it is. I remember those days well."

"Me too," said Dowdy. "I remember how much I hated it when I'd look in my rearview mirror and see a cop behind me. I just knew he was going to flip the light switch any second and pull me over for any number of things that were either wrong with my car or that I was doing wrong in my driving."

"It was a bitch, wasn't it?"

"Let's bag this hat and get back to looking for some blood and a deer."

Two hours later, when they had completed searching to the north, west and southeast of the crime scene with no luck finding blood or a deer, Dowdy finally conceded, "I'm convinced that if a deer was shot by Bruington or the killer, it wasn't around here. What do you say we head out?"

On the drive down from Fall Creek, Dowdy said, "Buddy, I want you to help me with this investigation. I want to keep you up-to-date, bounce things off you, and maybe see what you can come up with on your own."

"I appreciate that, Lieutenant Dowdy. I don't know how much time I can give you, but maybe you can talk to the captain and work something out."

"That's what I was planning on. It will help me and be good for your resume."

"I don't know about the resume part—at least not if we don't solve it."

"It'll help either way, trust me. You're due to put in for sergeant pretty soon, aren't you?"

"Yes, I am."

"So something like this will help, on top of your other investigative experience."

"It can't hurt."

"What do you have, eight years on the force?"

"That's right."

"You were in the Navy for four years right out of high school, too, weren't you?"

"I see you've been looking at my profile."

"Good men don't go unnoticed."

"Thanks for the vote of confidence, Lieutenant."

"It's the truth. Oh, by the way, I've got a meeting with Dick Eastbrook tonight. Do you care to come along?"

"Sure."

12

The Team

Wednesday and Thursday were the state trooper's days off this month, so on Thursday he got together with the hippie, who took him for a drive way up Lost Creek outside of the small town of Dexter. They drove the winding mountain road that took them up to Mt. June, the highest mountain in the area at 4,616 feet. They hiked to the peak on the trail which took them up the final 1,000 or so feet of elevation from the end of the logging road they drove in on.

When they reached the summit at 12:40, they took a seat overlooking the entire Lost Creek Valley. Miles to the northwest, they could see much of Eugene and Springfield and a lot of the surrounding areas, including many miles of the Willamette River. Even though they couldn't see Fall Creek to the northeast, because of the Lookout Point and Winberry Divides, their thoughts were there.

As they sat looking out over the vast expanse below, the hippie said, "Have you heard any more about the hunter?"

"No I haven't. I have to be careful how much interest I show, although I'm sure they would expect me to want to keep up on it."

"So you don't know if they've searched anymore for the missing hat?"

"As far as I know, no one has gone back up there since we were there Tuesday morning doing the search. But I know the hat is a concern to the hunter's buddies. And I think it bothers the investigating officer, Lieutenant Dowdy, more than he let on. I can tell you this, the hunter's rifle being off-safe and having a spent round chambered really set Dowdy's mind to work."

"Do you think they'll search any farther up that mountain?"

"I don't know what to expect. We could have avoided all of this if we hadn't killed him."

"There's no point in going back over that ground again. What's done is done," said the hippie.

"If that guy had just not happened upon our shack, none of this would have happened."

"If that guy had just minded his own business when he saw the shack, none of this would have happened."

"Maybe we should just burn it up?" suggested the trooper.

"I thought about that. But it took me two years to get it built and outfitted. I can't just walk away from it because some guy doesn't know how to leave well enough alone. Besides, if we were going to burn it, we would have had to do that instead of what we did."

"I wish we had."

"Like I said, it don't mean nothin'."

"It means plenty to his wife and kids."

"You gotta get that out of your mind. I told you, it'll eat you up if you don't. You know how many widowed Vietnamese women I saw? And orphaned kids? You gotta let it go."

"We could have just confronted him, found out if he would keep his mouth shut."

"Yeah, we just walk up to him in the woods, while you have your uniform on, carrying our rifles, and ask, 'What did you think of our shack? Did you happen to take anything from in there, any little keepsakes? You do know how to keep a secret don't you? Oh, the uniform? Don't mind that. It's just for looks.'

"And then he volunteers, 'Of course I know how to keep a secret. *I was in the Nam.* Trust me; I really know how to keep things secret. You guys have nothing to worry about. Like we used to say over there, "It don't mean nothin'."'" Come on Butch, nothing is that simple."

"But maybe since he was a Vietnam vet, he would've understood how hard a time you've had since you got home... how you can't hold down a job, how you can't sleep, how you can't get all of your war-time experiences out of your head?"

"Yeah, and he's a well-adjusted Nam vet that thinks those that can't adjust just took the easy road—like it's been an easy road. How many like him did solo sniper missions and killed over thirty Vietcong and North Vietnamese on those runs? How many of them went from being the valedictorian of their 1964 high school graduating class to being drafted and sent to a quagmire of a war, thousands of miles away from everything they ever knew, to fight an enemy they never saw, to be eaten alive by every bug known to man, to slog around in a foot of water when it's been raining non-stop for days, to have leeches sucking on every part of their body?"

He was crying now. "You get to where you shoot first, and ask questions only on the rare occasions that what you were shooting at somehow lives. Then you find out that you just shot up the good guys... and sometimes you actually did shoot up the good guys because an American patrol approached your position in the jungle without making radio contact first. So then you call in the medevacs, they arrive fifteen minutes later, you load the Americans you just shot up on to the Hueys. They take off, but then suddenly they're hit with a rocket propelled grenade, and they fall back down on top of your own guys, chopping them up and throwing pieces of them at you. You pick the pieces off your face, and tell yourself, 'It don't mean nothin'.'"

The hippie was bawling like a baby now; he didn't even seem to know where he was. It was the first time he had been able to let any

of it out since returning home in 1972. The Army didn't debrief him
or offer him any psychological help for what he'd been through.

He stood up. He was getting angrier and more belligerent by the
second. Butch wanted to help him, somehow, but didn't know how.
And he was afraid of him now. He thought he might kill anything
that touched him.

"One day in November 1966, we're on patrol west of Pleiku.
Your dad's on point and I'm following next behind him about thirty
feet away in the jungle. There's an explosion. Your dad screams
out. Me and everyone behind me hit the ground and crawl into the
brush. I can hear AK 47 automatic fire behind me. Immediately our
guys open up with the M16s and *the pig* (M60). Leaves are falling,
bullets are flying, and I can still hear your dad screaming. So I crawl
ahead to where the screaming is coming from. But before I reach the
voice, I find his legs and what is left of his pelvis. But the screaming
is farther away. Then I see him—half of him—his arms flailing
around. He's laying ten feet away, screaming, 'Del, Del.'

"I don't know what to do. I don't know whether to bring his legs
to his body, or try to bring his body to his legs. But then I realize it
won't do any good either way. So I go to his body. He's screaming
at me, 'Shoot me, Del. Please, shoot me.' But I can't. He's my best
friend."

Butch was crying like a baby himself now. He never knew the
details of his dad's death, just that he was killed in a firefight
outside of Pleiku.

"'You've got to shoot me, Del.' He's begging me. His M16 is
broken in half and laying off to the right. 'Do it Del,' he yells. 'Do
it, shoot me. It don't mean nothin'.'

"*I don't know what to do.* He's my best friend. I only have *one*
best friend. Finally I know I have no choice. I point the muzzle of
my M16 at the center of his forehead from a foot away and, before I
could stop myself, I pulled the trigger. A three-round burst exploded
from my rifle; he was dead. My best friend was dead. I killed my
best friend. I'm so sorry, Butch. I killed your Dad. I killed your
Dad."

Del collapsed to the ground, sobbing and saying over and over, "I killed your Dad. I'm so sorry. I killed your Dad."

Butch crawled to Del, hating him for what he did—but loving him at the same time for sparing his dad anymore suffering. He wrapped his strong arms around him, and as both of their bodies shook with each sob, said, "It's okay Del. It's okay. It don't mean nothin.' You had no choice."

They both sobbed for several minutes. There is so much that Butch doesn't know about his dad that he wants to know, that he thinks Del knows. That he thinks Del has held back from him. But right now, just letting out the pain is all that matters.

After what seemed like an eternity, Del got somewhat of a grip and stiffened up. Butch sensed it and gently pulled away, knowing to give space. They were sitting a foot apart now both looking off into the distance toward Mt. Zion and Eagles Rest below them to the north, but neither was seeing anything. Their eyes were clouded over from all the tears.

Finally Butch said, "I forgive you, Del. You did the only thing you could have done. You have to forgive yourself, not only for my dad, but for all of it."

"I don't know if I can ever forgive myself," he said, wiping his eyes on his green army shirt-sleeve. "I've needed to let it out for so long, but I couldn't. I knew if I ever let it out, this would happen."

"It's okay, Del. It's okay. It needed to happen."

"One time last summer I went to a meeting at Shiloh Inn in Springfield where an evangelist was giving his testimony about the severe injuries he suffered in Vietnam. He was a gunner on a patrol boat and got blown up by a white phosphorous grenade. His name was Dan Rover or something like that. His face was all messed up. He goes around the country giving his testimony and holding men's retreats. When he gave the invitation at the end for any Vietnam vets that needed to, to come forward, I came so close to going. I wanted to. I needed to. But I saw the way other vets were going to pieces up there, and I just couldn't let myself become that vulnerable. I haven't let myself feel anything since that day with your dad. I wished I hadn't gone to the meeting, but something inside me thought maybe I could get some answers.

"Your dad was my best friend. He was like the older brother I never had. You were almost ten when he shipped out to Nam a few months after I did. As fate had it, we ended up in the same company. He had done three years in the Army when he got out of high school in the early 50s. But when things heated up in Nam in '65, he enlisted. He wanted to help America help the little country of South Vietnam from being taken over by the communists. Like so many Americans in those days, he was patriotic and wanted to stem the tide of communism that was spreading like gangrene.

"The leaders of our country were saying that if South Vietnam fell to communism, it would be the first domino of many to fall. They said Cambodia, Laos, Thailand, and all of Indochina would go next. Your dad and thousands of other American men believed that and wanted to do their part in stopping it from happening. But the situation was much more complicated than that. I wish I could tell you your dad died for a worthy cause. But all I can say is he died a worthy American, not for a worthy cause."

Now that Del was opening up, Butch wanted to find out as much as he could before he closed back down. "How did you know my dad? I don't even remember that."

"When I was a sophomore at Cottage Grove High School, your dad was helping coach the baseball team. I was a starter on the JV squad. I guess he saw some potential, because after practice he took me aside and worked with me on my fielding and hitting. A couple weeks after I met him, he introduced himself to my parents and asked if I could come over to his house for dinner that weekend and to field some balls afterwards. My parents were thrilled.

"From that first dinner on, it seemed like I spent half my time there each week. You were only six then. Before the year was over, I got moved up to the varsity team. Over the next three years I grew closer and closer to your dad, you and your whole family. But then I was drafted into the Army when I was nineteen and left for basic training at Fort Ord a month later. Your dad signed up about the time I went to advanced infantry training."

"How could he leave me, my mom and sister to go in the Army?"

"Believe me, Butch, when I say, he loved all of you to pieces. But he felt he needed to give two years to the Army for such a worthwhile cause. He knew you would still only be twelve or so when he returned, and you guys would have plenty of time to be father and son together. I also think it had always bothered him that he didn't do any time in Korea on his first stint in the Army."

"It was a war. Didn't he consider that he might not come back?"

"When he joined in June of 1965, there were less than a hundred Americans dying there every month. Of course neither he nor many other people who weren't on the ground in Vietnam, realized just how much America's role there would escalate over the next couple years. Or how many Americans would be killed and injured. But even at that, I don't think it would've made any difference to your dad. He was like many of the soldiers who volunteered in the early part of that war, he never envisioned himself being killed there."

"I guess it's just all their loved ones at home that worry themselves sick about it."

"I know your mom worried a lot about him, but you kids were young enough that your time and minds were filled with all kinds of other things. Kids are very resilient. They don't spend a fraction of the time worrying about the big things in life, like adults do."

"I may not have worried, but the day I found out he died, I cried my eyes out. I would never have a dad again. And he would never get to see me play sports or take me fishing and hunting again." Butch got choked up and swallowed several times to keep from shedding anymore tears. He had to man-up now. They'd had their good cry and that had to be enough. He didn't want Del thinking he was weak inside. He had never seen any weakness in Del before today. And what he saw today wasn't weakness—it was years of pent up pain and guilt pouring out.

"I never did talk to your mom about it when I came home. I never talked to anyone about it. I couldn't. You saw why."

"It's okay, Del. I don't think any less of you for letting it out. You needed to. Maybe if you could have let it out a long time ago, both of us would have been better off for it."

"You're probably right, Butch. But I'm afraid of what this means. I don't want to feel anything. It's easier to keep it all locked up safe inside myself. I've told myself for years that it don't mean nothin'. I'm afraid if I let myself believe it did mean something, I won't be able to function."

"Honestly, Del, have you been functioning?"

"I've been surviving, which is more than a lot of combat veterans have done. I've seen some of the statistics and read an occasional magazine or newspaper article on the incidence of suicide among Vietnam veterans. It's not a pretty picture. And the suicides are just the physical death of the soldiers. Thousands more have died psychologically. At least I'm surviving."

"Are you really?"

"Yes. I am."

Butch was afraid to point out to him otherwise. He'd seen his anger before and some today and didn't want to incite it again. So he left it at that. There would be other times to talk about all of it. At least he hoped there would. But maybe Del would go back to being the closed down, non-feeling, non-communicative zombie he seemed to be much of the time for the last eight years.

Butch had wanted Del to fill the role that his dad should have filled, but he wasn't up for it. In fact he wasn't really up for anything other than getting high, getting drunk, or both.

"When you came back home in 1968, after your discharge from the Army, why didn't you stick around? I needed you. My mom needed you. We all needed you."

"You don't understand the way it was for me. I tried to do what your dad asked me to, but I was haunted by everything over there. It wasn't long before I got to smoking dope and dropping some acid with this group of longhairs outside of town. There were girls. I had all the women I could want. It was free love. It was a place that I could escape to and not have to face what I had seen over there. And what I had done."

"So you just quit hanging around to help my mom with us and to support her in the ways she needed?"

"It wasn't my intent to let all of you down. You've got to understand what I was going through."

"What do you think we were going through?"

"I couldn't take on anyone else's burdens back then. It was all too hard."

"So why did you go back into the Army and back to Vietnam in 1970? I mean if it was the cause of all your pain and suffering?"

"I couldn't make it in the world. The free-love and all the dope just didn't give me any meaning. The longer I did them, the less they took my memories and pain away. Finally, I realized the only place I could ever be right was back in the Nam, killing. I was a killer and a killer needed to be where he could kill. Can't you understand that?"

"I'm so sorry for all you went through, Del. I can only imagine what any of it was like."

"Don't be sorry. And you not only can imagine some of what I went through, I know you're going through it now yourself."

"It's not the same. It was one man, compared to dozens and my dad for you."

"I've listened to your remorse since the day you did it," said Del. "I hear you saying the same things I said, and thought, and still think."

"Sometimes I think the only thing that is going to make it go away, or make it right, is if I turn myself in," said Butch.

"What are you saying? Don't even think about it!"

"I'm saying, I've been thinking about turning myself in for killing that hunter."

"You know you can't do that. You wouldn't do that would you? You can't do that!"

"Why can't I?"

"Because you'll get a minimum of life in prison, maybe even the death penalty. You're a cop. When a cop kills in cold blood, they treat him even worse. You're sworn to uphold the laws, not go out and kill innocent people."

"I know that. But what am I supposed to do?"

"You're supposed to suck it up and be a man."

"Like you? Suck it up and be a man the way you have been?"

"That sounded disrespectful. Is that how you meant it?"

"I didn't mean any disrespect. What I meant is, it's hard for me to see how shutting everything up inside for all these years has been good for you."

"Look Butch, I wish we could undo the deal with the hunter. But we can't. Is it going to help the man's family or anyone else get along better if you turn yourself in?"

"I don't know. Maybe. That way they'd get some closure."

"Well they might get closure, but their lives wouldn't be any better for it. And here's a couple other things to consider. If you turn yourself in, I'm going down too, as an accomplice. That's over twenty years for me. And on top of that, your mom and sister lose you too.

"So what do we do?"

"We just make sure we don't get caught and charged with the crime—whatever that means. And we live our lives from here out the way we should. We don't have any other options."

"Maybe we'll have to burn the shack?"

"We might. But that's a last resort."

They talked about other things for another half hour or so, then hiked down off the mountain.

13

Eastbrook Meeting

In the Eastbrook living room Thursday evening—

Eastbrook's wife, Wanda, asked, "Can I get you deputies some coffee?"

"That would be great," said Dowdy, for both of them. "Black, please."

She left to go to the kitchen to pour the deputies and her husband each a cup of the coffee she had brewed just before they arrived.

"Do you have any new evidence on the case, Lieutenant Dowdy?" asked Eastbrook.

"Well, Corporal Easton and I returned to Puma Creek this morning and looked around."

"Were you looking for the hat?"

"Actually we were looking for blood."

"For blood? I thought you found enough blood already."

"We weren't looking for Bruington's blood."

"What blood then? Is there something you haven't told me?"

"Actually Mr. Eastbrook—"

"Call me Dick, would you."

"Okay. Actually Dick, I'll tell you a little more about the case, but at this point I need you to promise me you won't talk to anyone else about it. Is that a deal?"

"Of course. If you want me to keep quiet, I can definitely do that."

"That goes for your wife and your hunting buddies, too. Got it?"

"I've got it. No problem."

Just then, Eastbrook's wife came back into the living room with the coffee on a tray and each of the three men took a cup. She then announced, "I'll be in the family room watching some TV if you need anything."

"Thanks honey." He winked at her. After she walked into the other room, he said, "You don't have to worry about her, she's never been one to eavesdrop on my conversations."

"That's good."

"So what blood were you looking for today—the shooter's? What would cause you to think the shooter was bleeding?" He was obviously puzzled. "There's got to be something you haven't told me. Do you think Roger might have shot the shooter before he got shot himself? So he may have been shot in self-defense. I don't believe that for a minute."

"You just laid out quite a scenario, Dick. I hadn't even thought of the possibility that Roger was anything other than the victim. That's an interesting theory."

"Hold the fort, Lieutenant. I'm not suggesting for a second that Roger was anything but the victim. I was just brainstorming. That's all, and nothing more. You said you were looking for blood that wasn't Roger's. What other blood—than the shooter's—could you be talking about?"

"Where were you last Saturday, Dick?"

"Wait a minute here. Where are you going with that?"

"I just want to know where you were last Saturday when Roger was shot."

Aghast, Eastbrook said, "I told you Monday afternoon up at Puma Creek that I was hunting with Dave Stevens outside of

Creswell on Saturday."

"Relax, Dick. I don't think for a minute that you had anything to do with Roger's death. Sometimes I get so locked into a line of questioning, based on what I'm hearing from the person I'm talking to, that I can put them on the defensive and not even mean to. Trust me. You're not a suspect. And neither are your buddies, in case they've gotten that impression somehow."

Getting the color back in his face and breathing normally again, Eastbrook answered, "That's good to know. I'm not used to being on the defensive, in case you didn't know that. I'm president of the 'Sure Door and Window Manufacturing' plant here in Springfield."

"Nothing hurt then, right?" said Dowdy.

"Sure. Nothing hurt."

Easton sat silently in his chair, sipping his coffee, and taking the conversation in with great interest. He had been on site with Dowdy at a number of incidents over the years, but had never actually sat in on one of his interviews during a murder investigation. Dowdy kind of reminded him of Lieutenant Columbo on TV. He didn't know that Dave Stevens had that same impression of him just last night, only from a less comfortable vantage point.

"Now, Dick, if you want to do some more brainstorming, Corporal Easton and I would love to hear some more of your theories."

"I'm not taking that dive again, Lieutenant," he responded, while grinning. "I didn't like the way that last BS session turned out for me."

All three of them laughed. Easton didn't realize he was seeing Dowdy replay a technique he often used in interviews. Put the interviewee on the defensive, then relieve the pressure.

"Okay, Dick, I'm going to lay it all out there for you now. Tell you everything we know that you haven't been aware of up until now. Alright?"

"You bet."

"When we found Roger Monday night, I checked his rifle and, to my surprise and bewilderment, found that the safety was not engaged and the chamber held a spent shell casing."

"You're kidding?"

"No, I'm not."

"Why didn't you tell me that earlier?"

"One of the first rules in crimes is to never rule anyone out as a suspect prematurely. Another one is, do not disclose the evidence; it may prove to incriminate or exonerate a potential witness. That, of course is why it is vital that you not say anything to anyone about what you learn here today, except for what *I say* you can say. Do you follow me?"

"So you did consider me, Dave and Aaron suspects?"

"Not particularly. I just wasn't going to rule any of you out. So, obviously, I wasn't going to put all my cards on the table."

"I see your position, Lieutenant. So what is your explanation or theory for Roger's rifle being in that condition?"

"I've discussed it with the two state troopers who were there that night, Martin and Wilson, as well as the coroner, his assistant, Deputies Bradshaw and Lohner, my captain, and, of course, Corporal Easton. The theories that we've come up with, as I mentioned, didn't include your brainstormed idea that Roger may have been the assailant and the guy, or gal, who shot and killed him may have actually been acting in self-defense."

"Roger was shot in the back of the head. That's not an act of self-defense."

"You're the one who came up with that theory, remember."

"That wasn't a theory at all. I was simply throwing out what I thought you guys might have thought was a possibility."

"I know you were, Dick, but it was something we hadn't considered. And, frankly, we should have considered it."

"So now, because of me throwing that out there, you're going to consider that as a possibility. Or do you have evidence that definitely rules that option out?"

"Here's the evidence we have to consider, Dick. Roger was shot in the back of the head. He must have been looking down toward the water, with his head bent down slightly. The shot was probably taken from about seventy yards, near as we can tell. And he was wearing his orange hunting hat when he got shot—"

"You know for certain he was wearing his hat, or is that based on everything his wife, me and the other guys said?"

"He *was* wearing the hat."

"But you told me that you didn't find the hat when you searched for evidence on Tuesday."

"That's right, Dick. When I talked to you Tuesday afternoon, I was being truthful with you. But the hat missing and the safety off and the empty shell tormented me constantly the last two days. So this morning when Deputy Easton and I returned to the scene of the crime—"

"You found the hat?"

"Yes, Deputy Easton found the hat."

"And it had blood on it? It must have, or you wouldn't be so sure it was on Roger when he was shot."

"Yes, it had blood splattered all over the underside of the bill."

"Oh no."

"I know this whole thing has been hard on you, Dick. Again, I'm deeply sorry."

"Where did you find the hat? I mean you guys did a thorough search of the area Tuesday morning, right?"

"Deputy Easton and I expanded the search area considerably. The hat was on the ridge over 150 yards to the northwest from where we found Roger."

"So an animal must have carried it up there, right? The killer wouldn't have taken it up there and left it, not with the blood all over it."

"When I found the hat," Easton spoke up, "we could see immediately that it had teeth marks on the bill. Some small animal, probably a raccoon, a 'possum or a fox had carried it up there."

"Was it wet? Or did it look like it had been wet, like the animal picked it out of the water?"

"No," Easton said, "none of the blood splatters were diffused. The hat must have landed on the opposite side of the creek and been picked up there by the animal."

"You said you went back to look for blood. Did you find any, other than what was on Roger's hat?"

"No, we didn't. Nor did we find a dead deer like we were hoping to find," said Dowdy.

"You've got me confused now. What do you mean you didn't find a dead deer? I'm a pretty smart guy, but I'm lost."

"The blood we were searching for was that of a deer. We speculated that Roger, or the person who killed him, may have shot at a deer just before Roger was killed."

"So you think Roger's gun had a spent casing in it, and the safety off, because he may have shot at a deer just before he was killed?"

"Well, it doesn't make sense to any of us that Roger, a Vietnam veteran, would have taken one shot at the guy who killed him, then turned his back to him without reloading first."

"That's right. There's no way he would have done that."

"So what scenarios does that leave us with?" Dowdy asked rhetorically. "One, Roger took a shot at a deer earlier in the day and forgot to reload."

"Not hardly. No one could have the success record he has and make that stupid a mistake," Dick assured them.

"Our thoughts exactly. So, two, he took a shot at the same deer his killer was interested in, and the killer shot him over it. Three, he took a shot almost simultaneously with the shot fired at him by the killer, who thought he was shooting at a deer himself. Or, four, he took a shot at a deer almost simultaneously with the shot fired at him by the killer who hadn't seen, or didn't care about, the deer Roger was aiming at. Of course he didn't hit the deer or we would have found it or evidence it was hit."

"Which scenario *do you think* is most likely?"

"That's a hard one. We were hoping to find blood or a dead deer nearby."

"Or," Easton interjected, "a gut pile."

"And a gut pile would add credence to the shot over the same deer theory," said Eastbrook.

"Exactly. But we also thought we might find a dead deer that was shot by either Roger, or his killer, in competition with each other, but then the killer decided to get out of the area as fast as possible after shooting Roger."

"There's no way Roger would've been in competition with another hunter to shoot a deer."

"At least not knowingly," said Easton.

"I see what you mean. But since you didn't find a dead deer, a gut pile, or any deer blood, where does that leave you?"

"Speculating," said Easton.

"Roger could have taken a shot and missed, but we figured that was unlikely," said Dowdy. "You saw the terrain in the area. The shot couldn't have been too long. I figured from Roger's position, no shot at a deer could have been much over a hundred yards. And that's pushing it. Oh, Dick, what we didn't tell you is that what we were hoping to find more than anything was a dead deer with an entry wound and no exit hole."

"So you could recover the bullet and try to match it to Roger's gun or have it for evidence if you ever come up with a suspect?"

"That's right."

"So you're still left with no proof that Roger, or the other guy shot at a deer. Honestly, Lieutenant, what are the odds of ever figuring this thing out?"

"I'm afraid we'll need an unexpected break, Dick. If you wanted to kill someone, you couldn't pick a better time than during deer season, or a better place than a barren forest that gets no hunting pressure."

"Do you have anything else to go on?"

"I'm checking into some other things, possible connections

Roger might have had with anyone that would have a motive to kill him, checking his military background, that sort of thing. I don't plan to leave any stones uncovered. Trust me I want to get to the bottom of this as much as you do, even if he wasn't my best friend."

"I believe you Lieutenant. And I also believe that if anyone can figure it out, it's you."

"Well thanks for the vote of confidence. Before we leave I wonder if there's anything you might be able to tell us about Roger's military background?"

"Not much. I'd suggest you get a hold of Roger's service record. Start there. After you've looked at that, come talk to me. We'll compare notes."

"That sounds like a plan. I'm hoping they arrive tomorrow. I ordered them sent by Express yesterday morning. Well, I think that will do it for this evening, Dick. You will honor our deal, won't you?"

"You have my word, Lieutenant Dowdy. Is there anything I can tell my wife and buddies?"

"You can tell them we found the hat. But don't mention the safety or empty casing."

"No problem."

"Thank your wife again for the excellent coffee, will you?"

"Done. Let me escort you guys to the door," he said getting up from his chair, as Dowdy and Easton both stood up from the couch they were sitting on.

14

Bruington's Service Record

At 9:30 Friday morning, Lieutenant Jim Dowdy received a copy of Roger Bruington's military service record by Express Delivery. It didn't take him long to determine that he wasn't going to get all the answers he had hoped for from its contents.

Roger Dale Bruington; Active Duty- 13 November 1968 to 20 October 1971; **Served in Vietnam** from 25 August 1969 to 15 September 1971; Honorable Discharge; E-5, Sergeant; Medals/Awards- Army Purple Heart, Vietnam Service Medal, Republic of Vietnam Campaign Medal, National Defense, Army Good Conduct Medal, Army Commendation Medal, Bronze Star Medal, Expert Rifle Medal.

After looking Bruington's record over, Dowdy called Deputy Easton to his desk and let him have a look. Easton shook his head as he scanned the pages, then said, "It's obvious that Bruington did some serious combat and who knows what else during his two tours in Vietnam. But we sure aren't going to figure it out from this, are we?"

"My thoughts exactly. Here's what we can assume, I believe, based on the awards. The Purple Heart means he was wounded. The Army Commendation Medal and, especially, the Bronze Star tell us that he performed some extraordinary and heroic actions of some kind."

"And the Expert Rifle Medal tells us that he could have qualified to be a sniper."

"Yeah, and I'd bet that's part of the reason he had so much success hunting big game."

"No doubt about it," said Easton.

"Now, hypothetically," Easton continued, "let's just assume Bruington had actually shot at a nice buck. If the shot was taken in the area where his body was found, we both already agreed that, because of the terrain, the shot would have been a hundred yards or less. If you were a betting man, how much of your money would you put on him hitting the buck in the vitals at that range, based on his expert marksmanship medal, his other medals, and his past success on big game?"

"I wouldn't want to have to shoot against him, I'll say that."

"How many deer have you shot in your life, Lieutenant?"

"Close to twenty."

"And how many of those did you hit in the vitals?"

"At least eighty percent."

"How many of the deer you hit in the vitals went more than a hundred or two hundred yards?"

"None of them. And a few dropped on the spot. Most went less than seventy-five yards."

"So between your experience and mine with vital shots on at least a dozen deer myself, we know Bruington's buck's body, or evidence that the deer had been dragged off, or gutted, would have been within the area we searched."

"I'm sure of it. Assuming he took the shot from where we found him. And we already know he must have, or he would have reloaded immediately and there wouldn't have been an empty casing in his chamber."

"The only possible explanation," said Easton, "is that Bruington pulled the trigger as a reflex upon being hit by the killer's bullet."

"I think that's the only thing that could have happened," said Dowdy. "He had to have been ready to pull the trigger on a deer at the instant he was shot. Now, getting back to the service record— Other than listing where Bruington went to Basic Training, AIT, and then the orders to **MACV** (Military Assistance Command Vietnam) in Saigon, Vietnam, there's nothing there to go on. All it says is, *UNDISCLOSED DUTIES IN SOUTH VIETNAM*."

"Sounds like something top secret to me, Lieutenant."

"Or a deliberate cover-up of some kind."

"Sure makes you wonder, doesn't it?"

"I'm going to call Dick Eastbrook up right now and arrange a meeting with him here at the station this evening. I'm curious what he knows about Bruington's military service."

Meeting with Eastbrook at the Lane County Sheriff's Office that evening—

Here's Roger's service record, Dick." He handed him the folder. Go ahead and look it over."

"Corporal Easton, would you mind getting all of us some coffee?"

"Sure, Lieutenant," he said, as he got up and went out to the machine.

After Easton had returned with the coffee, and Eastbrook had a few minutes to look over the record, Dowdy said, "What's your impression after looking that over?"

"I never got to see Roger's DD214 before, or any of the rest of his service record. And he never talked about or showed me any of his Army medals. I just accepted it as the way he chose to deal with whatever happened with him in Vietnam. And to be perfectly honest with you, there was always a part of me that felt guilty around him for being his best friend since third grade and not even being a military veteran or having gone to war like he did. I don't know if you guys can understand what I mean or not?"

"I understand perfectly," volunteered Dowdy. "I still have a couple friends from my high school that aren't comfortable talking about Korea with me. I volunteered to go in the marines and go there, while they didn't think it was a good idea—they stayed out of the service. So we just never talk about the military when we're together. Honestly, I think most non-veterans aren't nearly as interested in that stuff as we vets are."

"You're probably right about that, Lieutenant."

"So, Dick, does that 214 tell you anything you already knew? And does it raise any questions in your mind?"

"Right off the bat, it causes me to have even more respect for Roger than before. I mean the Bronze Star and a Purple Heart. Those are a big deal—especially that *Bronze Star*. I'm no expert on military medals, in fact, I don't know much about them. But I know I've read plenty of articles and books over the years that mentioned soldiers receiving the Bronze Star, and it was always for some heroic action."

"You're right about that, Dick. It is a big deal. So is the Army Commendation Medal, though not on the same plane as the Bronze Star. Deputy Easton and I discussed the fact that the service record has copies of the citations connected with those medals and the Purple Heart, but the descriptions don't say anything specific, such as where he was, other than in South Vietnam, or what specifically he did, to earn those medals. And on top of that, anything there that mentions his duty stations or activities gives no description of anything once he got to Vietnam. Alls they say is, UNDISCLOSED DUTIES IN SOUTH VIETNAM. Doesn't that strike you peculiar?"

"Yes, it certainly does. I've seen hundreds of job applications and looked over probably three dozen DD214s and various other military commendation forms that were turned in with applications or resumes, and I've never seen any as vague as Roger's. It makes me wonder about what he told me last summer after meeting with his ex-Vietnam buddies for their annual get-together."

"You've got our attention. Go on."

"After Roger got back from the weekend in Seattle in early August, he told me he had given one of his buddies some important information regarding something to do with Vietnam. And he also said if anything ever happened to him, I was to let his buddies know that he appreciated their friendship and loyalty over all the years. That struck me odd, I mean that last thing. But, of course, you never asked Roger to tell you more than he volunteered when it came to his military duty."

"It wasn't until you called me this morning to say you had received and reviewed his military record and wanted to get together this evening that I even thought about what Roger had said. You know how it is, when you're our age, you figure you and your buddies are going to live for years. So I just let that remark go after a week or so—never thought anymore about it. Do you think it could mean anything?"

"I don't know, Dick. What else can you tell me about his Army buddies or his military service?"

"That's about it. I think the record answers my questions about whether Roger did any combat. Don't you agree?"

"Yes, Deputy Easton and I are convinced that he not only did combat in Vietnam, but that he was probably involved in covert operations. Why else would the service record be so vague about his duty there?"

"I agree, Lieutenant. But what could that possibly have to do with his death last Saturday? Or do you think there's any chance it does?"

"I don't know what to think, honestly. What you said about him giving his Vietnam buddies some information and then telling you that if anything happened... Well, then this happens. It makes you wonder."

"Are you going to try to contact his Vietnam buddies?"

"You bet I am. Whether they'll tell me anything, I don't know. If they're anything like Roger... But then, since I'm investigating Roger's death, maybe they will talk to me. Do you have their names, addresses or phone numbers?"

"Sorry Lieutenant. He never talked to me about them, never gave me their names, anything. His request last summer was the first time he said anything, other than that he was getting together with them each year."

"Do you happen to know how many guys he got together with?"

"Yes. It was just two guys."

"So now there's just those two left."

"I don't know what other Army guys could be connected. Maybe the two he met with each year have other guys they hook up with."

"If Roger told you what he did after returning last August, he must have figured you'd have a way to contact those buddies. What do you think? Do you think his wife might have the contact information?"

"I couldn't say, since I've never talked to her about any of it."

"I guess we'll start there. With any luck she'll be able to help us. Or at least look through all his stuff to see what she can turn up.

"Sounds like a plan, Lieutenant. Now, let's assume the Army connection has nothing to do with Roger's death, do you have a backup plan?"

Dowdy laughed. "You know I do. But right now, especially after what Roger told you last summer, I think that's a good lead to follow. I'm going to continue to dig around and see what I can turn up as far as who could possibly have a motive." Dowdy took a long drink from his coffee, then said, "What do you think Deputy Easton?"

"I'm with you, Lieutenant."

"Dick," said Dowdy, "I'm sure you've had plenty of time to consider a lot of possible scenarios. We know you've BSed at least one." They all laughed. "So I want you to tell me whether you think there is the slightest possibility that Aaron Howe could have been involved?"

"That's ludicrous, Lieutenant. You're still curious about him

because of the comment he made about Roger's wife, aren't you?
He told me how he stuck his foot in his mouth. If you hung around
him much, you'd see that's how he keeps his toenails clipped."

They laughed some more.

15

The Funeral

Lieutenant Dowdy had the weekend off, so he attended Roger Bruington's Memorial service in street clothes. Of course he kept his eye open for anything that might benefit his investigation. Bruington's Vietnam buddies were not there, because no one had figured out who they were, let alone gotten their hands on contact information.

The local Army Guard unit sent three representatives, dressed in their Army dress greens, to the service held at the River Road Evangelical Church where the Bruingtons were members. Bruington's closed casket sat in front of the sanctuary with an American flag draped over it. Numerous flower displays rested on a table behind it, and flowers in pots were spread across the front of the altar. Several tall candles burned on their stands just behind the casket above and behind the flowers. Off to the right of the casket was a four-foot by five-foot poster board with numerous photos of Roger when he was a kid, in his various uniforms while in the Army, and then the majority of the photos were of him with his wife and daughters.

Toward the conclusion of the service, the Army detail folded up the flag that was resting on the coffin and presented it to Jan Bruington, **"On behalf of a grateful nation."**

She had maintained her composure pretty well up until that point, but broke down crying when she took hold of the flag. Her young daughters, seated on each side of her, hugged her and each placed a hand on top of their dad's flag as they also cried.

Later, after a catered reception meal, the three guardsmen accompanied Bruington's body, his family and friends to West Lawn Cemetery in west Eugene for Roger's internment. One of them played taps on the bugle, as Bruington's casket was lowered into the ground. *Another soldier* from the Vietnam War—laid to rest prematurely.

At nine Monday morning, November 1st, Lieutenant Dowdy received a telephone call from Oregon State Police Trooper Wilson.

"Lieutenant Dowdy, I was just talking with State Trooper Martin last night, and we're both curious how the Bruington case is coming."

"We found Bruington's hat on Thursday, over a hundred and fifty yards up hill to the northwest."

"Was there blood on it?"

"Plenty. And there were small teeth marks. Obviously some small animal had carried it up there. The funny thing is we weren't there specifically to look for the hat."

"What were you there for?"

"We were searching for blood, a gut pile, or a dead deer. We thought it was possible Bruington or his assailant shot a deer."

"Did you find any of that?"

"No."

"At least now you know he was wearing the hat. So that satisfies his hunting buddy and his wife. Did you tell them yet?"

"I told his best friend, Dick Eastbrook, and told him he could tell the others, though not to tell his wife. I felt like I wanted to be the one to do that."

"You're brave, Lieutenant. How did she react?"

"I haven't told her yet. I figured I'd let her get through this weekend first with the service, and family in town and all. But I'll be meeting with her this afternoon."

"I think that was a good call, sir. Especially since the hat had blood on it, and you know she's going to ask about that."

"Yeah, when I told Eastbrook about the blood, he was upset by it.

"Well, Lieutenant, is there anything more you can tell me?"

"I'm afraid that's it for now. If anything breaks, I'll definitely let you and Trooper Martin know."

"I would appreciate that, sir. Good luck in the investigation."

"Thanks." They both hung up.

Dowdy wasn't one to talk much about his cases to other law enforcement officials who weren't part of the investigation. Consequently he didn't have to spend his precious time answering everyone's questions and keeping them apprised of an investigation's progress, and there was less chance information would leak.

16

Jan Bruington Meeting

Monday afternoon, Lieutenant Dowdy and Deputy Easton met with Jan Bruington in her home. Her sister and brother-in-law were still staying there, but were spending the afternoon at Jan's mother and fathers' place in Coburg. She put two trays containing cookies and various other goodies, left over from the weekend festivities, on the coffee table in front of the blue couch they were sitting on in the living room. She also served them some freshly brewed coffee. The men wasted no time grabbing some peanut butter cookies and brownies.

As Dowdy watched Jan bringing things in for them and then finally settling herself down in a blue rocking chair nearby, he couldn't help but notice how beautiful she was. She couldn't be more than five-foot two, nicely shaped, a hundred pounds or so, he thought. With her medium-length, flowing brown hair, green eyes, perfect complexion, full lips and naturally rosy cheeks, Dowdy could see that the other night, Aaron Howe had just stated what was probably on the minds of many men who had been in her presence.

Then he thought of his own beautiful, high-school sweetheart wife, Katie, and how devoted to him and their kids she had always been. How she had been there to hold him when he came home on some of his worst days, such as the day three teenagers, who were driving drunk, had run under a flatbed truck and been decapitated. He had even felt secure enough with her on several occasions to cry while she was holding him. And she was wise enough to just squeeze him tighter and not say anything other than, "It's okay, honey, I'm here for you, and always will be." He knew she would be, and he knew he was the luckiest man on earth.

"That was a very nice service Saturday for your husband. I know it must have been rough for you."

"Thanks so much for coming to it, Lieutenant. Yes, it was rough. But at the same time having family and friends so close for a few days was a big source of strength and comfort to me and the girls."

"Are your sister and brother-in-law going to be staying with you much longer?"

"Only for three more days. Then they have to get back home to Sacramento. His brother and his wife have been watching their three kids, and of course they miss them very much. They call them every day."

"It's nice of them to be here for you. I guess you probably have plenty of food around the house for awhile, if this is any indication?"

"Yes, I do. People have been wonderful."

"Well, if there's anything we can do during this time, be sure to let us know."

"I appreciate that, Lieutenant. With my parents and my two brothers living in this area, I think I'll be okay."

"Okay, Jan, there are several things that I want to talk to you about. Deputy Easton is now on this case part-time with me, so I wanted him here when I met with you."

"That's fine, Lieutenant." Turning to Easton, she said, "I'm glad you're on the case, too Deputy Easton. If I can be of any help to you, let me know."

"I will," Easton answered, in between bites of a peanut butter cookie. "Thanks for your hospitality in sharing all this good food with us, and the coffee is excellent to."

"You're so kind, and you're welcome."

"Jan," said Dowdy, "from here out, I want to keep you closely updated on the progress of our investigation. I'm keeping Dick Eastbrook updated as well. I need you to keep most of what we talk about between you, Deputy Easton and me, and, of course, you may talk to Dick about it. I've asked him not to tell anyone else, including his wife, anything I share with him about the case."

"I appreciate your willingness to share everything with me, Lieutenant. But I think you could let Dick's wife know what's going on, too. She's the most honest person I know, besides Roger and Dick."

"I understand your feelings on that, Jan. And I know it would be nice for you to be able to talk to her about it. But you have to look at it from our perspective. There are things in these investigations that must be kept secret in order to protect the evidence, possible witnesses, and to prevent the assailant from knowing what we know. So, like we use to say in the service, if a person doesn't have the need to know, then they are not to know. You understand I'm sure?"

"Yes, I do, Lieutenant, and I will cooperate with you fully. I just want to get to the bottom of this."

"Good."

He wolfed down another peanut butter cookie, and drank some more coffee. Then said, "I'm not going to sugar coat anything Jan, though I will be sensitive."

"I know you will, Lieutenant." She shifted in the chair, getting more comfortable, and placed her hands together in the middle of her lap. Both men couldn't help but notice how feminine she appeared.

"A number of things about Roger's death are peculiar.

"Have you found the hat yet?"

Dowdy cringed. "Yes, Jan, Deputy Easton and I found the hat Thursday. It had been carried off by a small animal."

"Answer me honestly, Lieutenant. Was there blood on the hat?"

"I'm afraid there was." She put her right hand to her mouth and gasped. Then a trickle of tears drained out of the outside edge of each eye.

Immediately, Dowdy handed her a Kleenex from the box on the coffee table.

After giving her a minute to get a grip, he said, "I'm so sorry, Jan. I can't imagine what you feel right now. I'm sorry to be the one to tell you."

"It's okay, Lieutenant. It's not your fault. I'll be alright. Just give me a second."

He did, then said, "The night we found Roger, I immediately checked his rifle and was surprised to see that his safety was off. Then when I opened the bolt, I discovered a spent casing inside."

"What's that mean, the spent casing, I mean? I don't know much about guns; I'm sorry."

"What that means is that there was a shell in the chamber that had been fired. Roger had fired his rifle sometime, either just before, or when he was shot himself."

"Oh, dear God! What does that mean?"

"I believe it is the best evidence that this was no accidental shooting. We believe Roger was murdered."

"No," she sobbed. "It couldn't be. No one would have a reason to do that."

Dowdy, handed her another Kleenex.

"It's possible Roger was just in the wrong place at the wrong time when a lunatic was out in the woods. But we have to proceed as if someone somewhere had a specific motive for shooting him. A couple people have suggested that he could have been shot over a deer. But I don't buy that."

"The day we found Roger's hat, on Thursday," said Easton, "we actually went up there to try to find a dead deer, deer blood, or a gut pile that would indicate a deer had been killed by either Roger or the shooter."

"Did you find any of that?"

"No," said Dowdy, "which tells us that no deer was hit by Roger's shot. We believe in all likelihood, he pulled the trigger reflexively upon being shot himself, and missed the deer he was probably aiming at. We were unable to locate any empty shells that would have come from the killer's gun, or any footprints in the area. The ground is covered with a thick, dense moss. And a herd of elk worked the area over pretty good, too, before we got there and found Roger."

"So what you're saying is you have no solid evidence against the killer."

"What we're telling you, Jan," said Dowdy, "is we have nothing to identify or trace back to the killer. But, believe me—we're doing everything we can to figure this out."

"I know you are. And I'm sorry if I implied otherwise."

"Jan, Friday morning, I received a copy of Roger's military service record. Would you like to see it?"

"I'd love to see it, but I don't know if I'll be able to understand it. I've never looked at one of those before."

"I'll tell you this, Jan, you have a lot to be proud of Roger for when it comes to his military service. He received several medals, among them, the Purple Heart, Army Commendation Medal, and the Bronze Star."

"The Bronze Star? I've heard and read that is awarded for a very heroic action. And the Purple Heart, I know, is for being wounded. I sure wish he would have told me about those when he was alive. He just wouldn't talk about anything to do with that war."

"You're right about the significance of the Bronze Star and Purple Heart. The Army Commendation Medal is also only awarded for some kind of heroic or extraordinary action. You have a lot to be proud of. I know I'm not telling you anything new there. But I mean, in regard to Roger's military service in Vietnam, you have a lot to be proud of."

"And I am so proud. I miss him so much. He must have his medals and other service record information around here some place. I've always respected his space and never dug through his files or boxes or anything. And he didn't get into my personal things either."

"You're a good woman, Jan."

"And he was a wonderful man. I wish you both could have known him."

"So do we," said Easton.

"Jan, now that Roger is gone, I'm sure he wouldn't mind, in fact, I'm sure he would expect that you would go through his personal belongings, files and records. We really need some help on this investigation, some clues, or something to go on. I don't want you to do it tonight, but do you think tomorrow morning you could round up all of his personal items that you haven't looked through and see if there is anything—I mean anything at all—that might be of benefit to us. In fact, it would be even better if we could come back and look through his things ourselves."

"You guys are welcome to do it while you're here today, if you have the time. The kids won't be home until after six. They go to Brownies on Monday afternoons. I help out with that, myself, but I've taken this week off."

"That would be great, Jan. But before we do that, I need to ask you a few more questions."

"Go ahead."

"Aaron and Dick both told us that Roger got together once a year with some guys he served with in Vietnam."

"Yes, he always went out of town for a weekend in August to meet them."

"Was the meeting always in Seattle?"

"Oh, no. Just this last summer's meeting was there. They've met in a different place every year."

"What was the reason for that?"

"Roger said they just liked to see different parts of the country."

"Neither Dick or Aaron had any information on the names, phone numbers or addresses of his Vietnam buddies. Do you happen to have that information?"

"I'm sorry, Lieutenant. I can't help you there—although you might find something when you go through Roger's stuff."

"I sure hope so. Here, look at these records." Dowdy handed her several pages of Roger's service record, including the one that said, UNDISCLOSED DUTIES IN SOUTH VIETNAM. Dowdy hated that phrase. And he was beginning to wonder if it shouldn't have said, ILLEGAL COVERT OPERATIONS ALL OVER SOUTH-EAST ASIA.

After taking a couple minutes to look through the records, Jan said, "I don't have any idea what these things are supposed to say."

"Trust me, Jan—they're supposed to say a lot more than that. So are the citations for the medals," said Dowdy. Is there anything else you can tell us about Roger's military duty, or his Army buddies?"

"Not really. Well, I doubt this has anything to do with any of this."

"What's that, Jan?"

"After Roger got home from Vietnam, there was one time when he went to Thailand for several weeks back in the spring of 1974. He said he just wanted to go back to some of his old R and R stomping grounds. I was several months pregnant with our second daughter, at the time, so there was no way I could have gone. He didn't mention me going anyway. I just assumed it was something he and the buddies needed to do. I even thought that he might get some closure by going back.

"When he got home, did he tell you anything about his trip?"

"He said he spent some time in Bangkok and also visited Pattaya."

"Do you have any photos of his Vietnam buddies, the two he met with each summer?"

"I wish I did, Lieutenant. I'm not much help am I?"

"You're plenty of help, Jan. And if we're lucky we'll get what we need when we go through Roger's files. As a matter of fact, would you mind if we get on those files and the personal stuff now?" The suspense was killing him.

"No, I don't mind," she said. She got up from her chair and motioned for them to follow her. "Come on, I'll take you to his study." They each grabbed a couple brownies and their coffee cups and followed her out of the living room and into the first room on the left as they started down the hall.

"Make yourselves at home here. I'm going to grab a box from our closet. I don't think there's anything else in there that would interest you. Oh, while I'm at it, I'll get his wallet."

"That'd be great, Jan." said Deputy Easton.

After she was out of hearing range, Dowdy said, "That woman is gold, isn't she. Not only pleasing to the eyes and a wonderful personality, but she knows how to stay out of her husband's things."

"I don't know too many men that are that lucky," Easton responded, "to have their wives stay out of their things."

"Now let's just hope we can find something worthwhile." Handing Easton a box, he said, "Here, you can start with this one."

After over an hour of going through Roger's stuff and putting down the last folder, Dowdy said, "Can you believe this? That guy must have kept his military stuff somewhere else—maybe in a safe-deposit box. Or who knows where?"

When they had completed putting the last of Roger's things back in order, they walked into the kitchen where Jan was stirring a sauce she was heating for the spaghetti she and the girls were going to have for dinner.

"We went through all of his stuff and found nothing that answers any of our questions, Jan. It looks like I'm going to have to go about this the hard way."

"I'm sorry you didn't find anything helpful, Lieutenant. So what is the hard way?"

"I'll have to contact the government to try to get the names and contact information of Roger's buddies. Maybe I'll get lucky and someone in the government will help me solve this thing."

"I wouldn't count on that," said Easton.

"Jan, do you know if Roger had a safe-deposit box anywhere, or where else he might have kept military documents and such?"

"I don't have any idea. I thought you guys would find something today. Do you men want to stay for supper? The sauce and spaghetti I'm making were given to me by one of the best cooks in our church."

"We'd like to, Jan, but it's been a long day. The last week or so, our wives haven't seen much of us. We better pass."

She walked them to the door and said, "I really appreciate what you two are doing."

"Thank you, Jan, for being so open with us, and for the goodies and coffee," said Dowdy. "If there's anything we can do for you, call me, will you?"

17

Trooper and the Hippie

Monday Evening, Trooper Wilson, wearing street clothes, drove his green Ford pickup to the hippie's run-down house outside of Jasper, walked up the walkway, and pounded on the front door.

"Yeah, take it easy. One of the hinges is already cracked," said the hippie, as he opened the door.

"Del, I've got some good news."

"What's that?"

"They found the hat. I talked with Lieutenant Dowdy this morning. They found the hunter's hat that you had planted. Good going."

"Damn it! Finally something goes our way. Come on in." They each crashed in one of the two broken-down, torn-up upholstered chairs in the twelve foot by twelve foot living room that had peeling wall paper on one wall and rough-sawn, one by six fir boards nailed vertically on another one.

"What else did he tell you?" asked Del, after taking a puff on a roll-your-own cigarette, holding it in for several seconds, then

122

blowing the smoke out into the room.

"He and another deputy went up in the woods looking for blood, or a deer or gut pile outside the perimeter of our original search area."

"Why were they looking for that?"

"Lieutenant Dowdy thought maybe the dead hunter had shot at a deer just before he was hit. He figured if they could find the deer it would answer the question about why the hunter's rifle was off safe and held an empty shell in its chamber."

"Well, of course they didn't find any blood, or anything. So now what is Dowdy saying happened?"

"He still believes the hunter was about ready to shoot a deer when he was killed. But that he was shot before he pulled the trigger on the deer. They figure he pulled the trigger reflexively when he was hit. What do you think about that theory?"

"I think it's a bunch of crap. But hey, if it settles things for them, it's alright with me."

"What do you think happened, Del?"

"I don't have the foggiest idea. We know the hunter was looking at something through his scope when you shot him. But we know he never got a chance to take a shot. Shoot we don't even know what he was looking at."

"You know that whole question could have been avoided if we had just checked his rifle when we moved it."

"That's another one of your, 'we could have, we should have, we shouldn't have done that,' trips, Butch. When are you going to quit doing that to yourself?"

"You're right, Del."

"The fact is we didn't check the rifle. And I don't think in the end it's going to matter at all. You said yourself, Dowdy feels comfortable with the scenario he told you about. We don't have anything to worry over. It really doesn't matter what happened now, does it? We did such a good job of staging the crime scene when we planted the hunter's body that not one of them has said anything about the possibility of the body being moved to that location."

"Right. We did an excellent job with that." Butch hated himself for even thinking, 'excellent job', but even more that he had spoken it. "No one has said a thing about the body being moved."

"I guarantee you the thought hasn't even crossed one of their minds. We're in the clear!"

"I think you're right, Del."

"Damn it. I know I'm right. It's time to relax."

"I could sure stand to do that."

"You damn right you could, Butch." Del was showing emotions Butch couldn't remember seeing from him since he went to Vietnam fifteen years ago. He was happy. It was great to see him happy again. Maybe that burst up on Mt. June had freed him up at last.

And then Butch suddenly felt that weight that had been hanging on him for the last nine days, that remorse, come welling up inside again, pulling down his spirits. Maybe Del was finally free, but he wasn't. He knew he would never be free. He thought, you can't kill a man in cold blood and ever be free. Del killed because he was a soldier. So did Butch's dad. No matter what Del told Butch, he knew his killing was not the same. It did mean something. It meant he was a killer and the dead man's wife was a widow. And he made her a widow. And he made the two young girls fatherless, just like the Vietnam War had made him fatherless. He hated himself for it. His dad would have hated him for it. Why did he listen to Del in the first place? The man's crazy...

18

Closed Doors

After no luck picking up anything on Bruington's military background, or anything else to aid in the investigation, from Bruington's files and personal belongings in his house, Dowdy determined he had to track down Bruington's two Army buddies. He knew the likelihood of Bruington's death having anything to do with the military or his Army buddies was slim. But it offered more than any other direction he had gone.

What continued to bother him was what Bruington told Eastbrook after meeting his Vietnam buddies in Seattle: "*If anything ever happens to me,* tell my Vietnam buddies…" and Bruington giving them information. The timing. Did Bruington know his life was in danger? Dowdy had to ask Jan Bruington whether Roger had any life-insurance policies. And if so, when were they purchased?

The next morning, Dowdy learned from Jan Bruington that at the time of his death, Roger did, in fact, have two policies totaling $200,000. Each listed Jan as the beneficiary—with the daughters as the secondary beneficiary if she died at the same time as Roger did.

The first policy was for $100,000. When Roger originally pur-chased it in 1974, it was for a $50,000 benefit. But in 1976, he increased the coverage to the current $100,000. The second policy was purchased last July, 1980, and was for $100,000. That intrigued Dowdy. Why did he purchase the policy a month before giving his Army buddies the information and then tell Eastbrook what he told him? It could just be coincidence. After all, he had purchased additional insurance in 1976. Maybe he just added that last policy when he could afford it, and intended to add even more insurance in the years ahead.

Dowdy asked Jan if Roger had talked about the policies with her at the time he purchased them. She said he had and he just wanted to ensure she had plenty of money if anything ever happened to him. She didn't know if he planned to buy any additional coverage in the future, but she was very thankful for the coverage they had when he died. She had already talked with the two insurance companies, and they each assured her she would receive payoff within a month without any problem.

Dowdy also learned that Roger had even bought mortgage insurance which would pay their house off upon his death. Meriwether Bank, the mortgage holder, told Jan that policy would settle soon, as well.

Throughout the rest of November, Dowdy wrote a number of letters and made numerous phone calls to the military records office and to several different Army bases. He soon realized he was on a dead-end road. The recipients of his letters, and the people he talked to by phone, either didn't know anything, passed him on to their superiors who then gave him the brush off, or they deliberately avoided giving him the names and contact information of Bruing-ton's buddies. Whenever he asked anyone if they personally served in Vietnam, the person either said they didn't, or they hesitated to admit having served there. Dowdy found that puzzling. At the same time it gave him a greater desire to get to the bottom of the

Bruington-Vietnam connection thing. But he couldn't even get below the surface, let alone get to the bottom.

After more than two months of not getting any closer to obtaining the contact information, Dowdy figured at some point the Army buddies would try to contact Bruington to coordinate their annual get together the next summer. But it could be months before that happened. He alerted Jan Bruington to the importance of contacting him immediately if the buddies called her and Rogers' home. Of course, Dowdy was assuming that the buddies weren't in on Bruington's demise—he couldn't believe they possibly could be—or even knew anything about it. How would they know?

19

A Break for Dowdy

By February, Aaron Howe was spending more and more time at the Bruington residence. Many of Roger and Jan Bruington's friends and family were actually thankful he had stepped in to help with some of the guy projects around her place. Jan's brothers and their wives, along with her parents, were also a huge encouragement and help to her, and they took the girls overnight to their houses regularly. Jan's church was also a big support. Her grief was still strong, but as each week passed she sensed little by little she and the girls were making progress toward healing from their devastating loss.

There were a few people who still looked at Aaron Howe with suspicion, knowing he was a single friend to Roger and Jan Bruington and had said on several occasions how lucky Roger was to have a wife like Jan. And the fact remained, Howe was alone on the Saturday Roger was killed. Sheriff Deputies Dowdy and Easton, however, believed Howe had told them the truth about his whereabouts on that fateful Saturday.

In early February, Del and Butch once again began their production of methamphetamines in the shack on Slick Creek. It wasn't a big operation, but they both made a couple thousand dollars each month in drug shipments.

Since Bruington's death, Del had set up a warning system along the perimeter, a hundred yards out from the shack. Now they would have time to lock the shack up and escape through the tunnel to the underground bunker thirty yards away if anyone approached the shack.

In the early-evening on **February 26th**, Jan Bruington's telephone rang. When she answered it, a voice with a deep-southern drawl, said, "Is Roger there?"

"May I ask whose calling?"

"This is one of his Army buddies. Is Roger home?"

"Oh, Uh," she stammered. This was the call they had hoped for. "Roger passed away."

"What? He was fine last summer when we saw him."

"Yes. He was fine last summer. But he died in late-October."

"It wasn't that **Agent-Orange** crap was it? He didn't say anything about it last summer."

"No. No." She started crying. Roger had never said anything to her about being showered in Agent Orange defoliant on his first tour.

The voice on the other end was silent. Half a minute passed with Jan crying.

"I'm sorry," she finally said, "it's just been so hard losing him."

"I'm so sorry, Ma'am. I don't really know what to say. Maybe I should call back another time."

"No. No. Please don't go. I need to talk to you."

"I'm here." He paused several seconds, then said, "I'm afraid to ask what happened to Roger."

"It's okay. It's not okay. But it's okay that you asked. He was killed in the woods during deer season."

"He was shot by another hunter?"

"We really don't know. He didn't come home from his deer hunt one weekend, and when the search and rescue team searched above his camp site, they found he had been shot a couple days earlier." She broke down sobbing again.

Then after half a minute, she pulled herself together and said, "The sheriff's deputy who is head of the investigation, Lieutenant Dowdy, has run into nothing but dead ends. As a matter of fact, he has been trying to get a hold of your contact information for months, with no luck. We've been waiting for your call."

"Why would he be trying to get a hold of me?"

"I don't really know. He hasn't told me why. I just know it's very important that he talk to you."

There was silence on the other end of the line for ten seconds, then finally, Jan said, "Are you still there?"

"Yes. Yes, I'm still here. This whole thing has caught me totally off-guard. I mean I did a whole tour with Roger, and we lived through some tough situations over there. Then to find out he got shot in the woods in Oregon. It's hard to swallow."

"I still can't believe he's gone. It's been four months. Four months of hell."

"I'm so sorry, Ma'am." He paused, then said, "I'm sorry, Roger told me your name, but I can't remember it right now."

"It's Jan. Thanks. What's your name?"

He hesitated, realizing he had opened himself up to that question. He considered giving her a false name, but then felt guilty for even thinking that. He learned to cover things up so well in Southeast Asia, and in the years since returning home, that it came natural.

"I'm Marvin. Marvin Kennedy."

"Thanks Marvin. All these years of Roger meeting with you guys, and he never told me your names. You guys must have been through hell."

"Nothing we went through could be as bad as what you're going through, Jan. I'm terribly sorry."

"Thanks for understanding. Now it's very important that Lieutenant Dowdy talk to you."

"I understand. Why don't you give me his number, and I'll try to contact him in the next few days."

After she gave him Dowdy's number, he asked if there was anything he could do for her. She said, "Just call Lieutenant Dowdy. Then call me back some time. And don't wait too long. There are things I would like to know."

"I understand. But I don't know how much I can tell you."

"I would just like to know about my Roger. I prayed for him constantly when he was over in Vietnam. I wondered about him every day, if he was safe or not. But when he came home, he never would talk about anything that happened over there. I've wanted to know for so long. I thought some day he would be able to tell me about it. Then this happened. Now I'll never know unless one of you guys who was there with him tells me."

"I understand, Jan. I really do. It's just hard going back there. I don't know, maybe some time, okay?"

"Yes. Yes, some time."

"I'm going to go now. I'm really sorry for you losing Roger. It's a huge loss to me too. And *I will* call Lieutenant Dowdy. I want to know more about what happened to Roger."

As soon as the line was clear, Jan called Lieutenant Dowdy.

"He called!"

"I'm sorry, ma'am. Who called?"

"This is Jan Bruington. He called."

"Jan. Jan, it's great to hear from you. One of the buddies from Vietnam called? Did you get his name and number?"

"No. Well I did get his name, but not the phone number. I gave him your name and number and told him it was very important that he get a hold of you."

"Did he say he would?"

"Yes. He said he would call you in the next few days."

"That's great Jan. Good going. What's his name, anyway?"

"Marvin Kennedy. He has quite a southern drawl, so he must be from down south somewhere."

"This is great, Jan."

"Well I've got to go pick up the girls from the skating rink. Please let me know what you find out, would you Lieutenant?"

"I'll tell you what I can, Jan. That's all I can promise. Thanks again for this good news. Now let's just hope he actually calls me."

"I know. I really think he will. I'll talk to you later."

Monday afternoon, March 2nd —

"Yes, Lieutenant Dowdy speaking. How can I help you?"

"Lieutenant Dowdy, this is Marvin Kennedy. I served in Vietnam with Roger Bruington. His wife told me what happened and said it was important that I call you."

"Yes. Thanks, Mr. Kennedy, for calling me."

"What happened to Roger? Was it a hunting accident?"

"I wish I could tell you exactly. We still haven't figured it out."

"Where was he shot? Where on his body, I mean?"

"He was shot in the back of his head."

"Oh, no! Well at least it was over instantly. That sounds like a sniper shot to me?"

"That's our thoughts exactly, or at least someone that is good with a rifle."

"How can you possibly think it is anything other than a murder, Lieutenant, with a shot like that?"

"Because it happened during deer season and Roger was hunting."

"But a shot directly in the back of the head. That's no accident. I've seen too many of those to think otherwise."

"Were you a sniper?" asked Dowdy, taking a chance on picking up a little background.

"Look, I didn't call you to talk about my military service. What is it you want from me?"

"I understand how you feel, Mr. Kennedy. It's just that from reviewing Roger's service record, so much about it points to some kind of covert duty, possibly as a sniper. I thought if you were there with him... Well you know what I mean. And the only thing his record says about his Vietnam service is UNDISCLOSED DUTIES IN SOUTH VIETNAM. Everything about his service record screams cover-up."

The other end of the line was silent.

After ten seconds, Dowdy said, "Mr. Kennedy, are you there?"

"Yes. This is just more complicated than I wanted it to be. But I guess it couldn't be avoided, could it?"

"Trust me, Mr. Kennedy. I don't intend to make it complicated or to try to get more information out of you than necessary. I just want to get to the bottom of Roger Bruington's death, figure out who might have done it. I have a few questions for you, based on information Roger's best friend gave me. I don't know if it will matter to you, but I was a marine and served in Korea at the tail end of that war. I know your situation was completely different. I just want you to know that I'm a brother-in-arms and understand war from first hand experience."

"That's helpful to know. That tells me you're not one of those government bureaucrats that let everyone else fight their dirty wars for them."

"You have that straight. Now can I share what I know with you and why I think it may relate to Roger's death?"

"Go ahead. No one else can listen in on this call can they?"

"No. This is a line straight to my desk and no others. That's why I gave Jan this number." Dowdy paused several seconds, then said, "I'll just lay all my cards on the table, then let you respond."

"That sounds fair enough, though I can't promise what I can

say."

"Last July, 1980, Roger took out an additional $100,000 life insurance policy, with his wife as beneficiary. He already had a policy for $100,000. Then he met with you and your other buddy in Seattle in early August. A week after coming home from his visit with you guys, he told his friend Dick Eastbrook that he had given you some important information when he saw you. He also told Eastbrook that if anything ever happened to him to contact you guys and tell you he appreciated your friendship and loyalty over all the years. That struck Dick odd at first. Then Roger was shot to death with a perfect hit in the back of the head on October 25th. And to make matters even more puzzling, when we found him, his gun was off-safe and it had a spent round in the chamber."

"That's odd. Do you think he might have shot at the assailant before getting hit himself?"

"We considered that; but we determined he never would have turned his back on his assailant without reloading first. Seeing his service record cemented that further in our minds. And there were no empty casings laying anywhere near him, plus his magazine was full. He had only fired the one shot."

"I see what you mean. You're absolutely right. Roger never would have turned his back without re-chambering a round, though in Nam we used the auto-loading M16s and M21s. But if he emptied a magazine, he always reloaded before turning away from the enemy. We all did. At least the ones that wanted to stay alive."

"I thought M21s were accuratized M14s specifically improved for snipers in Vietnam."

"You obviously know more about military weapons than the average Joe, Lieutenant. I guess I tipped my hand there, didn't I. I'm not comfortable talking about this anymore over the phone. If you want anymore information, you'll have to talk to me in person."

"I can fly down there if you'd like, Mr. Kennedy. Where is down there, anyway?"

"I see I'm in deeper than I wanted to be already. I'm in Georgia."

"Like I said, I can fly down there, or we can fly you up here and put you up in a motel. The advantage if you come up here is that I can take you out to the woods where Roger was found and show you the scenario."

"That's a little heavy, I'm afraid. Why don't you let me think about it for a couple days and get back to you?"

"Can I get your phone number?"

"No. I'll call you."

"You sound like a man of his word. I'll expect your call. If you don't get me, try again, will you?"

"Oh, I will. I just need to absorb this. I'll talk to you in a couple days, Lieutenant."

"Okay, Mr. Kennedy."

On Thursday, March 5th, Kennedy called Dowdy and agreed to fly up to Oregon.

Del and Butch at the Slick Creek shack above Fall Creek, on Friday afternoon—

"I got word that Dowdy's flying in some Vietnam buddy of Bruington's on Monday. I don't know what that's all about. Do you have any idea what it could mean, Del?"

"Who knows? Dowdy must be off on some wild goose chase. As long as he's still looking in another direction, we're off his radar. In fact, we'll never be on the radar."

"Dowdy's definitely not going down without a fight is he?"

"Decision or knockout, either way he loses. It's no skin off my back. Keep your ears open—see if you can pick up anything while the vet is here. Dowdy's really grasping at straws trying to figure out this killing, isn't he?"

"Do you have to say it like that?"

"Sorry, Butch. Sometimes I slip back. Over there you just said it the way it was, no sugar-coating it."

"I gathered that."

20

Vietnam Buddy

After picking Marvin Kennedy up at the Eugene Airport on Monday, March 9th, and getting him checked into the Eugene Hilton Hotel, Lieutenant Dowdy and Deputy Easton took Kennedy out to Puma Creek Campground. There Dowdy showed Kennedy where Bruington had camped, and then the three of them hiked up into the woods to the crime scene on Jones Creek, on the north side of Fall Creek.

Once on the scene, Dowdy explained the evidence they had found, including the position of Bruington's body and rifle, the blood, cheekbone, and also where Easton had found the hat. He then explained all the scenarios they had considered. Kennedy said he would have come to the same conclusion they had, based on the evidence as they presented it to him. He was sure it was not a hunting accident. So far Kennedy had asked all the questions and Dowdy and Easton had given all the answers.

Then as they all sat up against some old downed logs nearby, munching on sandwiches and candy bars, Dowdy said, "Marvin, now we would like to learn more about yours and Roger's military duty in Vietnam, or perhaps, more specifically, what information Roger gave you last summer."

"I'm going to forewarn you," Kennedy said, "that the inform-ation I give you two today could get me and other people in trouble. And I believe it may have gotten Roger killed. You can take notes, but don't write my name down as a source, nor ever reveal me as a source. I'm only going to tell you this stuff because Roger and I watched each other's backs for Roger's entire last year in Asia. But I wasn't here to watch his back, and now he's dead. The information that I share with you today, that probably got him killed, was new information to me a few days ago when I opened Roger's envelope for the first time after learning about his death. I knew nothing about it before that."

"So you're saying Roger was involved in something you didn't know about, and that got him killed?"

"Let me cross that bridge when I get to it. No matter what, you have to realize there are some powerful people out there in our government that will go to great lengths to keep what you're going to learn under the carpet. Do you understand what you're exposing yourselves to?"

"I think so," said Dowdy.

"And me too," said Easton. "We're law-enforcement officers and we put our lives on the line every day in the line of duty. If the buck can't stop with us, where does that leave everybody else?"

"I hear what you're saying, Deputy. But I'm talking about the possibility of ending up like Roger at the hands of the U.S. government."

"That's about as straight forward as you can be," said Easton.

"Yes, it is. But this isn't a game, believe me. Do I know that Roger must have been killed by the government? Of course not. But that is a definite possibility. As long as I never bring up any of the same issues that Roger was involved in, they won't know that I have any information. The same will be true of both of you. Do you follow?"

"We follow, alright," said Dowdy. "But we'll have to cross some of those bridges ourselves when we come to them."

"And you will never reveal me as the source of your information? I've got to have your assurance of that."

"You've got it," they both said simultaneously. Both Dowdy and Easton pulled out their four by six spiral notepads and black pens and wrote a few notes down, then got ready for some fast and furious writing.

While they were doing that, Kennedy pulled out his pack of Marlboros and lit one up. After sucking in and blowing out several puffs of smoke, Kennedy said, "This is a bit complicated, so if you need clarification don't hesitate to stop me and ask.

"Roger and I both served in separate Army infantry divisions north of Saigon during our first tours of duty in Vietnam. During that time, we never met each other and had no idea that the powers that be were already formulating plans for the sniper team that he and I would be on during our second tours. We both achieved Expert Rifle status in Boot Camp, but that is very common. So that alone didn't mean much. But the Army was always on the look out for potential snipers."

Answering the unasked question, he said, "Yes, the first criterion was to be an expert marksman. But being able to hit a human at a long distance is a completely different animal than being able to hit a target precisely. So many soldiers that were great on the shooting range couldn't hit a human at long range if their lives depended on it. It's the nerves. Are you a veteran, too, Deputy Easton?"

"Yes. I did four years in the Navy right out of high school."

"Are you a Vietnam veteran?"

"No—just Vietnam era. I served on a submarine in the Atlantic ocean."

"But you had to qualify on weapons in the Navy and as a cop."

"Yes. In the Navy, we qualified on the Colt .45 and on the M14." He didn't tell Kennedy that they qualified on a shooting range with the .45, but that they qualified on the M14 while at sea. If they could hit the water in the open ocean with their ten rounds, they qualified. At least that was the popular joke of the day.

"You guys may not be aware that the Army actually did a study in the wars and years prior to Vietnam about the value of soldiers using fully-automatic small arms over semi-automatic weapons. There was a debate over which was more effective in a battle situation. The two main arguments were that when using a semi-automatic weapon like the M1 or M14, soldiers were more likely to take careful aim at the enemy's body and therefore expend far less ammunition in accomplishing the same thing. The argument against that was that most soldiers, even in a battle situation, shied away from actually aiming directly at a human's body. They had such an aversion to killing another human—even the enemy—that they subconsciously did not want to aim at the person's head or torso."

"That's quite interesting, Marvin," said Dowdy. "And what did their study determine?"

"It verified the second argument. And that is one of the biggest reasons why the Army and the Marine Corps finally made the switch to the Colt M16 machine gun. The M14, of course, never panned out as a fully automatic weapon."

"So the soldier armed with an M16 can spray bullets back and forth across the target, the enemy's body, and not have that same sense of zeroing in and killing him."

"That's right. A lot more ammo is expended, but killing doesn't have the same impact on the soldier's mind. I'm not downplaying the traumatic effect that the killing has period, but rather, there is a consolation in the subconscious of not aiming specifically at the enemy's body to kill him. And in a platoon situation where a bunch of one's fellow soldiers are also spraying ammo at the enemy, you might rarely know for sure whose bullets killed any one guy. Sure, we all know that soldiers would sometimes talk about how many men they had killed. But bragging about it in public was often a cover for the remorse many of them felt when alone."

"That's some interesting stuff, Marvin. By the way, what rank were you when you got out?"

"I was a staff sergeant."

"Would you like us to call you sergeant?"

"No. That's behind me. You're doing fine just calling me Marvin. Anyway, getting back to Roger and me. Both of our platoon sergeants, already having been informed that the Army needed more snipers, recognized our strong nerves under fire and our accuracy in shooting the enemy and each recommended us for sniper duty.

"So two months or so before our first twelve month tours were over, we were pulled out of our companies and groomed for sniper duty, taught how to live off the land, and all that stuff. That's when I met Roger and the other guys that would be on various sniper teams. After that we were allowed only a two week leave instead of the customary thirty days. When we arrived back to MACV in Saigon, we were put together in teams of two, briefed and flown by chopper to the Vietnam-Cambodia border north of Saigon. Three teams were dropped there and other teams were dropped farther north."

"From our drop point, Roger and I were to hump it deep into Cambodia and snipe along the Ho Chi Minh Trail. This was in September 1970, shortly after the American forces who had invaded Cambodia in late April and May had withdrawn. As you probably know, officially no Americans were supposed to be operating in Cambodia or Laos at any other time except during the 1970 invasion. And that invasion, which was considered illegal, proved to be a huge point used by the war protesters at home. It was okay for the North Vietnamese to stock pile arms and supplies and train troops and attack South Vietnam from there, but we weren't allowed to go in there to fight them. It was bull!"

"So Roger's service record says UNDISCLOSED DUTIES IN SOUTH VIETNAM, because a lot of his duties actually occurred in Cambodia and Laos, where he wasn't supposed to be," said Easton.

"That's right. Mine says the same thing. But the CIA, Green Beret, Rangers, SEALS—you name it, special forces had been operating covertly in small groups there since the beginning of the war. Unfortunately, the amount of damage any of those groups or our sniper teams could do was minimal in the huge picture. What we needed was for our main forces to go right in from the start of the war and do whatever needed to be done. We could have completely dried up that Ho Chi Minh Trail—and probably won the war by 1968, instead of eventually losing it. But that was another example of trying to fight a war with your balls tied in a knot."

Dowdy and Easton both wanted to chuckle, but Kennedy's tone made it clear that he didn't say it as a joke.

"Of course all the bombing we did on the Ho Chi Minh Trail through 1971 made a big dent on the NVA activities. But they still got massive amounts of supplies, arms and soldiers through.

"So after you and Roger infiltrated Cambodia, you spent the next year sniping Vietcong and North Vietnamese regular soldiers?"

"We didn't do much with the VC. They were mostly in South Vietnam. It was the NVA regulars that we worked over. And we had to be careful to keep from getting caught. One shot deals— picking off officers, the more senior the better. He'd shoot, I'd spot. I'd shoot, he'd spot. Make the kill and get the hell out of Dodge City. We'd lie low for several days, while moving up the trail another ten kilometers. Then we'd put the lights out on another one. Obviously as the year moved on, our mission became tougher. There were more and more NVA patrols sent out into the perimeter areas of the Trail to seek out snipers like us. It wasn't like they were sitting ducks that just let you pluck away at them. After a couple months, it got downright risky getting anywhere near The Trail. Several of the sniper teams that trained with us were caught and executed. But we were lucky."

"How did Roger get his Purple Heart?"

"He should have received three Hearts. He received the one in his records the first year while still operating in the infantry division. He was shot in his right thigh muscle. It was a clean, through and through soft tissue wound, and he was back out for duty within a couple weeks or so. But the two he should have earned while working with me, he never received. That's another story.

The first one was a few weeks into our Cambodia tour, when we inadvertently walked into a small band of Pathet Lao, taking a lunch break while operating at the Laos-Cambodia border. They went for their guns and we opened up on them. Thought we had killed them all, but one wasn't quite dead and stabbed Roger in the left thigh as he passed by. Roger finished him off with a rifle butt to the side of his head. It wasn't pretty. Nothing over there was.

The third injury involved a swinging wicker basket filled with mud, leaves and punji sticks. Roger had tripped the hidden wire and managed to duck out of the way when it swung down like a pendulum, but he was grazed on his left shoulder. The wound was actually pretty deep and bled a lot, but I got him wrapped up. Trust me, he wrapped me up a few times himself. Anyway, that's about the whole of it, as far as our duty in Cambodia."

"Obviously none of that could have anything to do with his being killed," said Dowdy. "So are you going to share the information that Roger gave you last summer?"

"Yes. I'm even going to do better than that. I'm going to let Roger share it with you. He taped all the information, along with typing it all out. I brought my pocket recorder and the tape with me. I guess here in the woods is a perfect place to listen. This will be only the second time I've listened to the tape. The first time was the night after I initially talked with you. Forgive me if I get a little emotional."

"Don't worry about that."

21

Bruington Tape- Cambodia

Kennedy pulled the compact recorder out of his pack along with a packet that looked like it probably contained some written documents. He set the packet beside him and then pressed the play button on the recorder. Dowdy and Easton put their notepads down and listened.

Roger began speaking, in his deep, manly voice. Both Dowdy and Easton wished they had gotten to know him.

"This is **Roger Dale Bruington**, former Army sergeant who served his country in Vietnam from 25 August 1969 through 15 September 1971. If you are listening to this tape and I am not present, I am most likely dead as a result of the information I am about to share with you."

Kennedy hit the stop button and put his chin down to hide his face beneath his Army ball cap. Dowdy and Easton understood, and both actually had an eerie feeling come over themselves at those words. Kennedy picked up a small, dead branch from beside him and started breaking it into small pieces, piling them together

144

between his out-stretched legs. Then he hit the play button again, and Bruington continued.

"Everything I am about to say is taken from a journal I kept meticulously, beginning with the first letter from my Thai contact until now, regarding the POW issue and my correspondence with military and government authorities after my own trip to Thailand and Cambodia. Along with these tapes, I have the written version from which I made this tape verbatim included in the packet, as well as the actual evidence itself, written and photographic."

Dowdy and Easton looked at each other with that look that said, *this is going to be real good.*

"I served as a sniper for the U.S. Army along the Ho Chi Minh Trail in northeast Cambodia and southern Laos from September 1970 until September 1971. My partner and I killed forty-two North Vietnamese officers during that time. There were numerous other American sniper teams operating up and down the Trail in both Cambodia and Laos, and they took a heavy toll. But none of them, nor my partner or I, have ever been recognized publicly for what we accomplished, because those activities were covert and considered illegal by not only the U.S. Government (though some U.S. Officials were aware of the activities, and many of those favored our actions), but the governments of all the nations in southeast Asia, with the exception of South Vietnam, as well as many countries around the world.

It was okay for the North Vietnamese to use Cambodia and Laos as staging areas for prosecuting their war in South Vietnam and for refuges following their hit and run missions there. But we were not allowed to pursue them when they crossed back into these two countries. It was bull! So we snipers did what we could.

During my time in Cambodia, I established several reliable

contacts with Cambodian government soldiers. After leaving Vietnam for good in September 1971, being debriefed and then discharged immediately by the Army, I maintained contact with one particular Cambodian Government soldier through a mutual contact in Thailand.

As everyone knows, America's combat involvement in Vietnam ended in 1973, and the last known American POWS were released in March of 1973. In early March 1974, I received a letter from my contact in Thailand informing me that my soldier friend in Cambodia had proof that American soldiers were still being held prisoner in Northeast Cambodia, though he didn't specify how many.

That was disturbing news to me. But at the same time, I was glad to know that more of those never recovered, and listed as missing in action, were still alive. I had to do something about it. But before I could go to any U.S. authorities, I wanted conclusive evidence of the accuracy of my Cambodian contact's claim. I called my Thailand contact at the number he had given me in his letter and told him I wanted to come to Thailand, that he could put me in contact with our mutual contact in Cambodia. I said I wanted to see the American prisoners myself. He said he had already planned on it. I didn't want to wait until after the summer monsoon season to go; so I asked my Thai friend to work things out on his end with our Cambodian contact and get back to me ASAP.

On 15 April 1974, I flew out of Portland, stopped in Hawaii, stopped in Guam and then flew on to Bangkok, Thailand. Over the next two days, my Thai friend drove me, by way of numerous small towns and villages, to the Thailand-northern Cambodia border, within 75 kilometers of Laos, where we hooked up with our Cambodian contact at a predetermined location in Thailand. He had been waiting there for a day.

It was great to see both of my friends. My Cambodian friend was very excited about the information he had for me. But he immediately put a damper on my enthusiasm when he said that in the last month conditions throughout northern Cambodia had deteriorated markedly as the Khmer Rouge were clashing there with the North Vietnamese, who were previously their allies. He warned me that he didn't know if we could reach the camp where the American soldiers were being held, or if they might have been moved. The North Vietnamese detention camp we needed to get to was across the Mekong River, 300 kilometers southeast of our present position, seventy kilometers northeast of Lumphat, Cambodia.

He handed me the envelope at the same time I asked him, "How many American soldiers are being held?"

He said he didn't know if there were others some place else but he knew of a dozen. I couldn't believe it. A dozen American soldiers still alive and being held prisoner over a year after all prisoners were supposedly released. How many more there must be, I wondered. And, how would our government get them released? Or would they?

I then dumped out the contents of the folder. Four 8 by 10, black and white photos of American soldiers, obviously being held prisoner, flopped out on the ground in front of me. I looked at each photo, then realized there were only three different Americans shown. They were wearing dingy, white and gray striped pajamas, and looked like they were malnourished, but not down to just skin and bone like many previous POWs in Vietnam had been.

I asked, "Do you have photos of the other nine?"

He said, "No. No more photo, but have name of all twelve."

I dug through the first three sheets with information written in broken English. Then I got to the fourth page, a ruffled up half sheet listing the names of the POWs. It was obvious it had been passed along by an American. The names were written in order of rank from highest to lowest.

Wittmer, Dale M., LCDR, USN
Bender, James J. III, Lt., USN
Fields, William R., Capt., USMC
Kennedy, Rodney B., Capt., USAF
Rice, Anthony W., 1rst Lt., US Army
Holbrook, James. T., 1rst Lt., USAF
Polanski, Holden R., 1rst Lt., USAF
Bridgeforth, Kyle S., Sgt., US Army
Everly, Robert. C., Corp., USMC
Minnick, Frederick D., PFC, USMC
Wiedenower, Andrew J., PFC, USMC
Willingham, Tiller W., PFC, US Army

Upon seeing the list and seeing it was obviously written by an American prisoner, I broke down crying. I cried for these POWs, wondering if they knew the Vietnam War was over for America and that all known POWs had already gone home. I cried wondering if they knew that no one knew about them, and maybe few cared. I cried for what they must have been through, and for what they were still going through. I cried for their families. I cried at the thought that our government didn't know about them, and at the thought that our government would find out about them and maybe not do anything to get them released. I cried at the devastating cost America and Americans had paid in this war so far from home. I cried for all I had lost in this war. I cried that I couldn't even open up to talk about this war with the person I loved more than any other—my wife."

At that point Kennedy had to stop the tape again. Dowdy and

Easton were also deeply moved by what they were hearing. All
three men wiped their cheeks and eyes. Kennedy then pulled the
papers and photos from the packet and passed them to Dowdy, who
took his time looking at each photo and each written page before
passing each on to Easton. They couldn't believe what they were
hearing and seeing.

Dowdy said, "This is hard to take. Indisputable evidence of
American soldiers not released at the end of the war."

"You're not telling me anything, Lieutenant. And you haven't
heard the worst of it."

"I suspected that."

Kennedy pressed the start button again, and Bruington
continued,

"My friends understood what I had to be going through. My
Cambodian soldier friend had lost most of his family at the hands of
Pol Pot already, and had no idea if the killing would come to an end
soon or not.

Of course, in retrospect—as I make this tape in June 1980—I
know that hundreds of thousands, in fact, somewhere between one
and two million Cambodian citizens and soldiers were murdered by
Pol Pot and the Khmer Rouge before he was defeated. Whether my
Cambodian friend, and what was left of his family, survived, I don't
know. Neither I, nor my Thai friend, have ever heard from him
again.

Back to April, 1974—I asked my Cambodian friend how long
ago the photos were taken and when the prisoner list was made out.

He said, "Secret Cambodian soldier take photo in February this
year. He get list same day from this American prisoner and give to
me." He pointed at the tall, thin, dark-haired white man that he
identified as Navy Lieutenant James Bender. Bender was in three of
the photos. The other two Americans that also appeared in more

than one photo each were identified as Marine Captain William Fields, a white man, and the black man was Air Force Lieutenant James Holbrook.

After satisfying myself with the evidence my friend had given me, I replaced it in the packet and gave it to my Thai friend to hold until we returned. If he didn't hear from us in four weeks, he was to contact my American friend, whose name and number I won't mention now, but which I did give to my Thai friend. If I was captured, I didn't want to alert either the Khmer Rouge, or the North Vietnamese of an American having knowledge of American POWs still being held by the North Vietnamese.

After we were outfitted in full camo army fatigues, packs with supplies we needed, canteens and carrying M16s, Colt .45s and plenty of ammunition, my Cambodian friend and I said farewell to our Thai friend, who wished us good fortune. We then rode the motorcycles that the Cambodian had borrowed, and headed to the southeast into northeast Cambodia. We were stopped at several check points along the way, but my friend had obviously done his homework and knew what to say, because we were not detained anywhere.

On the second day, we reached the drop off point for the motorcycles, hid them, and proceeded on foot toward the Mekong River which was over seventy-five kilometers away. I had kept myself in top condition since my discharge from the Army and it was a good thing. It took us three days to get to the Mekong River. My friend knew the area very well because he had grown up in the region. This shortened our travel time considerably, but we still had to be careful to avoid detection by the Khmer Rouge soldiers.

When we got to the Mekong River we boarded the fishing boat of my Cambodian friend's allies and were taken across to the east. He would be waiting there for us upon our expected return in eight days. He warned us that the region was crawling with Khmer Rouge and farther east with North Vietnamese and that they were involved in many skirmishes. The farther we went the more obvious it became that our chances of getting into the camp where the

American POWs were being held, or had been held, were slim.

As it became increasingly more difficult to avoid contact with the Khmer Rouge soldiers, I thought more and more about my wife, my 18-month-old daughter and the baby my wife was pregnant with. When I had been in Cambodia and Laos in 1970 and 71, I wasn't a father. I felt guilty for what I was doing, for even risking my life when I should be back home with my wife and baby and the little one on the way. But then I felt guilty for even thinking of not going on for the sake of these American prisoners of a war that was already over for America. We stopped.

My Cambodian soldier friend could sense the internal battle I was fighting.

He said, "It okay. You have evidence you need now."

I said, "I know. But I wanted to verify it for myself, so I could tell my government that I saw the soldiers with my own eyes."

"It no matter now. You have photo and list by American soldier. You have all you need. I understand. You have baby and wife now, and baby to come. Not same as before. Baby need father. Wife and baby need you stay alive."

"But these American prisoners need me, too."

"You go back to wife and baby. You tell your government about soldier prisoners. Your government help you then."

"I don't know if they will do anything."

"You already do all you can. You good man. You good soldier. You good friend. Tell your government. That all you can do now. We go back now."

Reluctantly, and with a heavy heart, but at the same time a sense of relief from the fear and tension I had been feeling for the last twenty-four hours, I followed my Cambodian friend back through the jungle to the west. Now that I had let myself think of home, my wife and my daughter, now that I had let myself feel, I was almost overwhelmed with anxiety, with a sense of desperation. I had to stay alive. I had to get home to my family. That's where I belonged. My war was over two and a half years ago. What was I doing?

We reached the Mekong River in late afternoon the next day. We waited until dark to make the crossing. I always felt safer in the dark when I was over there before. When I was a kid I was afraid of the dark. But as a sniper, I learned to love it, just the opposite of when I was a grunt during my first tour in Vietnam. Then Charlie owned the night. We always worried that Charlie would ambush us in our sleep. It was so hard to sleep—*Charlie...and the bugs...and the snakes.* But as a sniper, my partner and I could sleep where no one would find us. We even slept in trees.

After crossing the river, my friend and I found a place to sleep for the night. Then the next morning we humped it back by the way we had come. He really knew his way.

Two days later, just when I thought we had it made, when we were only a few kilometers from our motorcycles, we were detected by a small patrol of Khmer Rouge, five soldiers. They yelled for us to stop. But we knew we were dead if we did. We dashed into heavy cover, just as they opened up on us with their machine guns. We knew we had to kill all of them, or we would never make it. As my friend returned intermittent fire moving back and forth from side to side behind trees to give the impression of both of us shooting, I did a flanking maneuver and came in from their side. I caught them all by surprise and slaughtered them. I wept. My war was over already. I wasn't supposed to be a soldier any more. I didn't want to kill anymore.

We hastily left that area and ran to our motorcycles. Fortunately, we had no more problems and made it back to Thailand and contacted our Thai friend to come pick me up.

I said goodbye to my Cambodian soldier friend for the last time. My Thai friend drove me to Bangkok where he waited with me for a day to get a plane back to the United States, carrying the evidence of American POWs.

When I got home, I made several copies of the papers and the photos. I struggled with who I should go to with the information, because I was aware of the controversy throughout the country over the fate of so many of those listed as MIA. There were reports that the Pathet Lao, particularly, were still holding American POWs in Laos. I had kept up on how the supposed discrepancies in the number of reported POWs and the number released in 1973 was being investigated. From all indications the U.S. government and armed forces had gradually determined that none of the reports of more Americans being held in Southeast Asia could be substantiated.

I knew I had positive evidence from a reliable Cambodian contact, but wasn't sure which channel I should take in reporting the information I had. Our government authorities had proven again and again throughout the Vietnam War that they could twist information around in whatever manner they wanted to accomplish various political objectives, often with seemingly little regard for the effect their actions had on the men fighting the war on the ground, in the water, and in the air.

22

Bruington Tape- General Overgard

Finally, I made the decision to start with the man who had commanded our armed forces in Vietnam from July 1968 to June 1972, General Travis Overgard. I fully believed if anybody would be interested in my reports, he would. And I proved to be correct, that is, when I was finally able to talk with him.

When I called his office at Fort Bragg, I was given the run around by the gate keepers saying the general was a very busy man, and "perhaps I can help you, etc." I wasn't about to give any details to anyone but the general, nor did I give my true identity. After a week of getting nothing but the runaround, I knew I had to get creative. So I said that I knew of three American soldiers' bodies that had been brought to Thailand and were being held there waiting for the general's instructions. Within three minutes General Overgard himself came on the telephone.

9 June 1974—
"This is General Overgard. I was told you had information

regarding three American servicemen's bodies being held in Thailand. And your name is Randal Millican?"

"Yes, General Overgard. It's great to finally get through to you. Your people have given me nothing but the run around for over a week now."

"I'm a busy man, as you can surely understand. I have to have a filter system or I'd be on the phone half the day. Now what is it that you have to tell me, Mr. Millican?"

"First, General, I have to confess that I am not Randal Millican. I used a false name for necessary reasons which I believe you will understand after you hear what I have to say. My name is actually Roger Dale Bruington. It was Sergeant Bruington when I was discharged from the Army in 1971 after two tours in Vietnam, the second spent as a sniper along the Ho Chi Minh Trail."

"Thank you for your service son. Those were some rough times. Where are you calling from?"

"I'm in Springfield, Oregon, where I live with my wife and family."

"Now what is this about three American soldiers' bodies being held in Thailand awaiting my instructions? And why would you have that information and not our ambassador in Thailand, or one of our Air Force superiors there?"

"Sir, what I have to tell you is far more important than three bodies in Thailand. That was a last ditch effort to get through to you personally."

"'I understand. Now you have my attention. Speak freely, son. We're both on the same team."

"I know that, sir. I have the utmost respect for you. I really need to meet with you so you can see first hand what information I am holding. I will tell you this much over the phone. There are confirmed reports of American POWs still being held by the North Vietnamese as we speak."

The line was silent. I figured General Overgard was undoubtedly wondering if he was dealing with another quack that was out to get attention for himself. I thought, surely the general still had doubts about the POW/ MIA situation, and hated the thought that American soldiers might still be detained in Southeast Asia.

After what must have been ten seconds, he said, "What kind of information do you have Sergeant Bruington, and where did you get it?"

"Sir, I got back from a trip to Thailand and Cambodia just two weeks ago. Trust me; you will want to see personally what I am holding."

"I need to know more than you're telling me, Bruington. I get reports like this fairly regularly, and they always turn out to be some guy or group wanting attention for themselves or wanting to keep the POW/MIA issue at the front of the news."

"I understand your position, General. While serving as a sniper in Cambodia and Laos, I made numerous contacts with Cambodian Government soldiers and one man in Thailand. It was through that chain of connections that I gained the information I now have. I have photos and a prisoner list written by an American prisoner, Lieutenant James Bender, US Navy. Lieutenant Bender also appears in three of the photos."

"Hold on for a minute, son. I'm going to dig up the MIA list; I have to see if your Lieutenant Bender is on it." A minute later he came back on and said, "Yes, Lieutenant James Bender, US Navy was shot down in his F-4 over Cambodia on 3 March 1972. His wingman observed a single parachute drifting toward the ground prior to the plane crashing, but had no idea whether it was Bender or his crew mate. We never heard from whoever it was after they made the ground; he never popped smoke, nor did our follow up sorties find any sign of him. Of course with our troop strength severely reduced by then, and the political situation being what it was regarding our presence in Cambodia, we were unable to send ground troops over there to try to locate him. So, he made it. Doggonit! One of my boys is still alive there."

I was excited at the general's enthusiasm and knew I had gone to the right man.

"You said you have a list of prisoners that Lieutenant Bender wrote up and gave to your Cambodian contact; and he is also shown in prison garb in three photographs?"

"That's correct, sir."

"I want you down here by Wednesday morning. I'll see that the Army pays for your flight. Will that work for you?"

"Yes General. That sounds great."

"Will you fly out of Springfield?"

"Actually out of Eugene—just across the river from Springfield."

"I'll take care of arrangements and get back to you, let's say at 11 o' clock. Will that work for you?"

"Yes sir."

Kennedy stopped the tape, turned it over, and then hit the play button.

Wednesday, noon, Fort Bragg—While at Bragg, I discreetly recorded my conversation with General Overgard.

After being picked up at the airport by a corporal and driven to the Fort Bragg Army Base, I met immediately with the general. At fifty-eight, the six-foot three-inch, gray-haired general was still a powerful looking man.

We shook hands, then he invited me into his military, all-business-like office. As we walked in, I observed an American flag hanging from its stand to the right of the door. Numerous plaques, awards and photographs lined the walls on either side along with a couple of large paintings. A wide, partially-shaded window took up much of the wall behind his desk. It gave the general an excellent view over-looking the parade grounds two stories below.

He took a seat in his cushioned, swivel, office chair behind the desk, while motioning for me to take a seat in one of the three wooden chairs in front of the desk. Besides his chair, there was only one other cushioned chair in the room, an army-green, upholstered rocking chair at the right end of his desk. I got the impression a visitor had to pass muster with the general before being allowed to sit in that chair. Or perhaps sometimes the general himself kicked back in it with his feet propped up on his desk. At any rate, he didn't offer it to me.

After exchanging some pleasantries, and my giving the general a summary of the information I possessed, I handed the folder containing the evidence to him. Upon seeing the POW information, including the photos, he seemed quite moved. He then took his time comparing Lieutenant Bender's hand-written POW list to the official MIA list on his desk. He found only one discrepancy. He immediately called his assistant, a sergeant, in the front office and gave him the information to see what he could find out. In two minutes the sergeant called him on the intercom and gave the general the information he wanted.

PFC Andrew J. Wiedenower, USMC, was not listed among the MIAs. The Marine Corps record reported him as AWOL on 23 April 1972. Apparently there had been a mistake, and he was actually POW/MIA, not AWOL.

Of the other ten men listed besides Lt. Bender, all were reported missing between 21 Sept 1970 and 6 Jan 1973. The other Navy officer and the three Air Force officers were all shot down while on bombing sorties. The circumstances of the other soldiers listed were vague. Since none of the eleven, excluding Wiedenower, turned up on POW lists or were ever seen alive by the POWs released during Operation Homecoming in 1973, or by anyone else, they were listed as MIA/presumed dead.

After General Overgard had looked over all my evidence and told me what his official information said about each troop listed, and I had explained the details of my trip to Cambodia, he said, "Sergeant Bruington, America should be very proud of you for the risk to your own life, particularly as a civilian, that you willing took on behalf of the men listed on this sheet and in these photos. You knew when you brought this information to me that there was no easy or quick solution to these alleged POWs' situation."

"Excuse me, sir. What do you mean, 'alleged POWs?' You do believe these men are still alive and being held captive in Cambodia, do you not? I mean, surely you can't deny this evidence."

"Of course I don't deny the evidence, particularly the three men in the photos. And one thing I want to do is get hold of a sample of Lieutenant Bender's handwriting from either his wife, his family, or preferably evaluations, reports and other documents that he filled out in the Navy. If the handwriting checks out, it would be very hard for anyone to deny the accuracy of this list and the fact that it was compiled by Lieutenant Bender. And combined with the four photos, which clearly show him in typical NVA prison clothes, it would be incontrovertible evidence that at some point since the last of these men were reported MIA, in Jan 1973, they were seen, or known to be, imprisoned by the NVA, and Lieutenant Bender had somehow learned of it."

"Sir, my Cambodian contact told me the Cambodian soldier who took the photos and received this POW list from Lieutenant Bender this past February, counted twelve American POWs in that NVA camp. That is indisputable evidence."

"I understand what you're saying, Sergeant Bruington. But you are the third man down the chain. You said that yourself. You, your Cambodian soldier contact, and then his Cambodian soldier contact. Things could have gotten confused somewhere along the way."

"Damn it, sir!" Then checking myself, "I'm sorry, sir. If I was still in the Army I wouldn't have said that. But you know darn well this is rock solid evidence. You know it is!"

"Sergeant, I definitely believe your story, and I believe the evidence. I do. Believe me, I do. But convincing the secretary of defense or the president, could be another matter. And when you consider the president is up to his ears in this Watergate Scandal, POWs alive in Vietnam wouldn't even cause him to blink.

"Hell, if he really cared about Vietnam, he would have let us do what we had to those last few years to win the war, including sending more troops, instead of withdrawing them. We could have won that damn war, you know. The way things are going over there right now, it's looking more and more like we're going to lose South Vietnam to the communists eventually, anyway. And all the nearly 58,000 men who died there, the hundreds of thousands who were wounded there, and the multiplied millions who served there, will have done it all for nothing. This president isn't going to send troops back into an area that we weren't supposed to be in in the first place—even when we were deeply involved in the war—to try to recover some ghosts. Even if he wanted to, he couldn't. Hell, he doesn't even have the power to take a leak anymore without a catheter."

"I don't believe this, sir. Are you saying that our country—the greatest country on Earth—is going to leave these men's fate in the hands of our communist enemies? It's going to do nothing about them?"

"Trust me, son, I'm going to do everything I can to get something done toward recovering these men. I'm just being honest with you about what to expect. Do you really believe our government, which, quite frankly, is in a shambles right now from the top down, is going to risk the lives of countless more men for these twelve?"

"But these men risked their lives for their government and their country. So now the country is just going to turn its back on them and leave them to fate? What about sending in a small team of special forces?"

"Look, son, I will do everything I can to see that we do something about these soldiers. But in the end, it's out of my hands, and you know that. What I need from you is a copy of all this information, including the photos."

"You can keep everything I gave you, General."

"Good. Now, you and I need to get one thing clear. I need your cooperation on this whole POW/MIA issue. By that I mean I can't have you talking to anyone else about this unless I tell you. You said you hadn't told anyone up to now, is that correct?"

"Yes sir. I've told no one. I know how precarious this whole thing is. If word was to get out, it could mean the death of those prisoners. I understand that."

"Good, it looks like you have the whole picture clearly in mind, son. Trust me—I will go through the right channels to see if I can get some action on this, okay? But it is critical that the media doesn't get a hold of this, or we can kiss those boys good bye."

"Yes sir. I agree with you, sir. I trust that you will do everything in your power to get these men home."

"Sergeant Bruington, I want to thank you again for your service to your country in Vietnam and your service to these men in what you are doing now. I'll have my assistant take you to your room and show you around the base, show you the chow hall and then make sure you catch your plane home in the morning. It's been nice to meet you, and I know we will be talking again soon."

We both stood, saluted, and I left his office with his assistant.

23

Bruington Tape- The Cover Up

My wife was curious about my trips to Southeast Asia and North Carolina, but I kept her in the dark with half-truths. I felt guilty about doing that, but I did it to protect her, both from worrying about me and to ensure she didn't have any information that could be used against her or me.

After hearing nothing from General Overgard in the three weeks following my meeting with him, I called his office. I correctly identified myself, but was told he was busy and couldn't talk to me. So I left my name and number. Over the next ten days, I called the general's office six more times, but got the same run around and left my number each time. The general never returned my calls.

Then, on 18 July 1974, after completing my swing shift as sawyer at the All American Stud Company in Jasper, Oregon, I was greeted at my truck in the parking lot by two surprise visitors, who identified themselves as CIA agents with information regarding my POW inquiries. They then directed me to follow them in their vehicle, which I did. I was leery of why the CIA was sent, rather than the general calling me.

They drove to an isolated location along the Willamette River and parked. After we got out of our vehicles, they told me in no uncertain terms that I was not to pursue the POW issue any further. They said our government had the information I had given to General Overgard and would handle the situation in the manner deemed necessary. They warned me that if I spoke to anyone about any of it I would undermine efforts to resolve the issue. They said there were some powerful people working to resolve the POW/MIA issue and it was vital that I not leak anything to anyone.

They went on to say that the situation was far more complicated than just sending in a team of special forces. It had huge political implications, not only for the American public, but around the world. It sounded like the usual CIA/Government BS to me. But I fully believed General Overgard was a good, honest man who genuinely cared about those men still being held in Cambodia, and for whatever other men might be held in Cambodia, Laos, and North Vietnam, and—maybe even in the Soviet Union, as well. I believed he would make sure his boys were brought home.

Two days later the CIA agents showed up at the end of my shift again. I was surprised to see them, and thought maybe there had been a good development regarding the POWs. Instead, after getting to our spot along the Willamette River, they handed me a large manila folder containing something with some weight to it. When I opened it and slid the contents out onto the hood of my pickup, I saw there were eight stacks of $100 bills. They told me each stack contained twenty-five bills, for a total of $20,000. I had never seen that much cash before in my life.

From the little interaction I had with the CIA while I served in Cambodia, I knew it was a common practice for them to make deals involving large sums of money, mostly U.S. Government money. And sometimes the deals involved trading arms or drugs, rather than money. I never liked the idea, but accepted what the CIA did as a necessary function in somewhat the same way I accepted what I did as a sniper. Who was I to judge or condemn other operatives within our government in light of what I did.

After the agents told me how much money was there, I asked, "What is this money for?"

"You were in Cambodia for your last tour. You know that things aren't always black and white. What do you think the money is for?"

"I don't want to guess, but I have a bad feeling about it."

"It has come down from our superiors that right now, with things being the way they are in our government, this POW/MIA issue has got to stay under-the-carpet at all costs. The President of the United States is facing almost certain impeachment for his illegal wire-tapping and the Watergate break-in. The American public has lost almost all faith in the government. The country's morale is at or near an all-time low. Inflation has almost doubled in one year to 14 percent. The Stock market has fallen nearly 15%. Gas is being rationed, and we have gas lines at stations all over the country because of the Arab Oil Embargo."

"And then on top of all the problems in America, the Army of the Republic of South Vietnam is being beaten back more every day, and its government is in political shambles. They continue to hold out hope that President Nixon and our government will send the B-52s and troops back in there to rescue them at any hour. That's never going to happen. You know that as well as we do. It's only a matter of time before the South falls and everything American soldiers fought and died for there will be lost."

"So are you telling me our government isn't going to do a darn thing about our POWs still being held?"

"I'm not saying that at all. And you have to trust me on that. (Like I was going to trust anyone in the CIA.) It's just a precarious situation that will have to be handled very carefully."

"So this $20,000 is payoff money for me to agree to keep my mouth shut?"

"You know how it works."

"Yeah, I know how it works? As soon as I accept your deal, I'm a criminal."

"You can't look at it that way."

"How am I supposed to look at it? I know if I take this money, I will be getting into bed with a government that wants to cover up the entire POW/MIA issue and pretend it doesn't exist."

"You're coming to some incorrect conclusions, Bruington, regarding this whole POW/MIA issue. Our government has every intention of doing everything within its power to look into the evidence and the reports you provided. After all, those are American citizens, American soldiers over there, and the government isn't going to rest until that issue is finally resolved."

"I'm supposed to believe that?"

"You met with General Overgard. Don't you trust him to stay on top of things? Those are his men that were left behind. They are his boys. He feels a deep responsibility to them, and their families. Didn't he communicate that clearly to you?"

"I thought so at the time. But I haven't been able to reach him by phone, nor has he returned any of my phone calls."

"That doesn't mean anything. He's a very busy man. You have to trust that he will stay on top of things."

"So, let's say I take the money today—"

"Look Bruington, you don't have any choice—"

"What do you mean I don't have any choice?"

"I mean, you don't have any choice. You have family who need you."

"Are you saying that my own government would hurt me over this?"

"I wouldn't use the term, 'hurt.'"

"Kill me? My government would kill me over this?"

"I don't know what they would do. We're just the messengers. But it was made clear to us that you needed to understand what is at stake here for the country and for yourself."

"I'm getting your message loud and clear now."

"Besides this $20,000, you will have $1,000 a month wired to the bank account of your choosing until this POW/MIA issue is resolved."

"You do mean indefinitely, don't you?"

"Like I said, we're just the messengers. We need to wrap things up now. Here is the number where you can reach us to give us the banking information, or to contact us any further." He handed me a slip of paper with his name and contact information. I knew I had no choice. Besides, like everyone else, I could use the money. And *I really didn't* have any choice. My own government told me so. Even at that, I was naïve enough to believe that General Overgard would stay on this whole POW/MIA issue until our boys were home.

Two weeks after receiving the $20,000, I learned that the General was being relieved of his command. Did that have anything to do with the POW/MIA issue? Perhaps he made waves with the wrong people, insisting that positive action be taken regarding "his boys" that were still being held prisoner in Southeast Asia. I may never know, because General Overgard died two months later from complications resulting from lung surgery. At least that's what the published reports said.

Over the next five years, despite occasional warnings from the CIA, I continued to try to stay on top of the progress regarding the POWs I knew of. But at every juncture, I was passed along to someone else or given evasive answers.

24

Bruington Tape- A Fatal Decision?

When the six-year anniversary of my trip to Cambodia came around in the spring of 1980, I was bothered more and more by nothing having been done to bring those twelve POWs home. At least I couldn't see where anything had been done. We were in the middle of an election year, and a lot had changed in our country over the last six years. We'd had a democratic president, Jimmy Carter, since January 1977. President Nixon, who had resigned in August 1974 instead of being impeached, had been pardoned of all wrong-doing in the Watergate Scandal by his former vice president and successor, President Gerald Ford. South Vietnam had collapsed and been taken over by communist North Vietnam in April 1975, so that chapter in American history had been closed.

"The Vietnam War was still not discussed openly by most people. The nation had wanted to forget about that war. The families of the 2,500 plus listed MIAs, a small percentage of Vietnam veterans, and a small percentage of the American population were seemingly the only folks keeping the POW/MIA issue alive. But in the last year, the climate throughout the country regarding the Vietnam War had seen a very slow shift from pretending it never happened, and trying to forget everything attached to it, including the soldiers who fought it, to actually accepting it as a painful part of America's history.

By June 1980, I knew I could no longer carry my secret. And I felt America was ready to hear my story. Through the media, I was going to make public my whole story, including all the evidence I had been holding for the past six years. I would make it known that I had turned a copy of my evidence over to General Overgard in June 1974. I was also going to detail the government cover up of that evidence. I felt that if I handled things correctly and went to all the major media with my information, and only agreed to tell them my story if they all released the story on the same date, that it was very unlikely that I or my family would be harmed.

At any rate, I couldn't be certain of my safety, so I took out an additional $100,000 life insurance policy, I made a copy of all my evidence and this entire write-up, plus—as you who are listening now know—I made a tape recording of everything I had written out. I will give a copy of all of it to my Vietnam buddy, whose name I will not reveal. If something happens to me, he can decide whether to turn the information over to the proper channels or reveal his identity.

So what did I do with the nearly $100,000 that I have received from the U.S. Government over the last six years? My wife will need to know.

I took the initial $20,000 and used it for down payments on two different houses and properties on the Oregon Coast. Every dime I've received for keeping my mouth shut since then has gone into those two properties to pay them off long before the original thirty-year mortgage period. Both properties are in the name Randy Millican and list my wife (real name) as heir if anything should happen to me.

For all the years since I bought the properties, I've had a contract with a local property management company on the coast, to rent both places out and make necessary repairs as problems come up. My wife knows nothing about the properties or the bank account in which any extra cover-up payoff-money is deposited.

I will close this tape by saying that I will continue to journal the progress of the MIA/ POW issue after I give this to my buddy, even after all of it is made public. The additional information will be with the original evidence and documentation in a blue cooler which I keep safely in the crawl space above the ceiling in my home in Springfield, Oregon. The addresses, property management company and account information, along with the attached bank account number are also in the blue cooler.

At that point the tape went silent, and Kennedy said, "That's all of it. Everything you heard has been typed out verbatim. Even in Nam, Roger kept a written record of everything we did. Of course over there he had his own code system, so if he was ever captured or killed the enemy couldn't figure out how many officers we'd sniped or where we had operated. I think you guys better get up in that crawl space and get that cooler."

"We'll see if we can get it tonight. Would you like to go over to the Bruington's place when we do and meet his wife?"

"Oh, no. I'm not ready for that now. But sometime I *would* like to meet her. He always said he didn't deserve her."

"She's definitely the pick of the litter," said Easton. "From what we've heard from Eastbrook, the last few months Roger's hunting buddy, Aaron Howe, the Army veteran, has been making regular rounds there. Eastbrook said it seems harmless enough and he's probably been a big help with some of the guy chores."

"Roger mentioned one of his good friends was an Army veteran. He said he liked him a lot and had elk hunted with him every year since getting home from Nam. As I remember, Roger once said he wondered what strings he had pulled to stay out of Nam. I sensed a little irritation when he said it, but it was just a passing thought. It only came up because somehow our discussion that weekend dealt with how a bunch of politicians' sons or relatives managed to avoid duty in Vietnam by some string pulling at the upper end. And you didn't even want to get Roger going on the draft-dodger issue."

"That draft-dodger situation and the string pulling," said Dowdy. "I often heard how a much higher percentage of blacks and boys from poor families ended up over there. Then you had all the war protesters and people even burning the American flag. Those were some complex issues, some tough times."

"And while you're at it," said Easton, "you better throw in the civil rights movement, women's lib, abortion rights, and the drug culture. It was something else."

"Well, it looks like some of that stuff has pretty well ironed itself out now," said Kennedy."

"And I don't know if our country is better off for all of it," said Dowdy. "I have some serious doubts about that,"

"I do too," said Kennedy.

They hiked out to Dowdy's rig, drove back to Eugene, let Kennedy off at the Hilton Hotel, then returned to the station, where Dowdy then called Jan Bruington. She said it would be no bother if Easton and him came over.

25

The Cooler

At the Bruington's in early evening, Easton pulled down the ladder leading to the overhead crawl space above the hallway outside the main bathroom and proceeded to climb it. No sooner had he stuck his head and shoulders up there, and made a sweep with his flashlight, when he noticed the small blue cooler behind one of the supporting spans of a roof truss a few feet away.

"I think I found it, Lieutenant. Give me a second."

He crawled up the rest of the way and reached the cooler, which he opened right up. Upon shining his flashlight inside and picking through the first couple papers, he said, "Lieutenant, we've definitely found what we're looking for."

He then closed the lid and passed the cooler down to Dowdy, who wasted no time popping the lid open and looking inside. He pulled out a handful of papers, and said, "You're right, Corporal. It's got military records, medals, commendations and who knows what else. All this time, and it was right under our noses."

"Actually right over them, sir."

"I stand corrected—right over them."

As Easton was making his way back down, Dowdy found a manila folder with papers and photos that appeared to be the originals of the information Kennedy had shared with them earlier in the day. There were also a couple of compact tapes. Just then Dowdy heard the door bell ring.

"I've got to get this stuff put back in the cooler; someone's at the door. "

Easton folded the ladder back up, then lifted the door up until the springs caught and carried the ladder and door back up into closed position.

Dowdy immediately recognized the voice at the door as Aaron Howe's. Jan hadn't said anything about him coming by, but their relationship had progressed to the spontaneous drop-by stage. Dowdy and Easton had come in Easton's family car, and were dressed in street clothes. Dowdy wondered if Howe would have come to the door if he knew he and Easton were the visitors.

With Dowdy carrying the twelve by sixteen inch cooler, he and Easton wasted no time getting to the entryway where Aaron was now standing with Jan.

"Aaron, what a surprise to see you, or I should say, *to see you here*," said Dowdy, using the put-em-on-the-defensive technique that he was so good at.

"Uh, yeah, Lieutenant. Nice to see you. Uh, how's your investigation coming? Anymore progress?" Aaron said, showing obvious interest in the cooler Dowdy was holding.

"It looks like your hunch paid off, Lieutenant," said Jan, noticing the cooler. "You found what you were looking for?"

"Yes, Jan, we found what we wanted. If you don't mind, I'd like to take this cooler with me down to the station. I'll get back to you later about its contents, if that's okay with you."

"You know it is, Lieutenant," she said, stepping aside so Dowdy and Easton had a clear path to the door that was still open.

When they got to their vehicle and opened the doors to get in, Easton commented, "Howe sure had his eyes locked on that cooler; I wonder why it intrigued him so much?"

Dowdy bent down and got in, holding the cooler on his lap. After they both shut their doors and Easton started the car, Dowdy said, "Put your self in his shoes. You come to your best friend's widow's house and are surprised to see a couple of sheriff's deputies, including the one who put you on the defensive the first week of your friend's murder investigation and made you feel like a possible suspect. You had made some dumb comment during your conversation with the cop that you always envied your good friend for having a wife like he does, and then you show up at her house months later while the cop's there still trying to put a case together. And on top of that, you see immediately that he's holding a case that must have important information in it. Would you be nervous, curious or what?"

"You have a good point there, Lieutenant. I guess part of me has never entirely ruled Howe out as a suspect."

"That's exactly the kind of thinking that makes you a good cop, Easton. As a matter of fact, I've always kept Howe simmering on my own back burner."

"Thanks for the compliment, Lieutenant. It just strikes me that Howe wasted no time moving in on Bruington's wife. What do you think?"

"I think it's a two-way street. They both have needs for companionship, and by being around each other, they also have a sort of connection to Roger. Though I think the connection thing is probably much more important to Jan. And let's face it, if you or I were single and suddenly our good Army friend was murdered and his wife was left alone with her two young daughters, would we take advantage of the situation? *Advantage* is the wrong word, but you get my meaning."

"Yeah, I get your meaning. And I think if I'm honest with myself, I would be doing the same thing Howe is doing. Why wait around and take a chance that some other guy might catch her in her time of vulnerability, and you miss out on the opportunity of a lifetime."

"It doesn't sound so good when you put it like that, Buddy. It's like the guy's been hanging back like a vulture waiting for the eagle to eat its fill. Then when the eagle flies off, the vulture swoops in to cleanup what's left of the carcass."

"I guess it did sound kind of crude, didn't it."

When they got back to the station, Dowdy and Easton looked over the contents of the blue cooler and discovered the additional documentation that Bruington had put together between August and his death. In addition to one tape marked, "POW/MIA Documentation March 1974-July 1980, they found a second tape that was labeled "POW/MIA Documentation August 1980- . They listened to enough of each side of the first tape to determine that it was the exact recording they had listened to in the woods with Kennedy.

Then Dowdy started playing the second tape:

"This is Roger Dale Bruington, former sergeant in the United States Army. This is tape number two beginning in August 1980 documenting my findings and action regarding the Vietnam POW/MIA issue—"

Immediately Dowdy stopped the tape and said, "I don't want to listen to anymore of this until we can listen to it with Kennedy present."

"I totally agree, Lieutenant. Let's call him up and tell him we found the cooler, and it contained everything we hoped it would."

Dowdy reached Kennedy by telephone at the Hilton and told him they had found the blue cooler. He arranged for him and Easton to pick Kennedy up in an hour. They would go to a local park to listen to the new tape, and then get dinner at the Olive Garden.

At Alton Baker Park, next to the Willamette River in Eugene, the three men sat at a table under a light and looked through the contents of the cooler. Besides the new information Dowdy and Easton had discovered earlier, they also found the contact information for Kennedy and the other Vietnam buddy, Jimmy Davenpool.

While Kennedy was perusing the cooler contents, he explained that Davenpool was the third soldier that Kennedy and Bruington met with each summer. Kennedy said Davenpool and another soldier—who was killed in Vietnam in January 1972—had served as the middle men between Kennedy, Bruington, and MACV. The four of them met every six weeks for mission briefing and re-supply. Two days ahead of the rendezvous, Davenpool and the other soldier would be dropped by chopper somewhere in South Vietnam, a few kilometers east of the Cambodian border. Two days after the four of them met, Davenpool and the other soldier would be extracted from somewhere else.

After Kennedy had looked the cooler contents over to his satisfaction, Dowdy put the new tape in the recorder and pressed play.

"This is Roger Dale Bruington, former sergeant in the United States Army. This is tape number two beginning in August 1980 documenting my findings and action regarding the Vietnam POW/MIA issue—

In August I met with my Vietnam buddies in Seattle for our annual reunion. At that time I gave one of them a large envelope that contained copies of all my information and documentation concerning the POW/MIAs and the U.S. Government cover up. I did not tell him what the envelope contained, or that I intended to go public with the information inside the envelope. I asked him not to open the envelope until I told him to, and said that if anything ever happened to me, I wanted him to at least have the information I had put together. I knew he would follow my instructions. In Vietnam,

Cambodia, and Laos, we had always watched each other's backsides, and I knew he would watch mine."

Kennedy stopped the tape and wiped his eyes, believing he had failed to watch Roger's backside this time. *And now he was dead.* In a minute, Kennedy pressed play, and Bruington continued.

"The first week of September, I called my CIA contact to ask one final time for information regarding the fate of the twelve POWs in Cambodia and what progress had been made, if any, in getting the issue resolved. He informed me that as far as it concerned me, the issue had already been resolved. That I was to drop it and be happy with the monthly payments I was still receiving and would likely receive indefinitely. I told him that my conscience would no longer allow me to do that, and I was going to seek resolution to the POW/MIA issue by channels of my own choosing. He strongly advised me against doing that, and warned that to do so would be a huge mistake for everyone involved, opening up old wounds and causing new ones. I wasn't sure how to take the "causing new wounds," but understood that to be a threat to my health and well being.

My CIA contact's name and phone number are on a half sheet of paper which, if you haven't found already, are also in the cooler where you found this tape.

It is now October 10th, 1980. I intend to call a meeting of all the major media in America by November 17th of this year, 1980, and hand over copies of all of my POW/MIA information and documentation since I began keeping records of it in March 1974. Before I release any of this information to the press, and before any media members are allowed in the locked conference center where this meeting will take place, I will require that they sign a legal document agreeing to release the news on November 27th, Thanksgiving Day. The document will also stipulate the severe penalty to any media person, and his/her company, if they choose to release the information to anyone in any form before that date.

I know some will say the timing of November 27th—
Thanksgiving Day could have been much better. And I agree. It
should have come out years earlier. But since it didn't, when you
stop and think about it what better day of the year to tell the truth to
Americans than on America's Thanksgiving Day.

The next time you hear from me will be after the POW/MIA
news breaks on Thanksgiving Day.

The tape went silent.

"Boy, that's hard to take," said Kennedy, wiping more tears from
his cheeks.

"Your buddy Bruington was a special kind of hero, Marvin. You
were very lucky to have a partner and friend like him."

"I just wish he had told me about all this a long time ago. Maybe
it all would have turned out differently. Maybe I could have
watched his back and prevented his death."

"Son," said Dowdy, "you've got to let that go. None of this is
your fault. And we still don't know for sure that any of this had
anything to do with Roger's death. Yes, the timing of everything
seems too coincidental. But we can't be certain. Deputy Easton and
I will continue to look into all of it and do our best to find out what
happened and why."

"I appreciate that, Lieutenant Dowdy. So what are you going to
do with this information?"

"I'm going to try to get the answers we need the quiet way. But
if that doesn't work, I'll have to consider other options."

"Like taking it to the media?"

"We'll have to cross that bridge when we come to it."

"Well no matter what you do, never mention my name."

"You have nothing to worry about," Dowdy assured him. "Now
let's go get some supper."

"Sounds good, Lieutenant."

Over their pasta dinners at the Olive Garden, Dowdy realized he hadn't considered his captain and the district attorneys' expectations of being kept up-to-date on any new developments in the Bruington case.

"What about the district attorney and my captain?" Dowdy said to Kennedy. "I'm expected to keep them up to date on the progress of our investigation."

"Isn't it true that you don't have to turn potential evidence over to the district attorney, or discuss it with him, until you are pretty sure it will be used in prosecuting the case?" Kennedy asked.

"That's a big gray area, actually. We have some liberty, obviously, or we and the DA would be tied down reporting and discussing every detail of our investigation. That wouldn't work for either of us—"

"So that means that while you're gathering possible evidence, you don't have to tell him or your captain everything, right?"

"Well, yes."

"So until you can make some kind of connection between this evidence and a potential suspect, they can be left in the dark."

"That sounds good in theory. But you know what big egos DAs have, always puffed up with their own importance. You didn't hear it from me, but this DA is no exception."

"Look, Lieutenant. Why raise the curiosity of anybody else about any of this until you can nail down a connection?"

"You make plenty of sense, Marvin. And I think for right now, until Deputy Easton and I have turned over more stones and found something substantial, we can keep the whole thing between the three of us. Well, actually, I *would* really like to let Roger's best friend, Dick Eastbrook, see and listen to what we have. He can be completely trusted to keep his mouth shut. And I think he could be of some value along the way. Plus I believe Roger would want him to know about it."

"You're probably right about Roger. I guess that would be okay with me.

26

Revelation to Eastbrook

At the Eugene Airport the next day, Lieutenant Dowdy assured Kennedy that he would keep him posted on whatever he learned regarding a connection between the POW/MIA cover up and Roger Bruington's death. Kennedy gave Dowdy his consent to go to the press if he decided to, but under no circumstances was he to ever name Kennedy or connect him to Bruington's information.

Over the next three days, the only person Dowdy contacted was the CIA agent who, in September 1980, had warned Bruington not to go to other channels with his POW information. The agent acknowledged having a conversation with Bruington, but denied knowing anything about any actual POW/MIAs. He lied to Dowdy, saying he had known Bruington since their days in Cambodia and had remained friends ever since then. He also said Bruington had fabricated a bunch of information and photos of supposed POWs held in Southeast Asia sometime after the war, because he could never accept that all the Vietnam POWs had been released and

179

returned home in 1973.

Dowdy saw it all as more CIA BS, and came to the conclusion he would get no where dealing any further with the CIA.

Dowdy knew the whole situation was ticklish. He also knew he could never go to the media with the information without having the material reviewed by his superiors in the Sheriff's Department, as well as the district attorney and probably a judge or two. They would be the ones who made the decision to involve the media. At times like this, Dowdy wished he wasn't a county employee. He never did like kissing butt, but accepted it as part of the job.

He thought one way he might get around his superiors was if Dick Eastbrook took Bruington's information to the media. In fact, that was an additional reason he wanted Kennedy's permission to let Eastbrook see all of Bruington's evidence. Dowdy could claim he didn't know Eastbrook would take it public. Cops twisted things like that all the time to get around the chain-of-command BS.

Four days after Kennedy returned to Georgia, Dowdy took Dick Eastbrook for a hike in the woods north of Springfield, in the hills above the Mohawk River, where they had plenty of privacy, and let him see and listen to Bruington's account.

At several points while listening to the tapes, Eastbrook was moved to tears. When they had finished listening to both tapes, he said, "This is amazing stuff, Lieutenant. All these years Roger was carrying this around, unable to tell anyone, and waiting for the government to resolve the situation. And they had him over a barrel as soon as he accepted their money, and he knew it. But in the end he was going to follow his conscience and go public with the whole thing. I admire him for that. Do you think that is what got him killed?"

"I'm not sure what to think. Whoever shot him was obviously a marksman. It very well could have been a CIA hit. But if it wasn't, then what do I have? I would be falsely accusing my own government, and its branches, of the cold-blooded murder of a decorated Vietnam veteran. Then where does that get me?"

"I don't envy your situation. Wouldn't you have to go through your chain of command first anyway, before you could ever go public?"

"Only if I wanted to keep my job. Though I could probably write a best-selling book about the whole thing and make a hundred times what I'm making with Lane County."

"But wouldn't there be the risk to your life and maybe even your family's lives?"

"I've thought of that. But honestly, I agree with Roger's plan of getting all the major media in the country together at one place and make them sign written contracts agreeing to all release their stories on the same date, before giving them what would be one of the biggest breaking news stories in decades. I think where Roger may have screwed up was informing his CIA contact of his intentions of trying to resolve the POW/MIA situation through other channels of his own choosing. I don't think he mentioned the media to his contact, at least he didn't say he did. But it wouldn't take a brain surgeon to put two and two together and see the media as a huge possible channel."

"So what are you going to do about it, Lieutenant?"

"For the time being, I'm going to try to pick around to see if I can turn up anything regarding the status of the POWs on Roger's list. I have to be so careful, and really think things through before proceeding. I will tell you this Dick, I have considered the one way to get around jeopardizing my job is if I claimed ignorance on the whole thing, with Deputy Easton agreeing to do the same, and you were the one to go to the media."

"Hold on there, Lieutenant. I don't know that I would want to do that."

"I understand your feelings about that, Dick. It's just one of the options I've considered."

"So that's really why you're sharing all this with me, isn't it?"

"Not at all. Before I even came up with the idea of you being our possible media contact, I had already mentioned to Deputy Easton and Roger's Vietnam buddy that I wanted to let you, as Roger's best friend, see and hear all of his evidence."

"Well I'd really have to do some heavy thinking before getting involved that way."

"Really, Dick, *who more likely* to know or find out about all this stuff Roger was involved in than his life-long best friend? And you would just be going to the media with the same evidence Roger was going to go there with. You would be the messenger and nothing more."

"I see what you're saying, Lieutenant."

"And as Roger's best friend, wouldn't you want to help him resolve the issue that had been so heavy on his heart and mind for so long? You did tell me early on that you occasionally felt a tinge of guilt around Roger over your not serving in the military. Maybe those men are still alive in Cambodia, or more likely now, Vietnam, and could still be recovered and united with their families. Imagine being a part of that."

"I can't imagine how good that would be. I'll definitely think it over."

From mid-March through early May of 1981, Deputies Dowdy and Easton made no more progress on the Bruington case or the POW/MIA issue. Dowdy decided his best recourse was to take Bruington's information to the media through Dick Eastbrook.

27

Breaking News

On May 11th, Dowdy and Easton met with Dick Eastbrook and gave him the latest scoop on Bruington and the POW/MIA issue. Eastbrook agreed to go to the mass media with Roger's documentation, but said he wanted to reveal some of it to Jan Bruington first. He didn't want her to learn of it second-hand through the media. Dowdy agreed that Eastbrook should definitely tell her first.

On Tuesday, May 19th, Dick Eastbrook met with dozens of newspaper, television, and radio reporters in a locked, close-door session in Portland, Oregon. Prior to the meeting the media people were told the news concerned the Vietnam POW/MIA issue, but were given no details. In the closed room, each news reporter signed a legal contract agreeing to release the news on Monday, May 25th, and not before then. If a reporter broke that agreement, he or she would forfeit their right to ever report news again, and their news agency would pay Roger Bruington's wife three million dollars and the family of each military member named five million dollars for breech of contract. The media members chomped at the bit to hear what could possibly be so important.

Eastbrook had made up dozens of packets—each containing a copy of each Cambodia POW photo and verbatim detailed documentation of Bruington's records, along with a cassette copy of each of his tapes—to give the reporters at the end of the session. No cameras or tape recorders were allowed in the room. Eastbrook did not even give the reporters his real name. He didn't want to be connected to, or receive any personal recognition for, the evidence that Roger Bruington had collected on the POW/MIA issue. He made it clear that he was nothing more than the messenger, finishing the mission begun by U.S. Army Sergeant Roger Bruington.

During the meeting, Eastbrook played the tapes of Bruington speaking. At various points, reporters all over the room could be seen wiping their eyes or blowing their noses. Hardly a soul in that big room wasn't moved to tears at some point.

On Monday, **May 25th, 1981**, news broke all over the country. Some of the headlines read:

"POWs Still Alive In Cambodia"

"Did CIA Assassinate Decorated Vietnam Veteran in POW/MIA Cover Up?"

"Vietnam POWs Still Held Captive Eight Years After War Ends"

"Is Your Vietnam Soldier Still A POW?"

"Why Hasn't U.S. Government Brought All POWs Home From Vietnam?"

"Live Vietnam POWs Buried In Government B.S."

"Vietnam MIA-CIA Cover up: Is Your Soldier Still Alive?"

"Bring Remaining Vietnam POWs Home"

By noon Monday thousands of protestors gathered with their signs in front of courthouses all across America. Thousands more marched on Washington, demanding that the government bring the POWs home.

"No More Cover Up! Bring Our Soldiers Home From Vietnam!"
"No More Cover Up! Bring Our Soldiers Home From Vietnam!"

The chants had a familiar ring to them, at least the, "Bring Our Soldiers Home From Vietnam!" did.

All of the newspaper articles were accompanied by one or more of the 1974 photos of the POWs being held in Cambodia, and many printed a list of the soldiers written up by Lieutenant Bender in 1974. The articles were each written with their own slant. Some focused on the alleged government cover up, and some on the death of Roger Bruington and its possible connection to the whole POW/MIA issue. Others focused on new hope for the families of the twelve POWs, and possibly others, to be re-united with their missing soldiers. Still others questioned whether the entire thing was a hoax to keep the POW/MIA issue alive, or asked whether the government would actually have left POWs to the fate of their captors for all these years.

There were dozens of variations to the story. Some papers took up the entire front page with photos, articles and sidebars, often quoting Bruington verbatim. Clearly the stories stirred the American people in a way they hadn't been since the announcement in the winter of 1973 that the war was over for America and the last of the soldiers and POWs were coming home.

Talk shows across the country were taking calls from irate listeners who couldn't believe their government had evidence that American soldiers were still being held prisoner in Vietnam, yet had done nothing to bring them home. Others claimed the government was actually behind the release of the news. Some said new President Ronald Reagan was just the leader our boys needed to finally bring them home.

At the Sheriff's Station, crap hit the fan, as Deputies Dowdy and Easton were brought before their superiors and asked how much they knew about the news released. Both admitted they knew of the information, but had nothing to do with Bruington's friend Eastbrook going to the media with it. When asked why they hadn't discussed any of it with their superiors, they said they highly doubted there was any connection between Bruington's death and the information being dispersed by the media, regardless of what anyone else thought or said. Lieutenant Dowdy reminded his captain that he was already aware that Dowdy had looked into Bruington's service record and had made contact with Bruington's ex-Vietnam buddy.

Dowdy admitted he had not made anymore headway toward solving the Bruington case. But he assured his superiors that he believed sooner or later something would break.

As soon as his shift was over, Oregon State Police Trooper Wilson, buzzed up to Del's place on Wallace Creek in Jasper. He barged in the front door, carrying the Monday edition of the Eugene Register-Guard.

"Have you seen today's paper or been listening to the news?"

Unimpressed, Del exhaled a big puff of smoke from his roll-your-own Prince Albert cigarette, and said, "No, I haven't. I've been trying to catch up on some Zzs. What's the big deal?"

"You know the hunter from Fall Creek?"

"Yeah, did they catch the killers?"

"Funny. His picture is on the front page along with three photos taken in 1974 of American POWs still being held prisoner by the North Vietnamese in Cambodia. This Bruington, the hunter, was some kind of war hero, and had tried for years, after the war was over, to get the POWs in Cambodia released."

"Let's see that," said Del, grabbing the paper from Butch. "We shot a war hero? We shot a guy who was working to bring POWs home? There aren't anymore POWs. They were all released during the homecoming operation in 1973. Where are they getting this crap?"

"Trust me, Del, it's not crap. I read every word. This Bruington had documentation for all his claims."

"If he's been dead since last October, why the hell is this stuff just now coming out?"

"Apparently one of his friends got hold of the information back when Dowdy brought in the Vietnam vet from down south the first week of March. Do you remember me telling you something about that?"

"Of course."

"Now this friend believes the CIA or U.S. Government may have been the ones who murdered Bruington above Puma Creek last October to keep him from revealing publicly this same news that's all over everything today."

"That's bullcrap. You and I know what happened to him. It had nothing to do with this POW crap. It seems that guy had a knack for sticking his nose in where it didn't belong, didn't he? And it finally got him killed. The CIA killed him? That's bullcrap. What will they come up with next?"

"This is good then, really. Isn't it? I mean if they're convinced it was the CIA, then we're completely in the clear."

"You do have a point there, Butch. Yeah, you definitely have a good point there. Have you heard anything today about what Dowdy is saying about all this? Does he believe it was the CIA?"

"I haven't heard a thing about Dowdy. But I'm sure I will in the next couple days. Let's turn the news on. I heard it's all over the big three channels, on all the radio stations, talk shows. You name it. It's the biggest media blitz in years." Butch stepped over several Playboy magazines and turned on the fourteen-inch television."

"Look at that, all those people waving their signs and flags. We haven't seen anything like this since, well when I was home in '68 and '69, between tours in Vietnam. Back then there were protesters and riots on college campuses all over the country, calling for us to get out of Vietnam. You remember any of that?"

"Yeah, I remember. I didn't know for sure what to think. I knew the war had killed my dad, but I didn't know if the war itself was a bad thing or not. I wanted to believe he died for a noble cause. You know how idealistic you are when you're twelve or thirteen. Everything in the world is supposed to be okay. You're dad isn't supposed to be dead." He got a bit choked up and quit talking, as he continued to watch and listen to the protestors in front of a courthouse in Norfolk, Virginia.

"It'll blow over in a week or so, and everything will get back to business as usual, Butch. Trust me—this POW/MIA issue is dead. The only thing left in Vietnam, Laos or Cambodia are the *ghosts* of all the American, Vietnamese and communist soldiers who died there, and the hundreds of thousands of dead civilians murdered by the communists, and, of course, the million plus Cambodian civilians and soldiers killed by Pol Pot and the Khmer Rouge. But even that finally worked itself out. Don't worry. It'll all smooth out sooner or later. None of it means anything. Making a few bucks and surviving, those are the only things that mean anything in the end."

"You're probably right. But it's good to get people to believe in a cause."

"What do you know about that? Your dad and I believed in a cause once, and where'd it get us? He's dead, and I'm crazy."

"You're not so crazy anymore, Del. I can see it every day, you're getting better."

"If you say so."

On the White House steps first thing Tuesday morning, Secretary of Defense, Richard Moffit, made a statement to the press in response to the accusations that the U.S. Government has had knowledge since 1974 of the twelve POWs still being held in Cambodia and done nothing to secure their release, or to attempt to liberate them by covert actions.

"America, yesterday and this morning you read and heard stories that there are American soldiers still being held captive in Southeast Asia, particularly Cambodia. You were also told that your government has known about these POWs since 1974, and stood by and done nothing to secure their release."

"America has been through some of her toughest times over the last dozen or so years, and only in the last two years has she taken some big steps in returning to the greatness she has always been known for. The POW/MIA issue has never been an easy one. *Dealing with the communists on anything has never been easy.* But you have to know and believe that your government and the Department of Defense have always taken all claims regarding possible live American POWs seriously. We have always been tremendously grateful for the sacrifices made by our soldiers, marines, sailors and airmen in every war, and also during peace time."

"Trust me, when the Department of Defense received the photos, prisoner lists, and reports in June 1974, regarding possible POWs in Cambodia, Laos and Vietnam, it did, and has continued to do, everything in its power to resolve the situation. It is very disturbing that this information was released to the mass media which then failed to substantiate the claims made in these reports before taking them public and causing such an up roar. They have given false hope to the families of the men listed, and not only to them, but to all those families whose men are still listed as Missing In Action, and whose bodies have never been recovered, identified, or returned to the United States."

"None of our military intelligence during these last seven years validates any of the claims made by these reports. Am I saying definitely that there is absolutely no possibility of an American or Americans being held against their will in a foreign country—in Vietnam, Cambodia, or Laos? No. No man—no American—could say that. But *I am* saying that your government has done its best during these years to get a full accounting for every soul that served his country in Southeast Asia, and will continue to do so. The Department of Defense has checked out every report or name ever mentioned among our returned Prisoners Of War and have accounted for every soldier mentioned, either through the process of elimination or through comparative analysis, interviews and so on. Trust me when I say we will continue to do our best to resolve these delicate issues."

"We are continuing our efforts to communicate with the Vietnamese Government in Hanoi regarding our MIA's and to open the door for recovering the remains of American servicemen. But this will be an ongoing process for many years to come. We understand that without your son's, grandson's, brother's, husband's, or father's body, you will never have complete closure. It is our continuing goal to bring *closure* to that devastating chapter in America's history, *closure* for the country and *closure* for all the families whose sons, grandsons, brothers, husbands, or fathers are still listed as Missing In Action/Presumed Dead."

"Thank you—and God bless you. God bless America, the land of the free and the home of the brave, the greatest nation on Earth. May each of you have a day of peace and hope!"

The media and the American public received Defense Secretary Moffit's statement with mixed feelings. The majority of people questioned afterward for their reaction to the statement, said *it was just more government Bologna*. Others wanted to believe that the government was being honest with the public regarding the POW/MIA issue, that it had made every effort possible to get to the bottom of things and resolve the issue. Still others weren't sure what to think. On one hand they hoped there were still MIAs alive in Southeast Asia, that America might still get them home to their families and friends. On the other hand, some just wanted the issue, along with the war, to go back where it was a couple days ago, stuffed in the memories of America's past.

When asked specifically, "Do you think this whole thing is—or could be—a hoax perpetrated by either the media or possibly even by the government itself?" nearly twenty-five percent polled said that was a possibility. When asked why the media or government would do that, seventy percent couldn't come up with a reason. The other thirty percent came up with a number of reasons. The prevailing reasons were: the media wanted to stir up public anger toward the U.S. Government; or they wanted to bring the **POW/MIA** issue back to the center of the public eye in hopes the government would be forced to resolve the issue promptly instead of dragging its feet like many believed it had been doing.

On Tuesday afternoon, Lane County Sheriff, David Alford, along with Lieutenant Dowdy, Corporal Easton, and Captain McKluskey met with Dick Eastbrook in a meeting room at the Sheriff's Station in Eugene. Captain McKluskey asked Eastbrook why he took the information to the mass media.

"Captain, I was Roger Bruington's best friend. For all the years since he returned home from Vietnam, I knew there was so much he wasn't telling me about that war. In fact, he told me almost nothing. I knew he was deeply scarred by whatever he had seen and experienced over there. But I also knew *he* would have to decide if and when he ever shared any of that with me.

"Well he never got the chance to. His life was taken before he got that chance. So when I got to meet his ex-Vietnam buddy in March (Eastbrook never actually met Kennedy), along with Deputies Dowdy and Easton, and got to see the reports Roger had written up, and the photos of American POWs, and listen to the tapes he had made regarding his knowledge of the POW/MIAs being held in Cambodia--and which the U.S. Government, CIA, Department of Defense, or whoever else, had done there best to keep under the carpet—I knew someone had to carry the torch for Roger and see action taken to resolve the issue. It wasn't an easy decision for me to go to the press. But in the end, I was convinced that if Roger was going to take it to the press, and didn't get to, then by golly I was going to get it to the press for him."

"What is the Vietnam buddy's name?"

"He wants to remain anonymous."

"Did Deputies Dowdy and Easton know you intended to take the information to the press?"

"They suspected it."

"Did they tell you it wasn't a good idea?"

"They figured I could do what I wanted."

"And did you figure on the huge public reaction to your press release?"

"I knew it would be big news. You'd have to be pretty naïve not to, Captain."

"Did you suggest to the reporters that Roger had been killed by the CIA?"

"No. I didn't add any commentary to anything Roger had documented. I was just the messenger delivering Roger's evidence. I let the reporters come to their own conclusions. They always do anyway. You know that."

"You're right there. So now maybe you've complicated Lieutenant Dowdy and Deputy Eastons' murder investigation. Had you considered that releasing the reports might have that effect?"

"Honestly, Captain, I don't agree with that at all. If, in fact, some government entity was responsible for Roger's death, I mean if it was an assassination, then going public didn't change that fact. Nor did it make it any easier or more difficult to find the killer. If Roger was killed by someone other than the CIA or our government, I can't see where this will hurt at all, either. It may even help. The killer might figure he's in the clear and slip up, giving your guys the break they need to solve the case."

"You're pretty optimistic, Mr. Eastbrook. A killing in an isolated location in the woods, where the body is not discovered until two days later, and in which there seems to be no evidence left by the killer, is a long-shot from the start. But I know if it can be solved, Deputies Dowdy and Easton are the men who can do it."

"I agree with you there, Captain. Now are we done? I have to get back to my office."

"Yes, Mr. Eastbrook. We are done here. I can't say that I'm happy about what you have started. But on the other hand, who knows? It might turn out to be a necessary development, not only in solving your friend Bruington's murder, but in resolving the whole POW/MIA issue. I do understand why you did it, and I respect your loyalty to your friend. It took a lot of courage to go forward with that evidence. But now you may have a monkey on your back that you hadn't counted on."

"Oh, I counted on it. But I had to do it for Roger and for the POWs that I believe our government has ignored. You guys have a good day." He got up and left the room and the station.

After Eastbrook left, Captain McKluskey reprimanded Dowdy and Easton for withholding information from him. But then he said he agreed with them, that he highly doubted it was a government or CIA hit. He said he didn't believe for a minute that any government agency would assassinate a Vietnam War hero even if he did attempt to reveal a possible cover up in the POW/MIA issue.

Both Dowdy and Easton expected this response from the captain, and knew it hadn't changed their standing within the department.

Over the next several weeks, the activists' demonstrations throughout the country gradually diminished, but it was obvious to everyone that the **POW/MIA issue** was not going away. And it became clear that many people in America had turned a corner in regard to *their perception of the Vietnam War and the soldiers who fought it.* Suddenly it was okay to talk about Vietnam. It was okay to acknowledge the soldiers who sacrificed so much physically, emotionally and psychologically there. And, hopefully, in time even the soldiers themselves would open up and talk about the war.

The **Vietnam Veterans Memorial Wall**, which had been in the planning since the Vietnam Veterans Memorial Fund was established in April, 1979, was now in the early stages of design approval. The Wall would list the names of the more than 58,000 servicemen who were killed in the war, including the more than 2,500 soldiers listed as Missing In Action—Presumed Dead. Many veterans and non-veterans alike were getting excited about the memorial.

Many believed the Vietnam Veterans Memorial Wall would prove to be a huge vehicle of healing for veterans and for the nation.

Amen!

28

Mitch Walton

Mitch Walton, a handsome, brown-haired, twenty-four year-old fitness nut, lived near Lusk, Wyoming, a few miles from his sister Becky and her husband, Patrick. He had his own universal gym, which he worked out on four days a week, and he was also an avid bicyclist, logging over a hundred miles a week. He graduated in June 1980 from Nelson State University in Colorado, with a degree in wildlife biology. After graduating he took the next year off, paid his living expenses from a trust his parents had established years earlier for his college education and expenses, and spent that time doing hours of reading a day on top of his biking and workouts.

His plan was to spend June through September of 1981 touring the Pacific Northwest on his Trek, fourteen-speed, mountain bike, then begin applying for entry into a Wildlife Masters Program at the prominent West Coast Universities that offered it. He left Lusk on June 1st with the necessary cash, a Visa credit card, his sleeping bag, and his saddle packs filled with a few changes of clothes, extra tennis shoes, a light 10 foot by 10 foot tarp, and numerous other items he would need. He also wore a fanny pack and a backpack which was designed to leave space between the pack and his back.

Mitch's intention was to keep in touch with his sister and her husband by phone every three days or so to keep them apprised of his whereabouts, progress, and share some of his experiences. He figured he might even pick up a little extra spending money and local lore by occasionally spending an afternoon or evening washing dishes on a drop-in basis at a few local diners along his way. Of course, living in Lusk, Wyoming, he had no idea how few drop-in dishwashing jobs would be available along the way because of the tight job situation on the West Coast. It was the experience and local information he was really after anyway. He didn't need the money.

By the weekend of July 4th, Mitch had made it through Idaho and eastern and central Oregon, stopping to visit and enjoy numerous small towns, lakes and streams along the way. He purposely avoided larger towns and cities, except when they fell in his path; when they did, he pedaled his way through them as fast as he could. He was in excellent shape, in the prime of his life. Along with the bike riding, he did many pushups, sit-ups, windmills, treadmills, and various other strength and agility exercises each day. He ate and drank mostly good, wholesome foods, and some of the bounty he could collect from nature. The trip was going well for him. He had called his sister at least every third day and shared some of his exhilarating experiences with her and her husband.

Upon arriving at the white covered-bridge at the upper end of Dexter Reservoir in Lane County, just off Oregon State Highway 58, about noon on Friday, July 3rd, he stopped to eat. Sitting on the dike's big rocks just over the guardrail next to the historic covered bridge, eating a tuna-fish sandwich and drinking part of an orange Gatorade, Mitch looked over his Oregon State map.

With his keen interest in the outdoors and wildlife, he soon decided he wanted to check out the Fall Creek drainage of the Willamette River. He knew nothing about the area, but from the map, he could clearly see there were many smaller creeks that flowed into Fall Creek and that all of them originated far away from any towns. Fall Creek was in the Willamette National Forest—a portion of which he had passed through earlier in the morning—that extended north and south along the west slope of the Cascade Mountains in Lane County. Little did he know that his decision to check out Fall Creek *would seal his fate*. And no one could have imagined how.

After finishing his lunch, he pedaled the half mile to the historic two-story Lowell Store and called his sister Becky. That would be the last she heard from him.

At three-thirty in the afternoon, with temperatures nearing ninety, he reached Dolly Varden Bridge where a couple dozen people, from pre-teen kids to middle-aged adults, were standing near the guardrail on the left side, waiting to jump or dive the twenty-three feet into the twelve-foot-deep hole beneath. Others, soaking wet from having already made the jump, were walking toward them on the bridge. He stopped on the bridge near the crowd to watch for several minutes. Then, after seeing several people make the plunge, he couldn't resist the temptation to join in the fun.

He rode his bike to the east end of the bridge, parked and used his chain and padlock to secure it to a white-barked alder tree. So far, in the many similar stops he had made along his way, no one had taken anything from his saddle packs. But that possibility was always on the back of his mind. He took off his backpack, fanny pack, tee-shirt, tennis shoes and socks, and left them, along with his blue ball cap, next to his bike. He then walked to the crowd on the north side of the bridge wearing only his cutoffs and skivvies.

As he joined the other onlookers and participants, Mitch struck up a conversation with a beautiful, well-tanned, blue-eyed, blonde-headed babe, about five-foot-three, with a full bust that was pouring out of the edges of the white and red polka-dot bikini. He guessed her to be about twenty.

"Hi gorgeous," he said, with all the confidence he could muster.

"How's the water?"

She smiled at him, revealing her double dimples, while taking several seconds to admire his strong shoulders, bulging biceps, muscular thighs and calves, six-pack abs and dark tan. "It's great. It's a little cool on the initial plunge, but it's refreshing, and you get used to it fast. You going to jump or dive?"

"What have you been doing?"

"I jump. This is a little high for me to dive from."

"Well, I'll be diving. I actually prefer to dive when I get up this high."

"What are you, one of those Acapulco divers?" she said, doing her best to tease and flatter him.

"No, but I did dive from the Weimea Falls in Hawaii."

"How high are they?"

"You can dive from anywhere on the rock face, but the highest I dove from was about sixty feet."

"No way. This is twenty-four feet or so. You dove from almost three times higher than this?"

"Yes, I did."

"And you didn't break your pretty neck?"

"Of course not. I only dive into safe water. I've met too many paraplegics and quadriplegics that were paralyzed by hitting their head on boulders or the bottom when diving. I might take the dive from up high, but I'm smart enough to not do it when it isn't safe."

"Well it's safe here, as long as you don't play submarine after you submerge."

"Funny! You sure are cute. You from around here?"

"Thanks. You're not so bad yourself. Yeah, I live in Lowell. How about you, are you from around here?"

"No. I'm actually from near Lusk, Wyoming."

"You're a cowboy?"

"Not really. Not everyone in Wyoming is a cowboy, you know. Some of us are actually smart."

"I like cowboys."

"I'll be a cowboy if you want. I mean I was a cowboy growing up, but kind of changed my way when I went to college. We raised cattle and had several horses. Believe me, I can ride."

"Well let's see if you can dive."

"Okay, coming right up. You going to come in after me, or do I have to come back up to see your pretty face again?"

"I'll jump in after you. You sure are a sweet talker, aren't you?"

"I know how to treat a lady."

"We'll see about that."

"What's this beautiful lady's name, anyway?"

"I'm Monica."

"Nice to meet you, Monica. I'm Mitch," he said, extending his hand to shake hers. "M and M, it has a nice ring to it, doesn't it? And I know how good they taste."

"What you know is how to pour it on, don't you?"

"Only when I want to."

Mitch moved over to his left several feet, stepped up onto the top of the guardrail post, and stood there at attention, like divers do, letting the suspense build for everyone around. Many of the people playing in the water downstream from the bridge, as well as those sitting in the sand and gravel along the shore watched with interest. Jumpers and divers always attracted the attention of onlookers. And usually the spectators never knew what kind of show-off move the jumper or diver might try. Or what they might yell, which was often part of the ritual.

Mitch thought, I'm going to put on a show. I'll let this hot, little filly see what I'm made of. He took a long, deep breath, bent his knees, swung his arms back, and then swung them forward as he leapt up and out into the air several feet from the bridge. Just as he began falling, he tucked his knees and head in tight to his body and grabbed his shins. Instantly, the audience knew something good was coming and a couple people shouted a quick, "Alright!" as Mitch somersaulted downward. He came out of the one and a half just in time to enter the water in a straight vertical posture and with only a small splash.

"Yes!" several people yelled. "Great dive!"

"That was a ten!" yelled a couple others.

He couldn't hear them as he disappeared beneath the surface.

Those watching from the bridge couldn't see him descending toward the bottom because of all the bubbles rising from the depths—nor could those along the shore and in the water downstream.

When Mitch didn't come to the surface in the three or four seconds that was the norm, a few people, including Monica, who was holding her breath and, gripping the guardrail in front of her tightly, became a bit anxious for him.

The shadow that was caused by the bridge blocking the afternoon sun was over the water, and even though the bubbles were clearing, no one above could see Mitch.

Twenty seconds passed.

Then thirty.

Still he didn't surface.

"Help him! Someone help him?" Monica screamed. "It's been too long."

Two men and an older teenager who had been waiting for their turns, immediately climbed onto the guardrail, sat for a couple seconds peering into the water that had flattened out except for the slight riffle of the creek's current, then jumped. Moments later they each surfaced below the bridge, just as Mitch surfaced fifty feet upstream from them, at the opposite side of the bridge.

They knew the diver must have hit bottom and knocked himself out at a minimum. And they didn't even want to think about the worst case scenario.

Mitch spotted them at once and saw they were treading water while searching the depths beneath them.

Two women walked up and down the shoreline, scanning the water.

"Hey, I'm up here. It's okay. I'm fine," Mitch yelled. "What's going on?"

He hadn't considered how his antics would affect anyone but Monica. And he only wanted to impress her, not scare her. Not really. Just make her concerned about him.

The people on the bridge didn't hear him yell.

Several of them shouted to the three in the water, "Go find him. You've got to get him. He doesn't have much time."

Then one of the men in the water, who had heard Mitch, turned his head toward him but was unable to clearly see his face because of the lighting. "Are you the diver?" he yelled. "Are you the one who just did the one and a half?"

"Yes. I'm fine," Mitch answered. "I just swam upstream after the dive. It's okay."

"He's up there," the swimmer said to the people on the bridge, pointing upstream.

"He can't be up there. That's upstream."

"No, he's okay," said the swimmer. "He's okay. He's under the other side of the bridge.

The people on the bridge immediately turned and started to dart across the highway, but stopped just in time to keep from running into the red '68 Chevelle that was slowly cruising by. Almost everyone drives slowly over Dolly Varden Bridge, not only because of all the swimmers milling around there, but because they are either going into or coming out of the tight right-angle turn on the west side of the bridge.

As soon as they were clear of the car, people ran to the south edge of the bridge and leaned over the guardrail to look.

Monica was one of the first, and upon seeing him, yelled, "Mitch! Mitch, what are you doing?"

"It's okay, Monica," he answered, observing her long blonde hair hanging down in front of the top of her polka-dot bikini that was really struggling to hold things in now. Things turned out better than he had hoped. Or maybe they didn't. He didn't want everybody to think he had hit bottom. He hadn't really thought of that. He just wanted to excite Monica a little.

"Why did you do that to us, Mitch? We all thought you hit bottom or something."

"I'm sorry, Monica. I didn't mean to worry anyone. I was just having some fun."

"What did you think we'd think?"

"I guess I didn't think," he said, continuing to tread water. "I'll meet you on shore downstream from the bridge. I'll wait for you to jump."

"Are you serious? I'm not in the mood to jump now. You took the fun and games out of me."

"I'm sorry, Monica. I didn't mean to." He thought, man you've really screwed up now. A beautiful, hot-bodied babe like her—and you go and pull something stupid like that. I guess you are a cowboy. So much for this going anywhere, you stupid jackass. "Can we still talk? I didn't mess everything up with you, did I?"

Everyone leaning over the guardrail found this exchange interesting. One married man on the bridge, thought, you sure don't know how to stay out of trouble with your girlfriend, do you buster. If I had a hot broad like her, I'd do everything I could to stay on her good side. Man would I try to stay on her good side.

Mitch swam down through the pool under the bridge, but stayed off to the side of where anyone would be diving. As he stepped out of the water, he heard a yell and turned just in time to see and hear a splash. The fun had once again begun. As he walked up onto shore below the bridge, Monica walked back toward his bike, and upon reaching the end of the bridge, took the warn dirt trail to the beach where Mitch was waiting.

"I'm really sorry, Monica," he said, when she approached him. "I guess I didn't think things through too well. I just wanted to impress you."

"For future reference, that's not the way to do it. I really liked your dive, but you should have been happy with that."

"I know. Will you give me a fresh start?"

"We'll see."

"Who are you up here with anyway, Monica?"

"A couple of girl friends from Lowell. We come up here all the time. I take it you're by yourself?"

"Yeah. I'm on a bicycling tour of the Northwest."

"By yourself?"

"Yeah. I'm having a ball."

"I can see that."

"I really am sorry, Monica."

"I know you are. But *you are definitely* a cowboy, aren't you."

"I guess I deserved that," he answered. "How come a beautiful babe like you is up here with her girlfriends? I mean, I would think you would have to beat the guys off with a stick."

"I'm flattered. Actually, I had a boyfriend until a few weeks ago."

"So are you still hoping to get back together with him?"

"Oh, no. He tried to pick up on one of my girlfriends four weeks ago, and I found out about it."

"Are you kidding me?" The guy must be a complete idiot, he thought. Either that or ...

"Yes. I mean, no I'm not kidding. Do you have a girlfriend waiting for you back in Wyoming?"

"No."

"That's good," she said, smiling flirtatiously at him.

Alright, he thought. I'm back in the saddle. But what good is it going to do? Nothing is going to change my plans or cut this trip short.

"Would you like to come over to our fire and roast some hotdogs and marshmallows with us?"

"I'd love to. I need to get my bike. It's up there by the tree." He pointed in the direction of his bike, though he couldn't see it over the blackberry bushes between the creek and the bike.

"Oh, that's *your* bike?"

"Yeah. Do you want to walk up there to get it with me, then I'll just follow you to your site."

"Sounds like a plan."

They walked up, grabbed his clothes and shoes, and walked his bike to her camp site. After she introduced him to her two girl friends, they all sat around the fire and visited while roasting hot dogs and marshmallows on green willow shoots.

Later, as the sun dropped lower behind the fir trees to the west of them, Monica asked, "Do you want to sleep here in our camp site? What are you sleeping in anyway?"

"My shorts." All three girls laughed.

"No cowboy. I mean, do you have a tent?"

"I knew what you meant, I was playing with you."

"Sure you were," said one of the girlfriends, whose looks couldn't hold a candle to Monica.

"No really, I was. I actually have a small tarp that I hang up over me if it's going to rain. Otherwise I just lay in my sleeping bag under the stars."

"Well, it doesn't look like you'll need your tarp tonight," said the other girlfriend, a pretty fair looking red-headed chick.

"What are your plans tomorrow?" asked Monica.

"I figured I could hang out here with you gals for the morning, then I'm going to head farther up the creek."

"So how are we going to stay in touch?"

"We can exchange phone numbers, and I'll call you sometime when I'm back where I can get to a phone. And, of course, once I'm home in late-September. I'm planning to apply to the wildlife masters program at one of the big universities out here on the West Coast. I was looking at the map, and I see Eugene isn't too far from here. Does the University of Oregon have a good wildlife program?"

"Yes, as a matter of fact, they do," answered Monica. "I'll be a junior at the U of O this fall in biology, actually."

"I guess we missed that earlier, didn't we?" he said.

"We just got side-tracked."

The remainder of the evening went well. The four of them enjoyed the fire together, ate some s'mores, and drank hot cocoa. Then finally, Monica gave the girlfriends the hint that she would like some alone time with the hunk, and they went off to bed in the four-man tent. Mitch and Monica cuddled up close by each other as they sat on a blanket up against a big log and talked into the fire. Before she went in for the night he gave her a gentle short kiss on her lips, and thought, only a fool would leave this for the road.

The next morning, they ate an excellent French toast and sausage breakfast, which Monica cooked over the fire. Then they spent the remainder of the morning visiting and laughing. Mitch kept an arm around Monica for much of the time and managed to sneak an occasional kiss when the girlfriends were pre-occupied, and got a little more serious kissing in when they would leave for several minutes at a time.

Then he knew it was time to hit the road. After exchanging phone numbers and promising to stay in touch, he and Monica walked his bike up to the main road. There they held each other for a couple minutes, kissed at length, hugged once more and kissed a final time, then said their goodbyes. She would never see or hear from him again.

29

Puma Creek Campground

Mitch pedaled along on Fall Creek Road, heading east, and stopped at several of the pull offs and a couple of creeks. When he got to the Clark Creek area and saw all the old-growth Douglas firs, he had to stop and walk among them. They don't have trees like this anywhere I've been, he thought, they're magnificent. The largest trees were nearly eight feet at the base and towered over two hundred feet into the sky.

After leaving the Clark Creek area, Mitch continued east.

At five o clock, he pedaled into Puma Creek Campground. He knew at once that this was the spot, if he could find an unoccupied campsite. He pedaled around the loop and found only one of the eleven sites open. Immediately, he rode back around to get the site number, and then went to register. He signed in for site 7.

Little did he know that a man, a hunter, had been camped in the next site over, site 6, eight and a half months earlier and came up missing in the old-growth forest to the north across Fall Creek from the camp ground—or that when they found him, he was dead, lying partly in a creek, with his brains blown out.

After parking his bike and rolling out his sleeping bag on the moss not far from the fire pit and camp table, Mitch walked to the outhouse and took care of business. He then walked back to his camp site, and soon decided he needed to go gather some fire materials: moss, and small branches so he could build himself a fire after awhile.

After spending last evening with Monica and her friends, he wasn't looking forward to his time alone around the camp fire tonight. He knew he would miss all their giggling and being females. He already missed Monica. He knew he was definitely going to follow up with her. Mitch walked down the same trail the searchers had walked over eight months earlier until he came to Fall Creek, then followed it back to the west a few hundred yards, passing the foot bridge that crossed over the creek. He sat down by the water and chewed on the stems of some licorice fern he had picked off a rotting, moss-covered stump nearby. Fall Creek was noticeably smaller here than it was at Dolly Varden Bridge because several tributaries ran in between here and there.

Mitch hadn't done a lot of fishing in his life, but he knew enough about Fish and Wildlife to know good trout water when he saw it. And he had never seen better looking trout water than he had seen in the last two days he'd spent touring Fall Creek. He also knew trout liked eating the ripe salmon berries that fell into the creek from overhanging vines during the summer months. His curiosity got the best of him.

He got up and walked back to a patch of salmon berry bushes growing alongside the creek, and picked several of the yellow unripe berries. He ate a couple, but they weren't nearly as tasty as he'd hoped. He wished it was a little later in the summer, when the salmon berries and the abundant blackberries he had observed would be ripe.

After eating a couple more sour salmon berries, Mitch hiked down to the creek and sneaked along the bank among the white-barked alder trees until he saw just the hole to throw a berry into. He tossed a yellow berry with a gentle underhand swing of his arm, while standing behind a big rock in the shade, knowing trout spooked easily on small creeks.

The berry landed just above the base of the riffles, right where the water smoothed out into the long pool below, and began drifting downstream. He waited expectantly for the sudden rise of a trout, and just when he was beginning to wonder if this stream had been depleted completely of its trout, as so many other streams throughout Oregon and Washington had been in the last ten years, a silver-colored trout of about ten inches exploded from the water, taking the yellow berry and disappearing again to hide under the edge of the bedrock along the near bank.

Mitch was elated. Though he couldn't tell what specie of trout it was, from his studies he knew that most of Oregon's small streams were populated by the native cutthroat trout, so-named for the twin orange-red slashes on either side of the trout's throat, under its jaw, forward of the gills.

He tossed in another berry in the same location, and then immediately another, and another. Just as the third berry hit the water, the first one, which had drifted several feet downstream, was taken by the same-sized trout. He guessed it was probably the same one that had taken the first berry. Then, suddenly the second and third berries were taken at the same time, but by two different trout. They were smaller than the first one.

As he stood there leaning on the big rock he was hiding behind, looking at the water and watching a lonely, brown alder-leaf drift past, he contemplated the future of this creek and so many others like it. He had read in many sources about the decline in wildlife in certain parts of the country and how the trout and other fish that inhabited so many of the West Coast streams were only a shadow of the populations they once were. One of the reasons he had chosen his field of study was his desire to help solve the problem of the fish and wildlife decline. Seeing the trout today only reaffirmed his desire to do that so generations to come would get to experience what he just did.

He picked and tossed several more berries into the creek, then knew it was time to gather his fire materials. He walked back toward the campground and picked up small branches as he went.

While digging some instant coffee and instant soup out of his pack, an older couple from campsite 6 walked up to his table and struck up a conversation with him.

"Hi there, camper," said the man. "Isn't this a beautiful place to camp?"

"It's wonderful. We didn't have anything like this where I grew up."

"Where are you from, young man?" asked the woman.

"I was born and raised in Lusk, Wyoming."

"What are you doing out in these parts?" she said.

"I took the summer off so I could tour the Pacific Northwest on my bicycle. Where are you folks from?"

"We're from Florence, Oregon, over on the coast, next to the Siuslaw River. What's your name, son?" asked the man.

"I'm Mitch. Mitch Walton. And yours?"

"Nice to meet you, Mitch. I'm Bob Carter." He stuck out his hand, and, after shaking Mitch's, said, "This is my wife, Ruby." Mitch shook her hand.

"Glad to meet you folks. You been camped here long?"

"We got in two days ago," answered Bob. "We'll be here another three, then head back to the coast. We come up here over every fourth. Florence can get pretty wild over the fourth with all the tourists. We came up here and found this campground over ten years ago. Fell in love with it. We've been coming here every fourth since."

"Well I can sure see why. It's beautiful. I'm planning to do some hiking tomorrow, though I haven't decided exactly where yet. The exercise and fresh air are medicine to my soul."

"You've got that straight," said Bob. "Do you use a compass and map when you hike?"

"Most the time I at least have my compass on me. I just take some initial bearings, and then it's a piece of cake."

"You sound like you know your way around in the wild."

"Actually, I majored in Wildlife Biology at Nelson State University in Colorado; graduated a year ago."

"Good for you, Mitch" said Ruby.

"The way things are going with our wildlife and especially our fish out here on the West Coast, we need all the good men in that field we can get," said Bob. "We've got these, 'Save the seals and sea lions fanatics, and all kinds of other green peace and animal rights yeh whos... You aren't one of them, are you?"

"No, I'm definitely not one of them."

"They think the solution to all our problems is to stop all logging, hunting, fishing, trapping, and just about everything else that has always been a part of man's lifestyle. So many of these kids coming up today grow up in the concrete jungles of Portland, Eugene and all the other towns and cities. Talking to them, you get the impression they think even meat grows on trees."

"I guess growing up on a farm in Wyoming, raising cattle and other stock, along with growing our own vegetables every year, caused me to understand all that better than the city kids."

"Your mom and dad taught you well, Mitch. Now if we can just get you to come out to Oregon and work in our Fish and Wildlife Department..."

"That's very kind of you, Bob. It's funny you should say that. As a matter of fact, I just met a wonderful young lady yesterday when I stopped at Dolly Varden Campground. I spent the afternoon and evening getting acquainted with her and her two girlfriends who were camped there. Then I spent the night and hung out this morning until around noon, before heading up this way. We exchanged phone numbers and addresses. In fact, I'm planning to call the University of Oregon in a few days to see about any openings they might have in a wildlife masters program."

"It sounds like your tour up Fall Creek might pay some big dividends for you, Mitch," said Ruby. "Would you like to come over to our campsite next to you and join us for a nice batch of my spaghetti, with some green salad and garlic bread?"

"Ruby, you must have my number. Here I was intending to make myself some instant soup. How can I pick that over a home-made spaghetti dinner? I'd love to. Do you know I've only had three home-cooked meals since I've been on the road the last month?"

"Well you camped at the right campground tonight. I'm going to go get it started. Feel free to join us anytime. It'll probably be forty-five minutes to an hour before we're ready to eat."

"Alright, I'll be over in a little bit."

The Carters walked hand in hand back to their campsite. Watching them made Mitch miss his mom and dad; he lost them in a car accident two years earlier. Now he just had his sister, Becky, and brother, Larry.

After a tasty dinner with the Carters in site 6, Mitch rolled it in for the night. He was very tired from staying up late last night visiting with Monica. As he lay in his sleeping bag under the stars, he thought of how lucky he would be if something could actually work out with her. Man she's beautiful, he thought, and that body, it's enough to make a guy weak in the knees—and then to have a fun, sweet personality too. And she's interested in me, some hick from Wyoming.

He drifted off to sleep with her on his mind.

30

The Hike

At seven the next morning, Sunday, July 5th, Mitch sprang out of his sleeping bag, quickly drank a Grape Gatorade, did a little stretching, then rolled up his bag and put everything in his pack and saddle bags. He fastened the sleeping bag over the saddle bags, then pedaled away from campsite 7 as quietly as he could. He wanted to be up and out before the Carters awakened in order to avoid the possibility of getting hung up in an extended conversation with them. He figured if he was going to let himself get hung up anywhere it would have been with Monica.

He pedaled uphill on Jones Creek Road for about two miles, then doubled back to the south on a logging spur road. When he got to the landing at the end, he stashed his bike in some tall ferns down over the edge of the landing, and hiked to the west until he reached Jones Creek. He crossed the creek and climbed up the side of the ridge until he got to the top that sloped uphill to the north.

He had no idea that the hunter who was shot to death over eight months earlier had been found no more than a quarter mile downstream in Jones Creek.

After reaching the upper portion of the sloping ridge above the creek, Mitch sat down on a log, and drank some water from his quart canteen. He then removed his fanny pack and stretched out his arms, legs, and torso. He then did sixty pushups, a hundred sit ups and fifty windmills. He completed his mini-workout with another forty push ups, and then unzipped his fanny pack to pull out his brunch. After polishing off a peanut butter and jelly sandwich, a granola bar and an orange, he continued his hike up the mountain.

An hour and a half later, and over two miles to the northwest from where the hunter was found, Mitch stopped for another half a sandwich and some water. After a fifteen minute respite sitting against an old stump overlooking the uppermost reaches of Slick Creek, he headed down and across that drainage on an old deer trail that looked like it wasn't traveled much.

As he continued down the trail, he thought about Monica. He thought maybe he would surprise her and try to hook up with her that evening at Dolly Varden or, if she wasn't still there, in Lowell.

Thirty yards ahead he came to a broken three-foot-diameter log lying across the trail. He knew a deer would just jump over it, but he stepped up on the log and took a quick look. He saw there were no obstacles and took a decisive step placing his foot a couple feet ahead of the log. But the ground was soft. In fact, it wasn't ground at all. The fir-needle-covered surface gave way completely. As he tumbled forward, he instinctively yelled, "No!" and thrust his hands out to the sides to catch the edges of the hole. But it was *too late*. He was completely committed and fell into the seven foot wide and long hole. When he landed he screamed out in severe pain. He was impaled on several sharp pointed sticks.

Somehow none of them had pierced his head. Immediately he determined that his right arm was still free and uninjured. He was in excruciating pain and felt himself getting weak. Or was he? He wasn't sure. He must be losing a lot of blood, he thought. When he tried to move his head to turn it, he couldn't; there was a stick up against the middle of each ear, crowding his head. His face was lying in moss and his chest was bottomed out on moss and ground beneath that. But he could still get air and breath. He had no way to check the rest of his body.

Pain was coming from so many places, his pain sensors were overloaded. He groaned. He realized his left arm was bent backward with a stick stabbing through his bicep muscle. He tried to take a mental inventory of his wounds, based on where the pain was coming from. He really had to concentrate, and that was so hard. He started at the top of his body and tried to isolate that in his mind. Where was the pain coming from? He realized he had a stick poking into his upper chest on each side, beneath each collar bone. But he had no way of knowing how deep the sticks had penetrated. Nor could he tell how big they were.

Then he remembered his right arm was still free. He moved it and wrapped his fingers and thumb around one of the sticks and squeezed firmly. As near as he could tell the stick was about three-quarters of an inch in diameter. That wasn't good. Or was it? He tried to pull on the stick, to pull it upward, but it would move only a fraction of an inch. He knew it must be buried not only somewhat deep, but maybe it had an angle, like a hook, on the end to prevent it from being pulled out—another *point* against him. He thought, why would it have an angle? Then he realized he was probably just too weak to pull the stick up. And the angle for pulling with his arm was so bad. He thought if he could pull the surrounding sticks out with his free right arm, he might be able to get free. He tried pulling again, but couldn't do any good.

He didn't know if he was dying. He wondered if he was already dead. No, if he was dead, he wouldn't be feeling all this pain. He felt around to the surrounding sticks, trying to determine how far apart they were, and if they were uniformly spaced.

Suddenly he thought of his sister Becky, at home in Lusk, Wyoming. He wanted to go there so bad, to be there with her and Patrick. If only he hadn't come on this trip. How did this happen to him? He was impaled on punji sticks in a punji pit in America. He had read about these being used in Vietnam and other countries as booby traps and to catch large wild animals. But not here. Not in his own America. Not to him. *How could this be*? It couldn't be real. He was only dreaming.

He tried to wake himself up. But it wasn't a dream. He was awake.

He tried to determine the distance between the two sticks beside his ears and the two beneath his collar bones. He estimated they were about nine inches apart. Had they missed his lungs? They must have, he could still breath. And his heart was closer to the center of his body. It had to be fine.

He concentrated hard to isolate his body from his chest down, and considered where the next two sticks would be. It wasn't good. The one in his right side had to be in his liver. How long could he live with a pierced liver or kidney, or both? He had no idea. Was the spike on his left side in the kidney or spleen? He knew a ruptured spleen was an emergency that could kill a person if they didn't get medical help soon. Oh how he hoped it wasn't in his spleen. But a spike in the kidney might even be worse.

God. He thought of God. How could he not have thought of God much in recent years? God wasn't popular at Nelson State University. Probably not at many universities and colleges throughout America, he thought. This country, which was founded on godly principles, had drifted so far from God. *He had drifted so far from God.* His thoughts of God came quickly now, and very clear. He didn't even have to concentrate to think of God. Why was that?

Mitch remembered the fun he had as a kid at the Baptist church he and his family had attended. As a young boy he loved playing on the church's playground. He could see himself going up and down on the teeter-totter, and holding onto the bars as he hung way out from the edge of the merry-go-round as it spun around. He remembered pretending to be a jet pilot flying over the Andes Mountains as he swung above the bar on the chain-link swing.

He had accepted Jesus Christ as his savior when he was seven.

He'd even been baptized. His parents were faithful church goers, and he'd been involved in the church's small youth group when he was in high school. But after leaving home and going to college, he had left most of that behind him. At college everyone focused on obtaining knowledge, in philosophizing about the meaning of this or that. There was little room for God. Sure, plenty of students had discussed God and theology. But very few thought God had any relevance to life today. Besides they were in college to have fun, in addition to obtaining knowledge. God didn't fit into the kind of fun they had.

He pulled his thoughts back to his body. Where would the next spikes be? They had to be just above the top of his pelvis. What organs were there? He tried to remember. Then he realized the inventory was a waste of time. He didn't have a prayer anyway.

He prayed silently, "God, I'm sorry for forgetting about you in my life. I'm so sorry for following the thinking of so many of the people I interacted with at college. I studied all about nature and wildlife, your creation, and then lived my life as if you didn't exist. Please forgive me. Forgive me for being so angry at you when Mom and Dad were killed. I couldn't forgive you for taking them, good Christians, good parents. Forgive me for being so angry at you, for blocking all the things I had always believed about you out of my mind."

Mitch felt himself getting sicker, weaker by the minute. He was fading. This is it, he thought. And he couldn't do a thing to stop it. He would never get to see his sister and brother again. He would never get to experience the great outdoors again—God's wonderful creation that bore constant witness to His awesomeness. Yet people ignored God day after day. And he would never get to know Monica. Why God? Why?

He took comfort in knowing he would be seeing his mom and dad. He thanked God that he had been raised in a Christian home with Christian parents who had taught him to love God and His Son

Jesus.

Half an hour after landing in the pit, Mitch lost consciousness. But he had made things right with God. His heart stopped twenty minutes later.

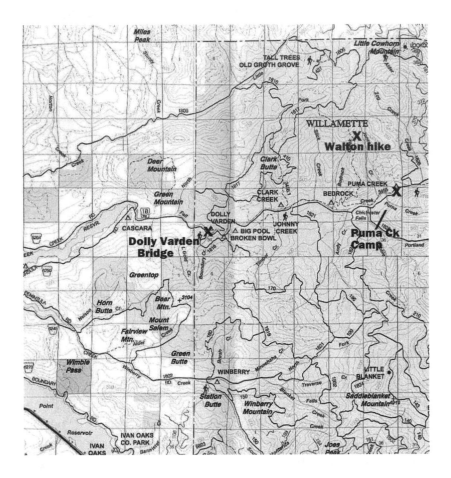

Mitch Walton camped one night at Dolly Varden Bridge, the next night
he camped at Puma Creek Campground, then took the fateful hike.
Each square is a square mile.
(See map on page 34 for larger area of coverage.)

31

Sister's Call to OSP

At 4 PM on Friday, July 10th, five days after Mitch died, his sister, Becky, called the Oregon State Police.

"My brother is missing in Oregon."

"Where are you calling from?" asked the woman trooper who answered the phone in the OSP office in Springfield.

"I'm in Lusk, Wyoming. My brother is in Oregon somewhere and hasn't called in since July 3rd."

"What do you mean he hasn't called in?"

"He's... he's been on a bicycle tour of the Pacific Northwest since the first of June and hasn't checked in with me for over seven days. He was checking in at least every three days."

"He's on a tour, so he's with other bicyclists, right?"

"No. He's doing a solo tour. No one is traveling with him."

"And you said he had been checking in with you every three days?"

"Yes, even less than that sometimes."

"And you haven't talked to him since when?"

219

"Since a week ago. Something's happened to him. He would never have gone this long without calling in."

"Wait a minute, Ma'am. What is your name? And what is your brother's name?"

"My name is Becky Randall. My brother's name is Mitch Walton. Mitchell Paul Walton."

The trooper wrote down the names and the other information Becky had given her.

"So you and your brother live in Lusk, Wyoming. Or does he live in Oregon?"

"No. I mean, yes, we both live in Wyoming."

"Where was your brother when he made his last call to you?"

"Lowell, Oregon. I saw on the map that was close to Springfield. That's why I called your number."

"Yes, Lowell is in our jurisdiction. So your brother called, what time of day, from Lowell?"

"He called me at one-thirty."

"Was that your time or his?"

"My time—Wyoming time."

"Do you know where he was going from Lowell?"

"He said something about some place called Fall Creek. Is that far from Lowell?"

"No, it's just over the mountain a little ways. So you're sure he was going up Fall Creek?"

"That's what he said."

"Do you know how long he was going to be up there, or where he planned to go after that?"

"No, I have no idea. He was just planning as he went."

"So he may have gone up Fall Creek for a day or so, and then took off to who knows where?" She was a little irritated, and showed it in her voice even though she wasn't supposed to. The OSP throughout Oregon got called regularly by people saying a friend or family member was missing, then it turned out the "missing person" would show up a day or two later.

"No. He would have called if he went anywhere else."

"Maybe he was having so much fun at Fall Creek that he just hasn't been back to a phone. Does he have a girlfriend?"

"No. What's that got to do with it?"

"Maybe he met a gal up Fall Creek and just decided to stay there longer. There are a lot of young gals up Fall Creek in the summer. Did he tell you to call the police if he didn't check in within a certain amount of time?"

"No!" said Becky, obviously frustrated. "But I know he would have checked in if something wasn't wrong."

"And he told you he would definitely call in at least every three days?"

"Well, he said, 'every three days or so.'"

"So maybe this is one of those, 'or so's.'"

"It's not! He never would have gone this long. You have to know my brother."

"I understand your concern, Ma'am, but this sort of thing goes on all the time—"

"You're not listening to me!" she shouted. "My brother has not checked in, and I know something has happened to him."

"I appreciate your concern, Ma'am. I really do. And I can understand how you feel. I've taken down your information. Can you give me a description of your brother?"

Feeling like maybe she was finally getting somewhere, Becky said, "Yes. Yes. He's twenty-four, five-foot eleven, 180 pounds, has long, brown hair, brown eyes, clean-shaven, very handsome, is very muscular, in excellent shape and has a nice tan."

"How long is his hair?" asked the trooper, though she wanted to say, "It sounds like he should be in the Mr. Universe Contest."

"It comes down to his collar."

"Okay, Becky, here is what I'm going to do—"

"Yes?"

"I want you to send me several recent photos of your brother. Send them overnight delivery, if you want."

"Definitely!"

"Send them to Attention: Trooper Murphy, Oregon State Police, 3620 Gateway Street, Springfield, Oregon 97477. Did you get that?"

"Yes. Trooper Murphy, Oregon State Police, 3620 Gateway Street, Springfield, Oregon, 97477."

"That's right. If you don't hear from him by Monday morning, call me back. We will have the photos by then if you send them overnight. Even if you do hear from him by then, please call me and let me know."

"You're going to wait three days?"

"Look, Becky, like I already said, he's probably hooked up with some babe somewhere and just hasn't gotten down to a phone. We need to give it two more days."

"That's wrong. Something is wrong with my brother. Something has happened to him in your jurisdiction, and you're just going to sit and do nothing for three days?"

"Becky, I need the photos. And I want to give this thing until Monday. If he hasn't checked in, trust me, we will get on it. In the mean time, I'll send a trooper up that way with the description of your brother, and ask him to keep his eyes open for him, maybe ask around a little."

"I don't like that at all."

"Well, I'm sorry, Becky. That's the way it's going to be. You have to understand things from our perspective here. Your brother's on a bicycle tour all over the Pacific Northwest by himself. That's what you told me. He said he would check in every three days or so, and *has up until now*. But the fact that he would take a trip like this by himself, tells me he likes to be on his own schedule. Since he didn't tell you to call the police if he didn't check in—and he did say every three days *or so*— we've got to give it a little more time before getting too excited."

"Okay, I'll get the photos out today. But if something has happened to my brother…"

"I'll talk to you Monday, Becky."

After getting off the phone, Trooper Murphy went to the dispatcher and asked, "Which trooper is on Fall Creek today?"

"Trooper Wilson has Fall Creek.

"Would you have him call me?"

"Yes. I'll get a hold of him right away.

Fifteen minutes later, Trooper Wilson radioed back in on his CB radio. The dispatcher patched him through to Trooper Murphy.

"Murphy here."

"This is Trooper Wilson."

"Yes, Trooper Wilson, I received a call from a woman in Lusk, Wyoming saying that something has happened to her brother out here in Oregon. She said he's been on a bicycle trip by himself out in the Northwest since June 1rst. Apparently he had been calling in every three days and now it's been a week since she's heard from him. His last phone call was made from Lowell, saying he was headed up Fall Creek.

"I got a description and asked her to overnight some recent photos and to call me back on Monday morning. You know how these things go. She wasn't happy about that. The usual. So I told her I'd at least have a trooper run through the area and keep their eyes open for someone matching his description."

"That can be like a needle in a haystack up here this time a year."

"I know that, but I said we would do that much."

"What's the guy's name and description?"

"His name is Mitch Paul Walton. He's twenty-four, five-foot eleven, 180 pounds, collar-length, brown hair, brown eyes, clean-shaven, very handsome, very muscular, in excellent shape, and has a nice tan."

"Sounds like at least a couple dozen other guys up here, maybe a hundred," Wilson answered, with obvious sarcasm.

"That's what I thought. I told her he's probably hooked up with some nice babe up there."

"Well, I'll keep my eyes out for him."

32

Definitely Missing

At 8:30 Monday **morning, July 13th**, the phone rang at the Springfield OSP Station.

"Oregon State Police. Trooper Murphy speaking. How may I help you?"

"Trooper Murphy, did you get the photos of my brother?"

"Ms. Randall. Yes, we got the photos. You still haven't heard from him?"

"That's right. I tried to tell you Friday that something terrible has happened to him."

"I believe your brother may, in fact, be missing. It has been, what, ten days now since he last contacted you. Is that right?"

"Yes, that's right." She broke down crying.

"Settle down now, Ms Randall. Would your brother have taken plenty of food with him, and water?"

"Not anywhere near ten days worth. Maybe enough food for four or five days, and a lot less water. He knew he could always stop somewhere for more water."

"You said he was in excellent physical condition. That's a big point in his favor."

"What if he had something go wrong on his bike and ran it off a ledge or something?"

"We have no way of knowing what happened. But I will tell you this, many of the roads, at least the paved roads, on Fall Creek have guardrails at those kinds of places. Would he have camped at a campground and left his bike there to go on a hike?"

"I don't know. He told me a couple times when he checked in that he had stayed one night in a few different campgrounds. But the rest of the nights, he just sacked out some place out of the way."

"On Saturday, we had a trooper drive through all the campgrounds on Fall Creek, and he didn't run across your brother. He did see and talk to a few young men who basically matched your brother's description—"

"Are you sure none of them was him?" Becky said, desperately hoping they had made a mistake.

"Yes, we're sure. Not one of them was your brother. And no one the trooper talked to knew anything about a Mitch that matched your brother's description."

"So now what will you guys do to try to find him?"

"We're going to get a few troopers up there, and I'm going to contact the Lane County Sheriff's Department to see what kind of help they can give us."

"Only three troopers, and maybe that's it?"

"No, Becky. Trust me, that's not it at all," assured Trooper Murphy. "We're taking this very seriously. Unfortunately, we may be on a wild goose chase. If your brother just rode up Fall Creek for a day or two, then left the area entirely, we may not even be looking in the right place."

"I don't believe that. He would have checked in with me at the first chance he had. I know he's up Fall Creek somewhere. Have you ever had someone abducted or murdered up there?"

"You don't want to look at it that way, Becky. It will just eat you alive if you start playing all the possible scenarios in your mind. It's still quite possible that your brother is fine."

"He would never have gone this long without letting me know. He would know I'd be too worried about him."

"All's I can say then, Becky, is that we will do all we can to locate him. You've got to trust me on that. We'll make copies of some of your brother's photos and make sure everyone involved has one and the description. For now, try not to worry. We'll keep you posted on what we find out."

Twenty minutes later, after being briefed on the case by Trooper Murphy, OSP Captain Miles Burton, of the Springfield office contacted the Lane County Sheriff's Department and requested to speak with Lieutenant Dowdy.

"Lieutenant Dowdy here."

"Yes, Lieutenant Dowdy. Captain Burton, Oregon State Police. We have another missing person in the Fall Creek area. Another male, but this one's twenty-four—a bicyclist."

"That's just what we need. We still haven't made any more progress on the Bruington case. Everything has been dead ends. I'm beginning to have doubts about solving that case. What are the details, Captain?"

"A woman called in from Wyoming on Friday to tell us her brother was in the middle of a solo bicycle tour throughout the Northwest, and that he hadn't checked in for seven days. She said he called her from Lowell on July 3rd and said he was going to check out the Fall Creek area. She hasn't heard from him since.

"Oh boy!"

"The woman said he had been checking in at least every three days. On Friday our trooper asked the woman to send some photos out by overnight delivery and told her to call back today. The trooper told her this sort of thing happens fairly regularly, and that we needed to give it a little more time, since he was doing this tour by himself and all. That same trooper just got off the phone with her twenty minutes ago. I have my doubts that he's even still in the area. I figured he may have hit Fall Creek for a day or so, then left the area. But the woman insists he never would have gone this long without checking in. The trooper is convinced something has gone afoul and it's time to get serious about trying to find the brother."

"I think you're right. But I'm sure this situation has nothing to do with the Bruington case," said Dowdy. "There's no reason it would."

"Well, let's hope not, Lieutenant. As soon as you and I get off the phone, I'm going to get three troopers out to Fall Creek with the photos and have them start asking questions. Did you want to get your department going on anything yet?"

"We don't even know if the guy is in the area. And with that area being so large, unless we can narrow things down to a specific area, I think we'd best hold off. If the guy is out there somewhere, and he's been missing for ten days, or at least six or seven, chances are he's dead. Did the sister tell you guys how long he's been on that tour of his?"

"Yes. He left Lusk, Wyoming on June 1rst and came through Idaho and eastern Oregon before getting to Lowell."

"Well, he's obviously in great physical condition. I'll send one of my men over to pick up some copies of the photos and get the description and any other information you can give us on the case. If you figure anything out will you let me know?"

"We'll be looking for him. I'll keep you updated Lieutenant."

"Good."

Thursday evening, on the phone with the hippie—

"Del, I hadn't told you any of this before now because I was hoping it would work itself out."

"What haven't you told me?"

"Last Friday, the OSP got a call from a woman in Wyoming concerned about her bicycling brother who hadn't checked in with her in a week. Apparently he was on a summer-long bicycle tour alone throughout the northwest states. He had been checking in every three days or less and hasn't contacted her since making the call to her from Lowell two weeks ago tomorrow."

"Why should I care about any of that?"

"He told the sister that he was going to check out the Fall Creek area."

"I'm listening."

"In six days, myself and the other troopers involved out there have not run across him or his bike. And no one we have talked to, or shown the photos of him to, knows anything about him."

"So, obviously, he's not out there. That doesn't take a rocket scientist to figure out, does it?"

"It's not quite that clear. The sister swears he wouldn't have left the area and gone somewhere else without first checking in with her."

"People do that kind of stuff all the time."

"Not this guy. At least not according to his sister."

"How old a guy is he?"

"He's twenty-four, a Nelson State University graduate with a bachelor's in Wildlife Biology. He was actually planning to go for a master's degree in a year or so. That's what the sister said, anyway."

"So he's touring all over by himself on his bike? If that were you or me and we ran across some babe bonanza like Fall Creek, what would we do?"

"Yeah, that's what I told them at the Department. And they all agreed. At least, when we first got the report last Friday, everyone agreed. The trooper who handled her call and requested the photos told the sister he probably hooked up with one of those hot babes in their skimpy bikinis, and is having the time of his life. But it's now been thirteen days since he last checked in. That's too long, and everyone that's heard about it believes something is afoul, that he's had an accident or something."

"But that could have happened a long way from Fall Creek."

"We know that. But still, that's the only place he was known to be going to."

"So how does that affect me?"

"Del, my captain contacted Lieutenant Dowdy about it on Monday."

"And Dowdy's on the case?"

"No. At least not yet, he isn't. But the captain said he's going to get back in touch with him first thing in the morning and bring him in on it."

"Has anything more been said about that hunter?"

"Yes, actually. Dowdy mentioned it as soon as the captain told him about the missing Wyoming man."

"Does anyone think there's a connection?"

"No. And, obviously, you and I know there isn't."

"So there's really no problem, right? You said yourself that neither you nor any other troopers have picked up any information indicating the Wyoming man was seen by anyone up there."

"That's true. But Dowdy's a good detective, and he has a nose."

"I guess his nose isn't that good. He hasn't figured out the other thing yet—nor will he."

"I'm still nervous about that, Del."

"Well don't be. And you better not say anything about anything around Dowdy."

"Don't worry, I won't."

"I've got to get going. Let me know whatever you hear."

"I will. I'd stay completely out of that area right now."

"You're probably right."

33

The Shack

The next evening, Friday, on the phone-

"Del, they've picked up a lead on the Wyoming man today."

"What kind of lead?"

"A swimmer at Dolly Varden Bridge, a middle-aged man, said the Wyoming guy was at the bridge two weeks ago with his girl-friend, some hot blonde babe that the man said he had seen there earlier in the summer."

"I thought you said the guy was on this tour alone?"

"I did, but apparently he's picked up some good baggage along the way. *The lucky stiff.*"

"Yeah, you said that right. The man was sure it was the Wyoming guy?"

"No doubt about it. Dowdy showed him two photos. Apparently the guy had done a show-off dive off the bridge. There was quite a fuss. A number of people, including this man, thought he'd had a diving accident. Three people jumped in after him, but it turned out the Wyoming guy was just pulling a gag for the benefit of his girlfriend. The man Dowdy talked to said he was on the bridge when the girlfriend chewed the guy out for scaring her and the rest of them. But he saw them on the beach together a little later and figured they must have patched things up."

"We've all been there, haven't we? So they know he's got a girlfriend with him now. He's probably holed up with her somewhere getting high and drunk and laid to his heart's content. If I were him, I wouldn't call my sister either. She'd probably lecture him on letting himself get side-tracked from his trip by a broad. The sister's probably a first class bitch too."

"You're sure assuming a lot, Del."

"I'd put all my money on it. That's how I'd handle it if I was that cowboy. Damn I'd like to have a hot, young babe myself."

"Too bad Dowdy isn't buying that whole scenario so cleanly."

"No? What's he saying?"

"I haven't talked to him myself. Just going on what the captain told me. Dowdy's going to try to find out if anyone else up there knows the girlfriend. He thinks it's possible they just met while he was up Fall Creek, and the gal could be someone from this area."

"Well let's hope so. Then they can track down the two of them and break up their love fest."

"You sure have it all figured out, don't you, Del?"

"Prove me wrong."

"I hope you're right, actually. I've just been thinking, maybe we should sneak into the shack and close down our operation."

"You're awful nervous, Butch."

"Tell me I shouldn't be. Let's just say Dowdy gets the information on how to find that gal, and the Wyoming guy isn't with her. Then what?"

"She'll probably know where he is."

"But still, he hasn't checked in with the sister since he was seen with the chick at Dolly Varden Bridge. They're going to believe he's still up Fall Creek. Maybe they'll even search for him from the air using light planes or helicopters. They might find the shack."

"You're worrying too much. We made sure you can't see the

shack from the air. Not with those huge trees as an overhead canopy and then the jungle netting and vines growing over it all. They'll never see it from the air."

"Don't you think we ought to go in there discreetly and make sure everything's alright? I don't know, Del. There's something about this guy missing, and knowing he was last seen for sure at Dolly Varden Bridge later the same day he called his sister in Wyoming. There's something about that that tells me he may still be up there.

"Come on, Butch. That's ridiculous."

"Oh, there's one other thing. The captain mentioned the possibility of putting the Wyoming man's photo in the Register-Guard, and on the local news channels, with an appeal for anyone that saw him in the Fall Creek area to contact either the Oregon State Police or Lane County Sheriff's Departments. I'm worried that will get a lot of people poking around up there."

"That definitely could be a problem," said Del. "Meet me at the Jasper Store in an hour in your camo's. We've got to get up to the shack by way of Little Fall Creek tonight and look around. We may have to move everything down into the tunnel for the time being.

That evening at the shack, well after dark, after lighting up the lantern inside and looking things over—

"There's no evidence anyone's been up in here, Del."

"If it wasn't for that damn deer hunter last fall, chances are we wouldn't have a thing to worry about now. But Dowdy's bound to try to make some connection between the two if that Wyoming kid doesn't turn up soon."

"Maybe we would have been better off to put that hunter in some other area of Fall Creek, completely away from this side of the hill?"

"We already discussed that earlier, don't you remember? We had to put him where we did since he was camped at Puma Creek. If we had moved him somewhere else, they'd have found this shack a long time ago searching this whole mountain for him. It worked out the only way it could have. If we're lucky, they'll put the appeal in the paper and the gal and him will see it and contact the police to say he's fine, that he just got side-tracked."

"It's possible they're not even together."

"Why would a young stud like that, who has the whole summer to do whatever he wants, and go anywhere he wants, not take advantage when he meets a hot, young filly?"

"Not everybody is like us, Del. Sometimes I think you forget that."

"Yeah, tell me one young, college-age guy that wouldn't love to be in the cowboy's boots right now. Though I doubt he's worn them much since he met that babe."

"What if something did happen to him somewhere up in these woods?"

"You said yourself, you and the other troopers have been all up and down Fall Creek and haven't turned up a thing on him, except for what that guy at Dolly Varden Bridge said. If he's got a bike, the bike would have been in a campground or somewhere, wouldn't it, Butch?"

"Not necessarily, he could have stashed it somewhere and then gone for a hike, had an accident in some canyon and who knows what."

"With the girl?"

"Your still assuming the girl is with him. What if the sister is right that he would have stuck to his tour and only been side-tracked temporarily by the girl? Maybe exchanged phone numbers and addresses to hook up later?"

"Alls I can say to that is, if that's true, he doesn't have half the libido I had at that age."

"Well, some people actually make plans, have goals, and stick to them, no matter what."

"What are you implying with that? I definitely didn't like the sound of that comment."

"Seriously, Del. They are the minority, no doubt about it. But some people do stick to their guns."

"Not this cowboy. Not in a babe bonanza like Fall Creek in the summer."

"Well, I think we need to keep all the options open."

"We will. Don't worry. We will. Now let's get all this paraphernalia, the propane tanks, everything, down into the tunnel. They'll never find the tunnel, or even think there could be one. As much as I hated those gooks, I learned a lot about jungle warfare from them. The tunnels were probably the most useful."

"How could you stand to go down in those holes? Just the thought of it makes me stir crazy, and that's without putting all the booby traps, or armed soldiers, down in there waiting for me."

"Yeah, most guys couldn't do it. You had to be built pretty small and wiry just to fit in there. And then you had to be crazy enough to do it."

"What'd you take down there with you?"

"I took a flashlight, a sawed-off shotgun, my Colt .45 with a couple extra magazines, and some grenades. If I was lucky, I'd actually have someone else to go down with me. That always gave you a little better feeling about doing it."

"Not me. No way you could have paid me enough to be that stupid."

"Stupid probably. Dumb as an ass, definitely." They both laughed.

Butch could see that Del had come a long way in his recovery in the months since coming apart up on the top of Mt. June last fall. He was seeing some of the Del he remembered years ago before he went to Vietnam. Butch had often wondered over the years, if his dad had lived if he would have come back from the war as screwed up as Del had. Sometimes he really missed his dad and all the fun they had together when he was a young kid. *That damn war!*

After they got their operation shifted below, leaving nothing incriminating in the shack, Del suggested they go check his punji pits to see if they caught the black bear that had broken into the shack five weeks back. Upon discovering the break in, Del had constructed the pits. Butch was impressed with their potential, but had expressed some concern over a human falling in them. Del had assured him they would only leave them unobstructed for a month or so, and they both knew no one, other than the dumb hunter, ever hiked up around that area. That was one of the reasons Del had chosen that location for building the shack and running his meth and marijuana operation from there to begin with.

Del didn't hold out much hope of getting a bear simply because they normally move slowly and deliberately. It was unlikely a bear would commit itself to that fatal step, though he thought if it came from the side the log was on at the one pit, it was possible. He did, however, believe they might get a deer in one, though. He figured once he had actually trapped a deer, he would go to checking the pits every couple days, so the meat could still be salvaged. He had only checked the pits twice before and been disappointed to have no action. This would be the first time Butch had gone along for the check.

The first pit, only two hundred yards away from the shack, was undisturbed.

"Let's get this thing covered up with those small logs there," Del pointed his flashlight at a fallen, broken up twelve-inch diameter alder tree thirty feet away. "Then we'll cover it up with some dead branches. We can't take a chance of anyone having an accident if they do end up getting a ton of people up in the woods looking for the cowboy and his girl friend."

After getting the pit safely covered and hidden, Butch said, "I feel a whole lot better now."

"It's just a safety precaution for the time being. I don't expect anyone will come within a mile of this area. After this all blows over, we'll put these pits back into action and see what we can scare up."

Del led the way by flashlight to the other pit two hundred yards away. When they got within about thirty yards, Del noticed a change in the way the ground looked on the near side of the log.

"Hey, I think we had some action, Butch." He sped up the pace, then said, "You damn right we had some action!"

They were both nervous with the excitement only a trapper can understand as they closed the final fifteen yards to reach the pit. As Butch hustled up beside Del to look into the pit, he said, "Oh no, Del. That's no animal!"

Del was speechless. It was like everything inside him had shut down. He dropped to his knees at the edge of the pit, sobbing. Butch couldn't believe their bad luck. He knelt down to see if there was any sign of life in the pit. But there was none. *The pit had worked perfectly.* It had done its job.

Butch suddenly turned and crawled a few feet away from the pit and vomited. The stench from the rotting flesh in the pit and the maggots was more than he could take. When he felt like he might have his stomach under control he returned to the edge, to the right side of Del, and peered in again.

They both stared for what seemed like several minutes at the mangled, bloody, rotting body, the tips of the home-made vine-maple punji sticks protruding several inches out of its back.

Finally Del said, "I didn't. I didn't. How could I have? This wasn't supposed to happen. No one ever comes up this way this time of year. Even you know that. We've never had anyone up here except that odd-ball hunter last deer season. What was this guy doing up here?"

"I don't know what to say, Del. I really don't. We already deliberately killed one guy over this drug operation. Now this. I can't be part of any of it anymore. I don't know how I'm going to be able to live with it. This has to be that biker from Wyoming."

"What the hell was he doing up here anyway? He has the whole United States of America to take his bike tour on and to hike in and he comes up into our woods. Damn him! It don't mean nothin'."

Butch was seeing first-hand the technique Del used many times in Vietnam when a terrible thing happened around him, to him, or because of him. He'd get terribly angry. By being angry he didn't have to feel any other emotions. He didn't have to feel any guilt. That technique had served him well in the Nam.

"It looks like birds have been tearing at the back through the clothes," said Butch.

"Yeah, and some animal has torn at his arm and chewed on his side. I saw plenty of this over there. It was bad enough when it was the enemy. But sometimes we found some of our own guys. One time we found three of our guys tied up off the ground on a tree trunk, stripped naked, with their bodies skinned from the neck down. Their balls were cut off and held in their mouths by a stick jammed through their lips. The Viet Cong played very dirty."

Butch didn't respond. This wasn't the enemy. And this was their doing, not the work of the Viet Cong.

He suddenly felt terribly sorry for Del. What that war had taken from him. Man, what that war had taken from Butch. And now that war had taken two other humans—one on purpose to avoid the complications of a drug bust and prison time for a crazy Vietnam veteran. And now an innocent hiker falling into a booby trap the crazy veteran learned in Vietnam. This can't be real, he thought. But he knew it was.

"What are we going to do, Del?"

"What can we do? It was an accident. Totally an accident! But this kind of trap is illegal on public lands. I don't know if it's legal anywhere other than in third-world countries. Damn it worked good. Damn it. Why did it have to be a human? Damn him for coming up here. We don't have any choice, Butch. We have to bury the whole thing right where it's at. If we reported it, they'd get us for first-degree murder. And then they'd find the shack, maybe the tunnel, then figure out that we were involved with the deer hunter. There's no turning back."

"So we just bury him right here?"

"Do you want to try to move that mess? You can't keep from

puking as it is."

"Are we going to burn the shack?"

"We can't burn the shack. The woods are too dry. We'd start a major forest fire. We both know that. But we come back up tomorrow and thoroughly wipe it down with cleaner to remove any fingerprints, anything that could connect us to it. Then tomorrow night we come back up and haul everything out of the tunnel, close off the entrance to it, then get our stuff the hell out of here. We'll have to come over from Little Fall Creek again. Chances are no one will even come anywhere near here looking for him. But we can't take that chance."

"I'm with you. We've got to clean that shack so they can't possibly connect it to either of us. Then we never come up here again."

"Right. End of story. Now get back to the shack and grab a couple of shovels. Too bad we couldn't just get a back-hoe in here."

"That's not even funny," said Butch, as he turned to follow the rays of his flashlight back toward the shack.

As Del continued to stare at the bloody mess in the hole—that until recently was a vibrant, intelligent, young man from Lusk, Wyoming—he wondered, why couldn't the war have ended over there? It seems like everything I do turns to crap. And now I've turned my best friend's son into a killer. I was supposed to be a dad to him, but not me. You can't make a dad out of a killer. I was a fool to ever try to be a dad to him.

Then he heard himself say out loud, "I'm sorry, Coach. I'm so sorry. I turned your wonderful son into a drug maker and a killer. I should have been the one who tripped that 'bouncing-betty' that day. Not you."

Ten minutes later, Butch returned with two round-tip shovels, and the two of them took the dirt that was piled up against the log and filled in the hole, covering up the bicyclist from Wyoming. As they worked, Del said, "We're going to have to find this guy's bike and get rid of it."

"He must have stashed it in the brush real well, because our troopers and the Sheriff's deputies have cruised the edges of all the paved and gravel roads in the whole area looking for him and his bike. But it's got to be off of one of the roads that encircles this area. Who knows how far he hiked. That bike could be who knows where. Obviously with the law all over Fall Creek we aren't going to look for the bike during daylight hours."

"Yeah, but in the beam of a flashlight, the reflection off it should be easier to find," Del suggested. "You're going to have to really stay on top of whatever the cops are doing up here."

After the body and punji points were completely covered, they both stepped around on the dirt in the pit to compact it down. Then they continued to add dirt and pressed it down some more.

"Tomorrow we can do a thorough job of blending this whole area into the surroundings, even set some small logs and brush in disarray over the grave," said Del.

"Yeah, when were done, nobody will ever find it."

"At least no one except maybe an *archeologist* in 2050, long after we're both dead."

34

Fall Creek Inquiries

First thing Saturday morning, the Oregon State Police and the Lane County Sheriff's Department sent several officers each to canvas the Fall Creek area in hopes of gaining more information about Mitch Walton or his girlfriend.

At just after two in the afternoon, while Sheriff's Deputy Ryan Folkner was parked at Dolly Varden Campground talking with several young adults at one campsite, a late-model compact Ford pulled off the edge of the campground road fifty yards away and parked. Four college-age gals got out carrying towels and started to double back toward Dolly Varden Bridge.

"That's her!" said one of the young women next to the deputy. "That's the girlfriend. I've seen her up here before."

"That is her!" chimed in another. "Let me see that photo of the boyfriend again?" She grabbed the photo out of one of the young men's hands. "Definitely. They were here two weeks ago. I talked to her that Sunday, early in the afternoon before they left. I think her name is Monique. No, it's Monica."

Deputy Folkner immediately took the photos back and told the young people to wait there. He then walked briskly up the road to catch up with the four young women who were all dressed in bikinis.

"Ma'am. Monica!" he shouted.

The girls stopped and looked around.

Upon seeing the sheriff deputy, Monica answered, "I'm Monica."

"Yes. Monica. I need to talk with you."

She couldn't imagine what the deputy could want with her, but the four girls waited for him to reach them near where the campground road met Fall Creek Road.

"Monica, I understand you were up here two weeks ago with your boyfriend. Is that right?"

"No," she said, puzzled. "I don't even have a boyfriend. We broke up over a month ago."

"Several people up here have said you were up here two weeks ago with your boyfriend."

Monica looked at her friends trying to figure out where the deputy could have heard that.

"This is your boyfriend, isn't it?" He handed her the two copied photos he had of Mitch Walton.

Immediately recognizing him, she said, "No, he's not my boyfriend. Not yet anyway. We met up here two weeks ago. We hung out for less than twenty-four hours."

"So you were here with him, right?"

"I met him for the first time here on the bridge. We hit it off real well. He hung out for the rest of that day, slept in our campsite and hung out for the next morning, then left on his bike. That's the only time I've ever seen or talked to him. Why, what's going on?"

"He's missing."

"What do you mean he's missing?"

"His sister in Wyoming called and reported him missing over a week ago. She said he should have called in to her three or four days before that, but never did. And he still hasn't called in."

"You're not serious are you, deputy?"

"I'm very serious. Do you know where he was going when he left here?"

"He headed farther up Fall Creek. Said he was going to check it out then continue his summer-long bicycle tour."

"You said he wasn't you're boyfriend *yet*. Did you guys exchange contact information, phone numbers or addresses, or anything?"

"Yes. Like I said, we really hit it off and were planning to keep in touch. He even mentioned maybe coming out here to go to the U of O, where I attend."

"And you haven't heard anymore?"

"He said he would call when he got back home, maybe before that. Nothing definite. But we both knew we wanted to get to know each other better."

As the young deputy admired Monica's beautiful, voluptuous figure he could certainly understand why Mitch Walton would want to get to know her better. What he couldn't understand is why he would have left her at all. He thought, she's got to be one of the hottest, most desirable babes I've ever seen. Then getting his mind back to business, he knew he needed to radio dispatch and report locating the girlfriend.

He immediately got on his radio and reported the girl. Within ten minutes a state trooper and another sheriff's deputy arrived at the campground, where he was now standing with the girls and other young people near his squad car. Detective Dowdy arrived twenty minutes later.

After talking with Monica, Dowdy said, we need to go through every campground from here on up the creek, get the registry information for the weekend of the 4th and see if Mitch Walton signed in anywhere. That should have been done earlier.

By an hour and a half later it was determined that Mitch had not signed in to any campgrounds on the nights of the 4th and 5th. Nor were there any single campers in any sites those nights. It seemed like another dead end.

Then Lieutenant Dowdy, speaking over his radio from Dolly Varden Campground said, "We're going to have to contact all these campers who were in any of these campgrounds those two nights and ask if any of them talked to a Mitch Walton from Wyoming. I'll get a couple people on that down at the station as soon as we get a list of the names, addresses, and license plate numbers back there. For now talk to everyone you can and find out if anyone remembers seeing this kid or talking to him on the 4th or 5th."

He then said to Monica, "You said you live in Lowell. When did you go home from your camping trip that weekend?"

"My girlfriends and I only stayed here Friday and Saturday nights. I got home about three-thirty Sunday afternoon. With it being so close to home, we pop up here anytime we want."

"I don't blame you," said Dowdy. "But that means Mitch Walton could have come back through here anytime after you left on his way out and you wouldn't have been here."

"That's right. Do you think that's what he did?"

"I can't say. I have no idea. You were the last person that we know of, so far, to talk to him. I'm sure if you had been here when he came back out he would have stopped. What do you think?"

"I'm sure he would have. We really hit it off well. I was really excited about the possibilities. I think he was too."

Dowdy thought, I can understand why he would be.

Monica actually reminded Dowdy of an older version of his own beautiful cheerleader daughter who would be a senior in the upcoming year. He was also reminded of how beautiful, how youthful, how care-free his wife, Katie, was at that age. He thought, she's still the most beautiful woman in the world, maybe not as carefree as she was back then, but even more beautiful.

Dowdy hoped that somehow there would be a happy ending to this Mitch Walton-Monica story. But he seriously doubted there would be. He knew it had been way too long since Mitch had contacted his sister in Wyoming, and the chances that he was still alive, wherever he was, were slim.

Only one other person up Fall Creek over the weekend had ever seen or knew anything about Mitch Walton. A man in his late-twenties had also seen Mitch on Dolley Varden Bridge on the 4th. Unfortunately, none of the campers up Fall Creek the weekend of the 4th, who the sheriff's department had contacted, knew anything about him either. There were still a dozen campers that hadn't been reached and a deputy was still trying to contact them.

Dowdy had not activated the Lane County Search and Rescue Team yet.

Finally, late-Monday afternoon, the deputy making calls to the remaining Fall Creek campers made contact with a couple in Florence, Oregon that definitely remembered Mitch Walton. The deputy immediately patched the woman through to Lieutenant Dowdy, who happened to be in his office.

"This is Lieutenant Dowdy. I understand you talked with Mitch Walton up Fall Creek over the weekend of July 4th."

"That's right. A wonderful young man," said the woman. "He stayed in the campsite right next to us on Saturday night."

"He did? And which campground was that in? I didn't get that information from the other deputy before taking the call."

"Puma Creek."

The words hit Dowdy like a slap in the face. "You said, 'Puma Creek?'"

"That's right—Puma Creek Campground. We were in campsite 6, and he was in 7."

Dowdy was puzzled. He had looked at all the rosters for campsites that night and not one of them listed Mitch Walton. He thought there must be a mistake.

"Ma'am, I'm sorry, I didn't get your name."

"Ruby Carter. My husband Robert and I live on Rhododendron

Drive northwest of Florence."

"And you were camped in site 7 at Puma Creek Campground over the 4th of July weekend?"

"Campsite 6. The Walton boy was in 7."

"Can you hold for a minute Mrs. Carter?" Immediately he beeped the other deputy on the intercom and asked him to bring the camper roster into his office. In twenty seconds Dowdy had the list.

"Yes, Mrs. Carter. I see you were in campsite 6, but the only people signed into site 7 were a man and woman. A Will Bender and a Julie Temple."

"There must be some mistake," she said. "Here, I'll let you talk to my husband, Robert."

"This is Robert Carter. My wife said there seems to be some confusion on the name of the person camped in site 7 at Puma Creek. What's this all about anyway?"

"Yes, sir. Mr. Carter, our deputy contacted you folks because we are trying to get information on a missing person, Mitch Walton, from Wyoming—"

"That Walton boy is missing? Since when?"

"We're actually still trying to figure that out. So you definitely met and spoke with a Mitch Walton on Saturday July 4th at Puma Creek Campground?"

"Absolutely. Wonderful young man. Very respectful—not one of those 'earth first' hippies, just a wonderful young man. Even joined us in our campsite for spaghetti dinner. My wife's an excellent cook."

"How many nights was he there?"

"Well, that was the only part that struck us a bit odd." Dowdy wondered what was coming. "He came in some time after five Saturday evening, took the only open campsite, number 7 next to us, and then was gone when we got up at 7:30 Sunday morning. We were both surprised. We were hoping he would stick out the week-end. But he was on a summer-long bicycling tour by himself. We figured he was just independent and wanted to keep moving. He said something about going for a hike on Sunday."

"Did he say where he was going hiking?"

"No. We figured it would probably be somewhere up Fall Creek. But that would only be a guess. For all we know he rode back down from Fall Creek and headed somewhere else miles away."

"That's what I'm afraid of," said Dowdy.

"Do you have any idea what might have happened to him?"

"I don't know, but I don't think it was anything good. I probably shouldn't tell you this, but a hunter who was camped in your site, number 6, last October during deer season, came up missing and was found shot to death in the hills to the north of there."

"Oh, my gosh!" He turned away from the hand piece and told Ruby.

Dowdy heard her say, "Oh my dear God."

"Have you solved the other murder, I mean that shooting?"

"No. We're still working on it. In the beginning we thought it could have been an accidental shooting by another deer hunter, but we ruled that out. Anyway, I'm sure it's totally unrelated to the Walton boy."

"I sure hope so. Do you think he's in that area?"

"Like I said, I don't know what to think. Fall Creek is a huge area. He could be anywhere. In fact, there's probably a good chance he's not even up there. Without his bike or a campsite with his gear in it, we have nothing to go on. No starting point for a search... Well, I really appreciate the information you folks have given me. I'm going to let you go for now, but I have your number if I need to talk to you further."

"Will you please let us know when you find out what happened to that boy?" said Robert Carter.

"I certainly will. Thanks again for your time and the information. I really am sorry that I had to give you the news."

"If you need any other information, call us."

"I will."

35

No Where to Search

After Lieutenant Dowdy got off the phone with the Carters, he immediately relayed the information he had gleaned to his captain. The captain then contacted the local media requesting they run Walton's photo accompanied by a short explanation saying, "Mitch Walton is a twenty-four-year-old man from Lusk, Wyoming, who was on a summer-long, solo bicycle tour of the Pacific Northwest. He went missing after being last seen in the Fall Creek area on Sunday, July 5th. If anyone has seen or heard from him since then—or found an abandoned, Trek, fourteen-speed, mountain-bike—please contact the Lane County Sheriff or the Oregon State Police."

Dowdy was puzzled why Walton signed in to Puma Creek Campground as a couple under a different name. He guessed it meant one of two things. Either Walton was up to something he shouldn't be, or he just didn't want anyone to be able to keep track of him. With all of the positive he had heard about him, he was certain it was the latter; just a young man who was enjoying his independent summer and didn't want to be accountable to anyone.

He probably wouldn't have even kept in regular contact with the sister in Wyoming if she hadn't insisted on it.

Wednesday, late-afternoon, July 22nd—Dowdy on the phone with Mitch Walton's sister in Lusk, Wyoming. He had spoken to her the first time four days earlier, on Saturday evening; it hadn't gone well for him.

"Ms. Randall, Lieutenant Dowdy, Lane County Sheriff."

"Have you found my brother?"

"No we haven't, but I wanted to update you on the situation."

"Have you searched the woods for him yet?"

"If you'll allow me, Ms. Randall, I'll get to that."

"Go ahead."

"Thank you. I want to start by telling you that on Monday evening we talked with an older couple from the Oregon Coast who talked with Mitch—"

"He's at the Oregon Coast?"

"No, no. This older couple had camped in the same campground at Fall Creek as Mitch did on Saturday night, the 4th, actually in the site next to him. He even had dinner with them. But when they woke up the next morning, he had already pulled out on his bicycle. They had no idea where he was going, but he had said something to them about maybe going for a hike."

"So you know where he went hiking; have you searched there?"

"The couple had no idea where he was going to hike. And here's another problem. Your brother signed in Saturday night in the camp site under the name of Will Bender and he put down the name Julie Temple as a female camping with him. He said they were from Moscow, Idaho. But the couple from the coast said the guy in that campsite that they had over to dinner with them in their campsite was definitely your brother. Do you know anyone by either of those names, or do you have any idea why he would have used those names instead of just his own?"

"I've never heard of those people. Are you sure it was Mitch then?"

"Definitely. The couple described your brother perfectly, he told them he was from Wyoming, gave his real name, all of it. It was definitely Mitch they met."

"I don't know why he would do that. Do you have any idea?"

"I figure he probably didn't want to have to be accountable to anyone, because he was free-lancing the whole trip."

"That sounds reasonable. But he still would have kept in contact with me like he was doing."

"I'm not questioning that. I wish I could tell you that I know he's alright. But at this point, I think even you know that's not likely the case. The Oregon State Police and the Lane County Sheriff's Department have been making every reasonable effort to find your brother, and will continue to. We've even run his photo, and said he was missing, in the local newspapers and on TV. We included an appeal for anyone with possible information to contact local law enforcement. We've received several calls from people offering to help in a search, or just asking about him. But only two who reported seeing him or knowing anything about him. And unfortunately, they only confirmed what we already knew about him."

"But you haven't searched the woods yet, have you?"

"Look, Ms. Randall. We've had people drive every bit of the hundreds of miles of roads up there looking over the banks and in the ditches. Nothing. And yesterday and today, we sent up a helicopter and a small plane to search from the air. Unfortunately, other than the roads, they really can't see much. Have you ever been out to Oregon? Have you ever seen what the forests in Western Oregon are like?"

"No, I haven't."

"This isn't Wyoming or the Midwest. The timber here is dense. You can't just fly over it and see everything."

"Then why don't you get people searching the woods on foot?"

"You just don't understand, Ma'am. It isn't that simple. There are over two hundred and fifty square miles of rugged, heavily-timbered woods in the Fall Creek area. And, frankly, without a starting point we aren't going to do it. We have no bike, no camping gear. Nothing whatsoever to go on. We can't just send search and rescue people into an area that vast to conduct a search when we don't know your brother is even in that area. He could very easily be many miles away from Fall Creek."

"You don't understand, Lieutenant. I've been trying to tell you, and the state trooper, that Mitch would never have left that area without calling me first."

"I understand what you're saying, Ma'am. Trust me, I really do. But the fact remains, it would take us weeks to search that entire area on foot."

"So you're not even going to look. Is that right?"

"Not until we can nail down a starting point. I know that isn't what you want to hear. But there are a lot of other considerations. Trust me, if we find a starting point, we won't hesitate to get our people into the woods on foot. That's the best I can tell you. I've got to get going now. But we will keep you informed of any new developments. I know this is difficult for you, and I completely understand. We will keep looking. I will talk to you later."

"Thanks a lot," she said sarcastically.

After Lieutenant Dowdy got off the phone with Becky Randall, and had a conversation with his own captain, he called and talked to OSP Captain Burton telling him of his conversation with Walton's sister. The OSP captain said his trooper had run into the same attitude from the sister. But none of them could blame her for feeling the way she did.

Dowdy concluded the conversation by telling Captain Burton that he and his own captain felt at this point both departments had done about all they could. Dowdy said they weren't going to send the chopper or plane back up because they didn't feel it would accomplish anything. None of the lawmen had any way of knowing if Walton's disappearance involved a crime, an accident, or if he just skipped the country. If they received any helpful information from the public, they would move forward. Otherwise, all they could do now was to continue to keep a presence with the two departments in the Fall Creek area, talk to swimmers and others on the weekends and hope something turned up.

On the phone the next morning—

"Del, my captain has informed us that because there is no starting point, there won't be a search on foot for the Wyoming man in the Fall Creek area. We're in the clear."

"That's great news, Butch. And here we cleared everything out of there."

"Don't get any ideas, Del. I'm done up there. I meant it. I've been involved in far too much already."

"Don't get on your high horse with me. We made our mistakes. But it will all pass and things will get back to normal."

"It'll never pass for me, Del. Don't you understand. I'm not like you. I can't just compartmentalize all this crap and go on with my life as if it never happened."

"Well you damn well better never say a word to anyone. I mean it. I made my mistakes. But I can't bring anybody back to life, and I've already lost so much of mine. I'm not going down because of your weakness."

"Damn it, Del! I'm not going to tell anyone anything. But I have to live with what I was part of, and what I did, for the rest of my life. And I'm telling you, I'm through dealing in the drugs or ever doing anything illegal again. The price was way too high for me, and for those two dead men."

"So..."

"Don't worry. I'll still keep in touch with you. But I don't want to be around the dope anymore."

"So you're getting religious on me, huh?"

"Call it whatever you want. I never should have done any of it anyway. I guess I justified it by telling myself the government killed my dad by sending him off to war. That there were no absolutes, that nothing really mattered in life except surviving by whatever means I had to. That's what you always told me. It was all a sort of self-deception. *There is right and wrong*—and I can't live on the wrong side any longer."

36

The Evonuks

From the end of July through mid-September Lieutenant Dowdy, the Lane County Sheriff's Department, and the Oregon State Police accomplished nothing more in solving either the Roger Bruington death or in learning the fate of Mitch Walton. Both cases had gone completely cold, and no more than the normal summer patrols made their rounds in the Fall Creek area. High school and college classes had begun in the last two weeks, and combined with the gradually lower night-time temperatures resulting in a dip in water temperatures, the crowds at Fall Creek had petered out. But there was still a string of campers and other outdoor enthusiasts determined to draw the summer out to the very end.

One such early-fifties-aged couple—Roderick and Sandy Evonuk, from Cave Junction, Oregon—was on the final road trip of the summer when they drove their Ford pickup, pulling their sixteen-foot camp trailer, into Puma Creek Campground late in the afternoon on Tuesday, September 15th. There was one other couple camped there when they arrived, but they were planning to pull out in the morning.

After the Evonuks parked their trailer and got signed in to site 9, they decided they wanted to stretch their legs a bit, so they took a walk along the trail that followed the south bank of Fall Creek on the north side of Puma Creek Campground. It was the same trail Mitch Walton had walked two and a half months earlier, the night before he came up missing. And it was the same trail Roger Bruington's body had been carried over by the rescue team eleven months earlier. But neither of the Evonuks knew any of that. They had been on the road so much of the summer this year that they scarcely had time, or taken the opportunity, to keep up on any of the news happenings in Oregon.

All four of the Evonuks' children were raised and out of the house, the three youngest were still going to college. Their oldest, a son, was married, had a son and daughter and worked as an engineer in Klamath Falls. The Evonuks planned to swing over to spend a few days with him and his family after leaving Fall Creek in four or five days, before returning home.

The Evonuks had met in college years ago when they both attended Oregon State University. Roderick had a master's degree in Cultural Anthropology, while Sandy had a doctorate in *Archeology*. Both had worked long tenures as professors in a couple different universities over the years, and both had done extensive research and written many reports and articles that were published in magazines in their fields.

Both Rod and Sandy had always prided themselves on staying in excellent physical condition. But in recent years, Rod had taken to drinking too much, too frequently, which had put a strain on his and Sandy's relationship. He had always liked to tip the bottle when the occasion presented itself, and had always been a barrel of laughs when he drank too much. But nowadays he often became belligerent once he had half a dozen or more beers under his belt.

After walking perhaps two hundred yards, along the high bank of

Fall Creek, the Evonuks dropped down to the creek. After getting a refreshing drink, Sandy pulled out her topographic map of Fall Creek. The two of them looked it over, and plotted their hike for the next day. They would go up into the old-growth area northwest of Puma Creek. Since it was one of the largest road-less areas in the vicinity, Sandy was sure few people probably ever went in there. She also liked the potential of finding an overhang or two in what showed up on the map as a steep area back up there, not far from Slick Creek.

That evening as they sat at their fire the couple from the other occupied site came over and struck up a conversation. Sandy could see that Rod had drunk enough to begin feeling pretty good, and she was concerned that he was only a couple more beers from moving into the belligerent stage. She quickly discouraged the other couple from staying long by saying, "Rod and I are celebrating our twenty-seventh wedding anniversary by ourselves," In fact, their anniversary was actually two weeks earlier. The other couple picked up on her hint and made a tactful exit five minutes later.

Early the next afternoon, as the Evonuks were hiking toward Slick creek, over two miles north of Fall Creek, Jan noticed something.

"Rod, look at that area over there near that log. Something just doesn't look right about it."

"I can't see what you're talking about."

"Let's get a closer look," she said, immediately heading in that direction.

Upon getting within twenty feet, she said, "Something's been digging under the edge of that brush."

"Do you smell that?" said Rod. "It smells like something dead."

Moving right up to the brush, she said, "Something's definitely dug around here."

"That's probably a bear or cougar kill."

"You're right, Rod. It looks like the animal piled brush over it."

"That's got to be a very possessive animal."

"I don't like it, Rod. We didn't even bring any pepper spray with us."

"If we get caught at this kill by a bear or puma, it may not be repelled by pepper anyway. They can get very cantankerous when anything messes with their food. Why don't you get your camera out and at least get a few quick shots. Then I think we better get away from here."

"Maybe we could come back up here tomorrow and dig it out to see what it is. You could bring your .38 with you."

"It's most likely a deer," he said. "Probably a fawn, but who knows?"

She pulled her 35mm Nikon Camera out of her backpack and snapped several photos from different angles. Then they walked away.

After going a hundred yards, she said, "I don't know what it is, Rod, but I have the feeling we're being watched."

"Oh, you're just nervous because of that stash."

"No, Rod. I really feel like something is watching us."

They both looked all around them, but saw nothing suspicious.

"Let's get out of here," Sandy said. "With all that thick brush, something could be watching us and we'd never see it. I just don't have a good feeling about it."

Though he didn't share Sandy's concern, Rod looked around on the ground as they walked and located a couple of three and four foot branches. He handed one to Sandy and said, "Here, if anything comes out of the brush, at least we'll have something to fend it off with."

Back at their camp site at Puma Creek that evening they had T-bone steaks, tossed green salad, and garlic bread for dinner, and then relaxed near the campfire reading. The other campers were gone, and they were actually glad to have the camp to themselves.

By 7:30 the dark had closed in and they could see the shadows dancing around them as glowing sparks floated away above the fire and quickly went out. In the last hour, the sky that was clear during the day had turned dark. An end-of-summer thunderstorm was in the making. Sandy moved her lawn chair right up against Rod's, and he took the hint by wrapping his right arm around her. He was already feeling good, and continued to swig away at a beer.

At 8:20 they heard a vehicle driving their way. Someone had pulled into the campground. A minute later, an early-seventies vintage, green Ford pickup pulled up at the edge of their campsite and stopped. They were both a bit uncomfortable with that, but figured it was probably just someone wanting some information or looking for someone. By the firelight, they could see there was only one person in the truck, and that there were a couple of rifles resting on the gun rack just in front of the cab's rear window; that made them both a little nervous. But their fears were quickly alleviated when the person got out of the truck without grabbing either gun. As he came around the front of the truck and walked over to them, they could see he was a husky man, probably about six feet and going a couple hundred pounds.

"How are you folks doing tonight?" he asked.

"We're just enjoying the serenity of the evening," Sandy answered, guessing the man to be in his mid-twenties.

"Been camping here long?"

"This is our second night," said Rod, with his speech slightly slurred.

The man looked at the beer can Rod held in his left hand, spotted several empties on the ground beside his chair, and then looked with interest at the full six pack of Schlitz on the table beside him. Sandy noticed, thought about offering him one, but decided to wait.

"You guys from around here?"

"Cave Junction, actually," answered Sandy, a bit nervous that Rod might be approaching that mouthy stage in his drinking.

Then obviously noticing the screening pan and small shovel laying on the opposite end of the wooden picnic table, the stranger asked, "What brings you folks up into these parts?"

Sandy, growing more concerned by the second, quickly answered for both of them, "We've been doing a lot of camping this summer. This is our last stop."

"What are you doing with that screen and shovel?"

"We're scientists. My husband's an anthropologist, and I'm an archeologist."

"Did you find anything interesting today?"

All of a sudden, both Rod and Sandy felt a chill run up their spines wondering if Sandy had actually been right that something had been watching them in the woods. Could this man have been watching them?

"Nothing special," Rod got an answer in.

"I was beginning to wonder if you always let her do all your talking for you."

Rod, a slightly built man at only five-seven and a hundred forty pounds, suddenly wished he had the .38 pistol that was in a drawer in the camp trailer. He didn't know what to say, but had enough beers in him to know he wasn't going to let this stranger disrespect him.

"Cat got your tongue? I was just funnin' with ya."

"We're both a bit on the tired side," said Sandy.

"We're not much into entertaining this evening," added Rod. Sandy couldn't believe he could be so dumb, since this guy seemed to be asking for trouble. In the last three years, she had seen him stick his feet in his mouth more times than she could remember while he was under the influence. But they had never been camped alone way out in the woods with a husky, armed, abrasive stranger when he had done it before. She felt herself beginning to tremble.

"I didn't come here to be entertained either. I was just out for an evening drive and figured I'd swing through here to see if anyone was camping."

"Well you sure ask a lot of questions," said Rod.

"I don't want any trouble with you folks, so I'd suggest that you don't push it with me."

"We were having a good time until you showed up, now would you mind continuing on your evening drive?"

Looking right at Sandy, the stranger said, "You're husband may be smart enough to be a scientist, but when it comes to controlling his mouth when he's been drinking, he doesn't seem to know when to shut up."

"Please, mister, we don't want any trouble. My husband has had a few too many to drink." She suddenly got up from her chair, grabbed the six pack and said, "Here, you can have these. But would you please just leave us be."

Rod immediately stood and tried to grab the beer back from her while saying, "You aren't giving my damn beer to some damn, rude stranger."

The man stepped back and said, "You better take a seat, mister, while you still can. The only reason I haven't dealt with you before now is because I don't want to bloody your face in front of your beautiful wife. But you've about pushed me to my limit."

"Please," Sandy begged him, "would you please leave. We don't want any trouble. Please. My husband doesn't mean anything."

"I can speak for myself, Sandy. The guy's a complete idiot thinking he can come into our campsite and threaten me in front of my wife."

Rod lunged at the man with his right fist. The man caught his hand in his own right hand and grabbed his right triceps with his left, swung him past him on the right and flung him to the ground.

"You barked up the wrong tree tonight you old bastard. I just wanted to be a friendly neighbor. Now look what you've done."

"That's bullcrap!" Rod said, now trying to get back to his feet. "You ask us what we found. We know you were up in those woods today. What are you hiding up there anyway?"

"You're a dumb old bastard. Can't you see you're whipped?"

Sandy begged, "Please, mister. Leave now, before it gets any worse. You can't hold what a drunk says against him."

"I'm a drunk? My own wife thinks I'm a drunk? I'll show you who's a drunk." Rod got to his feet and charged the big stranger.

The stranger was ready for him and under hooked his arms with his and slung him onto the edge of the table. There was an obvious cracking sound, as Rod cried out in pain and fell to the ground.

"Look what you've done to my husband," Sandy screamed, dropping the beer and then beating on the man's head and shoulders with her fists.

"You damn bitch!" The man grabbed her by the throat and began choking her, while Rod lay on the ground groaning and barely moving his arms. Blood trickled out the side of his mouth.

Sandy scratched the man's right cheek with her left hand, but within thirty seconds she quit struggling. The man laid her back on top of the table and held her throat for a few more minutes to make sure she was dead. Then he began kicking Rod in the head and face to finish him off. Five minutes later he was back in his truck on his way out of Puma Creek Campground and down Fall Creek Road.

37

They Got Him

At eleven fifteen the next morning, Thursday, September 17th, 1981—

"Lane County Sheriff's Dispatch."

A frantic voice on the other end said, "There's been a double murder!"

"Where are you calling from?"

"I'm at the last house on Fall Creek Road, above the reservoir.

"Are you sure the people are dead?"

"Yes, they're dead!"

"One second, please?" The dispatcher immediately relayed the caller's message to the closest deputy in the field, who was near the Jasper Store in Jasper.

"Are you by yourself?"

"Yes, except for the people who live here; they're letting me use their phone."

"Are the victims family or friends of yours?"

"No. I was just driving through the campground after fishing this morning and found them."

"So the victims are in a campground?"

"Yes."

"Which campground?"

"Puma Creek."

"Do you know how the victims were killed?"

"No. Well, the man looks like he was beaten to death. His face is all messed up and there's a pool of blood around his head. The woman is just lying dead on the top of a picnic table."

"So there is one dead man and one dead woman?"

"That's correct."

"I want you to stay where you are. We have a couple of deputies on the way now, and we'll have a couple state troopers in the area shortly as well. What is the address where you are calling from?"

He gave the address then stayed on the line until the first deputy had arrived at Puma Creek Campground thirty minutes later, and the dispatcher let him hang up after getting his name, address and phone number and telling him to stay where he was until a deputy had a chance to come by and speak with him. Lieutenant Dowdy and Doug Villard, the County Coroner, were also on their way to the campground.

At Puma Creek Campground at 1:20 pm—

"What is it with this Puma Creek Campground?" asked Coroner Villard, as he and Dowdy took photos of the victims and the crime scene.

"I'm beginning to think maybe we need to close it down," answered Dowdy. "It seems like I've been spending half my time out here the last year."

"Well you really can't make any connection between that Wyoming kid and any of this can you?"

"I'm beginning to wonder about that. What are the chances that none of these incidents is related?"

"It could just be a fluke, Lieutenant. This couple was beaten-to-death, not shot. And you don't have a clue about what happened to that kid, right?"

"No, I don't. But I think I'm going to have to go back over every scrap of evidence on him and the Bruington murder. As tantalizing as it's been to blame the government or CIA for Bruington's death, these killings and the Walton boy coming up missing from around here … I don't know. It's just too coincidental."

"We have no obvious evidence left here by the killer," said Villard.

"It's possible his fingerprints could be on one or more of these beer cans. We'll take them all in and dust them at the station. Judging by the condition of both victims' bodies, there was quite a struggle. If we're lucky, the killer had some physical injury, possibly to his face, that someone will notice. The news people should be here any minute. I talked to the Captain, and he's going to see that this ends up all over the news tonight and in the papers first thing in the morning. If the killer has been injured and has contact with other people, maybe someone who sees the news will contact us with a tip."

"Wouldn't that be nice."

"I think we have a much better chance with this guy than the other two situations."

At Del's house on Wallace Creek that evening—

"Del, you won't believe this."

"Won't believe what?"

"There was a double homicide at Puma Creek Campground last night, a husband and wife from Cave Junction."

"Are you serious?"

"I couldn't be more serious."

"How were they killed?"

"She was choked. He was beaten to death."

"Is Dowdy on the case?"

"Of course he is."

"Have you heard if they're trying to connect these two murders with the hunter last year?"

"Oh they're definitely looking at that possibility. And don't forget the other guy who was last seen and talked to at Puma Creek."

"Trust me, Butch, I'll never be able to forget the other one. I dream about that damn kid a couple times a week."

"Me too. We'll I've got to run."

"Keep me posted."

At the Sheriff's Office Friday morning—

"Corporal Easton, I really think it's time you and I get back up in those woods above Puma Creek and cover every inch of them. I have this darn feeling there's something yet to be discovered. And I believe these killings yesterday are somehow tied to all of it."

"I'm game, Lieutenant. Do we want to take anyone else up there with us?"

"Not right now. Other than I would like to take Dick Eastbrook."

"Why do you want him to go?"

"I just do. Call it instinct if you will. He knew Roger's hunting techniques. Maybe something will fall into place for him once we get back up in the woods."

"I'll trust your judgment on that Lieutenant."

That evening on Jasper-Fall Creek Road, OSP Trooper Bryan Wilson has just pulled over an east-bound, green, early 70's model, Ford pickup, with two rifles on the gun rack visible through the back window—

"Do you know why I pulled you over?" asked Wilson, as he pointed his flashlight beam into the Ford's driver's face.

"I don't have a clue."

"Your left tail light is broken. May I have your driver's license, vehicle registration and proof of insurance?"

The man retrieved his license from his wallet and then reached into the glove compartment for the other two items. As he did so, Trooper Wilson released the strap on his service .38 with his right hand and grabbed the pistol by its handle. At the same time he remained standing just back of the driver's side door, prepared to take evasive action if necessary.

After getting the three items from the pickup's driver without incident, Wilson proceeded cautiously to his truck and called in the license number to the dispatcher. He had previously called in the plate numbers upon pulling the pickup over. Dispatch came back two minutes later with the report the driver, Edward Dils Rierdan, was on probation for third-degree misdemeanor assault.

With that information, Trooper Wilson, walked cautiously back up to the driver's side door of the truck and handed the three items back to Rierdan. When Rierdan reached for the items, Wilson noticed a fresh scab on his left thumb, and asked, "What'd you do to your thumb?"

"Huh? Oh, I did that working on my truck a couple days ago."

Rierdan's hesitation aroused Wilson's skepticism and curiosity. Something about his response didn't seem right, so he said, "Have you been staying out of trouble? I understand you're on probation for assault."

At that comment, Rierdan unconsciously turned his head more toward the open driver's window allowing the light from Wilson's flashlight to illuminate the right side of his face for the first time. Rierdan said, "I catch enough crap from my probation officer. I don't need it from you too."

With the new view, Wilson noticed something on Rierdan's right cheek. Between the scab on the thumb and the mark on Rierdan's cheek, Wilson's mind went into overdrive. Then it hit him. The Puma Creek killings… *The killer might have fresh wounds.*

He said, "Wait here, I've got to take a call on my radio." As Wilson started to move away from Rierdan's truck, suddenly Rierdan reached for one of his rifles. Wilson immediately drew his pistol and took three quick steps to the open driver's window of the truck and pointed his barrel into Rierdan's face.

"Put your hands on the steering wheel NOW, where I can see them, and stay in the seat!"

With his left hand, Wilson removed his radio and said, "Code 11-99, milepost 8 Jasper-Fall Creek Road."

Dispatch acknowledged Wilson's request and said they were sending deputies to his assistance.

Five minutes later, the first Lane County sheriff deputy pulled in behind Trooper Wilson's pickup, immediately got out, drew his pistol and moved to the front edge of the OSP rig. Upon seeing that Wilson was standing two feet away from the green Ford with his pistol pointed into the cab, Deputy Lohner, asked, "Is there just the one suspect?"

"Yes. I have him contained, but need your assistance in taking him into custody."

At once, Lohner moved in to assist.

"Now, get out of the vehicle keeping your hands in plain sight. We don't want this situation to get any worse for you."

Rierdan complied and was immediately taken to the pavement by Deputy Lohner. Both officers pulled Rierdan's arms behind his back while forcing his face against the blacktop. Deputy Lohner cuffed him, and quoted him his rights. Wilson then explained to Lohner how he had noticed the fresh wounds and how Rierdan had reached for his rifles.

Another sheriff deputy and a state trooper pulled up at the same time from opposite directions.

When questioned about the Puma Creek murders, Rierdan denied having anything to do with them, though he acknowledged seeing the stories in the news.

Thirty minutes later, Lieutenant Dowdy met State Trooper Wilson and Deputy Lohner, who transported Rierdan, at the Lane

County Jail. Rierdan was booked on endangering a police officer and suspicion of murder. Deputy Easton arrived as the booking procedures were completed and he, Dowdy, Lohner, and Wilson proceeded into an interrogation room. Rierdan was brought in several minutes later after the officers had time to go over the scenario and the possible connection to the Puma Creek murders.

"Why did you go for your rifle?" asked Wilson.

"I wasn't going for my rifle. I don't know where you got that."

"You reached up and put your hand on your rifle as I started to walk back to my vehicle. You're much better off to co-operate with us."

"You're lying! I did not go for my rifle. You wanted to harass me because I have a record."

"You don't just have a record. You're on probation for misdemeanor assault. Explain the cuts on your thumb and the scratch on your face."

"Like I told you out on the highway, I hurt my thumb working on my truck a couple days ago. I got the scratch on my face when I took my dog for a walk in the woods. I ran into a broken branch."

"We don't believe you," interjected Dowdy, who had an excellent nose for a skunk, at least most the time.

"I don't care whether you believe me or not; that's the truth."

"What were you doing at Puma Creek Campground Wednesday night?"

"I don't know where you got that. I was at home."

"Who can verify that?"

"I was alone."

"We have a witness that saw your truck screaming down Fall Creek Road Wednesday night," said Easton, bluffing.

"That's bull. If you had a witness, the trooper would have arrested me as soon as he pulled me over. Don't try your bluffing bullcrap with me. I'm smarter than that."

"If you were very smart, you wouldn't have made a play for your guns."

"I told you the Stater's lying. He made that up to give him an excuse to continue harassing my ass. He didn't like me as soon as he saw me. He uses his badge to harass people." Then staring right into Wilson's face, Rierdan said, "I'd like to see what you could do without that damn badge and gun to hide behind. I could kick your ass in a New York second."

"Lieutenant, do we have to sit here and listen to his crap?" asked Wilson.

"He's just making the situation worse on himself. He's already looking at a certain felony for endangerment of a police officer. And as soon as his vehicle is examined and his home searched, I'm sure we'll have all we need to put him in the chair. We know he killed that man and woman at Puma Creek. And he knows we know."

"I didn't kill anyone!" Rierdan shouted, stomping his feet on the concrete floor.

"Your only chance to avoid the chair is to cooperate with us."

"That's bullcrap! I'm not saying another word without a lawyer present."

"Do you have a lawyer?"

"No. And I can't afford one."

Dowdy called for the jail guards to take him away. They would talk to him later in the presence of his court-appointed attorney.

After Rierdan was removed from the room, the four lawmen discussed the situation and were all convinced that Rierdan was guilty in the Puma Creek murders, but that they needed to find incriminating evidence. His truck was impounded with the Sheriff's department, and Dowdy and Easton went over to see if the crime investigators had found any blood in it that could be from either victim. Rierdan's rented house on Little Fall Creek was also being searched for evidence connecting him to the victims.

Over the next twenty-four hours several pieces of evidence against Rierdan were turned up. The two rifles in his truck when he was arrested were both loaded, and one of them was a .270 loaded with hollow point rounds. A fully-loaded 9 mm, semi-automatic pistol was recovered from underneath the passenger seat. A single strand of long brown hair matching Sandy Evonuk's hair was recovered from the front seat of the truck. But the most incriminating evidence was a pair of leather boots found on Rierdan's back porch that had a significant amount of blood around the toes, and several drops of blood found on the floor mat of his pickup. The blood type found in both places was AB which matched Roderick Evonuk's blood type, and did not match Rierdan's or Sandy Evonuk's, which were both O positive.

None of Rierdan's fingerprints were found at the scene or on any of the beer cans recovered there either. All the prints on the cans and everything else around the table belonged to either Rod or Sandy Evonuk. Of course, there were so many fingerprints, old and new, on the table that none of them was useful.

The coroner's exam, which was completed shortly before midnight the day the bodies were discovered, had revealed that Sandy Evonuk died of suffocation from being strangled. She had significant post-mortem bruising on her neck and her hyoid bone was fractured. No evidence indicating she was raped was found. But skin and O positive blood were found dried under the fingernail of her left middle finger.

Roderick Evonuk died from numerous head traumas, but it was determined that he probably would have died anyway without immediate medical assistance because of a severely punctured left lung caused by two broken ribs, which most likely occurred at the same time his spine was broken. The coroner felt comfortable in his belief that Mr. Evonuk had been thrown down forcefully on the edge of the picnic table. He had significant pre and postmortem bruising across the middle of his back. Obviously the person, or persons, who killed the Evonuks was male and very strong.

38

Same Killer?

After their brief session with Rierdan, and putting together the evidence, Deputies Dowdy and Easton were convinced he killed the Evonuks. They also suspected he was probably responsible for the death of Roger Bruington and the disappearance of Mitch Walton. The coroner's exam of Bruington's head wound eleven months earlier revealed he had been shot with a .270 caliber rifle. With much of his face having been blown off, in all likelihood he had been hit with a hollow-point round, the same as Rierdan's .270 rifle was loaded with at his arrest.

The next step was for Dowdy and Easton to interview Rierdan again, this time in the presence of his court-appointed attorney.

On Wednesday morning, September 23rd, at the Lane County jail where Rierdan was being held without bail after his Tuesday hearing, Dowdy and Easton waited in the interview room. In ten minutes, Rierdan, handcuffed and wearing orange jail garb, and accompanied by his female attorney, was brought in the room by a guard. Rierdan and his attorney both took a seat on the opposite side of the wooden table from Dowdy and Easton.

The thirty-something-year-old, drab blonde-haired, plain-Jane, female attorney introduced herself as Melinda Holbrook.

Shaking her hand, Dowdy answered, "Ms. Holbrook, I'm Lieutenant Dowdy and this is Deputy Easton who is assisting me in this and other Puma Creek investigations. I'm just going to come right out and tell you that we have all the evidence we need for your client to be found guilty of both murders at Puma Creek on Wednesday, September 23rd. It would behoove him to co-operate in every way he can with our investigation."

"And what kind of supposed evidence do you have against my client?"

"A hair matching the female victim's hair was found in his pickup. And skin and O positive blood—the same as your client's— were found under one of her fingernails. As you can see, the wound on your client's face has not completely healed; and here are some photos of his wounds taken the night he was booked here, two nights after he killed the Evonuks."

"I didn't kill them. I was at home."

Immediately putting her right hand on Rierdan's left forearm, and turning her head toward him, Holbrook said, "You don't have to say anything. In fact, unless I tell you to speak, please don't."

"Lieutenant Dowdy, you and I both know the hair could have come from any number of women. My client is a handsome, strong, young man, as you can see, and has no problem attracting women. The hair could be from one of them. As far as finding O positive blood, there are more people in this country with O positive blood than any other type."

Dowdy wanted to say, yeah after he attracts the young women, he beats them. But instead he chose diplomacy, and said, "I'm sorry you can't see the forest for the trees, Ms. Holbrook. So I will show you a couple more trees that incriminate your client."

Dowdy then took out a folder, opened it, removed several 8 by 10 color photos, and spread them out on the table facing Holbrook and Rierdan.

Five of the photos were from the crime scene: a couple showing Rod Evonuk lying in a pool of blood with his face caved in, one with Sandy Evonuk lying dead on top of the picnic table, and two taken farther away picturing both Evonuks lying dead.

Dowdy said to Rierdan, who had quickly scanned the photos then stared at the front of Dowdy's shirt, "They look worse in daylight than when you left them in the dark, don't they?"

Rierdan didn't respond. Ms. Holbrook looked at the photos and shook her head.

"Those boots are on Rierdan's back porch. And as you can see in these blow ups, there is dried blood all over the toes. I'm sure that probably doesn't move you. So consider this, the blood type on the toes of those boots is AB which is the same type as Mr. Evonuk, the man whose head was caved in when he was kicked to death. Your client has O positive blood. But maybe you want to suggest that the blood, like the hair, came from one of his many women."

"That's enough of the wise cracks, Lieutenant," she said. "You have nothing placing my client at the scene of the crime."

"I'm sure the jury won't be bothered by that, especially when we tell them about the other two men your client killed in the Puma Creek area."

"Wait a minute. I didn't kill any other two people—"

"Don't say another word, Mr. Rierdan!" she said sternly. "You've said more than enough already."

"I don't know what you're trying to pull Dowdy, but your tactics stink. You don't have a solid case against my client, or you wouldn't be in here in the first place talking to us. You and I both know that."

"You're wrong there, Ms. Holbrook. We have a very solid case, *and you know it.* You undoubtedly are not aware that the round that killed the hunter, Roger Bruington, a year ago was the same .270 caliber hollow-point that one of your client's rifles was loaded with when it was recovered from his truck during his arrest last week."

Dowdy pulled out another 8 by 10 photo and laid it on top of the other photos in front of Holbrook and Rierdan. The photo was a close-up of the front of Bruington's head, his face missing from above his upper lip. "You're client is guilty in that death and the Wyoming bicyclist's death in July this year as well."

Partially grinning at Rierdan, Dowdy said, "I'm sure the district attorney will be in touch with you soon to attempt to get some co-operation from your client in solving the deaths of the other two people he killed. And if your client comes clean he might even avoid the death penalty."

"We're done here, Dowdy," she said, as she closed her notepad. "Guard?"

After Holbrook and Rierdan left the room, Easton said, "You definitely know how to go for the jugular, District Attorney Dowdy." They both laughed.

"Did you pick up on anything when Rierdan opened his mouth?" asked Dowdy.

"You bet I did, and his attorney obviously did too the way she tried to shut him up. It's hard for a guy like that to keep his mouth shut. You nailed him when you mentioned him being guilty in the *other two* killings. Considering we don't have any evidence confirming the Wyoming man's death, you obviously took some liberties."

"You know how it works with these thugs. Give them a little rope, even a weak one, and they're not smart enough to keep from hanging themselves."

"So do you think he will admit to these killings to keep from being charged with the other two?"

"I honestly don't know, Corporal."

"Do you really believe he might be guilty in the other cases?"

"I think there's a strong possibility—especially in the Bruington case. It's too bad we were never able to recover a bullet from the killer's gun. That would have been some hard evidence to refute."

"What kind of connection would Rierdan have with Bruington? I mean what motive could he possibly have for killing him?"

"I can't begin to say. And unless he confesses at some point to what happened with the Evonuks at Puma Creek that night, we'll probably never know what brought on that attack. We need to look into his background to see if there is anything that could give us a hint of any kind."

"I'm sure the DA will have his people on that, too," said Easton.

"I still want to get back up in those woods soon, with Eastbrook, and see if there is anything we might have missed."

"It's been an awful long time."

"I know that, but why has all this happened around Puma Creek? If this Rierdan did kill all four of them, there has to be a reason. Is he trying to hide something up in those woods?"

"It makes you wonder, doesn't it. When do you want to get up there?"

"We'll have to check with Eastbrook and see what works for him. I really want him along."

Early the next evening, Thursday, over the phone—

"Del, I talked to Dowdy today about the Rierdan case. He believes Rierdan is probably the killer in the Bruington case and he thinks he may have killed the Wyoming kid, too."

Blowing out a puff of marijuana smoke, Del said, "You and I know that's ridiculous. But hey, if the great detective Dowdy wants to believe that—that's all the better for us, right?"

"That's why I called now Del. Dowdy and some others are planning to get back up in the woods above Puma Creek. I hadn't told you this before, but one of the rifles in Rierdan's truck the night I stopped him was a .270 loaded with hollow points, just like the one we shot the hunter with."

"So now they're going back up to try to find the bullet, after all this time?"

"I don't know. I'm only telling you what he said. I didn't ask and he didn't volunteer any reason. I sometimes don't know what I could ask or say without giving him a reason to question me."

"You're a fool, Butch. Unless you came right out and admitted to anything, Dowdy wouldn't consider you a suspect in a hundred years. You remind him too much of himself at your age."

"How can you know that, you've never even met the man?"

"Trust me; I've seen his type all my life. They have this idealistic way of looking at everything. Every piece of his life's puzzle has always fallen perfectly into place—perfect childhood, perfect military duty, perfect wife and kids, perfect career. Guys like him can't possibly understand how some of the rest of us struggle from day to day. You gave me enough information about his background. I know I have him pegged."

"You always seem to have everything pegged, Del."

"When you've been through all I have and lived as long as I have, you pick up a thing or two along the way."

"So what are we going to do about the shack? The thunder-showers we had all last weekend soaked the woods pretty good. I don't think Dowdy is going to give up until he's covered that whole area. And if he finds the shack, he's going to go over it and all the surrounding area with a fine-tooth comb. What if we missed something?"

"You're right. These last two murders at Puma Creek have really complicated the situation. We don't have any choice. Pick me up here in an hour. We've got to get in there tonight. At least we know they'll never find the cowboy or, his bike—not without rounding all the pieces up from the Lane County landfill."

"Yeah, once the shack is burned, we're home free forever. I'll see you in a bit."

39

The Deer

One week later, Friday afternoon, **October 2ⁿᵈ**, Lieutenant Dowdy, Corporal Easton, and Dick Eastbrook, in the forest north of Puma Creek Campground, the first chance Eastbrook could get free for a couple days.—

"So you feel pretty confident Rierdan killed Roger too, Lieutenant?" asked Eastbrook, as the three of them headed west, crossing over a ridge east of Slick Creek, two miles north of Fall Creek.

"Yes. I think there's a good likelihood that he did kill Roger. And maybe even the Wyoming bicyclist. But proving it is another story. As you know, the whole CIA, government assassination-theory just hasn't panned out. It has to be something else.

"A couple weeks ago, I received a phone call from an Army officer who is a relative of the late General Overgard—"

"You did; how's he related?" asked Eastbrook.

"I can't divulge that."

"Was his call regarding Roger's death?"

"Dick, if you'll give me a chance, I will explain it."

277

"Sorry."

"Though I can't tell you how he's related to General Overgard, I will say he has access to the most important people in America."

"For Pete's sake, spit it out, Lieutenant."

Dowdy immediately stopped, and so did the other two.

"The officer told me he had talked to a number of people who would have been in the know on a cover up being taken to such lengths as to off a decorated Vietnam veteran. He assured me that he was absolutely convinced Roger was not killed by any government people, and wouldn't have been under any circumstances. He did concede that he believed the government had drug its feet miserably on the whole MIA issue and, specifically, on the Cambodian POWs reported to General Overgard by Roger in 1974. But he made it clear he would never go on record in that regard, and would deny even saying that.

"He also said the media blitz had definitely oiled some wheels and he already knew of two covert missions that had been carried out in Cambodia and Laos by small Navy Seal and Green Beret teams since the big news broke last May. He said, the special force teams had not actually located any American POWs, but had talked with a number of locals that gave every indication that Americans were, in fact, still being held against their wills by the Vietnamese and the Pathet Lao. He said more covert operations were in the works even as we spoke. That I could rest assured our government was now making a positive effort to recover any American GIs remaining in Southeast Asia, though neither he or the government had any idea how many might still be there."

"Have you gotten any kind of confession from Rierdan on the double murder at Puma Creek?"

"No. And, frankly, I don't expect one. The District Attorney has told me and my captain that he believes they don't need a confession to get a conviction on the double murder. He also said that unless some better evidence turns up, he has no intentions of charging Rierdan in Roger's death. He said, his having a .270 loaded with hollow points wouldn't hold water in the courtroom on its own. But if we could find something linking Rierdan to this area and give him a motive, such as trying to hide something, then he might be a little more interested in pursuing charges."

"Did you guys look into Rierdan's background? Does he have any military or shooting qualifications?"

"He joined the Army right out of high school, but was kicked out before completing boot camp," said Dowdy. "Supposedly he had absolutely no regard for authority, so the Army decided they didn't need the hassles he created."

"Sounds like the guy's a real winner."

"Yeah, he also has a history of abusing his girlfriends," said Easton.

After they'd each taken a good drink from their canteens, Dowdy led the way as they proceeded to the west down into the next draw. As they crossed a spring, Easton said, "You guys smell that?"

"Yeah," answered Eastbrook. "It smells like there's been a fire up here somewhere." All three of them instinctively checked the wind by wetting a finger and holding it up.

"It's coming out of the northwest," said Easton.

"Let's head up that way and see if we can find the source... That's coming in pretty strong all of a sudden."

They went another hundred yards and came up onto a bench, when suddenly Easton spotted something.

"I think I see the source of the smoke. Looks like there was a pretty large fire over there."

"Let's check it out," said Dowdy.

When they got near the charred wood, Eastbrook said, "This fire can't be more than a week old."

"Yeah, it looks like someone may have been living up here in this old shack," said Dowdy.

"That or they just used it for a trapping or hunting cabin," said Easton.

"Let's look it over real well," said Dowdy. "Maybe we'll find something that will tell us what the person or persons used it for."

They milled around among what remained of the burned wood. Everything was badly charred or completely turned to ash.

"Look here, Lieutenant," said Easton. "It almost looks like they had a cellar dug out in here."

"That's no cellar entry," Dowdy said, after they had cleared out some charred wood with gloved hands. "That looks like it might have been a tunnel at one time."

"Who would have a tunnel, especially way back up here in the woods?" asked Eastbrook.

"Drug dealers, who knows?" said Dowdy.

"I don't see anything around here that looks suspicious in that regard," said Easton.

"Makes you wonder if the fire was an accident, or set deliberately," said Eastbrook.

"You've got a little cop in you, don't you, Dick," said Dowdy.

"More like common sense."

"That's the best thing going for a cop," said Easton.

"What if this Rierdan guy was actually doing something up in here that was against the law?" said Eastbrook. "Maybe he was poaching deer or something else."

"I think it's more likely he was growing marijuana in the area," said Dowdy. "Or possibly making Meth."

"He's been in jail the whole time. He obviously didn't burn this down," said Easton.

"No, but someone he could have been involved with could have," said Dowdy. "I'm sure he had to have talked to someone he knew over the phone during the last week. He might have told them he was under suspicion for the other two cases as well."

"And if the other person was in on all of this, they would have figured out there might be a search for more clues up in here," said Easton.

"Yeah, it's all beginning to come together isn't it? I think Rierdan was up to a lot of no good. And I'm liking him more all the time as Roger's killer and probably even the Walton guy. Maybe the Captain and even someone from the DA's office will want to come up here with us to look around. Well, let's get our cameras out and get a bunch of pictures."

After completing the camera work and looking over the perimeter area, the three men swung uphill to the northeast. When they had gone half a mile they came to a heavy vine maple thicket still holding all its green leaves, though many had begun to turn yellow. With no way around but to cross down into the draw to their right, or climb the bank to their west, Dowdy said, "Let's just pick our way through this thicket. It won't take long."

Two minutes later, Dowdy said, "Look there, Corporal, just ahead of me and downhill."

"It's a dead deer, Lieutenant."

"That's not just a dead deer," said Eastbrook. "That's a real trophy."

As they moved in on it, they could see there was nothing left of the body except the skeleton and some dried hide on part of its mid section.

"*What a waste!*" said Easton.

"Judging by those antlers, this was one old boy," said Dowdy. "Undoubtedly died of old age."

"The heck he did," said Eastbrook, finally getting right up next to the deer and getting a hold of its antlers. "This is the big buck Roger told us about. See these two drop points. How many blacktail deer have these? Roger told us about these drop points. And these antlers are very close to the size Roger estimated them to be when he told us about having jumped a big, old buck up Fall Creek somewhere. That's why he came back up here the next week, the weekend he died. He was going to get this big buck."

"What do you think, Lieutenant?" asked Easton, scratching the side of his head."

"Well, that sounds too perfect. And what are the chances that we would find the very same buck that Roger had come looking for, I mean really?"

"Lieutenant, you said yourself there was a reason why you wanted me to come along with you two up here. This is the reason, and you didn't know it."

"I don't know about that, Dick. I'm not that telepathic."

"Call it a coincidence. Call it whatever. But I swear, this is the same buck Roger was after."

"Well, he obviously didn't get it. It's just a lucky find," said Dowdy.

"What if he did actually shoot at it, Lieutenant? I mean his rifle was off safe with a round spent."

"This is too crazy, Easton. And we already determined that he never would have not immediately re-chambered a live round."

"But Lieutenant—let's forget all the conclusions we have already come up with up to this point. You taught me that yourself. Then let's look at the evidence before us and see what it tells us."

"What's it telling you, Easton?"

"For one, with the rib bones on the right side chewed up by wild animals, we have no way of knowing whether they might have been damaged by a bullet. And there is no obvious damage to the spine or skull."

"What about the left side?" asked Eastbrook.

"Let's get some photos before we move it, men," Easton said, "just for the heck of it."

The lawmen pulled out their 35 mm cameras and snapped several shots apiece from various angles, using their flashes to even out the lighting.

"Now let's move him and get a better look at the left rib cage," said Dowdy.

"Lieutenant, is that possibly a bullet right there?" Easton said, as he pointed at something about half way down and a third of the way back between the left rib cage and the dried hide on that side."

"Unbelievable, Corporal," said Dowdy, as Easton pulled the ribs up into the air a few inches and they all saw a mushroom shaped bullet stuck to the dried hide. "We've got to get some photos of this.

Here, Dick, you hold the ribs up, while I snap a few shots."

"Now what's the evidence telling us, Lieutenant?" asked Eastbrook.

"It's telling us this deer was shot from the right side of it's rib cage and the core-lokt bullet expanded perfectly and hung up in the hide on the left side," said Dowdy.

After removing the bullet, Easton compared the butt of the bullet to a .38 caliber bullet he had taken out of his belt, and said, "And it looks like a .30 caliber bullet to me."

"I'm betting it came from Roger's gun," said Eastbrook, who suddenly broke into tears, taking himself and the lawmen totally off guard. But they understood. "Roger did kill the big buck he was after. And we all laughed at him when he told us he would. Damn us. He was the best friend a guy could ever have asked for. And I doubted him."

Dowdy and Easton each put a hand on Eastbrook's shoulders.

"You were just being his buddies, Dick," said Dowdy. "That's what buddies are for: to make life rough for their friends. I'm sorry once again for what you lost. Roger was obviously one heck of a special man. I wish I had gotten to meet him."

"Vietnam didn't get him, but that damn Rierdan did, in Roger's own home county. Damn him."

"We don't know for certain that this is Roger's bullet. Nor do we know that Rierdan was the one who killed Roger."

"You and I both know the truth, Lieutenant. And I know that when you compare this bullet to Roger's barrel, it will match up perfectly. *This is his buck!*"

"Why would Roger's buck be so far from where we found his body and the rifle off-safe and a spent round chambered?" asked Easton.

"That's the million dollar question, Corporal. And I can't give you a good answer. You have any ideas, Dick?"

"Maybe he shot this deer, but for whatever reason, didn't think he hit it, and didn't find any indication of a hit."

"Judging by where we found that bullet, the deer would have had an entry wound on the right side," said Dowdy. "But with no flesh, hardly any skin and very little rib bones remaining on that side, we have no way of knowing where the bullet entered."

"I think it's safe to say it had to at least been hit in the left lung since the bullet ended up directly beside the chest cavity there. But we don't know whether it was only hit in the left lung or both lungs."

"I agree with you Corporal Easton," said Eastbrook.

"We all know Roger was a dead-eye shooter, but we have no way of knowing whether this deer was hit with a running shot, a quartered shot, or what," said Dowdy. "Let's assume worst-case scenario. Say it was a rear-quartered angle shot from the right side and he hit the paunch and then the outside of the left lung. How far could the deer have traveled?'

"Several hundred yards, maybe more," said Eastbrook.

"And left very little external sign. No exit wound, where typically you get more bleeding. All the lung bleeding would have occurred inside the deer's chest cavity," said Easton. "And we all know you don't get a whole lot of bleeding on an entry wound going into the guts, unless you're lucky enough to hit a good vein or artery on the way in."

"And what would be the best-case scenario?" asked Dowdy.

"It's a broadside shot, you go directly through both lungs and the deer goes less than a hundred yards, probably a lot less. And you almost always get good bleeding from the entry wound, sometimes it pumps out of there, though not like an exit wound."

"Roger would have found the deer in that case," said Eastbrook.

"What if it was an uphill angle, or even a downhill angled shot?"

"An uphill angled shot with Roger lower than the deer, might have hit the deer in the heart."

"Look, you guys, we can speculate until the cows come home and it won't make any difference, will it? My best friend's dead, the killer is finally in custody, and we found Roger's buck. We have no idea why Roger's gun was off-safe and had a spent round remaining in the chamber. I don't know that we will ever be able to figure all of it out. But you have enough evidence right now to put the guy away for life and probably get the death penalty, even if he's never charged with Roger's death, right?"

"I'm sure we do, but you can never be certain," said Dowdy. "I like to get all the evidence I can."

"Well can we take this deer's skull with antlers attached with us? You've got the bullet and the photos, and I think that my reason for being here has been revealed. I'm not really in the mood to spend any more of the day up here in the woods. I hope you can understand."

"That's no problem, Dick. Of course we understand. This just brings all the pain back to the surface for you," said Dowdy. "And as far as I'm concerned, you've completed your mission here. Let's saddle up and get off the mountain. Deputy Easton and I can come back up on our own, or maybe, if we're unlucky, with someone from the DA's office."

Eastbrook immediately pulled out his hunting knife. As Dowdy grabbed each antler and twisted the big buck's head around, Eastbrook cut the skull free from the dried hide on the upper neck.

40

Confused

Later, that evening—

"Trooper Wilson, Lieutenant Dowdy here. I thought you'd be interested to know that Deputy Easton, Dick Eastbrook and I went back up into the woods north of Puma Creek today, like I had mentioned we would."

"How'd it go, Lieutenant, did you figure anything out?"

"Yes, as a matter of fact, that's what I wanted to tell you."

Wilson cringed at what might be coming. Nothing Dowdy could say would be good. "I'm listening."

"We found an old shack that had been burned down some time in the last week or so."

"Huh. Where was the shack?"

"It was way up there, a couple miles north of Fall Creek, not far from the upper reaches of Slick Creek."

"I wonder what that shack was doing there. Do you think it was burned accidentally, or what?"

"Oh, we definitely don't believe it was burned accidentally. We believe whoever was using it was probably connected to this

286

Rierdan fella, and they were undoubtedly using the shack for some-thing illegal. We think maybe some wildlife poaching or, more likely, for doing something with drugs, maybe growing some marijuana up in there somewhere or something. Rierdan probably talked with the other person or persons by phone from jail and told them he was suspected of killing the hunter to the north of Puma Creek a year ago and that there would likely be a search in the woods. Of course, calling from a jail phone, he couldn't have said anything about the shack directly."

"That's interesting. Did you find any marijuana plants or drug paraphernalia?"

"No. But whoever burned things down, undoubtedly removed anything incriminating first," said Dowdy. "What was interesting was that we found what I'm certain is the entrance to an under-ground tunnel of some kind."

"You did? Did you try to open it up?"

"No, it was filled up with a lot of charred debris and dirt. We might go back in there later to try to dig it out."

"Why would anyone have a tunnel up there?"

"Your guess is probably as good as mine. Maybe as an escape path should they ever get caught up there with their pants down by law enforcement."

"That's a pretty good guess, I'd say," Wilson agreed.

"But what's almost as interesting as finding the shack is that we found a buck deer that Roger Bruington had shot the weekend he was killed."

"Are you serious?" Wilson knew this couldn't be good.

"You bet I'm serious. And if we hadn't had Dick Eastbrook with us, we never would have made the connection."

"Why's that?"

"As soon as he saw the antlers on that dead buck in the vine maple thicket half a mile above the shack, he said it was Bruing-ton's buck. Eastbrook said the antlers were a perfect match for the one Bruington told him and the others about earlier that week. He had said he was going back in there to get the buck."

"How could Eastbrook possibly know they were the same antlers?"

"It wasn't just the size of the antlers, it was the double six-inch drop points coming off the right main beam."

"That would definitely make it unique," conceded Wilson. "What makes you think Bruington killed the deer and it didn't just die of old age?"

"We found a mushroomed .30 caliber bullet in the dried hide on the left side of the rib cage. And it turned out to be a perfect match to Bruington's 30.06 ammunition and to his rifle's barrel."

Terribly ill at ease, Wilson said, "What a coincidence, huh?"

"More like fate, I'd say. But it still leaves a lot of unanswered questions."

"Go on."

"For one, why Bruington didn't recover his dead deer, being the expert hunter and tracker that he was. And why was Bruington's gun off-safe and holding a spent round in the chamber when he was shot over two miles away from where we found the deer?"

"I see your point, Lieutenant. Do you have any theories?"

"I wish I did. I haven't got the foggiest idea about any of it."

Wilson breathed a bit easier, but not much. Dowdy had his darn nose going all-out. Them finding the shack would probably turn out to be good; it would make Rierdan look even guiltier. And there was no way anyone was going to believe a word that came out of his mouth. That is, unless he came right out and confessed to the other killings and explained what had happened, and then had a great alibi for the other two incidents.

"What if he actually shot the buck on Friday, and didn't know he had hit it? Then came back up into that basic area Saturday," said Wilson.

"Yeah, I suppose that's possible. But it doesn't answer the spent-round question, does it?"

"No, I guess it doesn't."

"Well, Trooper, I'm going to let you go. I just thought since you were there when Bruington's body was found and the next day, you would want to know. Would you be sure to tell Trooper Martin and your captain for me?"

"Thanks for the information, Lieutenant. I'll definitely pass it along."

As soon as Wilson hung up with Dowdy, he called Del—

"Del, they found the shack today."

"Good thing we burned it."

"That's exactly what I was thinking."

"What did Dowdy tell you?"

"They're pretty sure that Ricrdan guy and somebody else were doing something illegal out of it. Dowdy said possibly poaching wildlife, and almost certainly dealing in drugs, and probably growing marijuana."

"Those dirty scoundrels. How could they prostitute our forests that way? That Dowdy is pretty sharp, isn't he?"

"Too sharp!"

"Why do you say that?"

"They found a deer that the hunter we shot had killed, and it was only half a mile from the shack."

"What the hell? What do you mean?"

"I'm serious. They found a trophy buck that Bruington had shot. They found his bullet lodged inside the dried hide."

"How could they possibly have made any connection between a dead deer in the woods and Bruington?"

"It was Bruington's friend, Dick Eastbrook, who made the connection. He was up in the woods with the deputies."

"So what's that mean for us?"

"I'm not sure. But it has me pretty worried. They're really puzzled why Bruington wouldn't have recovered his dead deer."

"That happens all the time," said Del. "People wound deer and either don't know they hit them, or they can't track them down. So how was there a dead deer within half a mile of the shack?" asked Del. "You and I were in there all morning, before and after Bruington investigated the shack—that is until we started following him afterwards. We never heard any shots. I'm sure we would have heard a shot from that close."

"The only thing I could think of was that Bruington must have been up in there and shot the deer the evening before. Maybe if I would have stopped and talked to him when I saw him at his fire as I drove through Puma Creek Campground late that evening he would have told me about it."

"Yeah, he had to have shot at the deer Friday night. Is that what they think?"

"I don't know if they had considered it before I mentioned it as a possibility. But Dowdy thought it sounded plausible."

"Butch, I wonder if we shouldn't go back up there before they do and double check on things—especially the pit where the cowboy is buried. You never know. An animal could have come along and scrounged around there."

"I'm with you on that, Del. When do you want to go?"

"The sooner the better. When are you off during daylight hours?"

"How about tomorrow when we're hunting?"

"Did Dowdy say when he might be going back up there?"

"No, but I didn't get the impression it was going to be right away."

"Well, with tomorrow being Saturday, I'm sure nobody's going to be up in there then. See if you can find out when he's going back in there and volunteer to go with him. That will explain your call."

"I'll call him now and find out. We sure as heck don't want to be in there when they are, nor do we want them to get there first."

"Good idea. Call me right back if tomorrow's a go."

"Lieutenant Dowdy, Trooper Wilson here."

"Yes, Trooper Wilson."

"You mentioned maybe going back up Puma Creek to look around some more. I'd like to go with you if you wouldn't mind. I feel like I'm invested in this whole thing pretty good between Bruington and then arresting Rierdan. Do you know when you're going up there?"

I've got to talk to the District Attorney and see if they want to have someone go up there with us. They're out of the office until Monday, so I'll give you a call sometime probably Monday late-afternoon or evening."

"That's sounds great, Lieutenant. I appreciate it."

"No problem. Have a great weekend."

"I plan to. It's the opening day of deer season, and, for once, I don't have the duty."

"That's right," Dowdy said. "I've been so caught up in all this the last couple weeks, I completely forgot about it. I better get over to Bi-Mart and get my deer tag. I'm sure my wife would have reminded me. She's always so good about that stuff."

"You're a lucky man, Lieutenant."

"You're not telling me anything. Have a good one, Trooper."

"It's a go for tomorrow Del. Dowdy's going hunting and won't be back up Fall Creek before Tuesday. He's got to talk to the District Attorney's office on Monday to see if they want anyone to go with him when he goes back up. He said I could go along."

"That's good all the way around, Butch. We'll just include that area as part of our morning hunt. How's that sound to you?"

"Good. Maybe we'll kill two birds with one stone. Maybe we'll get lucky enough to get a chance at a trophy like the one they found."

"I don't care much about trophy hunting. The meat's all I'm after. Why don't you pick me up at 5:30? That'll get us up there before daylight."

"See you then."

41

Opening Day

Saturday, October 3rd, Opening morning of the Western Oregon General Deer Season: In the woods two and a half miles northwest of Puma Creek Campground, an hour after daylight—

Boom! Boom!

What the hell? Del thought. There shouldn't be anyone else up in this area.

At that moment a forked horn deer came running between Del and Butch—who were seventy-five yards apart—from the direction the shots had come from. Del spotted it immediately and shot at it with his open-sighted, lever-action, Winchester Model 94, 30-30. The young buck dropped to the ground, right beside a large patch of sword fern. "I got him, Butch."

"Good going, Del," he said, keeping a lookout for any other deer that might be scared their way. After three minutes, both men figured that was it and converged on the dead buck lying on the mossy ground between them.

"Those shots didn't sound too far away," said Butch.

"Yeah, they weren't far from the shack, maybe a couple hundred yards to the south."

"I guess it's real good that we got that whole thing wrapped up, isn't it."

"I'll say. These damn woods are getting to be like stink to flies. Every Tom, Dick and Harry seems to want to tromp around up here anymore."

"It had to happen sooner or later, Del."

"Well, hold that leg, while I get to work." Del took off his old army jacket, rolled up his shirt sleeves and pulled out his long-knife. He immediately cut around the deer's anus and then made a slit down the middle of its hind end to the genitals, which he cut free leaving the urinary tract in tact, all of it to be pulled through the anal hole once he had the body cavity opened up.

Just then Butch noticed movement out of the corner of his eye. Instinctively, he looked in that direction, and spotted a man coming down his side of the ridge.

"There's someone coming our way, Del."

"Just what we need, someone to coach us."

As the person closed to about seventy-five yards, Butch got a sick feeling in his stomach.

"You're never going to believe me, Del. It's Deputy Easton. He's dressed in hunter orange and carrying a rifle."

"Damn it. What the hell is he doing up here?"

"It just got worse, Del. Dowdy's with him and he's hunting too."

"That's the last thing we needed. Why the hell are they up here?"

"I'm sure they're wondering the same thing about me."

When Dowdy and Easton had closed to twenty yards, Dowdy said, "It looks like you guys had better luck than we did. My partner missed a running shot at a nice three-point that I jumped out of a thicket. Did you guys see him?"

"No. This is the only deer we saw, Lieutenant" answered Wilson.

"So you decided to hunt up in these woods today, huh, Trooper Wilson?"

"Yeah. After the buck you told me you guys found up here, I figured why not. And maybe I could get a look at that shack you told me about."

"Did you see it?" asked Easton.

"No. Where is it?"

"It's back that way," he pointed behind him and uphill, "over that ridge."

"This is my friend, Del Hensley, deputies."

"Nice to meet you Del," said Dowdy.

"Congratulations on the buck," Easton added.

Del mumbled something, continuing to work on his deer.

"Del, this is Lieutenant Dowdy, and Deputy Easton, of the Lane County Sheriff Department. You've heard me mention their names a time or two."

"Yeah, I vaguely recall the names," he said, as he pulled the deer's stomach and lower entrails free from the body cavity after making the necessary cuts. Then, as soon as he cut through the deer's diaphragm, blood poured out of the chest cavity. It was a double lung hit. Both lungs were bloody and deflated as Del cut them free, while leaving the heart attached to the wind pipe.

"You've obviously gutted your share of deer," said Easton.

Del didn't answer.

"Del is a Vietnam combat vet," said Butch. Del immediately looked up at him with as dirty a look as he could give, while angling his hat so the bill obscured his face from the view of the other two.

"You're a Vietnam vet, huh?' said Dowdy.

"That's right," Del answered, not volunteering anything more.

Observing Del's long hair which hung down well past his shoulders and seeing his long, straggly beard, the deputies glanced knowingly at each other and said no more on the subject.

"Do you guys want any help dragging that deer out of here?

Where are you parked?"

"We'll manage," said Del.

"Thanks for the offer" said Wilson.

"We'll leave you guys alone and get back to hunting," said Dowdy, as he turned back toward the direction they had come from.

After Dowdy and Easton had disappeared over the ridge, back in the direction of the burned-out shack, Del said, "Like hell they'll get back to hunting."

"Take it easy, Del. They're just up here hunting. Can you blame them after recovering a big buck up here yesterday? You have to admit, hunting in this old growth is nice. You have good visibility and nice terrain."

"You know damn well why they chose this area to hunt. They're looking to find something to hang our asses."

"I don't think we have anything to worry about, Del. They're headed completely away from the pit. And there's nothing else up here that could incriminate us. We made sure of that."

"Well you get up at the edge of that ridge and watch where they go. Signal me when the coast is clear, and I'll get my butt right over to the pit and check it out. I think I'll still be able to see you from there. If there's a problem, I'll deal with it while you keep a lookout."

"Alright, I'll wait until you're back up to the deer before I come back over."

"That Del is one seedy looking fella," said Easton, after he and Dowdy had gotten over the ridge. "I wonder what Wilson is doing, hooked up with a guy like that. He sure isn't very friendly."

"Well, let's not read too much into that. He looks like one of those Vietnam vets whose had a rough go of it since coming home."

"You're probably right, Lieutenant. But something about them being up in here, Wilson being with him? I don't know... something just didn't seem right about it."

"I know what you mean, Buddy. But you and I live on the good side of the tracks and only cross over to administer the law. Not all cops are like that. Some actually have a lot of interaction with the dregs of humanity. You haven't done any undercover work yet, have you?'

"No."

"Trust me, if you do, it will change your way of looking at things. On one hand you'll hate that sleazy way of life even more. On the other, you'll stop being so judgmental because you'll realize that if it weren't for your upbringing and lots of things going your way as an adult, you could be one of them."

"Not me, Lieutenant. No way!"

Butch walked up the ridge to the east and, as soon as he saw that Dowdy and Easton were safely in the distance toward the shack, gave a thumb up to Del who quickly dropped over to the pit where the Wyoming man was buried. Butch watched as he moved various small logs and brush around to completely cover the grave. Five minutes later Del gave the thumbs up and both men returned to the dead forked-horn.

"It's one helluva good thing we got up here. When I got close to it I could smell something dead. Some animal had gotten under our brush pile and dug up a fair amount of the dirt in the grave. I couldn't see any flesh, but if they came upon that it would've really raised suspicions, especially since they already found the shack."

"You got it all covered up so they can't possibly smell it?"

"Yeah, and I got it covered over real well with logs and brush. Don't worry, I took care of it. Now grab an antler and let's get out of here."

They each grabbed the base of an antler and drug the young buck out to Butch's truck, three-quarters of a mile to the west.

Deputies Dowdy and Easton decided to look the perimeter area above the shack over to see if they could find any sign where marijuana plants might have been grown. Twenty minutes later, Easton spotted something suspicious.

"Lieutenant, it looks like a shovel over there near that spring." He pointed to his left.

"Let's go see."

"It's a shovel alright. The handle's lying in some ferns."

"Don't touch it! This is a great find. We need to get some photos first."

After taking several photos, Dowdy said, "Alright, we don't want to touch that handle at all. It probably has a lot of finger prints on it. Grab it by the edges of the blade, and hide it in those ferns."

Easton grabbed the shovel with both hands and stuffed it completely into the ferns so they could finish searching the immediate area on the perimeter of the shack. Half an hour later, they had found nothing more that could be evidence, so they picked up the shovel and hiked the three-quarters of a mile back to the northeast to the road where their truck was parked. At the truck they stashed the shovel in the brush to be picked up at the end of the day when they were done hunting. Dowdy would take the shovel into the sheriff's office from there so the lab could process it on Monday morning.

In late-morning, Butch drove Del and the buck down to Del's place on Wallace Creek Road in Jasper and helped him get the deer hung up. Del then invited him into the house for a beer. He said he'd come back out in a little while to skin the deer and clean it up.

After drinking some beer and shooting the bull for ten minutes, Del said, "Why don't you come out back with me?"

When they got into the back yard, which consisted of a dried lawn, a fire pit and a couple of old wooden chairs near the pit, Del turned around and said, "Butch, I'm more worried than I've let on. You saw the way they looked at me. The same way a lot of people do—with suspicion."

"You're reading things into it. Give them the benefit of the doubt."

"You're not that big a fool are you, Butch? Why should I give them the benefit of the doubt? They don't give anyone the benefit of the doubt. They're police officers."

"I'm a police officer, and I've always given you the benefit of the doubt."

"It's not even the same thing, Butch. Sometimes you amaze me with how naïve you can be."

"Why, just because I don't consider everyone to be the enemy—like you do?"

"You'll never understand will you, kid? The war broke me, and I'm never going to get fixed."

"Don't say that, Del. You're already a lot better. I've seen you come a long way in the last year."

"I didn't want things to come to this."

"Come to what?"

"You still don't see it do you? Dowdy and Easton aren't going to give up on this case until they solve it. The only chance we had went out the window when they caught us up there today."

"That's not true, Del. Why are you saying that? You're worrying me."

Del stepped over directly in front of Butch, reached out and grabbed each of his biceps and squeezed firmly while looking him right in the eyes. Butch didn't know what to think.

"Butch, I love you. I always have. I don't think I ever told you that before, at least not since I left to go to Nam. I'm so sorry for getting you into all this. If it weren't for me, you never would have considered messing with the marijuana and drugs. And you sure as hell never would have had to shoot someone. You've got to hear what I'm going to say. I mean it. And if you respect me, you'll take what I say to heart."

"I don't like the sound of that, Del."

"Listen to me, Butch. Sooner or later they'll figure out that the guy you arrested for killing that couple at Puma Creek didn't kill Bruington."

"You're wrong about that. They're never going to believe a word he says. They already know he's guilty of killing Bruington too."

"You know that's not true. Something's going to go wrong and tip them off. In fact, it already did when they caught us up there today. We both would have been much better off if we hadn't killed the hunter and just took our chances with him knowing what he knew, or maybe even confronting him in the woods like you said earlier. I have to admit, I was wrong. But we can't undo any of it now. Now listen carefully. I'm not going to prison under any circumstances—whatever that means."

"We won't get caught, Del."

"We're already caught, Butch. It's all gone too far. You're already caught. I'm telling you, they will be questioning you. What will you tell them?"

"I'm not going to tell them anything."

"You aren't going to have a choice. Believe me."

"I'll never tell them anything about you."

"That's exactly what you must do. When they bring you in for questioning or however they handle it, you have to admit to knowing about what I was doing at the shack all those years. You also have to tell them you knew I shot that hunter."

"But you didn't do that."

"Yes I did. I may not have pulled the trigger, but I killed him all the same. You've got to get that through your head. And I killed the Wyoming biker in my pit."

"You're wrong, Del. And the biker was completely an accident."

"They're never going to handle it like that. You're smart enough to know that."

"They'll never find the biker. We don't have to say anything about that."

"Trust me, Butch. *They will find* the biker sooner or later."

"You said you completely took care of it."

"Look, Butch, all of that was just to buy us—me, some time to get ready."

"Ready for what?"

"I can't say. Just know that I'm not going to prison under any circumstances."

"Are you saying you're going to start a war?"

"No. That's not what I'm saying."

"Then what?"

"Leave it alone, Butch. I can't tell you anything. Leave it alone and don't ever ask me again."

"What are you saying then?"

"Here's how it's going down. At some point, and probably fairly soon, they're going to figure out that Bruington was not killed by Rierdan. They're going to question you and find some hole in your story, that is, unless you come clean."

"Come clean? If I come clean, I'm going to prison."

"You're going to prison either way, Butch. But if you handle things like I tell you too, come clean the way I tell you, you won't get a long sentence. I screwed up your life. I'm the reason you're guilty of anything."

"This is what you have to tell yourself over and over until it's the only truth you remember. You have to tell them you weren't there when Bruington was shot—that I got you to help me after I had shot him. That you helped me move the body and disguise the evidence, because I've been the only father you've had since your dad was killed in Nam. Then, if and when they bring up the pit, you have to tell them you know nothing about any of that."

"That's all a lie."

"Damn it, Butch! Do you want to go to prison for the rest of your life and probably even get the electric chair?"

"No. But what about you?"

"Forget about me. You still have your whole life ahead of you. Of course, you'll never be able to be a cop again, but you can still do good things with your life."

"I'll have to tell the truth."

"You dumb ass! *You will* tell the truth—the only truth that matters. The truth as I told it to you. Do you think you going to prison for the rest of your life is going to help either of those guys' families? No. Or do you think you going to prison for the rest of your life is going to help your mom, or your sister? No."

"But what about you, Del?"

"I'm just a *ghost*."

"Not to me you're not." Butch grabbed a hold of Del, hugged him, and wept. "I love you, Del. Please, there's got to be a better way?"

"There's no better way. My way now is the only way."

"What are *you* going to do?"

"Forget about me. You have to make your own life now, without me."

"I don't want to, Del. Please." Butch wept uncontrollably as he continued to cling to Del like a scared kid.

"There's no other way. Just know that no matter what happens, I love you."

"I love you, Del. I love you."

After getting home that evening, Dowdy thought about calling Trooper Wilson to ask if they had anymore luck with their hunt and to tell him he had found the shovel, but something told him not to. It was just a little too curious to him to find Wilson hunting in the area of the shack with the Vietnam hippie. He half expected Wilson to call him, but he didn't.

42

The Evidence

At 10:35 Monday morning, October 5th, Dowdy received a call in his office from the Sheriff's laboratory.

"Lieutenant Dowdy, Technician Sims here. I have some good news for you and some not so good news."

"Give me the good news first, Sims."

"You were right—the shovel handle was loaded with finger-prints."

"And some of them matched Rierdan's?"

"That's the bad news, at least as it relates to the Rierdan case. Not one of the prints on the shovel was his."

"They weren't. That is bad news. How many different sets of prints did you get?"

"All the prints came from two different people, but they didn't match any of the prints in the Oregon criminal files."

"Huh. Well maybe the other people involved don't have a criminal record, or if they do it's in another state. All that means is they either committed their crimes somewhere else or they've never been caught."

"That's right, Lieutenant. But is it possible that this shovel wasn't even used by whoever was running an operation from the old shack?"

"You know it is. But I was desperately hoping that shovel would tie Rierdan to the shack. I'm still looking for motive in the Evonuk double murder. After finding the shovel and screening pan on the camp table at their site and them both being into the earth sciences, I figured they might have hiked into the wrong area and done some digging. But then they were discovered by Rierdan, and whoever he's in on things with, and murdered to ensure they didn't say anything to the wrong people about their little discovery up in the hills above Puma Creek."

"That sounds like it came right out of a murder mystery, Lieutenant."

"Do you have any better theories?" Dowdy said, a bit irritated.

"I didn't mean anything by that, Lieutenant. What I meant is that it sounded real good."

"Well, apparently that's not the way things went. Darn it!"

"Do you have any suggestions as to where I might look to try to find a match for the prints?"

"I might. I'll have to get back to you on it. If you think of anything don't hesitate to check it out. We need a match on those prints, somehow."

"I'll do my best, Lieutenant."

In the afternoon, the district attorney returned Dowdy's phone call. Dowdy filled him in on his finding the burned-down shack, the dead deer, the shovel and running into Trooper Wilson and the hippie on their hunt. The DA said he personally wanted to visit the shack and surrounding area, and he would bring along one of his assistants, as well. They could go up on Friday when the DA had an open court date.

That night, Dowdy tossed and turned while lying in bed with his beautiful wife. Finally he got up and went into the living room and called Deputy Easton.

"Buddy, I can't get to sleep. I'm tormented by the details of this whole Evonuk—Bruington—Walton situation."

"I hear you there, Lieutenant. I'm having the same problem, though I'm sure I don't feel the weight as heavy as you do."

"We have all these pieces, but they're not fitting together. What are we missing?"

"I don't know, Lieutenant. I've been thinking, what if we lay aside all our notions about Rierdan being involved with the shack. What if the Evonuk killings are totally unrelated to the shack, Bruington and Walton? In fact, let's separate Walton. We have no idea what actually happened to him. We already guessed that it's very likely that he left the Fall Creek area altogether. You've said that all along yourself."

"I know I've said that, Buddy, but I've never totally believed it. There's always been part of me that wondered if there wasn't some connection to the Bruington case. And then when the Evonuks were killed at Puma Creek, it was like being hit in the middle of the forehead. I just knew somehow all three incidents had to be connected. And I really wanted them to be connected. That would settle the MIA cover-up assassination issue and make me feel better about my own government, knowing it wouldn't do such a thing to one of its war heroes."

"It's complicated, isn't it, Lieutenant. Who wants to believe that his own government would actually kill its own people to hide its own neglect and cover up? We know that stuff happens in many countries around the world. But not here in America."

"My sentiments exactly, Buddy. So where does all that leave you and me in this investigation?"

"That hippie in the woods this weekend... I don't know, something about him just rubbed me the wrong way."

"He got to you didn't he. He got to me too, I hate to say it. It just struck me odd that someone as friendly and straight forward as Trooper Wilson would have a guy like that for a hunting partner. Of course we know nothing about Wilson, any of his background, what his family situation is, or anything. For all we know he might be related to that guy in some way."

"Don't you think Wilson would've said that, I mean up there in the woods, Lieutenant? Instead, he just said he was a Vietnam combat veteran."

"I think maybe he said that for a couple reasons. One, anyone looking at him, the straggly appearance and the beat up army jacket lying beside him, would wonder. And two, he killed the running deer with one shot, after we had already said you missed two shots at a running deer."

"I see what you're saying, but are you completely comfortable with him... with him being with Wilson?"

"No, I'm not. In fact, since it has bothered you so much, too, how about if we look into his military service record a bit? In fact, I think I will have the Lab. Technician dig his fingerprints out of the military files. It could take a few days to get a hold of that inform- ation, but it sure isn't going to hurt anything."

"Now, you're talking, Lieutenant. I think maybe I can get some sleep now. We're moving this thing in a positive direction."

"Yeah, I think you're right Buddy. I'll talk to you in the morning. Get some sleep."

"You too."

When Dowdy received a copy of Delbert Dan Hensley's service record on Thursday morning, it looked all too familiar. He had served five total years in the U.S. Army on two separate enlistments with a break of nearly two years between them. All of his service was during the Vietnam War and, in fact, forty-seven months of his service was spent on UNDISCLOSED DUTIES IN SOUTH VIET- NAM. Dowdy hated that phrase. Then when he and Easton compared Hensley's record with everything they knew about Roger Bruington's military service, as well as his sniper partner, Marvin Kennedy's, they both believed Hensley probably served as a sniper as well.

While they were still going over Hensley's service record, Dowdy received a call from the Lab Technician.

"Lieutenant Dowdy, you're never going to believe this. The fingerprints from Delbert Hensley's military records match perfectly with one of the sets found numerous times on your shovel from Puma Creek."

"That's great news!" Dowdy answered, then suddenly felt a sickening feeling in the pit of his stomach when he considered what that could mean. "Let me talk this over with Deputy Easton and get back to you after a bit. Good work, Sims."

Dowdy told Easton the news, then they both sat pondering the meaning for a few minutes as they continued to pore back over Hensley's service record.

Finally Easton spoke up, "Are you thinking what I'm thinking, Lieutenant?"

"I don't like what I'm thinking one bit. What are you thinking, Corporal?"

"That Hensley and Wilson weren't up in that area together for the first time last Saturday."

"Yeah, and now that I think about that phone conversation, when Wilson called me back the night before wanting to know when we would be going back up there and wanting to go along..."

"Yeah, I'm having a bad feeling about all this," said Easton. "But I'm beginning to think some things are starting to come together."

"In a way a law enforcement officer never wants them to."

"With one of his own involved in a serious crime."

"Murder."

"We don't know that yet, Lieutenant. We need to be very careful how we proceed with this. It's possible that the Bruington shooting is unrelated to whatever Hensley was doing up at that shack."

"You don't really believe that do you, Corporal?"

"There are still so many unanswered questions."

Dowdy picked up his phone's handset and on the base punched in the numbers for the Lab.

"Technician Sims speaking."

"Sims, I have to ask you to do an unpleasant task."

"Yes, Lieutenant."

"Dig up the police personnel record on Oregon State Trooper Bryan Wilson."

"Did I hear you right, Lieutenant, Trooper Bryan Wilson of the Oregon State Police?"

"You heard me right, Sims. When you have found them, compare his finger prints to the other prints from the shovel."

"Let's hope not, Lieutenant."

"My feelings exactly."

Dowdy and Easton both went to the machine in the office and got a fresh cup of coffee. Neither of them spoke. They were both sick inside as they killed time waiting for the bad news they expected from the lab in a few minutes. They milled around for ten minutes looking at some of the missing person photos on the office walls, and finally went back into Dowdy's office and took their seats.

Three minutes later Dowdy's phone beeped. He didn't want to pick it up. As his message was about played out, he finally did.

"Dowdy here."

"You were right, Lieutenant. The prints match. I'm sorry to have to tell you that."

"They're definitely Wilson's on the shovel?"

"Yes, I'm afraid they are."

"Thanks. I'll be in touch."

"Sorry sir."

43

Back to the Woods

On Friday morning, October 9th, Lane County District Attorney, Miles Reed and one of his assistants accompanied Lane County Sheriff David Alford, Captain McKluskey, Lieutenant Dowdy, Corporal Easton and six other deputies into the woods above Puma Creek Campground, coming in from the north of the shack. State Trooper Wilson was not with them. Dowdy had a deputy call him Thursday night to tell him they wouldn't be going into the woods until the following week now.

After the District Attorney, the Sheriff and Captain McKluskey were satisfied they were not going to find any new evidence from the shack, including from the tunnel which was cleared of debris and searched, the lawmen spread out and did a broad sweep across the ridges and springs within half a mile of the burned-down shack. They didn't know if they would find anything else, but the DA and sheriff weren't leaving the mountain until they were certain they had all the available evidence.

Half an hour into the sweeps, one of the deputies said on his radio,

"I think I have something. It may be a grave."

All the men converged on his location beside a three-foot-diameter, fallen fir-tree and a huge pile of branches, small logs and a smattering of freshly disturbed dirt. There was a slight odor in the air that not all the men could detect.

"Someone has piled this stuff here," said the sheriff. "Let's get a bunch of photos, then tear it apart. We've got to see what has been covered."

After several lawmen and the district attorney's assistant snapped numerous photos, the men went to work pulling the brush and logs away. In less than a minute the ground by the log was cleared down to earth. More photos were snapped, then the moss, needles and twigs were swept away. At each step, more photos were taken. Then when the men had dug to about three feet below ground level with their folding shovels, they uncovered what appeared to be the tips of several sharp pointed sticks.

Dowdy said, "Are those what I think they are?"

Digging a bit more earth away by hand, one of the diggers said, "I'm afraid so. They're punji sticks."

By then the odor had grown distinct. Something dead was waiting to be discovered. They dug carefully with their gloved hands. Camera's continued to flash as progress was made.

Easton said, "We know Hensley did four tours in Vietnam. This is undoubtedly his work."

"Well let's hope we only find an animal in this pit," one deputy volunteered.

Just then, with every man present surrounding the area being dug out, another deputy said, "I'm afraid this is no animal," as he uncovered what looked like part of the skeleton of a human arm, with flesh and dried skin still attached.

They quickly dug some more and uncovered more of the skeleton and rotted flesh and skin partially covered by some deteriorated blue cloth from what looked to be a tee-shirt. Around the lower back was a brown nylon fanny pack in much better condition than the tee-shirt and the gray denim shorts. The blue tennis shoes on the dead person were in fairly good shape. The small word *Puma* was sown just above the wide stripe running most the length, across the outside of the shoes.

As more dirt was removed, the back of a skull with collar-length, brown hair matted around it, also came into view. A couple men stepped away from the pit, turned and vomited.

Cameras continued to flash.

"That's got to be that missing Wyoming man," said Dowdy. "All this time he's been right up here in these woods."

"Unbelievable," said the district attorney.

Lane County Coroner Doug Villard was called via the sheriff's dispatcher and summoned to the scene. Dispatch reported it would be at least an hour until the coroner team could reach the other sheriff's vehicles parked on the Clark Butte Road above the burned shack. One of the deputies would hike out and meet them to escort them to the grave.

The men doing the digging were careful not to disturb any of the punji sticks or the body as they continued working. As they dug out from under the body, the skeleton gradually dropped lower because what flesh and skin that remained was too fragile to support it on the punji sticks. They soon realized there was no point in digging anymore dirt from underneath it. Finally they had the entire corpse uncovered. One of the deputies used a two-inch-wide paint brush to sweep dirt, worms and various other bugs away.

As all the men stood or squatted around the edge of the pit, one of the deputies said,

"That had to be one hell of a way to die."

"Whoever did this should be put to death by the same means," said another.

"*Maybe it was an accident,*" suggested Easton.

"This was no accident, Corporal. You don't kill someone in a punji pit in the woods in the middle of America by accident."

"No. I mean, maybe the pit was designed to trap an animal, and it was merely an accident that this man walked into it."

"I say hang the mothers anyway. How would you like to die like that?"

"What do you think, Sheriff Alford or District Attorney Reed?"

"That's something we're going to have to really think about. But this is certainly one time when I wish I wasn't the DA."

"You don't want to hang the people who did this?"

"What I meant was that I wish I never had to see something this gruesome and then be involved in prosecuting it."

"Who is this Hensley guy that Corporal Easton said did four tours in Vietnam and probably built this pit?" asked one deputy.

"We can't discuss any of that right now," said Sheriff Alford.

"Is this connected with that deer hunter who was killed up here last year?"

"Or the couple killed in Puma Creek Campground?" said another deputy.

"It might be," said the sheriff. "We're still trying to figure all of it out."

The only lawmen present who knew there was any connection to a lawman were Dowdy, Easton, the sheriff, the captain, and the district attorney. However, the heavy weights presence was evidence enough that something big was going down.

Ten minutes after the corpse was completely uncovered, one of the deputies hiked out to the parking area. He returned thirty minutes later with Coroner Villard and Coroner Assistant Baird.

Looking into the pit, Villard said, "You weren't kidding when you said you had a first for me today. What a helluva way to die."

"I wonder how long the guy suffered." said the coroner's assistant. "Some judge and jury are going to give up their breakfasts when they see pictures of this."

"I sure as hell wouldn't want to be the defendant in the

courtroom when they show them," said Villard.

After the coroner and his assistant had taken their own pictures and completed their field work, the body, including the impaled punji sticks, was carefully removed from the pit and placed on its side on a stretcher and carried up to the coroner's van. All the other punji sticks in the pit were gathered up and bagged so they could be checked for blood and fingerprints.

Bruington's Deer Found; Walton's Body Found;

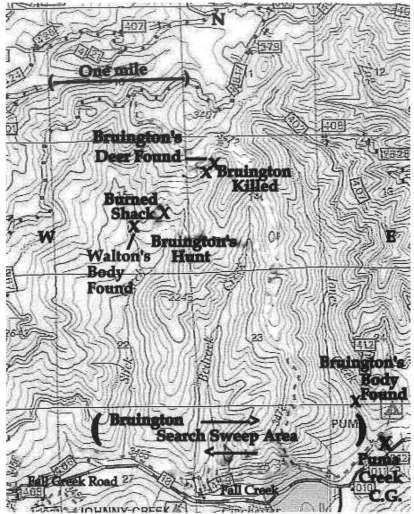

44

Trooper Wilson

Tuesday afternoon, October 13th, District Attorney Reed and the assistant DA met with Edward Rierdan's attorney, Melinda Holbrook, in the DA's office and offered her a plea bargain deal. She then met with her client at the Lane County jail to explain the DA's offer of two second-degree murder charges with life in prison and a chance for parole after thirty years, along with no charges being filed against him in the Bruington and Walton cases in exchange for his detailed confession of the events that occurred on the night the Evonuks were killed at Puma Creek Campground.

Rierdan did not want to accept the offer and insisted he had acted in self-defense that night. Holbrook finally convinced him that no jury in the country would see his actions as self-defense and that he was sure to get life with no parole or the death penalty if he didn't accept the DA's offer. And he would likely be charged in at least the Bruington murder, and possibly even Walton's disappearance.

On Wednesday morning the DA and his assistant, along with

Deputies Dowdy and Easton, met Attorney Holbrook and Rierdan in the interview room at the Lane County Jail. The session was recorded on audio and video tapes. Rierdan described the sequence of events leading up to the confrontation and killing of Roderick and Sandy Evonuk. He claimed he acted entirely in self-defense. But when the DA spelled out what the evidence said, he admitted he over-reacted and could have left before things escalated with old man Evonuk. He then insisted that he knew nothing about Bruington or Walton and, in fact, had never been in the woods above Puma Creek Campground.

The DA didn't tell him or his attorney that their investigation above Puma Creek had turned up the shovel with Hensley and Wilson's fingerprints on it, that they had found and identified, by dental records, Walton's body, or that many of the punji sticks had Hensley's finger prints on them. Since no charges had been brought previously against Rierdan in the Bruington and Walton cases, the DA's office was not obligated to reveal what evidence it had in those cases.

At 4:30 Wednesday afternoon, Sheriff Alford called Oregon State Police Captain Miles Burton and reluctantly filled him in on the Sheriff Department's findings. He then asked him to accompany himself, Captain McKluskey, Deputies Dowdy and Easton and several other deputies to Trooper Wilson's house in order to question him, and probably arrest him.

Captain Burton asked, "Why do you need so many deputies to go there. Wilson's been an excellent officer in his first three years. I think you're mistaken in your conclusions about his involvement in anything illegal."

"Look, Captain," said Sheriff Alford, "I totally understand how difficult it is to see one of your own in trouble. I've dealt with that a few times myself. But we are concerned that Hensley could be at Trooper Wilson's place and that, if he is, things could go south in a hurry. We want to be ready if they do."

"I understand. I hope you're dead wrong about Trooper Wilson."

"I do too. Believe me I do."

An hour later, Lieutenant Dowdy and Deputy Easton knocked on Trooper Wilson's door in Springfield. The other law enforcement officers, who had parked their vehicles down the road, were hidden behind nearby bushes, three of them armed with M16 machine guns and one with a twelve-gauge shotgun loaded with 00 buckshot.

Wilson opened the door, dressed in blue jeans, a brown tee-shirt and wearing house slippers. "Lieutenant Dowdy, what brings you out here?" he said, his stomach suddenly feeling sour.

"Trooper Wilson, Deputy Easton and I would like to ask you some questions."

"Sure, come on in," he offered.

"Actually, we'd like you to come on out. It's comfortable out here this evening and we'd just soon talk with you out here."

"Okay, no problem," said Wilson, though he knew there was a terrible problem.

He stepped out on to the front porch and then followed Dowdy to the rear of his unmarked car. Easton followed behind Wilson. Just then Wilson's captain, along with Sheriff Alford and Dowdy's captain approached from down the road.

Wilson was startled to see them, and asked, "Why are my captain and the sheriff here?"

"We think you have a pretty good idea, Wilson," said Dowdy. "We've found more evidence up in the hills above Puma Creek, and we need to talk to you about it. The sheriff wanted to be present and asked your captain to be here also."

Turning to his captain as he closed the final few feet, Wilson said, "What's going on, Captain?"

"I don't like it anymore than you do, Wilson. But some evidence that turned up in the Puma Creek woods needs some explaining. And unfortunately, you're the one who needs to explain it."

"We can all talk to you out here in your driveway or we can go down to the sheriff station," said Dowdy. "It's up to you."

"I don't want to go to the station," said Wilson, his mouth suddenly dry. "We can discuss things here."

"When Deputy Easton and I saw you hunting in the woods near the shack opening morning with your long-haired friend, it bothered us. We thought maybe he was a relative, but since you didn't introduce him as one, we figured he wasn't. It struck us odd that you would be up there the day after I told you we had discovered the dead deer with Bruington's bullet in it less than half-mile below the burned-out shack. And your call back to me that night asking when I planned to go back up there... it was just the combination of that and seeing you in there the next day.

"Well, later opening morning, Deputy Easton and I found a shovel north of the shack. We fully expected to find Rierdan's fingerprints on it, since we suspected that he and at least one other person were possibly growing marijuana and manufacturing drugs up in those woods and he had probably killed the archeologist couple at Puma Creek because they had wandered into the wrong area. Under the circumstances, we were pretty convinced he had killed Bruington, and maybe even the Wyoming man."

As Dowdy talked, Wilson glanced back and forth between him and his own captain's faces, while his right thumb fiddled nervously with his belt. The other four fingers were buried in his right front jean pocket. He was shocked that they found the shovel, and feared what was coming, but did his best to seem unmoved by the revelation. He knew all five lawmen were studying him carefully to observe his non-verbal response to Dowdy's words.

He also thought about what Del had told him eleven days earlier after they hung his deer. He had only talked with Del twice since then. In the first of those conversations, Del had said, "You better have your story figured out and cemented in your mind before anyone from either law enforcement agency speaks to you. And it damn well better be the story I told you to tell." Del said he would take care of himself, not to worry about him. "Just save your own butt from doing too much time." Butch knew not to bring the subject up in the second conversation.

"Well, guess what? We didn't find Rierdan's fingerprints on the shovel, but we did find numerous fingerprints from two other people." Wilson cringed. "Your hippie buddie's and yours." Dowdy let those words hang in the air. Neither he, the other four lawmen or Wilson spoke. All eyes looked at Wilson as if to say, please give us a logical explanation. We don't want you to be guilty. You are a lawman.

Wilson knew he'd been caught with his pants down. Even if he wanted to now, there was no way to separate himself from the shack. He rehearsed in his mind the story Del had told him to give.

After fifteen seconds of tormenting silence, that seemed more like five minutes, Captain Burton asked, "What would you like to tell us, Trooper Wilson? We want to give you every opportunity to be candid with us."

"If you will tell us the truth about everything, we will take that into consideration," said Sheriff Alford.

"Yes," Wilson finally spoke up. "I want to tell the truth. I'm going to tell you the truth."

"Good, we were hoping you would co-operate and make this easier on everybody," said Alford. "So what were your prints doing on that shovel?"

Wilson thought about telling them he had only loaned the shovel to Del and hadn't done anything at the shack with the shovel himself. But he knew they would know he was lying, so he chose Del's story.

"As you all probably know by now, Del Hensley served as a sniper in Vietnam for two years, his last two. He did four years total over there during the war. His connection to me was that my father was his baseball coach in high school and they became best friends. A few months after Del was drafted into the Army, my dad also joined to go help in Vietnam. Toward the end of Del's first tour there, he and my dad were in the same company."

"My dad was on point one day in November 1966, with Del the next man in the platoon behind him. Suddenly my dad tripped a mine and was blown in half, but was still alive. He begged Del to shoot him to put him out of his misery, and finally Del did."

Wilson paused to let that sink in, to possibly gain a little sympathy from the lawmen. They each shook their heads knowing the pain Wilson suffered over losing his dad was soon to be made worse.

"After my dad died and Del came home, he became like a surrogate father to me. He had plenty of problems, but he was all I had, as far as a dad goes."

"We're following you, Wilson," said Dowdy.

"Well, Del really struggled financially. In fact he couldn't hold down a job. He was too messed up in the head. He got heavy into dope and then figured out that he could at least survive by growing marijuana and making methamphetamines and selling them."

"So he used the shack?" said Captain Burton.

"That's right."

"And you helped him?"

"No. I didn't help him with any of the dope, just with packing materials in and building the shack and kind of keeping an eye out to make sure no one fooled around in the woods up there."

"People like Roger Bruington?" asked Easton.

"No, not people like Bruington."

"So you were an accessory to the production and sale of illegal drugs."

"What was I supposed to do, turn my surrogate father in after my own father had been killed in the war before I turned eleven?"

"That did put you in a difficult position," said his captain.

"Trooper Wilson, did you know Hensley had a punji pit in that area below where Deputy Easton and I saw you opening morning?"

"He had a punji pit up there?" Wilson asked acting surprised.

"Look Wilson, if you knew he had the pit, you better come clean with us."

"I didn't know anything about a pit. When did you find it?"

"We found it on October 9th."

"Where was it?"

"About seventy-five yards away from where you guys gutted out that deer," said Easton. "Are you sure you're being straight with us?"

"You bet I'm being straight." Wilson sensed they seemed to be swallowing his story so far. Maybe he could actually get out of this without doing too much time. Maybe Del was right.

"We found the missing Wyoming bicyclist dead in your buddy's pit."

"Oh no," Wilson answered, doing an excellent job of showing shock by his facial expression. "That had to be an accident. Del never would have trapped a human on purpose."

"Well, he had no problem covering the body up where it lay and going on about his business."

"I can't imagine how he would have felt when he found that guy in there," said Wilson. "You may not believe this, but Del does have a good heart. But *he is a survivor.*"

"Is that why he murdered Bruington with one of his sniper-grade shots to the back of his head, because he has a good heart?" asked Sheriff Alford.

"What are you saying?"

"What we're saying," said Dowdy, "is that we know that Hensley not only killed Walton—whether by accident or not—but that he deliberately shot Bruington because he came too close to, or perhaps even went inside, his shack and discovered incriminating evidence of a drug operation."

Rocking back and forth on his feet unconsciously, Wilson said, "How did you come up with that theory. Bruington was killed miles from the shack. His death had no relation to Del's activities at the shack."

"What if I told you that we now believe his body was moved after he was shot?"

"How could you come up with that? I was there when Bruington's body was found. There was no way his body was moved. I saw all the blood splattered there myself. And what about the piece of bone Trooper Martin found across the creek?"

"It was all just a little too convenient, Trooper Wilson," said Dowdy. "Now if there is something you're not telling us, this is your chance to come clean. If you don't, you're going away for life yourself."

"For what, being an accessory to a drug operation? Who are you trying to kid?" said Wilson, looking at his captain as if pleading for help in getting out of this fix. The captain's face was filled with sorrow. His eyes looked down at Wilson's feet, as he slowly shook his head.

"We know you knew about the pit and the dead Wyoming man, and we know you also knew about Bruington's murder. Now damn it!" Dowdy said, "Come clean while you still can!"

Wilson didn't know how Dowdy could possibly know the truth about either death, and he had no idea what Dowdy knew, or how he knew it. But learning Dowdy had found the shovel and the pit was a shock to him. Was Dowdy just bluffing, or what else was he hiding up his sleeve? Wilson weighed his options and decided to go with Del's story.

"It was that deer wasn't it? Finding that dead buck gave it away, didn't it?"

"Yes," Dowdy bluffed. "It was finding the dead deer with Bruington's bullet in it so close to the shack that gave us one of the pieces we needed to figure the whole thing out."

"Del called me early in the afternoon on Saturday, October 25th, a year ago, and told me he had shot a deer hunter who had gotten into his shack. He said he had no choice but to kill him, and that he needed my help in moving the body."

The lawmen looked at each other, but were careful not to show any surprise on their faces. This confession was far more than they could have hoped for. They had no idea Bruington had been moved. Dowdy had been grasping at straws when he bluffed about things being a little too convenient and the deer giving them the answer.

"I couldn't believe he had done that, but what could I do?" The other lawmen couldn't believe he had gone along with the whole thing, including helping move the body, and never once let on like he knew anything.

"Are you willing to go up into the woods with us tomorrow morning and show us exactly where you moved the body from?" asked the sheriff.

"You already know that. Why make me go through that with you?"

"It will ease your conscience to know you showed us yourself," said Dowdy.

Easton was thoroughly impressed with the skill Dowdy used to get at the truth, though he had no way of knowing that he was not actually getting the full truth—just Del Hensley's version of it.

"Yes, I'll go with you. This thing has been eating at me since the day it happened."

"Good. Now tell us about the Wyoming man in the pit."

"Tell you what? I told you I knew nothing about that."

"You expect us to believe Hensley told you about Bruington, but not Walton. We're not idiots, Wilson."

"I don't know anything about Walton other than what you just told me. Why would Del need to tell me about him? He didn't move the body, did he? He needed my help to move Bruington's body clear away from the shack to keep the shack from being discovered."

"He does have a good point there," said Captain Burton, doing what little he could to salvage something for his trooper.

"Okay then, Wilson," said Dowdy. "We'll buy your story. It does make sense."

"Take him into custody," said Sheriff Alford.

Easton, quickly patted Wilson down, then asked him to place his hands behind his back, which he did. Easton then cuffed him and quoted him his Miranda Rights. He then waited a minute for a deputy to move his squad car from down the road, and then loaded Wilson into it. Wilson was then transported to the Lane County jail and booked for accessory to illegal drug manufacture and sale, accessory to murder and obstructing a police investigation.

45

The Showdown

The next morning Wilson was taken into the woods below the
burned-out shack to what remained of Bruington's dead buck's
carcass. From there Wilson led the lawmen the short distance across
the draw and uphill to Bruington's position when he was shot and
described where Del supposedly told him he took the shot from,
farther up the hill.

The Sheriff, OSP Captain Burton, Dowdy, Easton and the other
three deputies searched for any remaining evidence, such as skull
fragments or a spent casing, in the area around the big fir, and up the
hill where Del's shot was taken from, but found nothing. Deputies
Dowdy and Easton paced off the distance to where the trophy buck
was found dead. It was only a hundred and ten yards from the huge
tree where Bruington was shot.

After completing their search, Dowdy asked Wilson, "Did you
hear Bruington's shot that killed the buck?" hoping to catch him in a
slip up.

"No. Like I said, I wasn't up here. When I mentioned to Del that

Bruington's gun was off-safe with a spent round chambered, he had no idea how that happened, unless Bruington took a shot from over the hill that morning and the sound never made it to the shack. Then two weeks ago when I told him about you finding the dead deer, he was completely at a loss how the shot could have occurred that close to the shack that morning without him hearing it."

"I'll tell you what I think, Lieutenant Dowdy," said Deputy Easton. "Based on where we found that deer, the fact that we know at least the left lung was hit and probably both lungs, and Bruington's position, I'm convinced that Bruington shot at the deer almost simultaneously with when Hensley shot him. Hensley never would have heard that shot because of the close blast to his ears from his own rifle occurring a split second later. What do you think, sir?"

"I think you've hit the nail on the head, Deputy Easton. That would explain all of it. Wilson, it seems the fact that neither Hensley nor you checked Bruington's rifle before or after you moved him has come back to bite the both of you squarely in the butt." Wilson didn't answer. He just stared at the mossy forest floor.

"Good work, deputies," said Sheriff Alford. "After all this time, you've finally put all the pieces together. And by this time two months from now, I will be calling you, Sergeant Easton."

"Thanks, sir. It wasn't easy."

"It sure wasn't," added Dowdy.

Friday, 10 A.M., October 16th, 1981: outside Del Hensley's house on Wallace Creek, near Jasper, Oregon. Hensley's old pickup was parked in the driveway thirty feet from the house. All the shades appeared to be closed, though the deputies and state troopers weren't sure about that. From behind a nearby three-foot-diameter maple tree—

"Delbert Hensley! This is Lieutenant Dowdy, Lane County Sheriff. Your house is surrounded. Come out with your hands on top of your head."

No answer from the house.

Besides deputies Dowdy and Easton out front, there were six

other deputies and five OSP troopers stationed outside the house. Along with their sidearms, half of the lawmen were armed with M16s and the other half had their riot shotguns. An old broken down cedar fence around part of the small backyard blocked some of the view of the back of the house.

Dowdy had learned from Trooper Wilson that Hensley owned six long guns (including a .270, an AR15, an AK47 and a twelve-gauge shotgun with the plug removed) and three pistols (including a military Colt .45 and a Smith and Wesson 9mm automatic.) Wilson knew of no other weapons other than various hunting knives, a couple of K bars, a bayonet or two and his butcher knives. He had pleaded with Dowdy for Del to be taken alive, and Dowdy had assured him that was their full intent. But, he said, in the end it would be up to Del. Wilson didn't reveal any of the conversations he had had with Del over the last two weeks in which Del had told him he wasn't going to prison, no matter what that meant. Wilson was scared to death that Del intended to shoot it out with the cops until he was dead.

Once more, Dowdy gave his order through the megaphone.

Still silence from the house. That was not the response Dowdy wanted.

"Delbert Hensley, this is Lieutenant Dowdy. This is your last chance to come out peacefully with your hands on your head, or we're coming in after you. Answer me if you're in there."

"Maybe he's not there, Lieutenant," suggested the deputy nearest him. "He had to have known eventually we were coming for him. Maybe he left his truck in the driveway as a decoy and already lit out of here."

"Wilson," said Dowdy, "when did you say you last talked with him?"

"Five days ago."

"Did he give any indication to you of his intentions?"

"No sir." Wilson knew if he admitted they had talked about

things, he would be looked at with more suspicion, and his story might not be trusted.

Dowdy said, "We're coming in Hensley. Come out peacefully while you still can."

Still nothing from the house. Dowdy drew his .357 magnum and signaled for Deputy Easton to move up to a tree closer to the house on the opposite side of the driveway from him.

When Easton stepped out, there was a sudden short-burst of automatic gunfire from the window to the right of the front door. Easton went right to the ground, his right lower leg bleeding. Dowdy immediately dove for cover behind the maple tree he had come from.

"I'm hit Lieutenant," shouted Easton.

"How bad?"

"Through my right shin; my leg's broken."

"Are you back out of danger?"

"Yes."

"Wilson," yelled Dowdy. "It looks like we're not going to be able to take your buddy out alive, unless you can talk some sense into him. Deputy, can you bring Wilson to me. I'll give him a chance to talk on the horn."

"Yes sir, Lieutenant. I'll use him as a body screen. I'm sure his buddy wouldn't shoot him."

When they started to walk toward Dowdy's position there was another burst of automatic fire that hit the ground ten feet in front of them.

"That's an M16 he's using, Lieutenant," yelled one of the deputies. "What do you want us to do now? He's shooting at his own friend."

"Lieutenant Dowdy," yelled Wilson. "He's not shooting to kill. He's shooting to keep you away from the house. If he wanted to kill anybody Deputy Easton would be dead already. For crying out loud, he was a sniper. He's not going to miss a close shot like that. Please try to resolve this thing peacefully."

"I hope you're right, Wilson. But I can't lose a man finding out.

What do you suggest?"

"Let me talk to him from here."

"Go ahead!"

"Del!" yelled Wilson, "There's no way out of there. You're surrounded. The lieutenant doesn't want to kill you. They know all about you killing the hunter and they found the biker in the punji pit. Why didn't you ever tell me about that pit and the biker? They know about the drugs. They know about all of it. I even told them about my dad. I told them the truth. I had too."

No sound from the house.

"Come on, Del, it's over, just like the war. You've got to give it up."

"It's not over!" yelled Del. "Neither is the war. We still have men over there and the government hasn't done a thing to recover them. You can't trust the government. You can't trust anyone."

"Del, you can trust me. You don't have to die."

"Everyone has to die!"

"You don't have to die today. Please, Del, they know the punji pit was an accident."

"There aren't any accidents, Butch. Everything happens for a reason."

"Please, Del, come out peacefully. No one else needs to get hurt."

There was no answer from the house.

"Del, you need to come out with your hands on top of your head," yelled Dowdy.

No Answer.

"Del, talk to me," said Wilson. "Tell me you're coming out."

Just then the shaded front door opened, and all the deputies in front trained their weapons there.

Easton, who had torn a sleeve off his shirt and wrapped it around his bleeding leg, yelled, "He's coming out, Lieutenant."

"Don't shoot him," yelled Wilson, relieved. "He's coming out peacefully."

Suddenly, automatic fire exploded from the front doorway spraying the front yard and Del's truck.

One of the deputies cut loose with his M16 in full-auto and sprayed the front door which was still partly open. Automatic fire broke out from all around the house, and shotguns loaded with 00 buckshot blasted away. The deputies were shooting at every window and door in the house.

"Hold your fire!" Dowdy yelled. "Hold your damn fire!"

But the shooting continued; they didn't hear him over the gunfire. Glass shattered and old, peeling, white paint fell away from the walls as bullets and balls pummeled the old, vertical, wood-strip siding.

Wilson cried, knowing his surrogate father was getting chewed up inside the house by the M16s and shotguns from all around the outside of the house.

"What's that sound?" yelled one of the deputies nearest the front of the house.

Finally Dowdy was heard as he continued to yell, "Cease Fire!" into the megaphone. The shooting gradually died off until it all stopped.

"What was that sound in the house?" said the same deputy. "It sounded like our shots were hitting metal."

"The shades are all shut," yelled another deputy, "at least what's left of them. I can't see inside except near the ceiling."

"Toss a flare up by that front window," Dowdy shouted.

A flare was lit and thrown in the grass near the window that Hensley's first shots had come from. Its bright light reflected off of something in the bottom third of the window.

"There's metal inside that window, Lieutenant," yelled the deputy, who had tossed the flare. "He's using steel plate to block the windows."

"He was ready for us then," said Dowdy, over the megaphone.

Thinking maybe Del had survived the onslaught, Butch felt a sense of relief. He was proud of Del for not being caught off guard.

And he felt a sense of love and respect for him that he'd never felt before. He was getting to see the soldier in action. He knew his own father must have been a hell of a warrior, too—just like Del.

"Del, are you okay?" yelled Wilson.

There was only silence. He didn't know what to think, but he didn't lose hope.

"Hensley," Dowdy yelled, "if you're still alive, give us some indication. If you can't talk, do something. Shoot one round into the ceiling. Just let us know that you're still alive."

Silence.

Dowdy conversed with the troopers in back of the house by radio. They hadn't observed any movement anywhere.

"Hensley, this is your last chance. Give us a signal."

Dowdy spoke on his radio, "I need two deputies and two troopers to quickly move up to the house. I want a lawman at each corner of the house. Do not go where you could be seen from any window. Once you are at the house, check in."

Two deputies in front and two state troopers at the rear of the house quickly made their way up against the house and checked in.

"Now move up to the nearest window, make sure the glass has been broken and toss in a smoke grenade at the top of the window. Be careful that the window is clear." They each acknowledged Dowdy's order.

Dowdy watched the deputy nearest to him toss in his grenade. Ten seconds later he saw smoke coming from the two windows at each end of his side of house. The house was filled with dark smoke in the rooms affected.

"Now toss in another grenade and then move up to the next window and do the same thing. Stay out of sight from the window. You officers on the perimeter outside, watch for movement above the metal in the windows. If you see or hear gunfire, return fire at the top of the window. Do not—I repeat—do not shoot in fully automatic mode, and do not use shotguns. I don't want us to hit our own men."

The four officers lofted in an additional smoke grenade and then moved up, staying next to the house, to repeat the sequence at the next window. After three minutes black smoke was coming from every window in the house.

"Hensley, if you can hear me, come out of the house."

Nothing.

The deputies outside waited five minutes for the smoke inside to gradually dissipate. Wilson wasn't sure what to think.

Five more minutes passed and then Dowdy gave the order, "I need two more deputies to move up to the front of the house. We're going in."

Two more deputies moved up going from tree to tree, then to Hensley's truck. No shots came from inside. They finally dashed from the truck to the front of the house, with still no shots being fired at them.

Over the radio, "We're going in now, from the front," said Dowdy. "Deputies in front enter carefully."

The first two burst into the house with their M16s. Instantly there was an explosion, then screaming from just inside the doorway.

"It's a booby trap!" yelled one of the deputies from just outside the front door. Groaning could be heard inside the entryway.

Then, "I'm okay. Are you okay?" said one of the deputies in the house.

"I'm okay. It was just a light concussion charge," yelled one of the men in the house. I tripped a wire right above the floor."

"We're alright," said the other deputy in the house over his radio. He's not in the living room."

"You other two men move in," ordered Dowdy. "Be careful. There are probably other booby traps. The men outside waited another minute as the smoke continued to gradually clear out giving them more visibility. Neither was excited about going in.

Finally they entered and joined the other two in searching the house from room to room. Pretty soon, over the radio,

"Lieutenant, we've completed searching the house. He's not here and there's no sign he's been hit."

"You're kidding me," said Dowdy. "He couldn't have escaped."

"He's got steel plating along the lower half of all the external walls in the living room. He was ready for us, sir."

"What's going on in there, Wilson?" Dowdy yelled. "What haven't you told me?"

"I don't have a clue, sir," said a very relieved, but curious, Wilson.

"He has to be hiding somewhere in that house," said Dowdy, over the radio. "Check the ceiling and under-floor crawl spaces."

Five minutes passed as the deputies used their flashlights to illuminate the attic and under floor space.

"Nothing sir. Nothing under the house."

"Nothing in the overhead crawl space either, Lieutenant. What do you want us to do?"

"He could not have just disappeared. He's not a ghost," said Dowdy, over the radio. "I'm coming in. Maybe he's got a tunnel out of his house, too."

"Wilson, does Hensley have a tunnel in there somewhere?"

"If he does, I didn't know anything about it. He's lived here for six years."

Dowdy entered the house with his .357 drawn and consulted with the four deputies inside.

"There's got to be a tunnel here someplace. He didn't just vanish. He had a good tunnel built under his shack in the woods. I don't know why I didn't consider that possibility in the first place."

After looking around in all the rooms and finding nothing, Dowdy, who was now in the kitchen, said, "There, pull out that cabinet. It's the only thing left."

Immediately, it was obvious. "There it is, Lieutenant. It looks like an opening in the wall."

"Darn it!" said Dowdy, who slid to the side the board that covered the back of the three foot by three foot opening. "Who will go in there?"

"Not me, Lieutenant," said one deputy. "They don't pay me enough to be that crazy."

"Me neither sir."

"Look, I think it's obvious he wasn't trying to kill anyone. He could easily have killed several deputies, not just with his machine gun, but with booby traps. He deliberately set the charge very light to avoid seriously hurting anyone."

"If you believe that, Lieutenant, why don't you go down there?"

"I will," said Dowdy. "Who's going with me?"

"I will, sir," volunteered Deputy Lohner.

"You can leave the 16 here. We'll just take flashlights and our handguns."

Dowdy shined his light into the opening and could see that the enclosed tunnel dropped down to the ground four feet below, and then went along horizontally under the house toward the backyard. The ground was covered in black plastic. He crouched down sitting on the edge with his light in his left hand and his .357 in the right. Then he jumped the twelve inches to the bottom. The plastic gave way, and he cried out in pain. His left calf muscle was pierced with a punji stick. His right foot landed on the tip of a sharp stick, but the steel plate in the bottom of his boot pushed the stick to the side, preventing an injury to that leg.

"Geez, the man has booby trapped this tunnel," said Lohner, as he pulled under Dowdy's armpits to help him get back up into the opening. "I'm not going any farther, sir. I don't need this crap."

"I don't blame you, Lohner. We'll call in the SWAT Team and let them handle it.

"We're lucky no one's been seriously hurt, or someone might have had your rear for trying to make this arrest without the Team in the first place," said another deputy.

"Hind sight's always 20/20," answered Dowdy, as Deputy Lohner drug him back through the opening into the kitchen.

Paramedics arrived fifteen minutes later to treat and transport

Easton and Dowdy. The deputies who set off the concussion charge needed only minor treatment for some scrapes on their lower legs.

The SWAT team arrived five minutes after the paramedics and took over the tunnel operation. Thirty minutes after beginning their search in the tunnel, one of the three SWAT members who had gone down said over his radio, "He's gone, sir."

"What do you mean he's gone?" asked Dowdy, who was laying on a gurney in front of the house next to the gurney Deputy Easton was laying on. "Where's that tunnel come out?"

"It came out inside an abandoned beaver lodge in the bank of this creek back here, a hundred yards behind the house. He had to have crawled out the den opening into the water and used the creek to escape. We went two hundred yards up and down the creek and found no sign that he had gone up the bank. He stayed in the creek."

"So he's got almost an hour and a half head start on us," said Dowdy. "Damn it! The damn *ghost of Vietnam*."

"What do you want me to do, sir?"

"Come on back in. It looks like we're in for a manhunt now."

Dowdy looked at Wilson who was in handcuffs beside him, wearing a huge grin.

"What are you smiling about, Wilson?"

"He once told me he was just a ghost. I guess he was right."

Despite an intense month-long county and state-wide manhunt by the Lane County Sheriff Department and the Oregon State Police, as well as the FBI, Delbert Hensley was not located. Numerous law enforcement agencies are continuing to look for him six months later, as he remains at the top of the FBI's Most Wanted List.

Former Oregon State Trooper Bryan Wilson was sentenced to ten years in Federal Prison for being an Accessory to First-Degree Murder, and for Obstructing a Police Investigation.

Although Aaron Howe continues to stop by Jan Bruington's place regularly, and she respects him and appreciates his friendship and support, in her eyes he will never be the man Roger was, and couldn't possibly be the husband to her, or the father to their daughters that she and they need. She continues to attend her church twice a week and receives constant encouragement from church members, her family, and many friends, especially Dick Eastbrook and his wife, Wanda.

Six more covert missions by U.S. Navy Seals, Army Rangers and Green Berets into Cambodia, Laos and Vietnam, from October 1981 to May 1982, have confirmed that American soldiers were, in fact, seen alive and being held against their wills as recently as March 1980. But currently it is not known how many men are still imprisoned, or in which countries they are being detained.

The public outcry has died down considerably since the big news break of May 1981. But the POW/MIA issue is alive and well— thanks to former U.S. Army Sergeant, **Roger Dale Bruington**. Thousands of local groups all across the country are continuing to hold the U.S. government accountable in its efforts to bring the remaining American GIs home to their country and families.

An Interview

with

Author Wesley Murphey

Lost Creek Books Consultant Marie Peterson: Wesley, in the interview that was printed in your book, **A Homeless Man's Burden,** you said that **Trouble at Puma Creek** was your favorite book of those you have written—why is that?

Wesley Murphey: I think it's because the book combines several of my greatest interests. Coming from a family filled with military veterans—among them, my dad was an Army medic at a bomber base in England during World War II, my older brother was a marine during Vietnam, my twin brother and I served four years each in the submarine force between 1974 and 1979, and my youngest sister served six years in the Army—I have always had a fascination with the Vietnam war, its soldiers, the War's aftermath and the whole POW/MIA issue. At the same time, I've always loved hunting and fishing and just being in the wild.

I also found the whole hippie movement intriguing. So much of what happened during the sixties and seventies, and even into the early eighties, was unlike anything this country has ever seen, before or after that, and probably won't see again. There were so many social issues at the same time the Vietnam War was going on and in the years immediately following the War. In **Trouble at Puma Creek**, I take the reader back to that period of time, alluding to actual historical events for part of the backdrop of the story, while using my characters to communicate the traumatic effects the War had on the soldiers who fought it, as well as their families.

Peterson: You've done a beautiful job of showing how devastating the War was for your good-guy-turned-criminal, hippie character Del Hensley. And the hippie on your book's cover is exactly the way I pictured Del being when I read about him in your manuscript. How did you find someone so perfect?

Murphey: Believe it or not, I ran a free ad for two weeks in two of the local weekly papers that said I needed a hippie-looking guy for a photo shoot. More than thirty-five hippies—or friends and family members speaking for their hippie-looking guys—called to volunteer for the part. When my actual hippie emailed me his photo, I knew I had hit pay dirt. If he isn't a hippie, hippies don't exist.

Peterson: Part of your story involves the cover up of the POW/MIA issue by the U.S. Government. Do you really believe there were American servicemen held captive in Vietnam or other parts of Southeast Asia after the Vietnam War ended—or perhaps still could be? And do you believe the government may have turned its back on known POWs?

Murphey: I'm not sure who you want to get me in trouble with if I answer that second question. But, yes, I do believe American GIs were held somewhere in Southeast Asia for years after the War ended. Like everyone else, I want to believe our government would have done all it could to obtain their release—though many people are skeptical that it did. I'll say no more, other than that I believe my book brings out some real possibilities. Could there *still be* American GIs held alive in Vietnam or other parts of Southeast Asia? What would be the point of that—for our former enemies, that is? If there were, in fact, GIs held after the War, it's hard to believe they would still be alive now, in 2011. It's sad.

Peterson: As I read **Trouble at Puma Creek,** I found myself deeply moved emotionally in a number of places.

Murphey: I've heard the same thing from readers of **A Homeless Man's Burden**—that and that they couldn't put the book down. That tells me as an author that I have succeeded—moving people emotionally, and having them tell me, "I couldn't put your book down." The Vietnam War was a big part of so many of our lives, and the way my book brings that out should move people. I'm really hoping even the younger generations, that weren't around during the Vietnam War, will read my book and learn a lot more about the War and the soldiers who fought it. There's some great history in this book.

Peterson: I understand there really was a double homicide at Puma Creek Campground. Was the double homicide at the Puma Creek Campground in your book related to that?

Murphey: Actually the true-life double homicide at Puma Creek Campground is where I got the idea for this novel. However, unlike my novel *A Homeless Man's Burden*, which was deliberately written using the Alice Lee true murder for its entire theme and in which I use a lot of facts related to the true crime, in *Trouble at Puma Creek* my story is only very loosely connected to the true murders at Puma Creek.

Some years back, I had a long conversation with retired Oregon State Trooper Al Jacobs about the actual Puma Creek murders. As a 46-year-old OSP officer he was the first law man on the murder scene at Puma Creek Campground on the night of September 15th, 1970. (Note my double homicide in the campground occurred on September 16th, 1981.) Jacobs arrived to find a 57-year-old woman (Maureen Schoenborn Mulvey) and her 27-year-old son (James Douglas Morris) shot to death. He said it was a grisly scene, as one can imagine.

The case went unsolved for nearly a year and it caused a lot of people to steer clear of remote campgrounds like Puma Creek when camping. But Al Jacobs solved the case himself when he determined that the murder actually happened as a sort of accident when a hunter who had been hunting deer in the High Cascades Buck Season without success decided to swing through Puma Creek campground to see if he could spotlight a deer there. Unfortunately the man and woman were in the wrong place at the wrong time and rather than poach a deer or two, the night hunter was shocked to find he had murdered two humans. He left the scene immediately, but Al Jacobs eventually tracked him down in a round-about way.

Peterson: That's amazing. Did you hear about those murders when you were a kid growing up in Dexter only 30 or so miles away as the crow flies?

Murphey: Yes. I was only 13 when it happened but I kept up on the news even then.

Peterson: Now tell me a little about your next novel in which a man seeks retribution on his mother-in-law.

Murphey: Most everyone has either experienced personally, or through a friend or relative, the negative impact a rogue mother-in-law can have on a marriage. I thought that issue would make a great novel, so I wrote one. Two women that read my manuscript thought it was excellent. The book is not for kids; its theme is pretty graphic. In fact, it's definitely outside my comfort zone as a Christian. At the same time, life is real, people deal with tough circumstances, and at times even good people cross lines in their thinking or actions that would shock anyone that knows them. That is true of my main character, Dan Thurmond, regarding his estranged wife and her mother, the marriage wrecker. But Dan's pastor, some of Dan's wife's relatives, and her best friend, are also targets because of parts they played in the demise of his marriage.

Peterson: That sounds interesting. I look forward to reading it.

About the Author

Wesley Murphey grew up in Dexter and Pleasant Hill, Oregon and lived in Lane County, Oregon until 2003, when he moved his family to beautiful Central Oregon where he now resides. He enjoys fishing, hunting, hiking, swimming, camping and numerous other outdoor activities. In addition to **Trouble at Puma Creek**, and the other books listed in the front of this book, Murphey has several other books in the works.

If you enjoyed this book or his others be sure to tell all your reading friends.

Wesley welcomes reader feedback on this book and also his others. Email him at <u>lostcreekbooks@netzero.com</u>.

Lost Creek Books
La Pine, OR 97739

email: lostcreekbooks@netzero.com
website- http://lostcreekbooks.com

Wesley Murphey's books make great gifts!

Get more information and order more of Wesley Murphey's books at lostcreekbooks.com. Credit cards accepted.
